1,000,000 Books
are available to read at

Forgotten Books

www.ForgottenBooks.com

Read online
Download PDF
Purchase in print

ISBN 978-0-259-39870-7
PIBN 10815515

This book is a reproduction of an important historical work. Forgotten Books uses state-of-the-art technology to digitally reconstruct the work, preserving the original format whilst repairing imperfections present in the aged copy. In rare cases, an imperfection in the original, such as a blemish or missing page, may be replicated in our edition. We do, however, repair the vast majority of imperfections successfully; any imperfections that remain are intentionally left to preserve the state of such historical works.

Forgotten Books is a registered trademark of FB &c Ltd.
Copyright © 2018 FB &c Ltd.
FB &c Ltd, Dalton House, 60 Windsor Avenue, London, SW19 2RR.
Company number 08720141. Registered in England and Wales.

For support please visit www.forgottenbooks.com

1 MONTH OF FREE READING

at

www.ForgottenBooks.com

By purchasing this book you are eligible for one month membership to ForgottenBooks.com, giving you unlimited access to our entire collection of over 1,000,000 titles via our web site and mobile apps.

To claim your free month visit:
www.forgottenbooks.com/free815515

* Offer is valid for 45 days from date of purchase. Terms and conditions apply.

English
Français
Deutsche
Italiano
Español
Português

www.forgottenbooks.com

Mythology Photography **Fiction** Fishing Christianity **Art** Cooking Essays Buddhism Freemasonry Medicine **Biology** Music **Ancient Egypt** Evolution Carpentry Physics Dance Geology **Mathematics** Fitness Shakespeare **Folklore** Yoga Marketing **Confidence** Immortality Biographies Poetry **Psychology** Witchcraft Electronics Chemistry History **Law** Accounting **Philosophy** Anthropology Alchemy Drama Quantum Mechanics Atheism Sexual Health **Ancient History Entrepreneurship** Languages Sport Paleontology Needlework Islam **Metaphysics** Investment Archaeology Parenting Statistics Criminology **Motivational**

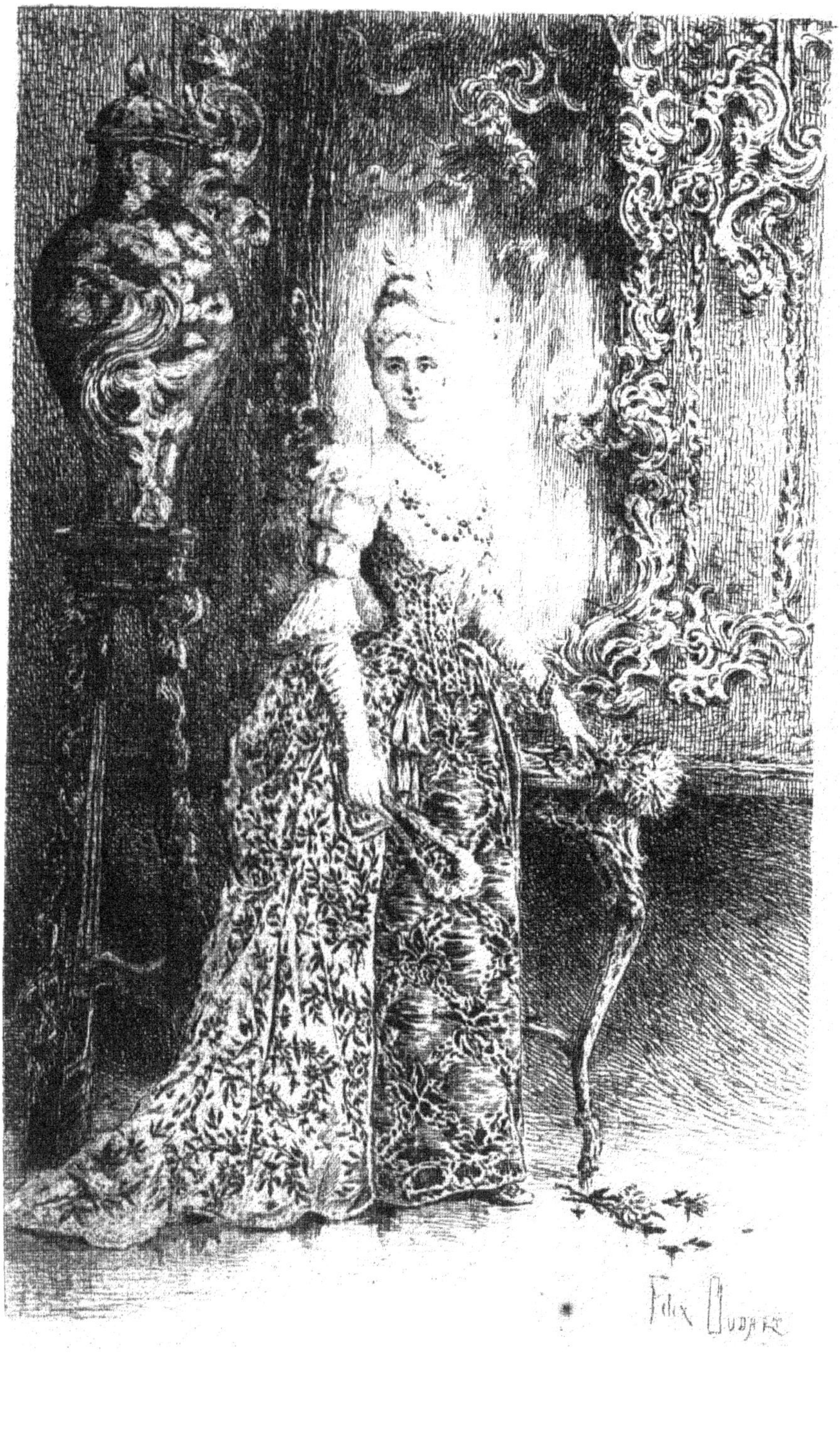
Félix Oudart

Andrée de Taverney.

MEMOIRS OF A PHYSICIAN.

BY

ALEXANDRE DUMAS.

Vol. II.

BOSTON:
LITTLE, BROWN, AND COMPANY.
1899.

Copyright, 1890, 1893,
BY LITTLE, BROWN, AND COMPANY.

UNIVERSITY PRESS:
JOHN WILSON AND SON, CAMBRIDGE, U.S.A.

CONTENTS.

Chapter		Page
I.	Who Monsieur Jacques was	1
II.	The Sorcerer's Wife	12
III.	Parisians	18
IV.	The King's Carriage	28
V.	The Bewitched	38
VI.	Le Comte de Fenix	55
VII.	The Cardinal de Rohan	72
VIII.	The Return from St. Denis	85
IX.	The Garden Pavilion	96
X.	The House in the Rue St. Claude	106
XI.	The double Existence — Sleep	114
XII.	The double Existence — Waking	122
XIII.	The Visit	131
XIV.	Gold	136
XV.	The Elixir of Life	149
XVI.	Inquiries	172
XVII.	The Apartment of the Rue Plastrière	184
XVIII.	Plan of Campaign	190
XIX.	Monsieur de la Vauguyon	201
XX.	The Wedding-Night	211
XXI.	Andrée de Taverney	223
XXII.	The Fireworks	233
XXIII.	The Field of the Dead	241
XXIV.	The Return	253
XXV.	Monsieur de Jussieu	262
XXVI.	Life returns	270

181617

CONTENTS.

Chapter		Page
XXVII.	The Aerial Journey	275
XXVIII.	Brother and Sister	283
XXIX.	What Gilbert had foreseen	296
XXX.	The Botanists	304
XXXI.	The Trap for Philosophers	311
XXXII.	The Apologue	319
XXXIII.	The Expedient of his Majesty Louis XV.	333
XXXIV.	How King Louis XV. transacted Business	342
XXXV.	The Little Trianon	351
XXXVI.	The Conspiracy is renewed	359
XXXVII.	The Sorcerer Chase	369
XXXVIII.	The Courier	382
XXXIX.	The Evocation	390
XL.	The Voice	402
XLI.	Disgrace	409
XLII.	The Duc d'Aiguillon	417
XLIII.	The King divides the Spoils	429
XLIV.	The Antechambers of Duc de Richelieu	438
XLV.	Disenchantment	450
XLVI.	The Dauphin's Family Repast	458
XLVII.	The Queen's Hair	469
XLVIII.	M. de Richelieu appreciates Nicole	479
XLIX.	The Transformation	490
L.	How Pleasure to Some is Despair to Others	496
LI.	The Parliaments	507
LII.	In which it is shown that the Path of a Minister is not always strewn with Roses	517
LIII.	Monsieur d'Aiguillon takes his Revenge	524
LIV.	In which the Reader will once more meet an old Acquaintance whom he thought lost, and whom perhaps he did not regret	531
LV.	The Confusion increases	542

LIST OF ILLUSTRATIONS

MEMOIRS OF A PHYSICIAN

Volume II.

Andrée de Taverney . . . . *Frontispiece*
Drawn and etched by Félix Oudart.

"A long train of carriages filled the avenues of the forest" . . . . *Page* 370
Drawn and etched by E. Van Muyden.

Andrée encounters Gilbert at Trianon . . . . " 459
Drawn by Eugène Courboin, heliogravured by Dujardin.

MEMOIRS OF A PHYSICIAN.

CHAPTER I.

WHO MONSIEUR JACQUES WAS.

GILBERT set to work with the greatest ardor, and his paper was soon covered with careful copies of what was placed before him. The old man looked at him for some time, and then sat down at the other table to correct printed sheets like those of which the bags containing the kidney-beans had been made.

They had passed three hours in this way, and the clock had just struck nine, when Thérèse entered hurriedly. Jacques raised his head.

"Quick, quick!" said she, "come into the other room! Here is another prince come to visit you. When will this procession of grandees be over? I only hope he will not take it into his head to breakfast with us, as the Duc de Chartres did the other day."

"Who is this prince?" asked Jacques, in a low voice.

"Monseigneur the Prince de Conti."

At this name Gilbert let fall on his paper a G which looked much more like a dinner-plate than a note.

"A prince! A grandee!" he muttered to himself.

Jacques left the study smiling; Thérèse followed, and closed the door behind her. Then Gilbert looked around, and finding that he was alone, sat bolt upright with astonishment.

"But where am I then?" exclaimed he. "Princes, highnesses, calling on Monsieur Jacques! The Duc de Chartres, the Prince de Conti calling on a copier of music!" He approached the door to listen; his heart beat strangely.

The first greetings were over between Jacques and the prince, and the latter was speaking. "I should have liked," he said, "to take you with me."

"Why so, Monseigneur?" asked Jacques.

"To introduce you to the dauphiness. A new era is opening for philosophy, my dear philosopher."

"A thousand thanks for your kindness, Monseigneur, but it impossible for me to accompany you."

"Yet, six years ago, you accompanied Madame de Pompadour to Fontainebleau?"

"I was six years younger then. Now I am fastened to my armchair by infirmities."

"And by misanthropy."

"And if it were so, Monseigneur, you must allow that the world is not worth the trouble of putting one's self out of the way for it."

"Well, I will let you off for St. Denis, and the grand ceremonial; but I must take you to Muette, where her Royal Highness will sleep the night after to-morrow."

"Then her Royal Highness arrives at St. Denis the day after to-morrow?"

"Yes, with all her retinue. Come, two leagues are easily travelled. Report represents her Highness to be an excellent musician, — a pupil of Gluck."

Gilbert heard no more. On the day after the morrow

the dauphiness and all her retinue would be at St. Denis; these words suggested but one idea to him, — that the next day but one, Andrée would be only two leagues distant from him. Of the two feelings which he experienced, the stronger overcame the weaker. Love put an end to curiosity. For a moment it seemed to him as if he had not room to breathe. He ran to a window to open it, but it was fastened inside with a padlock, — no doubt to prevent those on the opposite side of the street from seeing what took place in the study.

Gilbert sank on his chair. "Oh! I will never listen at doors again," said he; "I must not try to penetrate the secrets of this man, apparently so humble, whom a prince calls his friend and wishes to present to the future queen of France, — to the daughter of emperors, — whom Mademoiselle Andrée addressed almost kneeling at her feet. And yet perhaps I might hear something of Mademoiselle Andrée. No, no! I should seem like a lackey; La Brie used to listen at doors."

And he courageously retired from the door. But his hands trembled so much that he could not write, and indeed he required some more exciting pursuit to divert his thoughts; he therefore took a book from the table of Monsieur Jacques.

"'The Confessions!'" he read, with joyful surprise, "'embellished with a likeness of the author, Jean Jacques Rousseau;' and I have never yet seen a likeness of Rousseau!" and he hastily turned the silk paper which covered the engraving. No sooner did it meet his eye than he uttered a cry of amazement. At that moment Jacques opened the door. Gilbert compared his face with the likeness in the book, which he held in his hand, then, pale and trembling, he let the volume fall, exclaiming, "I am in the house of Jean Jacques Rousseau!"

"Let me see, my child, how you have copied your music," said Rousseau, smiling, and inwardly better pleased with this involuntary homage than with the thousand triumphs of his glorious life. And passing by the trembling Gilbert, he approached the table and began to examine his work.

"Your notes are not badly formed," said he, "but they are carelessly joined together. Here, there should be a rest, to make the time complete. Then see, the bars which divide it are not quite straight. Make the semibreves by two semicircles; it is not important that they should join. The note made perfectly round is ungraceful, and the stem does not join with it so well. Yes, my friend, you are indeed in the house of Jean Jacques Rousseau."

"Oh, pardon me, Monsieur, for all the foolish words which I have uttered!" exclaimed Gilbert, clasping his hands and ready to fall on his knees.

"Was it necessary that a prince should come to visit me," said Rousseau, shrugging his shoulders, "to enable you to discover in me the unhappy, persecuted philosopher of Geneva? Poor child, — happy in your ignorance of persecution!"

"Oh, yes, I am happy, very happy! But it is in seeing you, in knowing you, in being near you!"

"Thanks, my child, thanks. But it is not enough to be happy, you must work. Now that you have made a trial, take this rondeau and copy it on some proper music-paper. It is short and easy; above all things, observe neatness. But how did you discover — ?"

Gilbert, with a swelling heart, took up the volume and pointed to the portrait.

"Oh, yes, I understand, — my likeness burned in effigy on the first page of the 'Emile'! But no matter, flame is illuminating, whether it proceeds from the sun or from an *auto-da-fé*."

"Ah! Monsieur, my wildest dreams never exceeded this! To live with you! My highest ambition never hoped for more!"

"You cannot live with me, my friend," said Jean Jacques, "for I do not take pupils; as for guests, you perceive that I am not rich enough to entertain them, — certainly not to receive them as regular inmates."

Gilbert trembled. Rousseau took his hand.

"However," said he, "do not despair. From the moment I first saw you, I have been studying your character. In it there is much which requires to be corrected, but there is also much to esteem. Learn to subdue your inclinations. Distrust your pride, — that gnawing worm which is the bane of philosophy. Copy music, and wait patiently for better times."

"Oh, heavens!" said Gilbert, "I feel bewildered when I think of what has happened to me."

"What has happened to you is very simple and very natural, my child. You were flying, I know not whence, for I did not seek to know your secret, and in your flight you met a man gathering plants in a wood. He had bread, you had none; he shared his with you. You did not know where to seek an asylum for the night; he offered you the shelter of his roof. The man happened to be called Rousseau, — that is the whole affair. This man said to you, 'The first precept of philosophy is, "Man, be sufficient unto thyself."' Now, my friend, when you have copied your rondeau you will have gained your bread for to-day. Copy your rondeau, therefore."

"Oh, Monsieur, what kindness!"

"As for your lodging, that is yours into the bargain, — only, no reading at night; or, if you must have a candle, let it be your own, otherwise Thérèse will scold. In the mean time, are you hungry?"

"Oh, no, Monsieur!" replied Gilbert, in a choking voice.

"There is enough left from our supper of last night to serve for this morning's breakfast. Do not stand on ceremony; this repast is the last you will get at my table unless by invitation, if we remain friends."

Gilbert made a movement as if to speak, but Rousseau interrupted him. "There is in the Rue Plastrière," he continued, "a modest eating-house for mechanics; you can dine there on moderate terms, for I shall recommend you to the proprietor. In the mean time, come to breakfast."

Gilbert followed Rousseau without daring to reply. He was completely subdued; but at least it was by a man superior to most other men.

After a few mouthfuls he left the table and returned to his task. He spoke truly; his emotion was so great that it had taken away his appetite. During the whole day he never raised his eyes from the paper; and at eight in the evening, after having torn up three sheets, he had succeeded in copying legibly and neatly a rondeau of four pages.

"I will not flatter you," said Rousseau; "it is not yet well done, but it is legible. What you have done is worth ten sous; here is the money."

Gilbert took it with a low bow.

"There is some bread in the cupboard, M. Gilbert," said Thérèse, on whom the young man's modest demeanor, mildness, and industry had produced a favorable impression.

"Thank you, Madame!" replied Gilbert; "believe me, I shall never forget your kindness."

"Here!" said she, holding the bread out to him.

He was about to refuse, but looking at Rousseau, he saw, by the slight frown which contracted his piercing eye, and the curl which hovered on his delicately formed lips, that the refusal would wound him. "I accept your kind offer," said he.

He then withdrew to his little chamber, holding in his hand the six silver sous and the four copper ones which he had just received. "At last," said he, on entering his garret, "I am my own master! But stay,—not yet, since I hold in my hand the bread of charity!" And although he felt hungry, he laid down the piece of bread on the sill of the skylight, and did not eat it. Then, fancying that sleep would enable him to forget his hunger, he blew out his candle and stretched himself on his straw pallet.

Gilbert was awake before daybreak on the following morning, for in truth he had slept very little during the night. Recollecting what Rousseau had said about the gardens, he leaned out of the sky-light and saw below him the trees and shrubs of a very beautiful garden, and beyond the trees the hôtel to which the garden belonged, the entrance to which was from the Rue Jussienne.

In one corner of the garden, quite surrounded by shrubs and flowers, there stood a little summer-house, the windows of which were closed. Gilbert at first thought that the windows were closed on account of the earliness of the hour; but observing that the foliage of the trees had grown up against the shutters, he was convinced that the summer-house must have been unoccupied since the preceding winter at least. He returned, therefore, to his admiring contemplation of the noble lime-trees, which partially concealed from view the main body of the hôtel.

Two or three times during his survey Gilbert's eyes had

turned toward the piece of bread which Thérèse had cut for him the evening before; but although hunger pleaded loudly, he was so much the master of himself that he refrained from touching it.

Five o'clock struck. Gilbert was persuaded that the door of the passage must now be open; and washed, brushed, and combed, — for Rousseau had furnished his garret with all that was necessary for his modest toilet, — he descended the stairs with his piece of bread under his arm.

Rousseau, who this time was not the first to be up, and who from a lingering suspicion perhaps, and the better to watch his guest, had left his door open, heard him descend, and narrowly observed his movements. He saw Gilbert leave the house with the bread under his arm; a poor man came up to him, and he saw Gilbert give him the bread, and then enter a baker's shop, which was just opened, and buy another piece.

"Now," said Rousseau, "he will go to a tavern, and his poor ten sous will soon vanish."

But he was mistaken. Gilbert ate a part of his bread as he walked along; then stopping at a fountain at the corner of the street he took a long draught, ate the rest of his bread, drank again, rinsed his mouth, washed his hands, and returned toward the house.

"Ha!" said Rousseau, "I believe that I am more fortunate than Diogenes, and have found a man!" And hearing Gilbert's footsteps on the stairs, he hastened to open the door.

The entire day was spent in uninterrupted labor. Gilbert brought to his monotonous task activity, intelligence, and unshrinking assiduity. What he did not perfectly comprehend he divined; and his hand, the slave of his iron will, traced the notes without hesitation and without mistake. By evening he had copied seven pages, if not elegantly, at least with scrupulous correctness.

Rousseau examined his work with the eye both of a judge and a philosopher. As a judge he criticised the forms of the notes, the fineness of the joinings, the spaces for the rests and dots; but he acknowledged that there was a decided improvement since the day before, and he gave Gilbert twenty-five sous.

As a philosopher Rousseau admired the strength of resolution which could bend the ardent temperament and active and athletic frame of a young man of eighteen to such constant and unceasing labor. For he had discovered that in that young heart there burned an ardent passion; but whether ambition or love, he had not yet ascertained.

Gilbert gazed thoughtfully at the money which he had received; it was a piece of twenty-four sous and a single sou. He put the sou in his waistcoat pocket, probably with the other sous which were remaining from the little sum of the day before, and grasping the silver with evident satisfaction in his right hand, he said: "Monsieur, you are my master, since you give me work, and also lodge me in your house gratis. I think it only right, therefore, that I should communicate to you all my intentions, otherwise I might lose your regard."

Rousseau looked at him with a lowering eye. "What are you going to do?" said he. "Have you any other intention than that of working to-morrow?"

"Monsieur, for to-morrow, yes. With your permission, I should like to be at liberty to-morrow."

"What to do," said Rousseau, — "to idle?"

"Monsieur," said Gilbert, "I wish to go to St. Denis."

"To St. Denis?"

"Yes; Madame the Dauphiness is to arrive there to-morrow."

"Ah! true; there are to be festivities in honor of her arrival."

"That is it, Monsieur."

"I thought you less of a sight-seer, my young friend," said Rousseau. "I gave you credit, at first, on the contrary, for despising the pomps of absolute power."

"Monsieur —"

"Look at me, — me whom you pretend to take for a model. Yesterday one of the royal princes came to invite me to court. Well, observe: I, a humble citizen, refused his invitation, — not to go as you would go, my poor lad, on foot, and standing on tiptoe to catch a glimpse, over the shoulder of a guardsman, of the king's carriage as it passes, but to appear before princes, — to be honored by a smile from princesses."

Gilbert nodded his approbation.

"And why did I refuse?" continued Rousseau, with vehemence. "Because a man ought not to have two faces; because the man who has written that royalty is an abuse ought not to be seen bending before a king. Because I — who know that every festivity of the great robs the people of some portion of that comfort which is now scarcely sufficient to keep them from revolt — I protest by my absence against all such festivities."

"Monsieur," said Gilbert, "believe me, I comprehend all the sublimity of your philosophy."

"Doubtless; and yet, since you do not practise it, permit me to tell you —"

"Monsieur," said Gilbert, "I am not a philosopher."

"Tell me, at least, what you are going to do at St. Denis."

"Monsieur, I am discreet."

Rousseau was struck by these words; he saw that there was some mystery concealed under this obstinate desire, and he looked at this young man with a sort of admiration which his character inspired.

"Oh, very well!" said he; "I see you have a motive. I like that better."

"Yes, Monsieur, I have a motive, — one, I assure you, in no way connected with an idle love for pomp or show."

"So much the better; or perhaps I should say so much the worse. There is something unfathomable in your look, young man, and I seek in vain in its expression for the frankness and calm of youth."

"I told you, Monsieur, that I have been unhappy," replied Gilbert, sorrowfully, "and for the unhappy there is no youth. Then you consent to give me to-morrow to myself?"

"Yes."

"Thank you, Monsieur."

"Remember, however," said Rousseau, "that while you are gazing at the vain pomps of the world defiling in procession before you, I shall, in one of my herbals, be passing in review the splendor and variety of Nature."

"Monsieur," said Gilbert, "would you not have left all the herbals in the world the day when you went to visit Mademoiselle Galley after having thrown the bunch of cherries into her lap?"

"Good!" said Rousseau. "True, you are young. Go to St. Denis, my child." Then, when Gilbert, with a joyful countenance, had left the room, "It is not ambition," said he, "it is love."

CHAPTER II.

THE SORCERER'S WIFE.

At the moment when Gilbert, after his hard day's labor, was munching in his loft his bread dipped in cold water, and inhaling with delight the pure air of the gardens below him, a woman mounted on a magnificent Arabian horse was advancing at full gallop toward St. Denis, along that road which was now deserted, but which on the morrow was to be crowded with so much rank and fashion. She was dressed with elegance, but in a strange and peculiar style, and her face was hidden by a thick veil. On entering the town she proceeded straight to the Carmelite convent, and dismounting, knocked with her delicately formed finger at the wicket, while her horse, which she held by the bridle, snorted and pawed the ground with impatience.

Several inhabitants of the town, struck with curiosity, gathered around her. They were attracted in the first place by her foreign attire, then by her persistent knocking.

"What is it you want, Madame?" said one of them at length.

"You see, Monsieur," she replied, with a strongly marked Italian accent, "I wish to obtain admittance."

"In that case, you are taking the wrong way. This gate is opened only once a day to the poor, and the hour is now past."

"What must I do, then, to gain an audience of the Superior?"

"You must knock at that little door at the extremity of the wall, or ring at the grand entrance."

Another person now approached. "Do you know, Madame," said he, "that the present abbess is her Royal Highness, Madame Louise of France?"

"I know it, thank you," she replied.

"*Vertudieu!* What a splendid animal!" exclaimed a dragoon, gazing in admiration at the foreigner's steed. "Now, that horse, if not too old, is worth five hundred louis-d'or, as sure as mine is worth a hundred pistoles!"

These words produced a great effect on the crowd. At that moment a monk, who, unlike the dragoon, looked only at the rider, to the exclusion of her steed, made his way toward her, and by some secret known to himself alone, opened the wicket of the tower. "Enter, Madame," said he, "and lead in your horse, if you please."

The woman, eager to escape from the gaze of the crowd, which seemed to terrify her, hurried in, and the gate was closed behind her. The moment she found herself alone in the large courtyard she shook the bridle loose on the horse's neck, and the noble animal, rejoiced to feel himself at liberty, made his trappings clash, and pawed the ground so loudly that the portress, who happened for the moment to be off her post, hastened out from the interior of the convent. "What do you want, Madame?" she cried; "and how did you gain admittance here?"

"A charitable monk opened the gate for me," said the stranger. "As for my business, I wish, if possible, to speak to the Superior."

"Madame will not receive any one this evening."

"Yet I have been told that it is the duty of Superiors of convents to admit, at any hour of the day or night, their sisters of the world who come to implore their succor."

"Possibly so, in ordinary circumstances; but her Royal Highness, who arrived only the day before yesterday, is scarcely installed in her office yet, and holds this evening a chapter of our Order."

"Oh, Madame!" replied the stranger, "I come from a great distance,— I come from Rome. I have travelled sixty leagues on horseback, and am almost exhausted."

"What can I do? The orders of the Superior are positive."

"My sister, I have to reveal to your abbess matters of the highest importance."

"Return to-morrow."

"It is impossible. I have stayed one day in Paris, and already during that day— Besides, I cannot sleep at an inn."

"Why so?"

"Because I have no money."

The nun gazed in amazement at this woman, covered with jewels, and mistress of a fine horse, who pretended that she had no money to pay for a night's lodging.

"Oh, do not heed my words, do not examine my dress!" said the young woman; "perhaps I did not speak the precise truth when I said I had no money, for no doubt I could obtain credit in any inn. But what I want is not a lodging, but a refuge."

"Madame, this is not the only convent in St. Denis, and each convent has an abbess."

"Yes, yes! I know that well; but it is not a common abbess who can protect me."

"I think you are wrong in persisting thus. The Princess Louise no longer takes any interest in affairs of this world."

"What matters it to you? Only tell her that I wish to speak to her."

"She is holding a chapter, I tell you."

"After it is over, then."

"It has scarcely begun."

"I can go into the church and wait there in prayer."

"I am sorry, Madame, that I cannot permit you to wait there."

"Oh, then I am mistaken, — I am not in the house of God!" cried the stranger, with such vehemence of voice and look that the nun, alarmed, dared no longer oppose her wishes.

"If you are really in great distress," said she, "I will see what I can do."

"Oh! tell her Royal Highness," added the foreigner, "that I come from Rome; that I have made only two halts on the road, — one at Mayence, the other at Strasburg; that during the last four days I have rested only for the time absolutely necessary for myself and my horse to regain strength to continue our journey."

"I will tell her, sister;" and the nun hastened away.

A moment after, a lay sister appeared, followed by the portress.

"Well?" exclaimed the stranger, impatient to know what reply had been sent.

"Her Royal Highness says, Madame," replied the lay sister, "that it is quite impossible to give you an audience this evening; but that nevertheless the hospitality of the convent shall be extended to you, since you are in such urgent want of an asylum. You may follow me, therefore, sister, and if you have made so long a journey as you say, and are fatigued, you can retire to rest at once."

"But my horse?"

"Rest assured he shall be taken care of, my sister."

"He is as gentle as a lamb. He is called Djerid, and comes when called by that name. I entreat you to take care of him, for he is a most valuable animal."

"He shall be treated as if he were one of the king's horses."

"Thanks."

"In the mean time, conduct Madame to her apartment," said the lay sister to the portress.

"Not to my apartment, — to the church! I do not require sleep, but prayer."

"The chapel is open, my sister," said the nun, pointing to a little side door opening into the church.

"And I shall see the Superior in the morning?" asked the stranger.

"To-morrow morning? That is also impossible."

"Why so?"

"Because to-morrow morning there will be a grand reception."

"And for whom can a reception be more necessary than for an unfortunate like me?"

"Madame the Dauphiness will do us the honor to spend two hours here on her way through town to-morrow. It is a great honor for our convent, and a high solemnity for us poor nuns; so that, you understand, the abbess is most anxious that everything should be worthy of the royal guests we expect."

"But in the mean time," said the stranger, looking around with a shudder, "while I wait the leisure of your august Superior, shall I be in safety here?"

"Undoubtedly, my sister. Our house is a refuge even for the guilty; much more for —"

"For fugitives," said the stranger. "It is well; then no one can enter here?"

"No one, — that is, not without an order."

"Oh, but if he procures an order! Good heavens! — he who is so powerful that his power at times terrifies me!"

"He, — who?" asked the nun.

"Oh, no one, no one!"

"The poor creature is deranged," murmured the nun to herself.

"The church, the church!" repeated the stranger, so wildly as in some degree to justify this suspicion.

"Come, my sister, let me lead you to it."

"Yes, yes, I am pursued; look you — quick! The church!"

"Oh, the walls of St. Denis are strong!" said the nun, with a compassionate smile. "Believe me, after such a journey as you have described, you had much better go and rest in a good bed than bruise your knees on the stones of our chapel."

"No, no! I wish to pray; I wish to pray that God will rescue me from my pursuers!" cried the young woman, hurriedly entering the church by the door which the nun pointed out, and shutting the door behind her. The nun, curious, as all nuns are, hastened round to the principal entrance, and, advancing softly, saw the unknown praying and sobbing before the altar, her face bowed to the ground.

CHAPTER III.

PARISIANS.

THE nuns had informed the stranger correctly when they told her that the chapter of the convent was assembled in conclave. Madame Louise of France presided at the meeting, her first exercise of supreme authority, and assisted in their deliberation as to the best means of giving the daughter of the Cæsars a reception worthy of her august character and station.

The funds of the convent were rather low. The late abbess, on resigning her functions, had carried away with her a large portion of the lace, which was her private property, as well as the reliquaries and monstrances, which it was the practice of Superiors, who were all taken from the highest families, to lend to their convents, on devoting themselves to the service of God from the most worldly motives.

Madame Louise, on being informed of the intended visit of the dauphiness, had sent an express to Versailles, and the same night a wagon had arrived loaded with hangings, lace, and ornaments, to the value of six hundred thousand francs.

Consequently, when the tidings were spread of the royal splendor which was to be exhibited at the reception of the dauphiness, all the ardent curiosity of the Parisians was redoubled, — those Parisians whom Mercier describes as provoking only a smile when seen in private life, but assembled in masses, inciting rather to reflection and sorrow.

From earliest dawn the citizens of the capital, having learned from public report the route which the dauphiness was to take, began to issue from their dens, and at first in parties of ten or twenty, then in hundreds, and finally in thousands, they arrived at St. Denis.

The French and Swiss guards and the regiments stationed at St. Denis were under arms, and formed a line on each side of the road to keep back the waves of the living tide which rolled on toward the gates of the cathedral, and mounted even to the sculptured projections of the building. A sea of heads appeared everywhere, children's peeping from above the porches of doors, men's and women's thronging the windows. Besides these, thousands of curious spectators, who had arrived too late to secure places, or who, like Gilbert, preferred their liberty to the constraint and inconvenience of being shut up during the whole day in one spot, swarmed like ants on every side, climbing the trees which bordered the road from St. Denis to Muette, or dispersed here and there waiting for the procession.

The cortège, although still containing a numerous train of sumptuous equipages, and troops of domestics in splendid liveries, had considerably diminished after leaving Compiègne; for, except for the great lords, it was found impossible to keep pace with the king, who doubled and tripled the usual stages, by means of relays posted on the road.

Those of lesser note had remained at Compiègne, or had taken post to return to Paris, and give their horses a breathing-spell. But after a day's repose at their own houses, masters and domestics now thronged toward St. Denis both to see the crowd and to get another glimpse of the dauphiness, whom they had already seen once. And then, besides the court carriages, were there not at that period the carriages of the parliament, the financiers, the rich merchants, the ladies of fashion and of the opera? Were there not, also, hired horses and carriages, as well as public conveyances, which, crowded with good citizens of Paris, rolled toward St. Denis, moving slowly, and arriving later than if the journey had been made on foot? It may easily be imagined, therefore, what a formidable army directed its march toward St. Denis on the morning of the day when the gazettes and placards had announced that the dauphiness was to arrive, forming into a dense mass before the convent of the Carmelites, and when no more room could be obtained within the privileged enclosure, stretching away in long lines on the road by which the dauphiness and her suite were to arrive and depart.

Now, let any one picture to himself in this crowd, terrible even to the Parisian, Gilbert, insignificant in stature, alone, undecided, ignorant of localities, and too proud even to ask a question; for since he was in Paris, he had determined to pass for a Parisian, — he who had never before seen a hundred people assembled together.

At first he saw pedestrians thinly scattered along the road; at La Chapelle they began to increase, and at St. Denis they seemed to rise out of the ground, and presented much the appearance of an immense field bristling with ears of corn. For a long time Gilbert had seen nothing, lost as he was in the crowd; he could not look over the heads of those around him, and, swept along in the throng, he blindly followed where the concourse of spectators led him.

At last he saw some children perched on a tree, and longed to imitate their example; but he dared not take off his coat. He made his way, however, to the foot of the tree just as one of those unfortunates — who like himself were deprived of all view, and who staggered onward, stepping on the feet of others, and having their own feet trodden upon — conceived the bright idea of questioning their lucky neighbors perched on the branches, and learned from one of them that there was a large space vacant between the convent and the guards. Gilbert, encouraged by this first question, ventured in his turn to ask whether the carriages were in sight.

They had not yet appeared; but on the road, about a quarter of a league beyond St. Denis, a great cloud of dust was plainly visible. This was what Gilbert wished to know; the carriages not being in sight, it was needful only to ascertain precisely by what route they would approach.

In Paris, when one goes through a crowd without entering into conversation with any one, he is set down as either an Englishman or deaf and dumb.

Scarcely had Gilbert extricated himself from the multitude, when he perceived, seated behind a ditch, the family of a humble tradesman at breakfast. There was a blue-eyed daughter, tall and fair, modest and timid. There was the mother, a fat, laughing little woman, with white teeth and rosy cheeks. There was an aunt, tall, bony, dry, and harsh. There was the father, half-buried in an immense camlet coat, which was usually brought out of his chest only on Sundays, but which he ventured to put on on so grand an occasion as the present, and of which he took more care than he did of his wife and daughter, being certain that they could take care of themselves. There was the servant-maid, who did nothing but laugh. She carried an enormous basket containing everything necessary for breakfast, and even under its weight the stout lass had never ceased laughing and singing, encouraged as she was by her master, who took the burden when she was fatigued. In those days a domestic was one of the family, and occupied a position in it very analogous to that of the house-dog, beaten sometimes, excluded never.

Gilbert contemplated by stealth this group which was so new to him. Shut up at Taverney from his birth, he had hitherto seen only the lord and the lackey; the citizen was altogether a novelty to him. He saw these honest people employ in their domestic economy a system of philosophy which, although not drawn from the teachings of Plato and Socrates, was modelled much after that of Bias, *in extenso.*

They had brought with them as much food as they possibly could, and were determined to make the most of it. The father was carving one of those appetizing pieces of roast veal so much liked by the Parisian tradesmen. Nicely browned, dainty, and tempting, it reposed amid a bed of carrots, onions, and bacon, in the dish in which the day before it had been baked, carefully placed there by the good housekeeper. The maid had then carried it to the baker, who while baking his loaves, had given it an asylum in his oven along with a score of such dishes, destined to enhance the enjoyments of the following day.

Gilbert chose out a place for himself at the foot of a neighboring elm, and dusted it carefully with his checked pocket-handkerchief. He then took off his hat, spread his handkerchief on the ground, and seated himself. He paid no attention to his neighbors, and they, seeing this, naturally took notice of him.

"That is a careful young man," said the mother.

The daughter blushed. She always did so when a young man was mentioned before her,—a trait in her character which gave the highest gratification to her parents.

The father turned. "And a handsome lad too," said he. The daughter blushed still more deeply than before.

"He looks tired," said the servant-maid, "and yet he has not been carrying anything."

"Rather say lazy," said the aunt.

"Monsieur," said the mother, addressing Gilbert with that familiarity which is found nowhere but among the Parisians, "are the carriages still far off?"

Gilbert turned, and seeing that these words were addressed to him, rose and bowed.

"A most polite young man," said the mother.

This remark added a still deeper dye to the daughter's cheeks.

"I do not know, Madame," answered Gilbert; "I only heard that a cloud of dust was seen about a quarter of a league off."

"Draw nearer, Monsieur," said the honest tradesman, "and if you have not breakfasted —" and he pointed to the excellent repast which was spread on the grass.

Gilbert approached the group. He had not breakfasted, and the seducing odor of the viands tempted him strongly; but he jingled his twenty-five sous in his pocket, and reflecting that for the third of this sum he could purchase a breakfast almost as good as that which was offered to him, he would not accept any favor from people whom he saw for the first time.

"Thank you, Monsieur," said he, "a thousand thanks; but I have already breakfasted."

"Ah!" said the good woman, "I see that you are a prudent young man. But from where you are seated you will see nothing."

"Why," replied Gilbert, smiling, "in that case you will not see anything yourselves, as you are in the same position as I am."

"Oh, it is a very different matter with us! We have a nephew a sergeant in the French guards."

The young girl looked like a peony.

"His post this morning will be in front of the Paon Bleu."

"If I am not taking too great a liberty," said Gilbert, "may I ask where the Paon Bleu is?"

"Just opposite the Carmelite convent," replied the mother. "He has promised to keep places for us behind his detachment. He will then give us his bench, and we shall see at our ease all the company get out of their carriages."

It was now Gilbert's turn to redden; he had refused to eat with the good people, but he longed to be of their party. Nevertheless, his philosophy, or rather his pride, whispered: "It is very well for women to require some one to assist them, but I, a man, have arms and shoulders of my own."

"All those who do not reach that place," continued the mother, as if guessing his thoughts, "will see only empty carriages,— no great sight in truth, for empty carriages can be seen everywhere; it is not worth while to come to St. Denis for that."

"But, Madame," said Gilbert, "it seems to me that many besides yourself will endeavor to secure the place you speak of."

"Yes; but every one has not a nephew in the guards to assist them."

"Ah, true!" murmured Gilbert. As he said this, his face wore an expression of disappointment which did not escape Parisian penetration.

"But," said the husband, well skilled in divining the wishes of his wife, "this gentleman may accompany us if he pleases."

"Oh, Monsieur, I fear I should be troublesome," replied Gilbert.

"Bah! not at all," said the good woman; "on the contrary, you will assist us in reaching our places. We have only one man now to depend on, and then we should have two."

No other argument could have had so much weight in determining Gilbert. The idea that he could be useful, and thus pay for the favor which was offered him, put him quite at his ease and relieved him of every scruple. He accepted the offer.

"We shall see to whom he will offer his arm," said the aunt.

This assistance was indeed a real God-send to Gilbert. How, without it, could he have passed through a barrier of thirty thousand persons, each more favored than himself by rank, wealth, or strength, and especially by the practice they had acquired in obtaining places at fêtes, where every one seizes the best he can procure?

Had our philosopher been less theoretical and more practical, the present occasion would have furnished him an admirable opportunity for studying the dynamics of society.

The carriage with four horses burst like a cannon-ball through the mass; all fell back before its running footman, with his plumed hat, his gayly striped jacket, and his thick stick, who rushed on in advance, sometimes preceded by two formidable coach-dogs.

From the carriage with two horses was whispered a sort of pass-word in the ear of a guardsman, after which it proceeded to take its place in the square before the convent.

Single horsemen, although overlooking the crowd from their elevated position, were forced to advance at a foot-pace, and gained a good position only after a thousand jostlings, interruptions, and oaths.

Lastly, the poor pedestrian, trodden, trampled on, and tossed about, was driven forward like a wave urged on by thousands of waves behind. Sometimes raising himself on tiptoe to see over the heads of his neighbors; sometimes wrestling like Antæus, to fall like him to his mother Earth; seeking his way through the multitude, and when he had found it, dragging after him his family, — almost always a troop of women, — whom the Parisian alone ventures to attempt conducting through such scenes.

Lowest of all was the man of the dregs of the people. With unshaven beard and ragged cap, his arms naked to the elbow, and his garments held together by a string, indefatigably working with elbows, with shoulders, and with feet, and ever and anon uttering a savage and sardonic laugh, he made his way among the crowd as easily as Gulliver amid the Liliputians.

Gilbert, who was neither a great lord with four horses, nor a member of parliament with two, nor a soldier on horseback, nor a Parisian, nor a man of the people, certainly would have been trampled under foot by the throng had he not been under the protection of the tradesman. Backed by him he felt powerful, and boldly offered his arm to the mother of the family.

"Impertinent fellow!" said the aunt.

They set out; the father gave his sister and his daughter each an arm, and the maid-servant followed behind with the basket.

"Gentlemen, may I trouble you?" said the good woman, with her ready laugh. "Gentlemen, if you please, a little room. Gentlemen, be good enough — "

And every one fell back and yielded a passage to her and Gilbert, while in their wake glided the rest of the party. Foot by foot, step by step, they managed to advance five hundred paces, and then found themselves close to that formidable line of French guards on which the tradesman and his family rested all their hopes. The daughter had by this time regained her natural color. Once there, the citizen mounted on Gilbert's shoulders, and perceived at twenty yards' distance from him his wife's nephew twisting his moustache. The good man made such violent gestures with his hat that at last his nephew's attention was attracted to him; he came forward, asked his comrades to make way a little, and obtained a slight opening in their ranks.

Through this chink slipped Gilbert and the good woman, then the citizen himself, the sister and daughter, and after them the stout lass with the basket. Their troublesome journey was over, and mutual thanks were exchanged between Gilbert and the head of the family. The mother endeavored to detain him by their side; the aunt said he had better go; and they separated, not to meet again.

In the open space in which Gilbert now found himself, none but privileged persons were admitted, and he therefore easily reached the trunk of a large linden-tree, mounted upon a stone near it, and, supporting himself by a low branch, waited patiently. About half an hour after he had thus installed himself, the cannon roared, the rattling of the drums was heard, and the great bell of the cathedral sent forth its first majestic peal.

CHAPTER IV.

THE KING'S CARRIAGES.

A DULL heavy sound was heard in the distance, which became stronger and deeper as it advanced. As Gilbert listened, he felt every nerve in his body vibrate painfully.

The people were shouting "Vive le roi!" It was still the fashion then. Onward came a cloud of prancing horses covered with housings of gold and purple; these were the musketeers, the gendarmes, and Swiss horse-guards. Then followed a massive carriage magnificently decorated.

Gilbert perceived in the carriage a blue ribbon and a majestic head not uncovered. He saw the cold, penetrating light of the royal look, before which every form bent and every head was uncovered. Fascinated, motionless, breathless, he forgot to take off his hat. A violent blow roused him from his trance; his hat rolled on the ground. He sprang forward, lifted it up, and looking round, saw the tradesman's nephew looking at him with that truculent smile which is peculiar to the soldier. "Well," said he, "so you don't take off your hat to the king?"

Gilbert turned pale, and looked at his hat, covered with dust. "It is the first time I ever saw the king," said he, "and I forgot to salute him, it is true. But I did not know —"

"You did not know?" said the soldier, frowning.

Gilbert feared that he should be driven from the spot where he was so well placed for seeing Andrée, and love conquered pride. "Pardon me," said he, "I am from the country."

"And you have come to Paris to be educated, my little man?"

"Yes, Monsieur," replied Gilbert, swallowing his rage.

"Well, since you are seeking instruction," said the sergeant, arresting Gilbert's hand as he was putting his hat on his head, "learn this: you must take off your hat to the dauphiness as well as to the king, and to their Royal Highnesses the princes as well as to the dauphiness, — in short, you must take it off to all the carriages on which you see the *fleur-de-lis*. Do you know the *fleur-de-lis*, my little fellow, or must I show you what it is?"

"Quite unnecessary, Monsieur; I know it."

"It is well you know even that much," grumbled the sergeant.

The royal carriages continued to file past. As each reached the door of the convent, it stopped to permit its occupants to alight. This operation caused every five minutes a general halt along the whole line.

At one of these halts Gilbert felt as if a fiery sword had pierced his heart. He became giddy, everything swam before his eyes, and he trembled so violently that he was forced to grasp his branch more firmly to prevent himself from falling. About ten paces from him, in one of the carriages with the *fleur-de-lis* to which the sergeant had desired him to take off his hat, he had just perceived Andrée. Dressed in white, and dazzling with beauty, she seemed to his excited eyes some angelic being from a higher sphere. He uttered a stifled cry; but immediately afterward, conquering his agitation, he commanded his heart to be still and his gaze steady; and so great was his self-control that he succeeded.

Andrée, on her side, wishing to know why the procession had stopped, leaned forward out of the carriage, and directing her clear and limpid gaze around, she perceived Gilbert and at once recognized him. Gilbert feared that on seeing him she would be surprised, and would point him out to her father. He was not mistaken. With an air of astonishment she turned toward the Baron de Taverney, who, decorated with his red ribbon, sat with great dignity beside her, and directed his attention to Gilbert.

"Gilbert?" cried the baron, starting, "Gilbert here? And who, then, will take care of Mahon down yonder?"

The young man heard these words distinctly, and with the most studied respect he bowed to Andrée and the baron. It required all his strength to accomplish this feat.

"It is really he!" continued the baron, on perceiving our philosopher. "It is the little rascal himself!" The idea that Gilbert was in Paris was so far removed from his thoughts that at first he would not believe his daughter's assertions, and could hardly credit even his own eyes. As for Andrée, whom Gilbert examined closely, after the first slight shade of surprise had passed away, her countenance resumed an expression of perfect calm.

The baron leaned out of the carriage window and signed to Gilbert to approach; but as he attempted to obey, the sergeant stopped him.

"You see that I am called," said he.

"By whom?" demanded the sergeant.

"The gentleman in that carriage."

The sergeant's eye followed the direction of Gilbert's finger, and rested on the Baron de Taverney's carriage.

"Pray allow him to come this way, Sergeant," said the baron. "I wish to speak to the lad, — two words only."

"Four, Monsieur, four, if you like," replied the soldier.

"You have plenty of time; they are now reading an address at the gate, and I daresay it will occupy half an hour. Pass through, young man."

"Come hither, you rascal!" said the baron to Gilbert, who affected to walk at his usual pace, "and tell me by what accident it happens you are here, when you ought to be at Taverney!"

Gilbert saluted Andrée and the baron a second time, and replied : "It was no accident which brought me to Paris, Monsieur; I came hither of my own free will."

"Your free will, you scoundrel! Do you talk of your will to me?"

"Why not? Every free man has a right to his will."

"Oh, ho! Free man! You imagine yourself free, do you, you little wretch?"

"Certainly I am; I have never sold my freedom to any one."

"Upon my word, this is an amusing sort of a scoundrel!" exclaimed the baron, confounded at the coolness with which Gilbert spoke. "Your free will led you to Paris! And how did you travel; what assistance had you, if you please?"

"I came on foot."

"On foot!" said Andrée, with a slight expression of pity in her tone.

"And what do you intend to do in Paris?" inquired the baron.

"To get educated first, — then make my fortune."

"Educated?"

"Yes, I am certain of being educated."

"Make your fortune?"

"I hope to make it."

"And in the mean time what do you do, — beg?"

"Beg!" exclaimed Gilbert, with lofty scorn.

"You steal, then?"

"Monsieur," said Gilbert, with a look so proud and fierce that it fixed Andrée's attention on him for a moment, "did I ever steal from you?"

"What can your idle hands do but steal?"

"What those of a man of genius do, — a man whom I wish to imitate, were it only in his perseverance," replied Gilbert. "They copy music."

Andrée turned towards him. "Copy music?" said she.

"Yes, Mademoiselle."

"You know music, then?" she inquired, with the same contemptuous tone in which she would have said, "It is false."

"I know my notes, and that is enough for a copyist."

"And how the devil did you learn your notes, you rascal?" cried the baron.

"Yes, how?" added Andrée, smiling.

"I love music, Monsieur, passionately; and when Mademoiselle Andrée played on the harpsichord every day, I hid myself that I might listen."

"Good-for-nothing fellow!"

"At first I remembered the airs; then, as they were written in a music-book, by degrees I learned to read the notes from the book."

"From my music-book?" exclaimed Andrée, with the utmost indignation. "Did you dare to touch my music-book?"

"No, Mademoiselle, I did not permit myself to do so; but as it remained open on the harpsichord, sometimes in one place, sometimes in another, I endeavored to read in it, but without touching it. My eyes would not soil the pages."

"You will see," cried the baron, "that the fellow will assert next that he plays on the piano like Haydn!"

"I should probably have been able by this time to

play," said Gilbert, "had I dared to place my fingers on the keys."

Andrée in spite of herself again glanced at that face which was animated by a sentiment only to be compared to the fanaticism of a martyr; but the baron, who did not possess his daughter's clear and comprehensive intellect, felt his choler rise on reflecting that the young man was in the right, and that he had been treated inhumanly in being left with Mahon at Taverney. It is not easy to pardon in an inferior the wrong which he proves you have done him; and the baron therefore became more furious in proportion as his daughter became calm. "Wretch!" cried he, "you steal away; you go running about like a vagabond; and when questioned about your mode of life you utter such a tissue of absurdities as those which we have just heard! But it shall not be my fault if rogues and pickpockets infest the king's highways."

Andrée by a gesture entreated her father to be calm; she knew that ungoverned anger annuls superiority. But the baron thrust aside her hand, which she had placed on his arm, and continued: "I shall recommend you to the notice of the Comte de Sartines, and you shall speedily take a turn in the Bicêtre, scarecrow of a philosopher!"

Gilbert stepped back, crushed his hat under his arm, and pale with anger exclaimed: "Learn, Monsieur le Baron, that since I arrived in Paris I have found protectors in whose ante-chambers your Comte de Sartines would be glad to wait!"

"Indeed!" said the baron. "In that case, if you escape a prison you shall not escape a good caning. Andrée, call your brother!"

Andrée leaned forward out of the carriage and said imperiously to Gilbert, "Come, Monsieur Gilbert, you must withdraw."

"Philippe! Philippe!" shouted the old man.

"Leave us!" said Andrée again to the young man, who remained silent and motionless in his place, as if in ecstatic contemplation.

An officer, summoned by the baron's cries, hurried forward to the carriage door; it was Philippe, dressed in his captain's uniform. The young man was splendidly attired, and seemed in high spirits. "What! Gilbert?" he exclaimed, with a good-humored smile on recognizing the young man. "Gilbert here! How do you do, Gilbert? Well, what do you want with me, my dear father?"

"How do you do, M. Philippe?" replied Gilbert.

"What do I want?" said the baron, furiously. "I want you to take the sheath of your sword and chastise this scoundrel!"

"But what has he done?" asked Philippe, gazing by turns with increasing astonishment at the angry face of his father and the rigid and motionless features of Gilbert.

"Done? He has done—he has— Beat him, Philippe; beat him as you would a dog!" cried the baron. Taverney turned to his sister.

"What has he done, Andrée? Has he insulted you?"

"Insulted her!" repeated Gilbert.

"No, Philippe, no!" replied Andrée. "He has done nothing wrong; my father is in error. Gilbert is no longer in our service, and has a perfect right to go where he pleases; but my father will not understand this, and is angry at finding him here."

"Is that all?" said Philippe.

"Nothing more, brother; and I cannot imagine why my father should be so angry, particularly on such a subject, and about things and persons that do not deserve even a thought. Philippe, look and see whether the train is moving on."

The baron was silent, overcome by the lofty serenity of his daughter. Gilbert bowed his head, crushed by her contempt. For a moment a feeling akin to hatred darted through his heart. He would have preferred the mortal thrust of Philippe's sword — aye, even a lash of his whip — to her insulting scorn. He was almost fainting. Fortunately, the address had now ended, and the cortège once more moved on. The baron's carriage advanced with the rest, and Andrée disappeared from before his eyes like a vision. Gilbert remained alone. He could have wept; he could have groaned aloud. He thought that he could no longer bear the weight of his sufferings. Just then a hand rested on his shoulder. He turned and saw Philippe, who, having given his horse to a soldier of his regiment to hold, returned smiling toward him.

"Come, let me hear what has happened, my poor Gilbert," said he, "and why you have come to Paris."

His frank and cordial tone touched the young man's heart. "Oh, Monsieur!" he replied, with a sigh, his stern stoicism melting at once, "what should I have done at Taverney, I ask you? I must have died of despair, ignorance, and hunger!"

Philippe started. His generous heart was struck, as Andrée's had been, by the misery and destitution in which Gilbert had been left. "And you think, my poor fellow, to succeed in Paris without money, protection, or resources?"

"I trust so, Monsieur. A man who is willing to work rarely dies of hunger, where there are other men who wish to do nothing."

Philippe was struck by this reply; until then he had always looked on Gilbert as a commonplace domestic. "But have you any means of buying food?" said he.

"I can earn my daily bread, M. Philippe. That is sufficient for one who has never had any cause for self-reproach but that of having eaten bread he has not earned."

"I hope you do not say so with reference to that which you received at Taverney, my poor lad! Your father and mother were faithful servants, and you were always willing to make yourself useful."

"I only did my duty, Monsieur."

"Listen to me, Gilbert. You know that I always liked you. I have always taken a more favorable view of your character than others have, — whether justly or the reverse, the future will show. What others called savage pride, I regarded as sensitiveness; where others saw rudeness and ill-breeding, I perceived only honest bluntness."

"Ah, chevalier!" said Gilbert, breathing more freely.

"I really wish you well, Gilbert."

"Thank you, Monsieur!"

"Young like you, and like you also in an unhappy position, I was perhaps on that account more disposed to feel for and pity you. Fortune has blessed me with abundance; let me assist you until fortune smiles on you in your turn."

"Thanks, Monsieur, many thanks."

"What do you think of doing? You are too proud to accept of a situation as servant."

Gilbert shook his head with a scornful smile. "I wish to study," said he.

"But in order to study, you must have masters, and to pay them you must have money."

"I can earn money, Monsieur."

"Earn money? How much can you earn?"

"Twenty-five sous a day, and in a short time perhaps thirty and even forty sous."

"But that is barely enough for food."

Gilbert smiled.

"Perhaps," continued Philippe, "I am not taking the right way of offering you my services."

"Your services to me, M. Philippe?"

"Yes, my services. Are you ashamed to accept them?"

Gilbert made no answer.

"Men are sent on earth to aid one another," continued Maison-Rouge. "Are we not all brethren?"

Gilbert raised his head and fixed his intelligent gaze on the chevalier's noble countenance.

"Does this language surprise you?" said he.

"No, Monsieur," said Gilbert, "it is the language of philosophy; but it is not usual to hear such from persons of your rank."

"Yet it is the language of the times. The dauphin himself shares in these sentiments. Come, do not be proud with me," continued Philippe. "What I lend you, you can repay me one day or other. Who knows but you may yet be a Colbert or a Vauban?"

"Or a Tronchin," said Gilbert.

"Yes, or a Tronchin. Here is my purse, let me share its contents with you."

"Thank you, Monsieur," said the indomitable Gilbert, moved in spite of himself by Philippe's genial kindness; "but I do not want anything; only — only, believe me, I am as grateful to you as if I had accepted your offer." And, bowing, he disappeared in the crowd, leaving the young captain lost in astonishment. The latter waited a few minutes, as if he could not believe his eyes or ears; but finding that Gilbert did not return, he mounted his horse and returned to his post.

CHAPTER V.

THE BEWITCHED.

The noise of the carriages, the prolonged and merry peal of the bells, the joyful beating of the drums, all the pomp and ceremony of the day — a faint reflection of that world now lost to her forever — slipped away from the Princess Louise's mind like an idle wave which had rolled up to the walls of her cell and then retreated.

When the king had departed, after having once more endeavored, but in vain, to win his daughter back to the world by a mingling of paternal entreaty and royal command, and when the dauphiness, who had been at the first glance struck by the real greatness of soul displayed by her august aunt, had also disappeared with her gay throng of courtiers, the Superior of the Carmelites gave orders that the hangings should be taken down, the flowers removed, and the lace put away. Of all the sisterhood of the Carmelites she alone was unmoved when the massive gates of the convent, which had for a moment opened to the world, closed heavily again on their solitude. Then she summoned the sister who acted as treasurer of the convent. "During these two days of disorder," asked she, "have the poor received their usual alms?"

"Yes, Madame."

"Have the sick been visited?"

"Yes, Madame."

"Did the soldiers receive some refreshment before they departed?"

"They received the wine and the bread which you ordered, Madame."

"Then no one is ill or sick in the convent?"

"No one, Madame."

The princess approached a window and softly inhaled the cool and perfumed breeze which was wafted toward her on the humid wings of evening. The treasurer waited respectfully until her august Superior should give her an order or dismiss her. Madame Louise began to pluck off the leaves of the roses and jasmine which twined around the windows and climbed up the walls of the building. Heaven alone knows what were the thoughts of the poor royal recluse at that moment.

Suddenly the door of a detached building in the courtyard, close at hand, was shaken by the violent kick of a horse. Madame Louise started. "What nobleman of the court has remained at St. Denis?" asked she.

"His Eminence the Cardinal de Rohan, Madame."

"Are his horses here too?"

"No, Madame; they are at the chapter-house of the abbey, where he is to pass the night."

"What noise was that, then?"

"Madame, it was caused by the foreign woman's horse."

"What woman?" asked Madame Louise, endeavoring to recollect.

"The Italian who came yesterday to request the protection of your Royal Highness."

"Ah! true, I remember now. Where is she?"

"In her chamber, or in the church."

"How has she conducted herself since she came?"

"Since yesterday she has refused all nourishment

except dry bread, and has spent the entire night praying in the chapel."

"Some great criminal, doubtless?" said the Superior, frowning.

"I do not know, Madame; she has spoken to no one."

"What sort of a woman is she?"

"Extremely handsome, and with an expression at once gentle and haughty."

"This morning, during the ceremony, where was she?"

"In her chamber, close to the window, where I saw her, half hidden by the curtain, watching with anxious eyes every person who entered, as if in each she feared an enemy."

"She is some poor erring creature of the world in which I once lived and reigned. Admit her."

The nun made a movement to retire.

"Ah! what is her name?" asked the princess.

"Lorenza Feliciani."

"I know no one of that name," said Madame Louise, reflecting; "no matter, introduce her."

The Superior seated herself in her chair of state, which was of carved oak, made in the reign of Henry II., and had been used by the last nine abbesses of the Carmelites. It was a formidable judgment-seat, before which had trembled many a poor novice caught on the slippery path between spiritual and temporal things. A moment afterward the nun entered, leading in the strange lady, who was covered from head to foot with the long veil we have before mentioned.

The Princess Louise possessed the piercing eye characteristic of her family; and as Lorenza Feliciani appeared before her, she fastened a stern and searching glance on her. But she saw in the young woman so much humility, grace, and beauty, and in the large eyes, filled with tears, so much innocence, that her feeling of harshness gave place immediately to one of compassion and kindness.

"Draw near, Madame," said the princess.

The stranger advanced hesitatingly, and was about to kneel, when the princess prevented her.

"Is not your name, Madame," said she, "Lorenza Feliciani?"

"Yes, Madame."

"And you wish to confide a secret to me?"

"Oh! I am longing to do so."

"But why had you not recourse to the tribunal of penance? I have power only to console; a priest can not only console, but pardon."

"I require only consolation, Madame," replied Lorenza; "and, besides, it is to a woman alone that I dare relate what I have to tell you."

"Then it is a strange story which you are about to narrate?"

"Yes, strange indeed. But hear me patiently, Madame; it is to you alone, I repeat, that I dare confide it, both because you are all-powerful, and because the hand of God is almost necessary to protect me."

"Protect you? Are you pursued then? Are you in danger?"

"Oh, yes, Madame, yes!" cried the stranger, in wild alarm.

"But reflect, Madame," said the princess, "that this is a convent, and not a fortress; that those worldly thoughts which agitate the breasts of men penetrate here but to be extinguished; that this is not a house of justice, of force, or repression, but simply the house of God."

"Oh, that is what I seek!" said Lorenza. "Yes, I seek the house of God, for there alone can I find shelter and repose."

"But God admits not of revenge. How then do you ask his servant to avenge you? Address yourself to the magistrates."

"They can do nothing against him whom I dread."

"Who is he, then?" asked the abbess, with a mysterious and involuntary dread.

Lorenza approached close to the princess in a nervous and excited manner. "Who is he, Madame?" said she. "He is, I firmly believe, one of those demons who war against man, and whom Satan, their prince, has gifted with superhuman power."

"What do you say?" exclaimed the princess, recoiling as if to satisfy herself that she was not addressing a lunatic.

"And I — oh, how unhappy I am!" continued Lorenza, writhing her beautiful arms, which seemed modelled from those of some antique statue, "I crossed the path of that man, and now I am — "

"Go on."

Lorenza again approached the princess, and, as if terrified herself at what she was about to utter, she whispered hoarsely, "I am bewitched!"

"Bewitched?" cried the princess. "Take care, Madame! Are you sure you are in your senses? Are you not — "

"Mad, you would say. No, I am not mad; but I may become so if you abandon me."

"But permit me to observe that you seem to me in all respects one of the favored of Heaven. You are rich and beautiful, you express yourself rationally, and I see in your countenance nothing betokening that terrible and mysterious affliction."

"Madame, it is in my life, it is in the adventures which have befallen me, that the baleful secret lies which I would willingly conceal even from myself."

"Explain yourself calmly. Am I the first to whom you have disclosed your sufferings? Your parents, your friends —"

"My parents!" exclaimed the young woman, wringing her hands with agony, "my poor parents! Shall I never see you again? Friends!" added she, bitterly; "alas, Madame, have I any friends?"

"Come, let us proceed regularly, my poor child," said Madame Louise, endeavoring to restore order to the stranger's incoherent words; "tell me all. Who are your parents? How came you to abandon them?"

"Madame, I am a native of Rome, and I lived in Rome with them. My father belongs to the ancient nobility, but, like all our patricians, he is poor. I have also a mother, and a brother older than myself. In France, I believe, when a family such as mine has a son and daughter, the portion of the daughter is sacrificed to purchase the son's sword; with us the daughter is sacrificed to put the son forward in the church. Now, I have received no education, because an education was a necessity for my brother, who is studying, as my mother naïvely said, to become a cardinal; and to aid my brother my parents submitted to every privation, and decided on making me take the veil in the Carmelite convent at Subiaco."

"And you, what did you say?"

"Nothing, Madame. From childhood I had been taught to look forward to such an event as inevitable. Besides, I was not consulted; my parents commanded,— I had only to obey."

"But yet —"

"Oh, Madame, we Roman girls are helpless instruments in the hands of others. Almost all my young friends who had brothers had paid this debt for the advancement of their families. I had therefore no reason to complain, nothing unusual was asked of me. My mother merely caressed me a little more than usual as the time for my leaving her approached. At last the day for the commencement of my novitiate arrived; my father prepared his five hundred crowns, my dowry for the convent, and we set out for Subiaco. It is only about nine leagues from Rome to Subiaco, but the roads are bad, and our journey was slow and fatiguing. Nevertheless, it pleased me. I welcomed it as a last enjoyment, and whispered adieu to the trees, the shrubs, the rocks, and even to the withered grass which lined the road. How could I tell if at the convent I should see trees, rocks, or shrubs? Suddenly, in the midst of my fancies, as we wound along between a wood and a mass of overhanging rock, the carriage stopped. My mother shrieked; my father seized his pistols. My thoughts descended suddenly to earth, for those who had stopped us were bandits."

"My poor child!" said the princess, becoming more and more interested in the narrative.

"Well,—shall I confess it, Madame?—I was not much terrified, for these men had stopped us to take our money, and this money was the sum destined for my dowry to the convent. Consequently, if there was no dowry, my entrance into the convent would be delayed until my father could collect five hundred crowns more, and I knew well the time and trouble it had taken to amass these. But when the robbers, after having shared the booty, instead of permitting us to continue our journey, turned and seized me, regardless of the tears of my mother and the efforts of my father to defend me, I was struck with a sort of nameless terror, and shrieked aloud. They bound my hands in spite of my struggles, and held me while they threw the dice to ascertain to whom I should belong. I had abandoned all hope; my mother had fainted away, and my father lay writhing on the earth. At this moment a man mounted on horseback appeared among the robbers. He had spoken in a low voice to one of the sentinels, who had allowed him to proceed, exchanging a sign with him as he did so. This man was of the middle height, of commanding features, and had a resolute glance; he continued to advance calmly at the usual pace of his steed, and when he had arrived opposite me he stopped. The bandit who had already taken me in his arms and was carrying me away, turned suddenly at the first blast which the stranger gave on a little whistle fixed to the end of his whip, and allowed me to slip to the ground. 'Come hither,' said the unknown; and as the man appeared to hesitate, he leaned forward and whispered in his ear the single word, '*Mac.*' '*Benac*,' replied the bandit; and then, like a lion subdued and crouching under the lash, he proceeded to untie my hands as well as those of my father and mother. Then, as the money had been already divided, each man of the troop came forward in his turn to lay his share on a stone. Not a crown of the entire sum was wanting. 'Now, go!' said the unknown to the banditti, and instantly every man disappeared in the surrounding woods.

"'Lorenza Feliciani,' said the stranger then, addressing me and fixing on me a look which had more than human power in it, 'proceed on your way; you are free!'

"My father and mother thanked this stranger, who knew me, but whom we did not know, and entered the carriage again. I accompanied them with a sort of regret; for some strange, irresistible power seemed to attract me to the man who had saved me. He remained immovable in the same spot, as if to protect our retreat. As long as I could distinguish his form my eyes were fixed on him, and it was only when he was lost to view that the oppressive feeling which weighed upon my bosom was removed."

"But who was this extraordinary man?" asked the princess, interested by the simplicity of the narrative.

"Deign to hear me farther, Madame," asked Lorenza. "Alas! all is not yet told."

"I listen," said Madame Louise.

The young woman proceeded: "Two hours afterward we reached Subiaco. During the rest of our journey we never ceased conversing about this singular protector, mysterious and powerful, who had come so suddenly to our assistance like a messenger from heaven. My father, less credulous than I, thought that he must be the captain of one of the numerous troops of robbers which infest the neighborhood of Rome; but in this I could not agree, although I dared not openly oppose my opinion to my father's, which was the result of years and experience. My instinctive feeling of gratitude toward this man who had so wonderfully saved me revolted against the idea that he was a bandit; and every evening, in my devotions, I offered up a prayer to the Virgin for my unknown protector.

"The same day I entered the convent. I felt sadder, but also more resigned. An Italian, and consequently superstitious, I believed that God, by delivering me from the bandits, had wished to preserve me pure and unsullied for his service. I therefore gave myself up with ardor to the fulfilment of every duty of religion; and my father, learning this, drew up a petition to the Sovereign Pontiff to entreat him to shorten the period of my novitiate. I signed this document, which was expressed in terms so warm and earnest that his Holiness, seeing in it only the aspirations of a soul disgusted with the world, granted me a dispensation which fixed the term of my novitiate at a month instead of a year.

"This news, when announced to me, inspired me with neither joy nor grief. I was like one already dead to the world. For fifteen days I was kept closely confined, lest any worldly desires might arise in my breast. At the end of that time I was allowed to descend with the other sisters to the chapel. I entered and took my place behind the curtain which separated, or affected to separate, the nuns from the congregation. Looking through one of the openings, which seemed to me a loophole through which I could obtain a last glance at the world I was leaving, I saw a man standing up alone in the middle of the kneeling crowd. He seemed to devour me with his eyes, and I felt again that strange sensation of uneasiness which I had before experienced, — that superhuman power which seemed to draw me away from myself, as I had seen my brother draw a needle to the loadstone, even through a leaf of paper or a piece of wood.

"Overcome, subdued, unable to resist this attraction, I leaned forward, and with clasped hands I murmured, 'Thanks, thanks!' The nuns looked at me with surprise. They could not comprehend my words or gestures, and, following my glance, they rose on their seats and gazed down into the body of the church. I also gazed, trembling. The stranger had disappeared. They questioned me, but I only turned pale and red by turns, and stammered out some incoherent words. From that moment, Madame," cried Lorenza, in a despairing voice, "from that moment I have been in the demon's power."

"Nevertheless," replied the princess, smiling, "I see nothing supernatural in all that you have related. Calm yourself, my sister, and proceed."

"Ah, Madame! it is because you cannot understand

what I felt. Heart, soul, mind, — the demon possessed all."

"My sister, I fear greatly that this demon was only love," said Madame Louise.

"Oh, love could not have made me suffer thus! Love would not so have oppressed my heart; it would not have shaken my frame as the storm shakes a slender reed! Love would not have whispered in my ear the sinful thought which haunted me at that moment."

"What thought, my child?"

"Ought not I to have disclosed all to my confessor, Madame?"

"Doubtless."

"Well, the demon that possessed me whispered me, on the contrary, to keep it secret. I imagined, Madame, that there would be attributed to me with this man one of those intrigues which each one of us sisters before taking the veil has had with a regretted lover."

"An evil thought, indeed; but it is often a very innocent demon which puts such thoughts in the heart of a woman. Proceed."

"On the following day I was summoned to the parlor. I found there one of my neighbors of the Via Frattina at Rome, a young married lady, who regretted very much the loss of my society, because every evening we used to meet to talk and sing together. Behind her, close to the door, stood a man wrapped in a cloak, who seemed to be her servant. He did not turn toward me, but I turned toward him; he did not speak, yet I knew him. He was my unknown protector. The same thrilling sensation I had already experienced shot through my frame. I felt my whole being subdued by the power of this man. Had it not been for the bars which held me captive, I should certainly have followed him. Although enveloped closely in his mantle, rays of light seemed to shoot from him which dazzled me; profound as was his silence, it had sounds which spoke to me a harmonious language. I made a violent effort to subdue my feelings, and asked my friend who the man was who accompanied her. She did not know him. Her husband, who had intended to come with her, had been prevented by some engagement, and had brought this friend of his, a stranger to her, to be her companion.

"My friend was religious, and seeing in a corner of the parlor a Madonna who had the reputation of possessing miraculous powers, she would not depart without offering up a prayer before her. While she was engaged in her devotions, the man entered the room, approached close to me, uncovered his face, and fixed his glowing eyes on mine. I waited for him to speak; my bosom heaved as if in expectation of his words; but he contented himself with putting his arms through the bars which separated us, and extended them above my head. Immediately an inexpressible feeling of delight seized on my whole frame. He smiled; I returned his smile, closing my eyes, which seemed weighed down by an overpowering languor. Then, as if he had merely wished to assure himself of his power over me, he immediately retired. As he disappeared I recovered by degrees the use of my senses; but I was still under the control of this strange hallucination when my friend, having finished her prayer, rose, and embracing me, took her leave. When I was undressing at night I found in my bosom a note containing these words: 'In Rome, the man who loves a nun is punished by death. Will you give death to him to whom you owe your life?' From that moment the demon possessed me entirely, for I lied before Heaven, Madame, in not confessing that I thought of this man much more than of my salvation."

Lorenza, terrified at what she had disclosed, paused to discover what impression it had produced on the mild and intelligent countenance of the princess.

"Still," replied the princess, firmly, "all this is not possession by the Evil One; it is merely the result of an unhappy passion, and I must again repeat that such thoughts cannot be spoken of here, except to express regret for them."

"Regret, Madame?" cried Lorenza. "What, you behold me in tears at your feet beseeching you to rescue me from the power of this fearful man, and yet you doubt my regret! Oh, I feel more than regret, — I feel remorse!"

"And yet," said Madame Louise, "up to this point—"

"Ah, Madame, you have not yet heard all! Wait till I have finished, and then, I beseech you, judge me mercifully! Three days in the week we attended divine service in the chapel. The unknown was always present. I wished to resist him; I pretended that I was ill; I resolved not to go down. Alas! for human weakness. When the hour arrived, I descended with the nuns, as it were, in despite of my own will. If he were not in the church when I entered, I had some moments of calm; but as he drew near I felt him coming. I could have said, 'Now he is a hundred paces off; now he is at the door; now he is in the church,' and that without even looking in the direction from which he came. Then, when he had reached his accustomed place, although my eyes had been fastened on my prayer-book while I murmured the words before me, they turned involuntarily and rested on him. I could neither read nor pray; all my thought, all my will, all my soul were in my eyes, and my eyes were fixed on that man, who I believed was disputing possession of me with God. At first I could not look at him without fear; then I longed to see him; then my thoughts seemed to meet his. And often I saw him in the night as in a dream, and felt him pass beneath my window.

"The state of my mind did not escape the notice of my companions. The abbess was informed of it, and she in turn informed my parents. Three days before I was to pronounce my vows my father, my mother, and my brother — the only relations I had in the world — entered my cell. They came ostensibly to bid me farewell, but I saw plainly that they had some other motive; and when my mother was left alone with me she questioned me closely. And here the power of the Evil One may clearly be seen; for instead of telling all, as I ought to have done, I denied everything obstinately.

"On the day when I was to take the veil a strange struggle took place within me. I both dreaded and wished for the moment which was to give me up entirely to the service of God; and I felt that if the demon meditated a last effort to subdue me to his will, it would be at this solemn moment that he would make it."

"And had that strange man never written to you since the first letter which you found in your bosom?" asked the princess.

"Never, Madame."

"And at that time you had never spoken to him?"

"Never, except in thought."

"Nor written to him?"

"Oh, never!"

"Proceed; you were at the day when you were to take the veil."

"That day, as I have told your Highness, I hoped was to end my tortures, and I was impatient for the ceremony. 'When I belong to God entirely,' I thought, 'he will defend me as he defended me from the attack of the bandits.' I forgot that God had defended me only through the intervention of this man. In the mean time the hour arrived. I descended to the church pale, restless, but yet less agitated than usual. My father, my mother, my brother, my friend from the Via Frattina who had come before to see me, and many other of our friends, were there. The inhabitants of the neighboring villages also thronged the church, for the report had been spread that I was lovely; and a lovely victim, they say, is most acceptable to the Lord.

"The service began. I would have hastened it by my prayers; for he was not present, and in his absence I felt that I was mistress of myself. Already the priest had raised the crucifix before me, and I was just about to extend my arm toward it, when the trembling which invariably announced the approach of my persecutor seized me. Forced by an irresistible attraction, I turned round and saw him standing near the pulpit, gazing at me more fixedly than he had ever yet done. In vain I endeavored to keep my eyes on the priest; service, ceremony, prayers, faded from my sight. I believe I was questioned concerning the rite; I remember I was pulled by the arm to arouse me, but I tottered like some inanimate object trembling on its base. I was shown the scissors, from which a ray of sunlight was reflected back with dazzling brightness, but I did not even wink. Then I felt the cold steel on my neck, and heard its sharp points in my hair.

"At that moment it seemed to me as if all strength left me; my soul rushed from my body to meet his, and I fell motionless on the pavement, — yet, strange to say, not like one who has fainted, but like one overcome by sleep. I heard a loud murmur, and almost immediately after became insensible. The ceremony was interrupted with frightful tumult."

The princess clasped her hands with a gesture of compassion.

"Ah, Madame, was not that terrible?" said Lorenza; "and is it not easy to see in such an event the intervention of the enemy of man?"

"Take care, my poor girl," said the princess, in a tone of tenderness and pity; "I think you are too much disposed to attribute to miraculous power that which is simply the result of a natural weakness. On seeing that man you fainted, that is all. Proceed."

"Oh, Madame, do not say so, or at least wait till you have heard all before you judge. Had I fainted, should I not have come to myself in ten minutes or a quarter of an hour, or an hour at most? Should I not have been surrounded by my sister nuns, and have resumed courage and faith on seeing them?"

"Doubtless," said Madame Louise. "Well, was it not so?"

"Madame," said Lorenza, in a low, hurried whisper, "when I was restored to consciousness it was night. I felt a rapid, jolting motion, which fatigued me, and I raised my head, thinking that I was under the vaulted roof of the chapel, or within the curtains of my cell. I saw rocks, trees, clouds; then I felt a warm breath fanning my cheeks. I thought that it was the sick nurse who was endeavoring to restore me, and I made an effort to thank her. Madame, my head was resting on the bosom of a' man,—that man my persecutor! I looked at myself and felt of myself to become certain that I was alive, and that I was not dreaming. I could not restrain a cry of terror. I was dressed in white, and wore on my head a crown of white roses like a bride, or like a maiden dressed for the tomb."

The princess uttered an exclamation of astonishment. Lorenza hid her face in her hands.

"The next day," continued Lorenza, sobbing, "I made inquiries, and ascertained that it was Wednesday. For three days, therefore, I had remained insensible. I am ignorant of all that happened during that time."

CHAPTER VI.

LE COMTE DE FENIX.

A LONG and painful silence succeeded to this narrative, during which each of the two ladies seemed absorbed in her reflections. The princess was the first to break it.

"And you lent no assistance to this man to carry you off?" said she.

"None, Madame."

"You are ignorant how you left the convent?"

"I am quite ignorant."

"Yet a convent is kept carefully guarded; there are bars to the windows; the walls are very high; there is a portress who keeps the keys of the gates always at her side. That is especially the case in Italy, where the rules are even more severe than in France."

"Madame, I can only reply, that from the moment of my awaking from my trance until now, I have searched my memory in vain."

"But did you not reproach him for what he had done?"

"Oh, yes, Madame!"

"What was his excuse?"

"That he loved me."

"And what did you reply to that?"

"That I had a horror of him."

"Then you did not love him?"

"Oh no, no!"

"Are you quite certain?"

"Alas, Madame, what I felt for that man was singular indeed! When he was present I was no longer myself; what he willed, I willed; what he commanded, I did; my soul had no power, my mind no will; a look from him subdued and fascinated me. Sometimes he seemed to inspire me with thoughts which were not mine; sometimes he seemed to draw from me ideas so deeply hidden that I had never even guessed that I possessed them. Oh! do you not see, Madame, that there was magic in all this?"

"It is certainly strange, if not supernatural," said the princess. "But after you had been carried off, how did you live with that man?"

"He displayed the warmest affection for me, the sincerest attachment."

"He was a vicious man, no doubt?"

"I do not think so; there was, on the contrary, something lofty and inspired in his manner of speaking."

"Come, come! you loved him; confess it!"

"No, no, Madame," said the young woman, with mournful bitterness; "no, I did not love him."

"Then you ought to have left him; you ought to have appealed to the public authorities, and demanded to be restored to your parents."

"Madame, he watched me so closely that I could not fly."

"But why not write, then?"

"Wherever we stopped on the road, the house seemed to belong to him alone, and every one obeyed him. Several times I asked for pen, ink, and paper; but those to whom I applied were doubtless directed by him, for they never even answered me."

"And how did you travel?"

"At first in a post-chaise; but at Milan, instead of a

carriage we entered a kind of moving house, in which we continued our journey."

"But he must have sometimes left you alone?"

"Yes; but at these times, before leaving me, he approached me and said, 'Sleep!' I slept, and did not awake until his return."

The princess shook her head incredulously. "You would have been able to escape," said she, "had you seriously endeavored to do so."

"Alas, Madame! and yet it seemed to me that I did; but perhaps I was fascinated."

"By his words of love, by his caresses?"

"He seldom spoke of love, Madame; and except a kiss imprinted on my forehead in the morning, and one in the evening, he bestowed no caresses on me."

"Strange, strange indeed!" murmured the princess; then, as if some suspicion had crossed her mind, she said aloud: "And you are ready to assert again that you do not love him?"

"I do assert it again, Madame."

"And no earthly bond unites you to him?"

"None, Madame."

"Then should he claim you, he would have no right over you?"

"None, Madame, none."

"But," added the princess, after a moment's reflection, "how did you escape at last? I do not understand that."

"Madame, I took advantage of a violent storm which occurred while we were near a town called Nancy, I think. He left his place near me to go into another compartment of the carriage to talk to an old man who was with us. Then I leaped on his horse and fled."

"And why did you prefer remaining in France to returning to Italy?"

"I reflected that I could not return to Rome, since my parents and friends there would certainly imagine I had been the accomplice of that man, and perhaps refuse to receive me. I resolved therefore to come to Paris, and to endeavor to remain concealed; or to try to reach some other great city, where no eye — and, above all, his — could discover me. When I reached Paris, Madame, every one was speaking of your retirement into the convent of the Carmelites. They lauded your piety, your charity toward the wretched, your pity for the afflicted. A ray of hope darted through my soul, and I was struck with the conviction that you would be generous enough to receive me and powerful enough to protect me."

"You appeal always to my power, my poor child. Is he, then, so powerful?"

"Oh, yes, Madame!"

"But who is he, then? Through delicacy I have until now refrained from asking his name; but if I am to defend you, I must know against whom."

"Oh, Madame, even on that point I cannot enlighten you. I know neither who he is nor what he is. All that I know is that a king could not inspire more respect, a deity could not receive greater adoration, than he, from those to whom he deigns to reveal himself."

"But how do they address him? What is his name?"

"I have heard him addressed by different names; at present, however, I remember only two of them. One is given him by the old man, who, as I told you, travelled with us from Milan; the other he gives himself."

"What does the old man call him?"

"Acharat; is not that a heathenish name, Madame?"

"And what is his other name?"

"Joseph Balsamo."

"And what can you tell me of him?"

"That he seems to know all persons, to penetrate into all things; he is contemporary with all times, has lived in all ages. He speaks — may Heaven pardon such blasphemies! — he speaks of Alexander, Cæsar, and Charlemagne as if he had known them; yet I am sure they have been dead a very long time. But what is worse, he will talk of Caiaphas, Pilate, and our blessed Saviour as if he had been present at the crucifixion."

"He is some charlatan, I perceive," said the princess.

"I do not know exactly what that means, Madame; but what I do know is that he is a dangerous, terrible man. All yield to him, all bend before him, all fall prostrate at his word. You think him defenceless, he is armed; you think him alone, and he causes men to rise out of the earth; and that without an effort, — by a gesture, a word, a smile."

"It is well," said the princess. "Whoever he be, take courage, my child; you shall be protected from him."

"By you, Madame, by you?"

"Yes, by me; so long as you yourself do not abandon my protection. But cease from this time to believe, and above all do not seek to make me believe, in the superstitious visions which are the offspring of your diseased imagination. The walls of St. Denis will guard you securely against infernal powers, and against powers even more to be feared, — those of wicked men. And now, Madame, what are your intentions?"

"With these jewels, which belong to me, Madame, I wish to pay my dowry to some convent, — to this convent, if possible."

And Lorenza laid on a table precious bracelets, valuable rings, a magnificent diamond, and other jewels, the whole worth about twenty thousand crowns.

"Are those ornaments your own?" asked the princess.

"Yes, Madame. He gave them to me, and I devote them to the church. I have only one wish with regard to his property."

"What is that?"

"That his Arabian horse, Djerid, the instrument of my deliverance, be restored to him if he demands it."

"But with regard to yourself, you will on no account return to him?"

"On no account."

"Then what will you do? Am I to assume that it is your wish to enter this convent and continue in the practice of those duties which were interrupted at Subiaco by the extraordinary circumstances you have related to me?"

"It is my dearest wish, Madame; at your feet I supplicate its fulfilment."

"Be tranquil, my child. From this day you shall live with us; and when, by the exemplary conduct which I expect from you, you have shown that you deserve that favor, you shall take the vows, — and I answer for it, no one shall carry you away from St. Denis while your abbess watches over you."

Lorenza threw herself at the feet of her benefactress, and poured forth expressions of gratitude the most tender and the most sincere; but all at once, rising on one knee, she listened, turned pale, and trembled.

"Oh, heavens! Oh, heavens!" she exclaimed.

"What is the matter?" asked Madame Louise.

"My whole frame trembles. He is coming! He is coming!"

"Who is coming?"

"He who has sworn to destroy my soul."

"That man?"

"Yes, that man; do you not see how my hand trembles?

Oh!" continued she, in a tone of anguish, "he approaches! — he is near!"

"You are mistaken."

"No, Madame, no! Hold me! He draws me to him against my will. Hold me! Hold me!"

Madame Louise seized her by the arm. "Courage, courage, my poor child!" said she; "were it even he, you are in safety here."

"He approaches! He approaches!" cried Lorenza, with despair and horror in her voice, her eyes fixed, and her arms extended toward the door of the room.

"This is madness! Dare any one, think you, enter unannounced the apartment of Madame Louise of France? To obtain admittance, he must be the bearer of an order from the king."

"Oh, Madame, I know not how he procured an entrance," cried Lorenza, recoiling with terror; "but I do know that he is ascending the stairs, that he is scarcely ten paces distant, that he is here!"

At that moment the door opened. Alarmed at the strange coincidence, the princess could not prevent herself from starting back. A nun appeared.

"Who is there?" asked the abbess, hurriedly, "and what do you want?"

"Madame, a gentleman has just arrived who wishes to speak to your Royal Highness."

"His name?"

"Monsieur le Comte de Fenix."

"Is that he?" asked the princess, turning to Lorenza; "and do you know that name?"

"I do not know that name; but it is he, Madame, — it is he!"

"What does this gentleman want?" inquired the princess, addressing the nun.

"Having been sent on a mission to the king of France by his Majesty the king of Prussia, he wishes, he says, to have the honor of a moment's conversation with your Royal Highness."

The princess reflected for a moment; then, turning to Lorenza, "Retire into that cabinet," said she. Lorenza obeyed. "And you, sister," continued the princess, "admit this gentleman." The nun bowed, and left the room.

Having ascertained that the door of the cabinet was securely fastened, the princess seated herself in her armchair, and awaited the termination of the strange scene in which she found herself involved. Yet she could not subdue a certain degree of agitation.

Almost immediately the nun re-appeared, followed by the person who, as we have already seen, on the day of the presentation had caused himself to be announced as the Comte de Fenix. He was dressed in the same costume, — a Prussian uniform, with the military wig and black stock. His large, expressive eyes were cast down at first in the presence of the royal abbess, but only in a manner to indicate the respect which any gentleman, however high his rank, ought to show to a princess of France. But immediately raising them again, with a look which almost implied that he had already shown too great humility, "Madame," said he, "I thank your Royal Highness for the favor you have shown me. I confidently expected it, however, knowing that your Royal Highness is the generous patron of all the unhappy."

"Monsieur, I endeavor to be so," replied the princess, with dignity; for she felt certain that she should, before the lapse of many minutes, put to shame this man, who so impudently dared to claim her protection, after having deceived and ill-treated one confided to his care.

The count bowed, without betraying any consciousness of understanding the double meaning of her words.

She then continued, with something of irony in her tone: "In what way can I render you any assistance, Monsieur?"

"You can aid me in a matter of the greatest moment, Madame."

"Speak, Monsieur!"

"None but weighty considerations could have induced me, Madame, to intrude on your Royal Highness in this retreat which you have chosen; but you have, I believe, given shelter here to a person in whom I am deeply interested."

"The name of that person, Monsieur?"

"Lorenza Feliciani."

"And what is she to you? Is she your relation, your sister?"

"She is my wife."

"Your wife?" said the princess, raising her voice so that she might be heard in the cabinet. "Lorenza Feliciani is the Comtesse de Fenix?"

"Yes, Madame, Lorenza Feliciani is the Comtesse de Fenix," replied the count, with the utmost coolness.

"I have no Comtesse de Fenix in this convent, Monsieur," replied the princess.

But the count was not to be so repulsed. "Perhaps, Madame," said he, "your Royal Highness is not convinced that Lorenza Feliciani and the Comtesse de Fenix are one and the same person?"

"I admit it, Monsieur, — and your conjecture is correct; I am not well convinced on that point."

"If your Royal Highness will but command Lorenza Feliciani to be brought hither, you will soon have all doubts on that head cleared away. I entreat your Highness's pardon for urging the matter thus, but I am tenderly attached to the young lady, and she herself, I think, regrets being separated from me."

"Do you think so, Monsieur?"

"Yes, Madame, unworthy as I am, I think so."

"Ah!" thought the princess, "Lorenza was right; this is indeed a most dangerous man."

The count preserved unruffled calmness of demeanor and maintained the most courtly politeness.

"I must temporize," thought the princess to herself. "Monsieur," said she, "I cannot give up to you a woman who is not here. If you love, as you say you do, the person whom you seek, I can easily understand why you thus persist in endeavoring to find her; but, believe me, to be successful you must seek elsewhere."

The count on entering the room had cast a rapid glance on every article in it, and his eyes had rested for a single instant only, but that had been sufficient, on a table in a dark corner, on which Lorenza had placed those jewels which she had offered to pay as her dowry to the convent. He recognized them instantly.

"If your Royal Highness will have the goodness to recollect, — and I venture to entreat you to do so, — you will remember that Lorenza Feliciani was very lately in this room, that she placed on that table those jewels, and that, after having had the honor of conversing with your Royal Highness, she withdrew." Just then he caught the eye of the princess turning unconsciously toward the cabinet. "She withdrew," he continued, "into that cabinet; so that now I only wait for the permission of your Royal Highness to order her to return hither, which she will do immediately, I feel certain."

The princess colored with shame at the thought that she had lowered herself so far as to attempt to deceive this man, from whom, as it seemed, nothing could be hidden; and she could not conceal her vexation at the uselessness of all her efforts. She recollected, however, that Lorenza had fastened the door from within, and that, consequently, nothing but the impulse of her own free will could induce her to leave the cabinet.

"But even suppose she comes," said she, "what will she do?"

"Nothing, Madame; she will merely tell your Highness that she wishes to go with me, being my wife."

This last word reassured the princess, for she recollected the protestations of Lorenza. "Your wife!" she exclaimed, with indignation. "Are you sure of that?"

"Your Highness does not seem to believe me," said the count, politely. "Nevertheless, it is not quite incredible that the Comte de Fenix should have married Lorenza Feliciani, and that, having married her, he seeks to recover his wife."

"His wife!" she repeated, impatiently; "you dare to say Lorenza Feliciani is your wife?"

"Yes, Madame, I dare to say so," answered the count, with the most natural air in the world, "because it is true."

"You are married to her?"

"I am."

"Legitimately?"

"Certainly; and if your Royal Highness thus persists in doubting my word, I will place before your eyes the register of my marriage, signed by the priest who united us."

The princess started; so much coolness and self-possession shook all her convictions.

The count opened his pocket-book and unfolded a paper. "This is the register of my marriage, Madame, and the proof that I have a right to claim that woman as my wife; if your Royal Highness will read it and note the signature —"

VOL. II. — 5

"The signature!" repeated the princess, in a tone of doubt more insulting to the stranger than her indignation had been; "but if this signature — "

"This signature is that of the vicar of St. Jean de Strasburg, who is well known to Prince Louis, Cardinal de Rohan; and if his Eminence were here — "

"His Eminence is here!" cried the princess, fixing her flashing eyes on the count. "He has not yet left St. Denis, and is now with the canons of the cathedral; so that nothing is easier for us than the verification which you propose."

"That is indeed a fortunate circumstance for me!" replied the count, coolly putting up the paper again in his pocket-book. "When your Royal Highness has heard the cardinal's testimony, I trust that your Highness's unjust suspicions will be dispelled."

"Monsieur, this impudent perseverance is most revolting to me!" said the princess, ringing her bell violently.

The nun who had introduced the count appeared.

"Let my groom mount his horse instantly and carry this note to the Cardinal de Rohan; he will be found at the chapter of the cathedral. Let him come hither without a moment's delay, — I wait for him."

While giving these directions the princess wrote hastily a few words on a slip of paper, and handing it to the nun she added in a whisper: "Let a couple of archers of the guard be placed in the corridor, and take care that no one leaves the convent without my permission."

The count had followed all the movements of the princess, whom he now saw determined to contest the point with him to the very last; but, evidently decided not to yield the victory to her, he drew nearer to the door of the cabinet while she was writing, fixed his eyes on it, pronounced some words in a low voice, and extending his hands toward it, moved them to and fro with a regular and steady motion.

The princess, turning, saw him in this attitude, and exclaimed, "What are you doing there, Monsieur?"

"Madame," said the count, "I am adjuring Lorenza Feliciani to appear and declare to you of her own free will that I am not an impostor nor a forger. But this is not to prevent your Royal Highness from requiring the other proofs you have mentioned."

"Monsieur!"

"Lorenza Feliciani," cried the count, overpowering all opposition, even that of the princess, "leave that cabinet and come hither, — come!"

But the door remained closed.

"Come forth! It is my will!" repeated the count.

Then the key was heard turning in the lock, and the princess, with inexpressible alarm, saw the young girl enter, her eyes fixed on the count without any expression either of anger or hatred.

"What are you doing, my child?" cried the princess. "Why do you return to the man from whom you fled? You were in safety here; I told you so."

"She is also in safety in my house, Madame," answered the count. "Are you not, Lorenza? Are you not safe with me?"

"Yes!" replied the young woman.

The princess, overcome with astonishment, clasped her hands and sank back in her chair.

"And now, Lorenza," added the count, in a gentle tone, but yet with an accent of command, "I am accused of having made you act contrary to your wishes. Say, have I ever done so?"

"Never!" answered the young woman, clearly and

distinctly, yet without accompanying the denial by any movement.

"In that case," cried the princess, "what do you mean by all that story of an abduction which you told me?"

Lorenza remained silent, and looked at the count as if life and speech hung on his lips.

"Her Highness wishes doubtless to know how you left the convent, Lorenza. Relate to her all that happened from the moment of your fainting until you awoke in the post-chaise."

Lorenza was still silent.

"Relate all that occurred, from first to last; do not omit anything," continued the count. "It is my will."

"I do not remember," she replied.

"Search your memory, and you will recollect all."

"Ah, yes, yes!" said Lorenza, in the same monotonous tone, "I remember."

"Speak, then."

"When I fainted, at the very moment that the scissors touched my hair, I was carried back to my cell and laid on my bed. My mother remained with me until night, when, seeing that I continued in the same state of insensibility, they sent for the village surgeon. He felt my pulse, passed a looking-glass before my lips, and discovering no sign of life in me, pronounced me dead."

"But how do you know all that?" asked the princess.

"Her Highness wishes to know how you know that," repeated the count.

"Strange!" replied Lorenza; "I was able to see and hear, but I could not open my eyes, nor speak, nor move; I was in a sort of lethargy."

"In fact," said the princess, "Tronchin has sometimes spoken to me of persons who had fallen into a lethargy, and who, being to all appearance dead, were interred alive."

"Proceed, Lorenza."

"My mother was in despair, and would not believe that I was dead; she said that she would pass that night and the following day by my side. She did so; but the thirty-six hours during which she watched over me passed away without my making the slightest movement, or without a sigh having escaped my lips. Thrice a priest came to visit my mother; and each time he told her that it was rebelling against the will of God thus to persist in keeping my body on earth when He possessed my soul; for, as I had died at the moment when I was pronouncing my vows, he did not doubt, he said, but that my soul had winged its flight to heaven. My mother, by her entreaties, prevailed on him to allow her to watch by me another night, — that of Monday. On Tuesday morning they found me still insensible.

"My mother withdrew, vanquished, leaving me to the nuns, who by this time were loud in their exclamations against her impiety. The tapers were lighted in the chapel, in which, according to custom, I was to be laid out during one day and night. As I had not pronounced my vows, the sisters dressed me in a white robe, put a crown of white roses on my head, crossed my arms on my bosom, and placed my coffin on a bier. During this last operation a thrill of horror ran through my veins; for I repeat, although my eyelids were closed, I saw everything as if they had been wide open.

"The bier was carried into the church, and there — my face still uncovered, as is the custom in Italy — I was placed in the middle aisle, with lighted tapers around me, and a vase of holy water at my feet. During the day the peasants of Subiaco entered the church, prayed for me, and sprinkled my body with the holy water. Night came on; and as the visitors had ceased, the doors of the church were closed, except a little side door, and the nun who took care of the sick remained alone beside me.

"One terrible thought never left me during my trance, and now it became more dreadful. On the morrow I was to be buried, — buried alive, if some unknown power did not come to my aid! I heard the hours strike, one after another; first nine, then ten, then eleven. Each stroke found an echo in my trembling heart; for, oh, horror! I listened to my own death-knell.

"What efforts I made to break my icy sleep, to burst the iron bonds which held me down in my coffin, God alone knows; but he saw, and had pity on me. Midnight struck. At the very first stroke my frame was shaken by a convulsive shudder, like that which I always experienced when Acharat approached me; then my heart was stirred, and I saw him appear at the door of the church."

"Were your feelings at that moment those of fear?" asked the Comte de Fenix.

"No; they were feelings of happiness, joy, ecstasy! For I knew that he came to snatch me from the dreadful death which before had seemed inevitable. He advanced slowly toward my coffin, looked on me for a moment with a melancholy smile; then he said, 'Arise and walk!' The bonds which fastened me were broken at that powerful voice; I rose, and put one foot out of the coffin. 'Are you glad to live?' he asked. 'Oh, yes!' I replied. 'Follow me, then,' said he.

"The sister who was appointed to watch the dead had fulfilled this duty toward so many of the nuns that she had become careless and indifferent, and slept soundly in her chair. I passed close by her without awaking her, as I followed him who, for the second time, had saved me from death. We reached the outer court, and once more saw the cloudless firmament, studded with stars, and felt the cool night-breeze, which the dead feel not, but which is so grateful to the living.

"'And now,' said he, before leaving the convent, 'choose between God and me. Do you wish to be a nun, or to follow me?' 'I will follow you,' I replied. 'Come, then,' he said again. We reached the entrance-gate; it was locked. 'Where are the keys?' he asked. 'In the pocket of the portress, on a chair near her bed,' I replied. 'Enter the lodge without noise,' said he, 'take the keys, select the one that unlocks the gate, and bring it to me.' I obeyed, entered the lodge, found the key, and brought it to him.

"Five minutes afterward the gate was opened, and we were in the street. I took his arm, and we hurried toward the outskirts of the village of Subiaco. About a hundred paces from its last house a post-chaise was in waiting; we entered it, and drove off at a rapid pace."

"And no force was used; no threat was uttered; you followed that man voluntarily?"

Lorenza remained silent.

"Her Royal Highness asks you, Lorenza, if by any threat or any violence you were forced to accompany me?"

"No."

"And why did you go with him?"

"Speak, why did you accompany me?"

"Because I loved you," said Lorenza.

The Comte de Fenix turned toward the princess with a triumphant smile.

CHAPTER VII.

THE CARDINAL DE ROHAN.

STRONG as was the mind of the Princess Louise, all that she had just heard seemed so extraordinary to her that she could not help asking herself whether the man who stood before her were not a real magician, disposing of hearts and understandings at his will.

But the Comte de Fenix was not yet satisfied. "That is not all, Madame," said he; "and your Royal Highness has heard only a part of our history. Some doubts might remain on your mind did you not hear the rest from her own lips." Then, turning toward the young woman, "Do you remember, dear Lorenza," said he, "the rest of our journey, — how we visited Milan, the Lake Maggiore, the Oberland, the Righi, and the magnificent Rhine, the Tiber of the North?"

"Yes," she answered, still in the same monotonous voice, "yes; Lorenza saw all that."

"Dragged onward by that man, were you not, my child, — yielding to an irresistible power which you did not yourself comprehend?" asked the princess.

"Why should you think so, Madame, after what your Highness has heard? But if you wish for yet more palpable and material proofs, here is a letter written by Lorenza to me. I was obliged to leave her alone for a short time at Mayence. Well! she regretted me, and longed for my return; for in my absence she wrote me these lines, which your Highness may read."

The count took out of his pocket-book a note, which he handed to the princess. She read as follows:—

RETURN, Acharat! When you leave me, all hope and joy depart. Ah! when shall I be yours through all eternity?
LORENZA.

The princess rose, anger flashing in her eyes, and approached Lorenza with the note in her hand. The young woman appeared neither to see nor hear her. Her whole soul seemed to hang on the count's lips.

"I understand," said the count, quickly, before the princess could utter a word, "your Highness doubts whether this note be really written by her or not. That point can easily be settled. Lorenza, speak! Who wrote this note?"

He took the note, placed it in her hand, and she immediately pressed it to her heart. "Lorenza wrote it," said she.

"Does Lorenza know what it contains?"

"Yes."

"Then tell the princess what is in the letter, that she may believe me when I say you love me. Tell her; it is my will."

Lorenza appeared to make an effort; then, without opening the note, or turning her eyes on it, she repeated its contents.

"This is incredible!" said the princess. "I cannot trust the evidence of my own senses; there is something inexplicable and supernatural in all this."

"It was this letter," continued the Comte de Fenix, as if he had not heard what the princess said, "which determined me to hasten our marriage. I loved Lorenza as much as she loved me. We were in a position which might have given rise to unfounded suspicions. Besides, in the adventurous life which I lead, some accident might happen to me. I might be killed; I might die. And I wished, in case of such an event, that all my fortune should belong to Lorenza. On arriving at Strasburg, therefore, we were married."

" You were married?"

" Yes, Madame."

" It is impossible!"

" Why so, Madame?" said the count, smiling. " What is there impossible in the fact that the Comte de Fenix should marry Lorenza Feliciani?"

" But she told me that she is not your wife."

The count, without replying, turned to Lorenza. " Do you remember on what day we were married?" asked he.

" Yes," she replied; " it was the third of May."

" Where?"

" At Strasburg."

" In what church?"

" In the cathedral, — in the chapel of St. John."

" Did you offer any opposition to our union?"

" No; I was too happy."

" Because, Lorenza," continued the count, " the princess thinks that the marriage was forced on you, — that you hate me." As he said these words he took Lorenza's hand.

A thrill of rapture seemed to run through the young woman's frame. " I hate you!" she exclaimed. " Oh, no! I love you; you are good, you are generous, you are powerful!".

The count turned toward the princess as if he had said, " You hear?"

Seized with a kind of horror, the princess had recoiled from the pair before her, and sank at the foot of an ivory crucifix which was fastened against the black velvet hangings of the room.

"Does your Royal Highness wish for any further information?" asked the count, as he released Lorenza's hand.

"Monsieur," cried the princess, "do not approach me! — nor let her approach me!"

At this moment the noise of wheels was heard in the courtyard, and a carriage stopped at the entrance door.

"Ah!" exclaimed the princess, "here comes the cardinal, and we shall now know the truth."

The Comte de Fenix bowed, said a few words to Lorenza in a low voice, and waited with the calmness of a man able to control events. A moment afterward the door opened, and his Eminence the Cardinal de Rohan was announced.

The princess, reassured by the presence of a third person, resumed her seat, and desired him to be admitted. The cardinal entered; but scarcely had he made his salutation to the princess, when, perceiving the count, he exclaimed with surprise, "You here, Monsieur?"

"Do you know this person?" asked the princess, more and more astonished.

"Yes, Madame," said the cardinal.

"Then," she cried, "you will tell me who he is?"

"Nothing is more easy," replied the cardinal; "the gentleman is a sorcerer."

"A sorcerer!" murmured the princess.

"Pardon me, Madame," said the count; "but I trust that his Eminence will explain his words to your satisfaction."

"Has the gentleman been making any predictions to your Royal Highness, that I see you so much alarmed?" asked Monsieur de Rohan.

"The register of the marriage! The register, immediately!" exclaimed the princess.

The cardinal stared with the utmost surprise, not comprehending what this exclamation meant.

"Here it is," said the count, presenting it to the cardinal.

"Monsieur, what is this?" said he.

"I wish to know," said the princess, "whether the signature to that document is genuine or not."

The cardinal took the paper and read it. "Yes," said he, "it is a perfectly legal register of a marriage, and the signature is that of Monsieur Rémy, vicar of St. John's, in Strasburg. But in what way does that concern your Royal Highness?"

"Oh, it concerns me deeply, Monsieur! So the signature is correct?"

"Certainly; but I will not guarantee that it may not have been extorted."

"Extorted!" cried the princess. "Yes, that is quite possible."

"And the consent of Lorenza also?" said the count, with a tone of irony which was aimed directly at the princess.

"But by what means, Cardinal, — by what means could this signature have been extorted? Do you know?"

"By means which this gentleman has at his disposal, — by means of magic!"

"Magic! Is it you, Cardinal, who speak to me of magic?"

"Yes, I have said that this gentleman is a sorcerer; and I shall not unsay it."

"Your Eminence must be jesting!"

"By no means; and the proof is that I am going, in the presence of your Highness, to have a very serious explanation with him."

"I was myself going to request it from your Eminence," said the count.

"Excellent! But do not forget," said the cardinal, haughtily, "that it is I who am the questioner."

"And do not forget also," said the count, "that I will answer all your questions before her Highness, if you insist upon it; but I feel certain that you will not insist."

The cardinal smiled. "Monsieur," said he, "to play the magician well is, in our times, a rather difficult task. I have seen you at work, and you were very successful; but every one will not show the patience, and, above all, the generosity, of Madame the Dauphiness."

"The dauphiness!" exclaimed the princess.

"Yes, Madame," said the count; "I have had the honor of being presented to her Royal Highness."

"And how did you repay that honor, Monsieur? Come, speak!"

"Alas! much worse than I could have wished; for I have no personal hatred against men, and especially none against women."

"But what did Monsieur do to my august niece?" asked the princess.

"I had the misfortune, Madame, to tell her the truth, which she demanded of me."

"Yes," said the cardinal, "a truth which made her swoon!"

"Was it my fault," cried the count, in that commanding tone which he could at times assume, "was it my fault that the truth was so terrible as to produce such effects? Was it I who sought the princess? Did I request to be presented to her? On the contrary, I avoided her; I was brought before her almost by force, and she positively commanded me to reply to her questions."

"But what, then, Monsieur, was that truth which you declare to have been so terrible?" asked the princess.

"That truth, Madame? I drew aside the veil that hides the future."

"The future?"

"Yes, Madame, that future which appeared to your Royal Highness so threatening that you fled for shelter from it to a cloister to offer up tears and prayers before the altar."

"Monsieur!"

"Is it my fault, Madame, if the future, which was revealed to you as one of the sainted, was shadowed forth to me as a prophet, and if the dauphiness, whom it threatens personally, terrified at the sight, fainted when I declared it to her?"

"You hear him?" said the cardinal.

"Alas!" sighed the princess.

"For her reign is doomed," continued the count, "as the most fatal and disastrous in the history of the monarchy."

"Monsieur!" exclaimed the princess.

"For yourself, Madame," continued the count, "your prayers have perhaps obtained favor; for you will not see those events which I foretell. You will be in the bosom of the Lord when they come to pass. But pray! pray always!"

The princess, overcome by his prophetic tone, which agreed too well with the terrors of her own soul, sank again on her knees at the foot of the crucifix, and began to pray fervently.

The count turned to the cardinal, and, preceding him toward the embrasure of a window, "Let us be alone," said he; "what does your Eminence desire of me?"

The cardinal hastened to join him. The princess seemed

wholly absorbed in her prayers, and Lorenza remained silent and motionless in the middle of the room. Her eyes were wide open, but she seemed to see nothing. The two men stood apart in the embrasure of the window, half concealed by the curtains.

"What do you desire of me?" repeated the count. "Speak."

"I wish to know who you are," replied the cardinal.

"Yet you seem to know. Did you not say that I was a sorcerer?"

"Yes; but down yonder you were called Joseph Balsamo, and here you are called the Comte de Fenix."

"Well, that only proves that I have changed my name, nothing more."

"Very true; but are you aware that such changes may make M. de Sartines, the minister of police, rather inquisitive about you?"

The count smiled. "Oh, Monsieur," said he, "this is a petty warfare for a Rohan! What! your Eminence quibbles about names? *Verba et voces*, as the Latin has it. Is there nothing worse with which I can be reproached!"

"You seem to have become satirical," said the cardinal.

"I have not become so; it is my character."

"In that case I shall do myself the pleasure of lowering your tone a little."

"Do so, Monsieur."

"I am certain I shall please the dauphiness by so doing."

"Which may be not altogether useless to you, considering the terms on which you stand at present with her," answered Balsamo, with the greatest coolness.

"And suppose, most learned dealer in horoscopes, that I should cause you to be arrested?" said the cardinal.

"I should say that your Eminence would commit a very grave mistake in doing so."

"Indeed!" said the prince-cardinal, with withering contempt. "And who then, pray, will suffer from my mistake?"

"Yourself, Monsieur le Cardinal."

"Then I will give the order for your arrest this moment, Monsieur; and we shall soon know who this Baron Balsamo, Comte de Fenix, is, — this illustrious branch of a genealogical tree not to be discovered in any field of heraldry in Europe!"

"But why has your Highness not asked for information respecting me from your friend the Comte de Breteuil?"

"Monsieur de Breteuil is no friend of mine."

"That is to say, he is no longer so. Yet he must have been one of your best friends when you wrote him a certain letter —"

"What letter?" asked the cardinal, drawing nearer to the count.

"A little closer, Monsieur le Cardinal; I do not wish to speak loud, for fear of compromising you. That letter which you wrote from Vienna to Paris, to endeavor to prevent the marriage of the dauphin."

The prelate could not repress a gesture of alarm.

"I know that letter by heart," continued the count, coldly.

"Then Breteuil has turned traitor?"

"How so?"

"Because when the marriage was decided on, I demanded back my letter, and he told me he had burned it!"

"Ah, he dared not tell you he had lost it!"

"Lost it?"

"Yes, and you know that a lost letter may be found by some one."

"And so my letter—"

"Was found by me. Oh! by the merest chance, I assure you, one day when crossing the marble court at Versailles."

"And did you not return it to the Comte de Breteuil?"

"I took good care not to do so."

"Why so?"

"Because, being a sorcerer, I knew that although I wished to be of all the service I could to your Eminence, you wished to do me all the harm you could. So, you understand. A disarmed man who journeys through a wood, where he knows he will be attacked, would be a fool not to pick up a loaded pistol which he found at his feet."

The cardinal's head swam, and he was obliged to lean against the window-frame for a few minutes; but after an instant's hesitation, during which the count eagerly watched every variation of his countenance,— "So be it," said he. "It shall never be said that a prince of my house gave way before the threats of a charlatan. Though that letter should be shown to the dauphiness herself; though, in a political point of view, it should ruin me,— I shall maintain my character as a loyal subject and faithful ambassador. I shall say, what is the truth, that I thought the alliance hurtful to the interests of my country, and my country will defend me, or will lament me."

"But if some one should happen to relate that the young, handsome, gallant ambassador, confiding in the name of Rohan and the title of prince, and being most graciously received by the Archduchess Marie Antoinette, did not say that because he saw anything in the marriage hurtful to France, but because in his vanity he imagined he saw something more than affability in her manner toward him? What would the loyal subject and faithful ambassador reply then?"

"He would deny, Monsieur, that there ever had existed the sentiment that your words imply; there is no proof that it did exist."

"Ah, Monsieur, you mistake! There is the strongest proof, in the coldness of the dauphiness toward you."

The cardinal hesitated.

"Monseigneur," said the count, "trust me, it is better for us to remain good friends than to quarrel, — which we should have done before this, had I not been more prudent than you."

"Good friends?"

"Why not? Our friends are those who render us good offices."

"Have I ever asked you for any?"

"No, and that is where you have been wrong; for during the two days you were in Paris—"

"I in Paris?"

"Yes, you. Why attempt to hide that from me, who am a sorcerer? You left the dauphiness at Soissons, you came post to Paris by Villers-Cotterets and Dammartin, — that is to say, by the shortest road, — and you hastened to request your kind friends there for assistance, which they all refused. After their refusals you once more set out post for Compiègne in despair."

The cardinal seemed overwhelmed. "And what sort of assistance might I have expected from you," he asked, "had I addressed myself to you?"

"That assistance of a man who makes gold."

"And what matters it to me that you can make gold?"

"*Peste!* when one has to pay five hundred thousand francs within forty-eight hours! Am I not right? Is not that the sum?"

"Yes, that is indeed the sum."

"And yet you ask what matters it to have a friend who can make gold? It matters just this, that the five hundred thousand francs which you cannot procure elsewhere, you may procure from him."

"And where?" asked the cardinal.

"In the Rue St. Claude."

"How shall I know your house?"

"By a griffin's head in bronze, which serves as knocker to the gate."

"When may I present myself?"

"The day after to-morrow, Monseigneur, toward six o'clock in the evening; and afterward you may come whenever you please. But stay; we have finished our conversation just in time, for the princess, I see, has ended her prayers."

The cardinal was conquered, and, no longer attempting to resist, he approached the princess: "Madame," said he, "I am obliged to confess that the Comte de Fenix is entirely right; his register of marriage is authentic and valid, and he has explained all the circumstances to my complete satisfaction."

The count bowed. "Has your Royal Highness any further commands for me?" he asked.

"I wish to speak once more to the young woman," she replied. Then, turning to Lorenza, "Is it of your own free and unrestrained will that you leave this convent, in which you sought refuge?"

"Her Highness asks you," said Balsamo, quickly, "whether it is of your own free and unfettered choice that you leave this convent. Answer, Lorenza."

"Yes," said the young woman, "it is of my own free and unfettered will."

"And to accompany your husband, the Comte de Fenix?"

"And to accompany me?" repeated the count.

"Oh, yes!" exclaimed Lorenza.

"In that case," said the princess, "I wish to retain neither one nor the other; for it would be doing violence to your feelings. But if there is in all this anything out of the natural order of events, may the vengeance of Heaven fall on him who, for his own advantage or profit, has interrupted the proper course of nature! Go, Monsieur le Comte de Fenix! Go, Lorenza Feliciani!—only, take with you your jewels."

"They are for the use of the poor, Madame," said the count; "and distributed by your hands, the alms will be doubly acceptable to God. I seek to recover only my horse Djerid."

"You can claim him as you pass, Monsieur. Go."

The count bowed low, and gave his arm to Lorenza, who took it and left the room with him without uttering a word.

"Ah, Monsieur le Cardinal," said the princess, shaking her head sorrowfully, "there are incomprehensible and fatal omens in the very air we breathe!"

CHAPTER VIII.

THE RETURN FROM ST. DENIS.

AFTER leaving Philippe, Gilbert, as we have said, had re-entered the crowd. But not now with a heart bounding with joyful anticipation did he throw himself into the noisy billow of human beings; his soul was wounded to the quick, and Philippe's kind reception of him and all his friendly offers of assistance had no power to soothe him.

Andrée never suspected that she had been cruel to Gilbert. The lovely and serene young girl was entirely ignorant that there could be between her and the son of her nurse any point of contact either for pain or for pleasure. She revolved above all the lower spheres of life, casting light or shadow on them according as she herself was gay or sad. But now the shadow of her disdain had fallen on Gilbert and frozen him to the soul; while she, following only the impulse of her nature, knew not even that she had been scornful. But Gilbert, like a gladiator disarmed, had offered his naked breast to the full brunt of her haughty looks and disdainful words; and now his philosophy could suggest to him, bleeding at every pore, no relief but the consolation of despair. From the moment that he once more plunged into the crowd, he cared neither for horses nor men. Collecting all his strength, he dashed forward like a wild boar with the spear in its side; and at the risk of being crushed or trodden under foot, he opened a passage for himself through the multitude. When the very dense mass of people had been passed, he began to breathe more freely, and looking about him, he saw green grass, the cool water, and that he was alone.

Without knowing whither he was going, he had advanced toward the Seine; and he now found himself opposite the isle of St. Denis. Exhausted, not from fatigue of body, but from anguish of mind, he sank on the turf; and grasping his head with both hands, he began to roar hoarsely, as if by these inarticulate sounds alone he could express his rage and grief.

All those vague and senseless hopes which until then had shed a glimmering light on the darkness of his soul, and whose existence he scarcely ventured to confess even to himself, were now at one blow utterly annihilated. To whatsoever height genius, science, or study might raise him in the social scale, he must to Andrée always remain the Gilbert that he had been, — a thing or a man, to use her own words, not worth the slightest regard, not worth even the trouble of a glance. For a moment he had thought that, seeing him in Paris, knowing his resolution to struggle out of obscurity into light, — he had thought that Andrée would commend his endeavor; but instead of applause, what had he met with as the reward of so much fatigue and of such firm determination? The same scornful indifference with which he had been treated at Taverney. Even more, — was she not almost angry when she heard that his eyes had had the audacity to look on her music-book? Had he only touched that music-book with the tip of his finger, he would doubtless have been considered only worthy to be burned at the stake.

In weak characters any deception is but a blow under which love bends only to rise again stronger and more persevering than before. They vent their sufferings in complaints and tears, but their resistance is only passive, — nay, their love often increases by that which should destroy it; and they say to themselves that their submissiveness will at last have its reward. Toward that reward they steadfastly advance, whether the road be smooth or rough, — if the way be hard, they arrive later, that is all; but they do arrive. It is not thus with strong minds, obstinate natures, and powerful wills. They are indignant when they see their own blood flowing; at the sight their energy augments so furiously that they seem to hate rather than to love. Indeed, with them love and hate are so closely allied that they often are not aware of the transition from one to the other.

So it was with Gilbert. When he flung himself on the ground, overcome by his grief, did he love or hate Andrée? He knew not; he suffered, that was all. But not having the virtue of submission, he shook off his dejection of soul, and determined to carry into practice some energetic resolution. "She does not love me," thought he, "it is true; but had I any right to hope that she would? The only feeling that I had a right to hope for was that kindly interest which attaches to the unfortunate who strive with energy to rise above their wretchedness. Her brother felt this; she did not feel it. He said, 'Who knows? Perhaps you may become a Colbert, a Vauban!' If I should become either one or the other, he would do me justice; he would give me his sister as a reward for the glory I had won for myself, as he would now give her in exchange for my personal nobility, had I been born his equal. But as for her, — oh, yes! I feel it, — yes, although Colbert or Vauban, I should never be to her other than Gilbert! What she despises in me is what nothing can efface, nothing gild, nothing cover, — it is my humble birth. As if, supposing I attain my object, I should not then be greater, having risen to her level, than if I had been born beside her! Ah, senseless, unthinking creature! Woman! woman! — that is, imperfection! Do you trust in her open look, her expansive forehead, her beaming smile, her queenly carriage, her beauty which makes her worthy to be an empress? Fool! she is an affected, starched country-girl, bound up, swathed in aristocratic prejudices. The gay and showy young noblemen with empty heads — mere weathercocks — who have all the means and appliances for learning, but who know nothing, — they are her equals; they are men on whom she may bestow attention! But Gilbert? Gilbert is a dog, — nay, lower than a dog! She asked, I think, for news of Mahon; she did not ask how it had fared with Gilbert. Oh! she knows not, then, that I am as strong as they; that if clothed like them, I should be as handsome; that I have what they have not, — an inflexible will; and that if I wished — "

A threatening smile curled his lip, and he left the sentence unfinished: then slowly, and with a deep frown, he bowed his head on his breast. What thoughts at that moment entered his dark and gloomy soul? Under what terrible idea did that pale forehead, already furrowed with painful thoughts, droop? Who shall tell? Is it the boatman who slowly glides down the river in his skiff, humming the song of Henri-Quatre? Is it the laughing washerwoman who is returning from the splendid scene at St. Denis, and who, turning aside from her path to avoid him, probably takes the young loiterer for a thief, lying as he is at full length on the grass amid the lines hung with linen?

After half an hour's reflection, Gilbert arose, calm and resolved. He approached the bank of the Seine, and refreshed himself with a deep draught of water; then, looking around, he saw on his left the distant waves of people pouring out of St. Denis. Amid the throng he could distinguish the principal carriages, forced to go slowly from the crowd of spectators that pressed on them, and taking the road to St. Ouen.

The dauphiness had expressed a desire that her entrance into the kingdom should be a family festival, and the good Parisians had taken advantage of this kind wish to place their families so near the royal train that many of them had mounted on the seats of the footmen, and some held on by the heavy springs which projected from the carriages, without manifesting the least fear.

Gilbert soon recognized Andrée's carriage; Philippe was galloping, or rather, we should say, reining in his prancing horse, close beside it.

"It is well," said he. "I must know whither she is going; and for that purpose I must follow her."

The dauphiness was to take supper at Muette in private with the king, the dauphin, the Comte de Provence, and the Comte d'Artois. At St. Denis the king had invited the dauphiness, and had given her a list of the guests and a pencil, desiring her to erase the name of any one whom she did not wish to be present. Now, it must be confessed that Louis carried his forgetfulness of the respect due to her so far as to include in it the name of Madame Dubarry. It was the last on the list; and when the dauphiness reached it, her cheek turned pale and her lip quivered. But, following the instructions of the empress her mother, she recovered her self-possession, and with a sweet smile returning the list and the pencil to the king, she expressed herself most happy to be admitted thus from the first to the intimacy of his family circle.

Gilbert knew nothing of all this, and it was only at Muette that he discovered the equipage of the countess, followed by Zamore on his tall white charger. Fortunately it was dark; and concealing himself behind a clump of trees, he lay down and waited.

The king took supper with his daughter-in-law and his mistress, and was in charming spirits; more especially when he saw the dauphiness receive the countess even more graciously than she had done at Compiègne. But the dauphin seemed grave and anxious, and pretending that he suffered from a violent headache, retired before they sat down to supper. The entertainment was prolonged until eleven o'clock.

In the mean time the retinue of the dauphiness — and the haughty Andrée was forced to acknowledge that she belonged to it — ate in tents to the music of the king's private band, who had been ordered to attend for that purpose. Besides these, — as the tents could not accommodate all, — fifty gentlemen were seated at tables spread in the open air, waited on by fifty lackeys in the royal livery. Gilbert, still hidden in the clump of trees, lost nothing of this spectacle; and while the others were at supper he also ate his, — a piece of bread which he had bought at Clichy-la-Garenne.

After supper the dauphiness and the king appeared on a balcony to take leave of their guests. Madame Dubarry, with a tact which even her enemies admired, remained out of sight in the remotest part of the room. As each person departed, he passed below the balcony to salute his Majesty and her Royal Highness. The dauphiness already knew many who had accompanied her from Compiègne, and those whom she did not know the king named to her. From time to time a gracious word or a well-turned compliment fell from her lips, diffusing joy in the breasts of those to whom it was addressed. Gilbert, from his distant post, saw the meanness of their homage, and murmured, "I am greater than those people, since for all the gold in the world I would not do what they are doing."

At last the turn of the Baron de Taverney and his family came. Gilbert rose on one knee.

"M. Philippe," said the dauphiness, "I give you leave of absence, in order that you may accompany your father and your sister to Paris."

Gilbert heard these words distinctly, which in the silence of the night and amid the respectful attention of all around, vibrated in his ears.

Then she added: "Monsieur de Taverney, I cannot promise you apartments until I install my household at Versailles. You can, therefore, in the mean time, accompany your daughter to Paris. Do not forget me, Mademoiselle."

The baron passed on with his son and daughter. They were succeeded by many others, to whom the dauphiness made similar speeches; but Gilbert cared no longer for her words. He glided out from the clump of trees and followed the baron amid the confused cries of two hundred footmen running after their masters and calling to a hundred coachmen, while their shouts were accompanied by the thundering of numerous carriages rolling along the paved road.

The baron had one of the carriages of the court at his command, and it waited for them apart from the general crowd. When, accompanied by Andrée and Philippe, he had entered it, the latter said to the footman who was closing the door, "Mount on the seat beside the coachman, my friend."

"Why so? why so?" asked the baron, hastily.

"Because the poor devil has been on his legs since morning, and must be tired by this time."

The baron grumbled something which Gilbert did not

hear, while the footman mounted beside the coachman. Gilbert drew nearer. At the moment when they were about to start, it was perceived that the trace had become unbuckled. The coachman jumped down, and the coach remained for a few moments stationary.

"It is very late," said the baron.

"I am dreadfully fatigued," said Andrée. "Are you sure we shall get beds?"

"I hope so," said Philippe; "I sent on La Brie and Nicole from Soissons with a letter to a friend of mine, desiring him to engage a small garden pavilion for us, which his mother and sister occupied last year. It is not a very splendid abode, but it is suitable enough; you do not wish to receive company, — you want only a stopping-place for the present."

"Faith!" exclaimed the baron, "whatever it is, it will be better than Taverney."

"Unfortunately, father, that is true," replied Philippe, in a melancholy tone.

"Are there any trees?" asked Andrée.

"Oh, yes! and very fine ones too. But in all probability you will not have long to enjoy them, for as soon as the marriage is over, you will be presented at court."

"Well, this is all a dream, I fear," said the baron; "do not awake us too soon, Philippe. Have you given the proper direction to the coachman?"

Gilbert listened anxiously.

"Yes, father."

Gilbert, who had heard all this conversation, had for a moment hoped to discover the address.

"No matter," said he, "I will follow them; it is only a league to Paris."

The trace was fastened, the coachman mounted his seat,

and the carriage was again in motion. But the king's horses go fast when they are not in a procession which obliges them to go slowly, and now they darted forward so rapidly that they recalled to poor Gilbert's recollection the road to Lachaussée, his weakness, and his fainting. He made an effort and reached the footboard behind, which was vacant, as the weary footman was seated beside the coachman. Gilbert grasped it, sprang up, and seated himself. But scarcely had he done so when the thought struck him that he was behind Andrée's carriage and in the footman's place.

"No, no!" muttered the inflexible young man; "it shall never be said that I did not struggle to the last. My legs are tired, but my arms are strong."

Then, seizing the footboard with his hands, he followed at full speed, supported by the strength of his arms, and keeping his hold in spite of jolts and shocks, rather than capitulate with his conscience.

"At least I shall know her address," he murmured. "True, I shall have to pass one more bad night; but to-morrow I shall rest while I copy my music. Besides, I have still some money, and I may take two hours for sleep if I like." Then he reflected that as Paris was such a large place, and as he was quite unacquainted with it, he might lose his way after the baron and his daughter should have entered the house chosen for them by Philippe. Fortunately, it was then near midnight, and day would break at half-past three.

As all these reflections passed through Gilbert's mind, he remarked that they were passing through a spacious square, in the centre of which was a large equestrian statue. "Ha! this looks like the Place des Victoires," cried he, with a mingled sensation of surprise and joy.

The carriage turned. Andrée put her head out of the

window and looked back. "It is the statue of the late king," said Philippe; "we are now near the house."

They descended a steep street so rapidly that Gilbert was nearly thrown under the wheels.

"Here we are at last!" cried Philippe.

Gilbert sprang aside, and hid himself behind the corner of the neighboring street. Philippe leaped out, rang the bell, and turning, received Andrée in his arms. The baron got out last. "Well," cried he, "are those scoundrels going to keep us here all night?"

At that moment the voices of La Brie and Nicole were heard, and a gate was opened. The three travellers disappeared in a dark court, and the gate closed behind them.

The carriage drove off on its way to the king's stable. The house which had received the strangers was in no way remarkable in its appearance; but the lamps of the carriage in passing had flashed on that next to it, and Gilbert read over the gateway the words, "Hôtel d'Armenonville." It only remained for him to discover the name of the street. He proceeded to the nearest end of the street, — that by which the carriage had disappeared, — and to his great surprise he found himself close to the fountain at which he was in the habit of drinking. He advanced a few steps in a street parallel to that which he had left, and discovered the baker's shop where he usually bought his loaf. Doubting still, he went back to the corner of the street; and there, by the light of a neighboring lamp, he read the words which he had noticed when returning with Rousseau from their botanical excursion in the forest of Meudon three days before, — Rue Plastrière! Andrée, consequently, was not one hundred paces distant from him, — not so far off as she had been at Taverney when he slept in his little room at the castle gate! Then he regained his domicile, scarcely daring to hope to find the end of the cord left out by which the latch of the door was lifted. But Gilbert's star was in the ascendant; a few ravelled threads were hanging out, by which he pulled the whole, and the door opened gently at his touch. He felt his way to the stairs, mounted step by step without making the least noise, and at last put his hand on the padlock of the garret door, in which Rousseau had kindly left the key. Ten minutes afterward fatigue asserted its power over his disquieted thoughts, and he slept soundly, although longing for the morrow.

CHAPTER IX.

THE GARDEN PAVILION.

HAVING come in late and thrown himself hastily on his bed, Gilbert had forgotten to place over his window the blind which intercepted the light of the rising sun. At five o'clock, therefore, the rays of light beaming through the window awoke him. He sprang up, fearing that he had slept too long.

Accustomed as he had been to a country life, Gilbert could guess the hour at all times with the utmost precision by the direction of the shadows and by the paler or warmer tints of light. He ran, therefore, to consult his clock. The faintness of the morning beams, barely tingeing with their light the topmost boughs of the trees, reassured him; and he found that instead of having risen too late, he had risen too early. He finished his toilet at the garret window, thinking over the events of the preceding day, and exposing with delight his burning and oppressed forehead to the refreshing morning breeze. Then he remembered that Andrée lodged in the next street, near the Hôtel d'Armenonville, and he tried to guess in which of all the houses that he saw she might be. The sight of the lofty trees on which he looked down recalled her question to Philippe, " Are there any trees there ?"

" Might they not have chosen that uninhabited house in the garden?" said Gilbert to himself. This idea naturally led him to fix his attention on the garden pavilion, where, by a singular coincidence, a sort of noise and stir began to be apparent.

One of the window-shutters of the little abode, which apparently had not been opened for a considerable time, was shaken by an awkward or feeble hand. The wood yielded above; but held fast — by the damp, no doubt — to the frame at the bottom, it resisted the effort made to open it. A second shake more violent than the first had a better effect; the two shutters creaked, gave way, and falling back quickly, exposed to view a young girl all in a glow with her exertions, and beating off the dust from her hands.

Gilbert uttered a cry of surprise, and stepped back. The young girl, whose face was still flushed with sleep, and who was stretching herself in the fresh air, was Mademoiselle Nicole. There was no longer any room for doubt. The lodging which Philippe had said La Brie and Nicole were preparing was the house before him, and the mansion through whose gateway he had seen the travellers disappear must have its gardens adjoining the rear of the Rue Plastrière. Gilbert's movement was so abrupt that if Nicole had not been completely absorbed in the lazy meditation so delightful at the moment of waking, she must have discovered our philosopher at his skylight.

But Gilbert had retired all the more speedily, as he had no intention of being discovered by Nicole at a garret window. Had he been on a first floor, and had his open window showed a background of rich hangings or sumptuous furniture, he would not have been so anxious to avoid her eye; but a garret on the fifth story declared him to be still so low in the social scale that he took the greatest care to hide himself. Moreover, there is always a great advantage in seeing without being seen. And then, if Andrée should discover that he was there, would it not be sufficient either to induce her to change her abode, or prevent her walking in the garden?

Alas! Gilbert's pride still made him of too great importance in his own eyes. What was Gilbert to Andrée? Would she have moved her foot, either to approach or to avoid him? Was she not one of that class of women who leave the bath in presence of a lackey or a peasant because neither a lackey nor a peasant is a man? But these were far from being Nicole's sentiments, and her, consequently, he must shun.

He hid himself carefully, therefore; but as he did not wish to withdraw from the window entirely, he ventured to peep out cautiously at one corner.

A second window on the ground-floor of the pavilion, exactly below the first, just then opened, and a white form appeared there. It was Andrée, seemingly just awakened. She was enveloped in a dressing-gown, and was occupied in searching for the slipper which had escaped from her tiny foot and was lying beneath a chair. It was in vain that Gilbert, every time that he saw Andrée, vowed to build up between them a barrier of hatred instead of giving way to love; the same effect was produced by the same cause. He was obliged to lean against the wall for support; his heart palpitated as if it would have burst, and sent the blood in boiling currents through his whole frame. However, by degrees his throbbing arteries beat with a calmer motion, and reflection resumed her sway. The problem was, as we have said, to see without being seen. He took one of Thérèse's gowns and fastened it with a pin to one of the cords which crossed his window; and, sheltered by this impromptu curtain, he could watch Andrée without running any risk of being discovered by her. Andrée, following Nicole's example, stretched out her snowy arms, and then, folding them on the window-sill, she looked out on the garden. Her countenance expressed the liveliest satisfaction at all she saw. Lofty trees shaded the walks with their drooping branches, and everywhere verdure cheered her eye. She, who smiled so seldom on men, smiled freely on the inanimate objects around her.

The house in which Gilbert lived attracted her eye for a moment, like all the others which surrounded the garden; but as from her apartment only the garrets of the houses were visible, and, consequently, from them alone could she be seen, she gave those houses no farther attention. Of what interest to the proud young girl were persons living in garret chambers? Andrée was satisfied that no one saw her by whom it was of the least importance that she should not be seen, and that within the bounds of her tranquil retreat there would appear none of those prying or satirical Parisian faces so much dreaded by ladies from the provinces. The effect was immediate. Leaving her window wide open, so that the fresh and perfumed air might penetrate to the farthest extremity of her apartment, she proceeded toward the mantelpiece, rang a bell, and began to dress, or undress rather, in the shaded part of the chamber.

Nicole appeared, undid the straps of a shagreen dressing-case of the reign of Queen Anne, took from it a tortoise-shell comb, and began to comb out Andrée's hair. In a moment the long tresses and shining curls spread like a glossy veil over the shoulders of the young girl.

Gilbert gave a stifled sigh. At that distance he scarcely saw the beauty of her locks, but he saw Andrée herself, a thousand times more lovely in this dishabille than she would have been in the most splendid attire. He gazed with his whole soul in his eyes.

By chance, as Nicole continued to dress her hair, Andrée raised her eyes and fixed them on Gilbert's garret.

"Yes, yes!" said he, "look, gaze, as much as you

please; it is all in vain, — you can see nothing, and I see all."

But Gilbert was mistaken; Andrée did see something. It was the gown which he had hung up, and which, being blown about, had got wrapped round his head like a turban. She pointed out this strange object to her companion. Nicole, stopping in her complicated task, pointed with the comb which she held in her hand toward the skylight, and seemed to ask her mistress if that were the object which she meant.

All these gestures, which Gilbert devoured with the greatest eagerness, had, without his suspecting it, a third spectator. Suddenly a rude hand snatched Thérèse's gown from his head, and he was ready to sink with shame on seeing Rousseau beside him.

"What the devil are you doing there, Monsieur?" cried the philosopher, with a terrible frown, and a scrutinizing glance at the gown borrowed, without leave asked, from his wife.

"Nothing, Monsieur, nothing at all," replied Gilbert, endeavoring to turn Rousseau's attention from the window.

"Nothing? Then why did you hide yourself with the gown?"

"The sun hurts my eyes."

"This window looks towards the west, and the sun dazzles you when rising? You have very delicate eyes, young man!"

Gilbert stammered out some disconnected words; but feeling that he was only getting deeper in the mire, he at last hid his head in his hands.

"You are speaking falsely, and you are afraid," said Rousseau; "therefore you have been doing wrong."

After this terrible syllogism, which seemed to complete

Gilbert's confusion, Rousseau planted himself exactly opposite the window. From a feeling too natural to require explanation, Gilbert, who so lately trembled to be discovered at the window, rushed forward when he saw Rousseau standing before it.

"Ah, ah!" said the latter, in a tone which froze the blood in Gilbert's veins, "the garden-house is inhabited now."

Gilbert was dumb.

"And by persons," continued the philosopher, "who seem to know my house, for they are pointing to it."

Gilbert, trembling lest he had advanced too far, stepped back quickly; but neither his movement, nor the cause which produced it, escaped the jealous eye of Rousseau; he saw that Gilbert feared to be seen.

"No," cried he, seizing the young man by the arm, "you shall not escape, my young friend; there is some plot under this, — I know by their pointing to your garret. Place yourself here, if you please;" and he dragged him opposite the skylight, in the full view of those beneath.

"Oh, no, Monsieur, no! have mercy!" cried Gilbert, struggling to escape.

But to escape, which for a young and active man like Gilbert would have been an easy task, he must have engaged in a contest with Rousseau, — Rousseau, whom he venerated like some superior being; and respect restrained him.

"You know those women," said Rousseau, "and they know you."

"No, no, no, Monsieur."

"Then if you do not know them, and if they do not know you, why not show yourself?"

"Monsieur Rousseau, you have sometimes had secrets yourself. Show some pity for mine."

"Ah! traitor," cried Rousseau. "Yes, I know what sort of a secret yours is. You are a creature of Grimm or D'Holbach; you have been tutored to act a part in order to impose upon my benevolence; you have gained admittance into my house, and now you betray me to them. Oh, stupid fool that I am! Silly lover of Nature! I thought I was aiding a fellow-creature, and I was bringing a spy into my house!"

"A spy!" exclaimed Gilbert, indignantly.

"Come, Judas! on what day am I to be sold?" continued Rousseau, folding Thérèse's gown tragically about him, and thinking himself sublime in his grief, when unfortunately he was only ridiculous.

"Monsieur, you calumniate me," said Gilbert.

"Calumniate you, you little serpent!" exclaimed Rousseau. "Did I not find you corresponding with my enemies by signs,— making them understand, perhaps, what is the subject of my new work?"

"Monsieur, had I gained admittance to your house in order to betray the secret of your work, it would have been easier for me to copy some of the manuscripts in your desk than to inform others of the subject by signs."

This was true; and Rousseau felt so plainly that he had given utterance to one of those absurdities which escaped him when his monomania of suspicion was at its height that he got angry.

"Monsieur," said he, "I am sorry for you, but experience has made me severe. My life has been one long series of deceptions. I have been betrayed, sold, made a martyr, by every one that surrounded me. I am, you must be aware, one of those illustrious unfortunates on whom government has put its ban. In such a situation it is pardonable to be suspicious. Now, I suspect you, therefore you must leave my house."

Gilbert was far from expecting this peroration. He to be turned out! He clenched his hands tightly, and a flash of anger, which almost made Rousseau tremble, lighted up his eyes. The flash was only momentary, however, for the thought occurred to him that in leaving Rousseau's house he should lose the happiness of seeing Andrée every hour of the day, as well as forfeit the friendship of Rousseau; this would be to add misery to shame. His fierce pride gave way, and, clasping his hands: "Monsieur," said he, "listen to me! One word, only one word!"

"I am pitiless," said Rousseau; "men have made me by their injustice more cruel than the tiger. You are in correspondence with my enemies. Go to them, I do not prevent you. League with them, I do not oppose your doing so. Only leave my house!"

"Monsieur, those two young girls are not your enemies; they are Mademoiselle Andrée and Nicole."

"And who is Mademoiselle Andrée?" said Rousseau, to whom this name, spoken already two or three times by Gilbert, was quite familiar. "Who is Mademoiselle Andrée? Speak!"

"Mademoiselle Andrée, Monsieur, is the daughter of the Baron de Taverney. Oh, pardon me, Monsieur, for daring to say so to you, but I love her more than you ever loved Mademoiselle Galley or Madame de Warens! It is she whom I have followed on foot to Paris, without money and without bread, until I fell down on the road exhausted with hunger and fatigue. It is she whom I went to see yesterday at St. Denis, whom I followed, unseen by her, to Muette, and thence to a street near this. It is she whom by chance I discovered this morning to be the occupant of this garden-house; and it is she for whose sake I burn to be a Turenne, a Richelieu, or a Rousseau!"

Rousseau knew the human heart and the varying tones in which it speaks; and he felt assured that no one acting a part could speak with the trembling and impassioned accents of Gilbert, or accompany his words with gestures so true to nature. "So," said he, "this young lady is Mademoiselle Andrée?"

"Yes, Monsieur Rousseau."

"Then you know her?"

"I am the son of her nurse."

"Then you lied just now when you said you did not know her; and if you are not a traitor, you are a liar."

"Monsieur, you tear my very heart! Indeed, you would hurt me less were you to kill me on the spot."

"Pshaw! Mere phrases!—in the style of Diderot and Marmontel! You are a liar, Monsieur."

"Well, yes, yes!" said Gilbert; "I am a liar, Monsieur,—and so much the worse for you if you do not feel for one so forced to lie. A liar! a liar! I leave you, Monsieur; but I leave you in despair, and my misery will weigh heavy on your conscience."

Rousseau stroked his chin as he looked at this young man, in whom he found so many points of character resembling his own. "He has either a great soul or he is a great rogue," said he to himself; "but if they are plotting against me, why not hold in my hand a clew to the plot?"

Gilbert had advanced toward the door; and now, with his hand on the lock, stood waiting for the fiat which was to banish or recall him.

"Enough on this subject, my son," said Rousseau. "If you are as deeply in love as you say, so much the worse for you. But it is now late; you lost the whole of yesterday, and we have to-day thirty pages to copy. Quick, Gilbert; bestir yourself!"

Gilbert seized the philosopher's hand and pressed it to his lips; he certainly would not have done so much to a king's. But before leaving the room, and while Gilbert, still deeply moved, stood leaning against the door, Rousseau again placed himself at the window to take a last look at the young girls. Andrée had just thrown off her dressing-gown and taken her gown from Nicole's hands. She saw his pallid countenance and searching eye, and starting back, she ordered Nicole to close the window. Nicole obeyed.

"So," said Rousseau, "my old face frightens her; his young one would not have had the same effect. O lovely youth!" added he, sighing, —

"'O gioventu primavera dell' eta!
O primavera gioventu dell' anno!'"

and once more hanging up Thérèse's gown on its nail, he went downstairs in a melancholy mood, followed by Gilbert, for whose youth he would perhaps at that moment have exchanged his renown, which then rivalled that of Voltaire, sharing with it the admiration of the world.

CHAPTER X.

THE HOUSE IN THE RUE ST. CLAUDE.

THE Rue St. Claude, in which the Comte de Fenix had appointed to meet the Cardinal de Rohan, was not so different at that period from what it is at the present day but that some vestiges of the localities we are about to describe may yet be discovered. It abutted then, as it does now, on the Rue St. Louis and the boulevard, and descended toward the latter with rather a steep inclination. It boasted of fifteen houses and seven lanterns, and was remarkable besides for two lanes, which branched off from it, — the one on the left, the other on the right; the former passing by the Hôtel de Voysins, while the latter bounded the large garden of the convent of St. Sacrament. This last-mentioned lane, shaded on one side by the trees of the convent garden, was bordered on the other by the high, dark wall of a house, which stood in the Rue St. Claude. This wall, resembling the face of a cyclops, had only one eye, or, if the reader like it better, only one window; and even that, covered with bars and grating, was horribly gloomy. Just below this window, which was never opened, as one might perceive from the spider's webs that covered it on the outside, was a door studded with large nails, which indicated, not that the house was entered, but that it might be entered, on this side.

There were no dwellings in this lane, and only two occupants. These were a cobbler in a wooden box, and a stocking-mender in a cask, both taking shelter from the heat under the acacias of the convent garden, which after nine o'clock in the morning threw their broad shadow on the dusty ground. In the evening the stocking-mender returned to her domicile, the cobbler put a padlock on his castle, and no guardian watched over the lonely street, save the stern and sombre eye of the window we have spoken of.

Besides the door just mentioned, the house which we have undertaken to describe so accurately had another, and the principal, entrance in the Rue St. Claude. This entrance was a large gateway surmounted with carved figures in relief, which recalled the architecture of the time of Louis XIII., and was adorned with the griffin's head for a knocker which the Comte de Fenix had indicated to the Cardinal de Rohan as distinguishing his abode.

As for the windows, they looked on the boulevard, and were opened early in the morning to admit the fresh air. But as Paris at that period, and above all in that quarter, was far from safe, it occasioned no astonishment to see them grated, and the walls near them bristling with iron spikes. Indeed, the first story of the house was not unlike a fortress. Against enemies, thieves, or lovers it presented iron balconies with sharp points; a deep moat separated the building from the boulevard; and to obtain entrance on this side would have required ladders at least thirty feet long, — for the wall which enclosed, or rather buried, the courtyard was of fully that height.

This house, before which in the present day a spectator would be arrested by curiosity on beholding its singular aspect, was not very remarkable in 1770. On the contrary, it seemed to harmonize with the quarter of the city in which it stood; and if the worthy inhabitants of the Rue St. Louis, and the not less worthy denizens of the Rue St. Claude, shunned its neighborhood, it was not on account of its reputation, which was then unimpaired, but on account of the lonely boulevard of the Porte St. Louis and the Pont aux Choux, both of which were in very bad odor with the Parisians. In fact, the boulevard on this side led only to the Bastille; and as there were not more than a dozen houses in the space of a quarter of a league, the city authorities had not thought it worth their while to light such a desert region. The consequence was that after eight o'clock in summer, and four in winter, the place became a sort of chaos, with the addition of robbers.

It was, however, on this very boulevard, toward nine o'clock in the evening, and about three quarters of an hour after the visit to St. Denis, that a carriage drove rapidly along. It bore the coat of arms of the Comte de Fenix on its panels. The count himself, mounted on Djerid, who whisked his long and silky tail as he snuffed the stifling atmosphere, rode about twenty paces in advance. Within it, resting on cushions, and concealed by the closed blinds, lay Lorenza fast asleep. The gate opened as if by enchantment, at the noise of the wheels, and the carriage, after turning into the dark gulf of the Rue St. Claude, disappeared in the courtyard of the house we have just described, and the gate closed behind it. There was most assuredly no occasion for so much mystery, since no one was there to see the Comte de Fenix return, or to interfere with him had he carried off in his carriage the treasures of the Abbey of St. Denis.

And now we shall say a few words respecting the interior of this house, of which it is important that our readers should know something, since it is our intention to introduce them to it more than once.

In the courtyard of which we have spoken, and in which the springing grass labored by a never-ceasing effort to displace the pavement, were seen on the right the stables, on the left the coach-houses, while at the back a double flight of twelve steps led to the entrance door. On the ground floor the house, or at least as much of it as was accessible, consisted of a large antechamber, a dining-room, remarkable for the quantity of massive plate heaped on its sideboards, and a salon, which seemed quite recently furnished, — probably for the reception of its new inmates. From the antechamber a broad staircase led to the first-floor, which contained three principal apartments. A skilful geometrician, however, on measuring with his eye the extent of the house outside, and observing the space within it, would have been surprised that it contained so little accommodation. In fact, in the outside apparent house there was a second hidden house, known only to him who inhabited it.

In the antechamber, close beside a statue of the god Harpocrates, — who, with his finger on his lips, seemed to enjoin the silence of which he is the symbol, — was concealed a secret door opening with a spring, and masked by the ornaments of the architecture. This door gave access to a staircase, which, ascending to about the same height as the first-floor on the other staircase, led to a little apartment lighted by two grated windows looking on an inner court. This inner court was the box, as it were, which enclosed the second house and concealed it from all eyes.

The apartment to which this staircase led was evidently intended for a man. Beside the bed, and before the sofas and couches, were spread, instead of carpets, the most magnificent furs which Africa and India could produce. There were skins of lions, tigers, and panthers, with their glaring eyes and threatening teeth. The walls, hung with Cordova leather stamped in large and flowing arabesques, were decorated with weapons of every kind, from the tomahawk of the Huron to the kris of the Malay; from the sword of the Crusader to the kandjiar of the Arab; from the arquebuse, incrusted with ivory, of the sixteenth century, to the gun, damaskeened with gold, of the eighteenth. The eye in vain sought in this room for any other outlet than that from the staircase; perhaps there were several, but if so, they were concealed and invisible.

A German domestic, about twenty-five or thirty years of age, the only human being who had been seen moving about in that vast mansion for several days, bolted the gate of the courtyard; and, opening the carriage-door while the stolid coachman unharnessed his horses, he took Lorenza in his arms and carried her into the antechamber. There he laid her on a table covered with red cloth, and drew down her long white veil over her person. Then he left the room to light at the lamps of the carriage a large chandelier with seven branches, and returned with all its lights burning; but in that interval, short as it was, Lorenza had disappeared.

The Comte de Fenix had followed close behind the German, and had no sooner been left alone with Lorenza than he took her in his arms and carried her by the secret staircase we have described to the hall of arms, after having carefully closed both the doors behind him. Once there, he pressed his foot on a spring in the corner of the lofty mantelpiece, and immediately a door, which formed the back of the fireplace, rolled back on its noiseless hinges, and the count with his burden again disappeared, carefully closing behind him with his foot the mysterious door.

At the back of the mantelpiece was a second staircase, consisting of a flight of fifteen steps covered with Utrecht velvet; after mounting which, he reached a chamber elegantly hung with satin, embroidered with flowers of such brilliant colors, and so naturally designed, that they might have been taken for real flowers. The furniture was richly gilt. Two cabinets of tortoise-shell inlaid with brass, a harpsichord, and a toilet-table of rose-wood, a beautiful bed with transparent curtains, and several vases of Sèvres porcelain, formed the principal articles, while chairs and couches, arranged symmetrically in a space of thirty feet square, served to complete the decoration of the apartment, to which was attached a dressing-room and a boudoir. The latter had no windows, but lamps filled with perfumed oil burned in them day and night, and, let down from the ceiling, were trimmed by invisible hands. The sleeping-chamber, however, had two windows, hung with rich and heavy curtains; but as it was now night, the curtains had nothing to conceal.

Not a sound, not a breath, was heard in this chamber; and an occupant of it might have thought himself a hundred miles from the world. But gold shone on every side; beautiful paintings smiled from the walls, and lustres of colored Bohemian glass glittered and sparkled like glowing eyes, when, after having placed Lorenza on a sofa, the count, not satisfied with the trembling radiance of the boudoir, proceeded to light the rose-colored wax-candles of two candelabra on the mantelpiece.

Then, returning to Lorenza and placing himself before her, he knelt with one knee on a pile of cushions, and called softly, "Lorenza!"

The young woman at this appeal raised herself on her elbow, although her eyes remained closed; but she did not reply.

"Lorenza," he repeated, "do you sleep in your ordinary sleep, or in the magnetic sleep?"

"In the magnetic sleep," she answered.

"Then if I question you, you can reply?"

"I think so."

The Comte de Fenix was silent for a moment; then he continued: "Look in the apartment of Madame Louise, whom we left three quarters of an hour ago."

"I am looking."

"What do you see?"

"The princess is praying before retiring to bed."

"Do you see the Cardinal de Rohan in the convent."

"No."

"In any of the corridors or courts?"

"No."

"See whether his carriage is at the gate?"

"I do not see it."

"Follow the road by which we came. Do you see carriages on it?"

"Yes, several."

"Do you see the cardinal's among them?"

"No."

"Come nearer Paris, — now?"

"Now I see it."

"Where?"

"At the gate of the city."

"Has it stopped?"

"Yes; the footman has just got down."

"Does the cardinal speak to him?"

"Yes; he is going to speak."

"Lorenza, attend! It is important that I should know what the cardinal says."

"You should have told me to listen in time. But stop! — the footman is speaking to the coachman."

"What does he say?"

"The Rue St. Claude, in the Marais, by the boulevard."

"Thanks, Lorenza."

The count wrote some words on a piece of paper, which

he folded round a plate of copper, — doubtless to give it weight; then he pulled a bell, pressed a spring, and a small opening appearing in the wall, he dropped the note down. The opening closed again instantly. It was in this way that the count, in the inner apartments of his house, gave his orders to Fritz, his German servant.

Then, returning to Lorenza, "I thank you," he repeated.

"You are, then, satisfied with me?" asked the young woman.

"Yes, dear Lorenza."

"Well, reward me, then."

Balsamo smiled, and approached his lips to Lorenza's, whose whole body trembled at the touch. "Oh, Joseph, Joseph!" she murmured, with a sigh almost painful, "Joseph, how I love you!" And the young woman reached out her arms to press Balsamo to her heart.

CHAPTER XI.

THE DOUBLE EXISTENCE — SLEEP.

BALSAMO recoiled quickly, and Lorenza's arms, passing through the empty air, fell crossed upon her breast.

"Lorenza," said Balsamo, "are you willing to talk with your friend?"

"Oh, yes!" she replied. "But speak yourself the most, — I love so to hear your voice."

"Lorenza, you have often said that you would be happy if you could live with me, shut out from all the world."

"Yes; that would be happiness indeed!"

"Well, your wish is realized. No one can follow us to this chamber, — no one can enter here; we are alone, quite alone."

"Ah! so much the better."

"Tell me, is this apartment to your taste?"

"Order me to see it, then."

"I order you."

"Oh, what a charming room!"

"You are pleased with it, then?" asked the count, tenderly.

"Oh, yes! There are my favorite flowers, — my vanilla heliotropes, my crimson roses, my Chinese jasmines. Thanks, my sweet Joseph! How good you are!"

"I do all I can to please you, Lorenza."

"Oh, you do a hundred times more than I deserve!"

"You think so?"

"Yes."

"Then you confess that you have been very ill natured?"

"Very ill natured? Oh, yes! But you forgive me, do you not?"

"I will forgive you when you explain to me the strange mystery which I have sought to fathom ever since I knew you."

"It is this, Balsamo. There are in me two Lorenzas, quite distinct from each other, — one that loves, and one that hates you. So there are in me two lives; in one I taste all the joys of paradise, in the other experience all the torments of hell."

"And one of those is the life of sleep, the other is the life of waking?"

"Yes."

"You love me when you sleep, and you hate me when you are awake?"

"Yes."

"But why so?"

"I do not know."

"You must know."

"No."

"Search carefully; look within yourself; sound your own heart."

"Yes, I see the cause now."

"What is it?"

"When Lorenza awakes, she is the Roman girl, the superstitious daughter of Italy; she thinks science a crime, and love a sin. Her confessor told her that they were so. She is then afraid of you, and would flee from you to the confines of the earth."

"And when Lorenza sleeps?"

"Ah! then she is no longer the Roman, no longer superstitious; she is a woman. Then she reads Balsamo's heart and mind; she sees that his genius contemplates sublime things. Then she feels her littleness compared with him. Then she would live and die beside him, that the future might whisper softly the name of Lorenza, when it trumpets forth that of — Cagliostro!"

"It is by that name, then, that I shall become celebrated?"

"Yes, by that name."

"Dear Lorenza! Then you will love this new abode, will you not?"

"It is much more splendid than any of those you have already given me; but it is not on that account that I shall love it."

"For what, then?"

"I shall love it because you have promised to live in it with me."

"Then, when you sleep, you see clearly that I love you, — ardently love you?"

The young woman smiled faintly. "Yes," said she, "I do see that you love me; and yet," added she, with a sigh, "there is something which you love better than Lorenza."

"What is it?" asked Balsamo, starting.

"Your dream."

"Say, my task."

"Your ambition."

"Say, my glory."

"Ah, *mon Dieu! mon Dieu!*" and the young woman's breast heaved, while the tears forced their way through her closed eyelids.

"What do you see?" asked Balsamo, with alarm; for there were moments when her clairvoyant powers startled even him.

"Oh, I see darkness, and phantoms gliding through it! Some of them hold in their hands their crowned heads, and you,— you are among them, like a general in the thick of the battle. You command, and they obey."

"Well," said Balsamo, joyfully, "and does that not make you proud of me?"

"Oh, you are so good that you have no need to be great! And besides, I seek my own figure amid the throng which surrounds you, and I cannot see myself. I shall not be there!" murmured she, sadly. "I shall not be there!"

"Where will you be then?"

"I shall be dead."

Balsamo shuddered. "Dead, my Lorenza?" cried he, — "dead? No, no; we shall live long together to love one another!"

"You do not love me."

"Oh, yes!"

"Not enough, at any rate, — not enough!" she cried, putting her arms around his neck. "Not enough," she added, bestowing on his forehead many kisses with her glowing lips.

"With what do you reproach me?"

"Your coldness. See, you draw back! Do my lips burn you, that you avoid my kisses? Oh, restore to me my maiden tranquillity, my convent at Subiaco, the nights in my solitary cell! Give to me again the kisses which you sent me on mysterious wings of air, and which in my sleep I saw coming to me, like sylphs on wings of gold, and which filled my soul with delight."

"Lorenza! Lorenza!"

"Oh! do not avoid me, Balsamo; do not avoid me, I beseech you! Give me your hand, that I may press it, — your eyes, that I may kiss them; I am your wife."

"Yes, yes, my dear Lorenza, you are my well-beloved wife."

"And you suffer me to live near you, useless, abandoned! You have a chaste and solitary flower, whose perfume invites you, and you repulse its perfume. Ah! I see clearly that I am nothing to you."

"You, my Lorenza, nothing? You are my all, my strength, my power, my genius! Without you I should be nothing. Cease, then, to love me with that mad fever which disturbs the sleep of the women of your country. Love me as I love you."

"Oh! it is not love, it is not love, — the feeling you have toward me."

"It is at any rate all I ask from you; for you give me all that I desire. That possession of the soul suffices me for happiness."

"Happiness!" said Lorenza, with an air of contempt; "do you call that happiness?"

"Yes; for, in my mind, to be great is to be happy."

She sighed deeply.

"Oh, could you but know, my sweet Lorenza, what it is to read the uncovered hearts of men, and govern them with their own passions!"

"Yes, I serve you in that, I know."

"That is not all. Your eyes read for me the hidden book of the future. What I could not learn with twenty years of toil and suffering, you, my gentle dove, innocent and pure, can teach me when you wish. Foes dog my steps and lay snares for me; you inform me of every danger. On my understanding depend my life, my fortune, my freedom; you give that understanding the eye of the lynx, which dilates and sees clearly in the darkness. Your lovely eyes, closing to the light of this outward world, open to me a superhuman clearness of sight. They watch for me. It is you who make me free, rich, powerful."

"And you in return make me wretched," she exclaimed, abandoned to her emotions. And more eagerly than before she threw her arms around Balsamo, who, himself charged with the electric flame, could oppose but a feeble resistance. He made an effort, however, and unwound the living chain that was about him. "Lorenza! Lorenza!" he said, "for pity's sake!"

"I am your wife, and not your daughter. Love me as a husband loves his wife, and not as my father loved me."

"Lorenza," said Balsamo, trembling, "do not ask me, I beg of you, a love other than that which I can give you."

"But," said the young woman, raising her arms in despair, "that is not love; that is not love!"

"Oh, yes! it is love, — love holy and pure; it is that with which one ought to love a virgin."

The young woman made a sharp movement, and extended toward the count her white and vigorous arms in a manner almost threatening. "Oh! what does that signify?" she said, in a desolate tone. "And why have you made me abandon my country, my name, my family, everything, even my God? — for your God is not like mine. Why have you assumed that absolute empire over me which makes me your slave, which makes my life and my blood yours, — do you hear me? — why have you done all this, to call me the virgin Lorenza?"

Balsamo sighed in his turn, overwhelmed by the grief of that broken-hearted woman. "Alas!" he said, "it is your fault; or rather, it is the fault of God. Why has God made you that angel with infallible sight by whose aid I shall subdue the universe? Why do you read all hearts through their material covering, as one reads a book behind a pane of glass? It is because you are an angel of purity, Lorenza. It is because you are a diamond without blemish. It is because nothing casts a shadow on your mind. It is because God, seeing that immaculate form, pure and radiant, like that of the Holy Mother, sends to it, when I invoke him in the name of the elements which he has made, his Holy Spirit, which does not enter sordid and vulgar souls because it can find in them no place without spot in which to rest. As a virgin you are a seer, my Lorenza; as wife you would be only common clay."

"And you do not prefer my love," cried Lorenza, striking her beautiful hands together angrily, — "you do not prefer my love to all the dreams which you pursue, to all the chimeras you create? And you condemn me to maintain, in your presence, the coldness of a recluse. Ah, Joseph, Joseph! you commit a crime; it is I who tell you so."

"Do not blaspheme, my Lorenza," cried Balsamo; "for, like you, I suffer. Stay, read in my heart, and then say that I do not love you!"

"But, then, why do you resist your own desire?"

"Because I wish to raise you with myself to the throne of the world."

"Oh! your ambition, Balsamo," murmured the young woman. "Will your ambition ever give you what my love gives you?"

In his turn abandoned to his emotions, Balsamo allowed his head to lie on Lorenza's breast. "Oh! yes, yes!" she cried; "I see now that you love me more than your ambition, more than your power, more than your hope! Oh! at last you love me as I love you!"

Balsamo tried to shake off the intoxicating cloud which began to drown his reason; but his effort was useless. "Oh! since you love me so much," said he, "spare me!"

Lorenza no longer listened. She had made with her

arms one of those invincible chains that are more binding than clamps of steel, and more solid than diamond. "I will love you as you choose," she said, — "as sister or wife, as virgin or spouse; but give me one kiss."

Balsamo was conquered. Overcome by so much love, he had no strength for further resistance. His lips approached those of the young woman. Suddenly reason returned to him. His hands beat the air charged with intoxicating vapors. "Lorenza!" he cried, "awake; it is my will."

At once her arms released their hold, the smile which had played on her lips died away, and she sighed heavily. At length her closed eyes opened; the dilated pupils assumed their natural size; she stretched out her arms, appeared overcome with weariness, and fell back at full length, but awake, on the sofa.

Balsamo, seated at a little distance from her, heaved a deep sigh. "Adieu, my dream!" murmured he to himself. "Farewell, happiness!"

CHAPTER XII.

THE DOUBLE EXISTENCE — WAKING.

As soon as Lorenza had recovered her natural powers of sight, she cast a hurried glance around her. Her eyes roamed over all the splendid trifles which surrounded her on every side, without exhibiting any appearance of the pleasure which such things usually give to women. At length they rested with a shudder on Balsamo, who was seated at a short distance, and was watching her attentively.

"You again!" said she, recoiling; and all the symptoms of horror appeared in her countenance. Her lips turned deadly pale, and the perspiration stood in large drops on her forehead. Balsamo did not reply.

"Where am I?" she asked.

"You know whence you come, Madame," said Balsamo; "and that should naturally enable you to divine where you are."

"Yes, you do well to revive my recollection! I remember now; I know that I have been persecuted by you, pursued by you, torn by you from the arms of the royal lady whom I had chosen to protect me."

"Then you must know also that this princess, all-powerful though she be, could not defend you?"

"Yes; you have conquered her by some work of magic!" cried Lorenza, clasping her hands. "O Heaven, deliver me from this demon!"

"In what way do I resemble a demon, Madame?" said Balsamo, shrugging his shoulders. "Once for all, abandon, I beg of you, this farrago of childish prejudices which you brought with you from Rome; have done with all those absurd superstitions which you have retained in your mind ever since you left the convent."

"Oh, my convent! Who will restore me my convent?" cried Lorenza, bursting into tears.

"In fact," said Balsamo, ironically, "a convent is a place very much to be regretted!"

Lorenza darted toward one of the windows, drew aside the curtains, and, opening it, stretched out her hand. It struck against a thick bar supporting an iron grating, which, although hidden by flowers, was not the less efficacious in retaining a prisoner.

"Prison for prison," said she, "I like that better which conducts toward heaven than that which sends to hell." And she dashed her delicate hands against the iron bars.

"If you were more reasonable, Lorenza, you would find only the flowers, without the bars, at your windows."

"Was I not reasonable when you shut me up in that moving prison, with the vampire whom you call Althotas? And yet you kept me a prisoner, you watched me like a lynx, and whenever you left me you breathed into me that spirit which takes possession of me, and which I cannot overcome. Where is he, that horrible old man, whose sight freezes me with terror? In some corner here, is he not? Let us keep silent, and we shall hear his unearthly voice issue from the depths of the earth."

"You really give way to your imagination like a child, Madame. Althotas, my teacher, my friend, my second father, is an inoffensive old man who has never seen or approached you; or, if he has seen you, has never paid the least attention to you, immersed as he is in his task."

"His task?" murmured Lorenza. "And what is his task?"

"He is trying to discover the elixir of life, — what all the greatest minds have been in search of for the last six thousand years."

"And you, — what are you trying to discover?"

"The means of human perfectibility."

"Oh, demons! demons!" said Lorenza, raising her hands.

"Ah!" said Balsamo, rising, "now your fit is coming on again."

"My fit?"

"Yes, your fit. There is one thing, Lorenza, which you are not aware of, — it is that your life is divided into two equal periods. During one you are gentle, good, and reasonable; during the other you are mad."

"And it is under this false pretext of madness that you shut me up?"

"Alas! I am obliged to do so."

"Oh, be cruel, barbarous, pitiless, if you will; shut me up, kill me, — but do not play the hypocrite; do not pretend to compassionate while you destroy me!"

"But only reflect a moment," said Balsamo, without anger, and even with a caressing smile; "is it torture to live in an elegant, commodious apartment like this?"

"Grated windows, iron bars on all sides, — no air, no air!"

"The bars are for the safety of your life, you must know, Lorenza."

"Oh!" she cried, "he destroys me piecemeal, and tells me he cares for my life!"

Balsamo approached the young woman, and, with a friendly gesture, endeavored to take her hand; but recoiling as if from the touch of a serpent, "Oh, do not touch me!" said she.

"Do you hate me, then, Lorenza?"

"Ask the sufferer if he hates his executioner?"

"Lorenza, Lorenza! it is because I do not wish to be your executioner that I deprive you of a little of your liberty. If you could go and come as you liked, who knows what you might do in the moments of your madness?"

"What I might do? Oh, let me once be free, and you shall see what I would do!"

"Lorenza, you are treating unkindly the husband whom you have chosen in the sight of God."

"I chose you? Never! never!"

"You are my wife, notwithstanding."

"Yes; that indeed must have been the work of the demon."

"Poor insensate!" said Balsamo, with a tender look.

"But I am a Roman," murmured Lorenza; "and some day I shall take my revenge."

Balsamo shook his head gently. "You say that only to frighten me, Lorenza, do you not?" said he, smiling.

"No, no; I shall do what I say."

"Christian woman, what are you saying?" cried Balsamo, with authority. "Your religion, which enjoins the return of good for evil, is, then, an hypocrisy?— since you pretend to obey that religion and you return evil for good."

Lorenza appeared for an instant struck by these words. "Oh!" said she, "it is not vengeance to denounce to society its enemies, it is a duty."

"If you denounce me as a necromancer, as a sorcerer, it is not society whom I offend, but God; but if I offend God, who by a sign can destroy me, why does he not do so? Does he leave my punishment to weak men, subject to error like myself?"

"He bears with you," murmured the young woman; "he waits for you to reform."

Balsamo smiled. "And in the mean time," said he, "he counsels you to betray your friend, your benefactor, your husband?"

"My husband? Ah! thank Heaven, your hand has never touched mine that I have not blushed or shuddered at its contact."

"And you know that I have always endeavored to spare you that contact."

"It is true, — you are chaste, and that is the only amelioration of my misfortunes. Oh! if I had been obliged to submit to your love!"

"Oh, mystery! impenetrable mystery!" murmured Balsamo to himself, replying rather to his own thoughts than to Lorenza's words.

"Once for all," said Lorenza, "why do you deprive me of my liberty?"

"Why, after having given yourself voluntarily to me, do you now wish for liberty? Why do you flee from him who protects you? Why do you ask a stranger for protection against him who loves you? Why do you threaten him who has never yet threatened you, and say you will reveal secrets which are not yours, and of which you do not comprehend the import?"

"Oh!" said Lorenza, without replying to his questions, "the prisoner who has firmly determined to be free, will be so, sooner or later, and your bars of iron shall not keep me, any more than your moving cage kept me!"

"Fortunately for you, Lorenza, the bars are strong," answered Balsamo, with a threatening calmness.

"God will send me some storm like that of Lorraine, — some thunderbolt which will break them."

"Trust me, you had better pray God to do nothing of the kind. Do not give way, I advise you, to your romantic fancies, Lorenza. I speak to you as a friend."

There was such an expression of concentrated anger in Balsamo's voice, such a gloomy and threatening fire in his eyes, such a strange and nervous movement in his white and muscular hand, as he pronounced each word slowly and solemnly, that Lorenza, subdued in the very height of her rebellion, listened to him in spite of herself.

"You see, my child," he continued, in the same calm and threatening tone, "I have endeavored to make this prison a habitation fit for a queen. Were you a queen, you could here want for nothing. Calm, then, this wild excitement. Live here as you would have lived in your convent. Accustom yourself to my presence; love me as a friend, as a brother. I have heavy sorrows, — I will confide them to you; I am often and deeply deceived, — a smile from you will console me. The more I see you kind, attentive, patient, the more I shall lighten the rigor of your imprisonment. Who knows but that in a year, nay, in six months perhaps, you may be as free as I am, — always supposing that you no longer entertain the wish to steal your freedom."

"No, no!" cried Lorenza, who could not comprehend that so terrible a resolve should be expressed in a voice so gentle; "no more promises! no more falsehoods! You have carried me off, and by violent means. I belong to myself, and to myself alone; restore me therefore to the house of God at least, if you will not grant me my full liberty. I have until now submitted to your tyranny, because I remembered that you once saved me from robbers; but my gratitude is already weakened. A few days more of this insulting imprisonment, and it will expire; and then — take care! I may begin to suspect that you had some secret connection with those robbers!"

"You do me the honor, then, to take me for a captain of banditti?" said Balsamo, ironically.

"I know not what you are, but I caught certain signs and words."

"You caught signs and words?" exclaimed Balsamo, turning pale.

"Yes, yes, I intercepted them; I know them, — I remember them."

"But you will never tell them to any living soul? You will shut them up in the depths of your heart?"

"Oh, no!" exclaimed Lorenza, full of delight, in her anger, that she had found the vulnerable part of her antagonist, "I shall treasure them up religiously in my memory; I shall murmur them over to myself, and on the first opportunity shall say them aloud to others. I have already told them."

"To whom?"

"To the princess."

"Well, Lorenza, listen!" said Balsamo, clenching his hands till the nails entered the flesh. "If you have told them once, you shall never tell them again. Never shall the words you have spoken again cross your lips, for I will keep every door closely shut. I will sharpen the points on those bars, and raise the walls around this house, if need be, as high as those of Babel."

"I have already told you, Balsamo," exclaimed Lorenza, "that no prison can hold a captive forever, especially when the love of liberty is aided by hatred of the tyrant."

"Very well, leave your prison, then; but mark me, you have only twice to do so. The first time, I will beat you so cruelly that your eyes will have no more tears to shed; the second time, so pitilessly that your veins will have no more blood to shed."

"Great heavens! He will murder me!" screamed the young woman, in the highest paroxysm of fury, tearing her hair and writhing on the carpet.

Balsamo looked at her for an instant with a mixture of anger and compassion. At length compassion seemed to prevail. "Come, Lorenza," said he, "be calm; some future day you will be well rewarded for all you suffer now, or think you suffer."

"Imprisoned! imprisoned!" cried Lorenza, without listening to him.

"Be patient."

"Beaten!"

"It is a period of probation."

"Mad! mad!"

"You will be cured."

"Oh, put me in a madhouse at once! Shut me up at once in a real prison!"

"No; you have too well prepared me for what you would do in such a case."

"Death, then!" screamed Lorenza, "instant death!" and bounding up with the suppleness and rapidity of some wild animal, she rushed forward to dash her head against the wall.

Balsamo had only to extend his hand toward her and to pronounce, by his will rather than his lips, one single word to arrest her progress. Lorenza, checked in her wild career, staggered and fell into Balsamo's arms. She was asleep.

The strange enchanter, who seemed to have subdued in this woman all that belonged to her physical existence, without having been able to triumph over the moral life, raised her and carried her to her couch; then, having laid her on it, he imprinted a long kiss on her lips, drew the curtains, and left the chamber.

A soft and soothing sleep wrapped Lorenza in its embrace, as the mantle of a kind mother wraps the froward child after it has long suffered and wept.

CHAPTER XIII.

THE VISIT.

Lorenza was not mistaken. A carriage, after having entered Paris by the Barrière St. Denis and traversing the faubourg of that name throughout its entire length, had turned the angle formed by the last house and the Porte St. Denis, and was rapidly advancing along the boulevard. This carriage contained Monsieur Louis de Rohan, Bishop of Strasburg, whose impatience led him to anticipate the time fixed upon for seeking the sorcerer in his den.

The coachman, a man of mettle, and well accustomed to aid the handsome prelate in his gallant adventures amid the darkness and perils of certain mysterious streets, was by no means discouraged when, after having passed the boulevards of St. Denis and St. Martin, still thronged with people and well lighted, he received the order to proceed along the lonely and dismal boulevard of the Bastille. The carriage stopped at the corner of the Rue St. Claude, on the boulevard itself, and after a whispered order from its master took up a concealed position under the trees about twenty paces off.

Then M. de Rohan, who was dressed in the ordinary costume of a civilian, glided down the street, and knocked at the door of the house, which he easily recognized by the description of it given to him by the Comte de Fenix. Fritz's footsteps were heard approaching, and the door was opened.

"Is it not here that the Comte de Fenix resides?" asked the prince.

"Yes, Monseigneur."

"Is he at home?"

"Yes, Monseigneur."

"Well, say that a gentleman wishes to see him."

"His Eminence the Cardinal de Rohan, is it not?" asked Fritz.

The prince stood confounded. He looked all around him and at his dress, to see whether anything in his costume or in the attendant circumstances had revealed his rank; but he was alone, and in the dress of a layman.

"How do you know my name?" said he.

"My master has just told me, this very instant even, that he expected your Eminence."

"Yes, but to-morrow, or the day after?"

"No, Monseigneur, this evening."

"Your master told you that he expected me this evening?"

"Yes, Monseigneur."

"Very well; announce me, then," said the cardinal, putting a double louis-d'or into Fritz's hand.

"Will your Eminence have the goodness to follow me, then?"

The cardinal made a gesture in the affirmative. Fritz then advanced with a rapid step toward the antechamber, which was lighted by a massive bronze candelabrum containing twelve wax tapers. The cardinal followed, surprised and thoughtful.

"My friend," said he, stopping at the door of the salon, "there must be a mistake, I think; and in that case I do not wish to intrude on the count. It is impossible that he can expect me, for he was not aware that I intended to come to-night."

"Monseigneur is the Prince-Cardinal de Rohan, Bishop of Strasburg, is he not?" inquired Fritz.

"Yes, my friend."

"Well, then, it is Monseigneur whom my master the count expects." And lighting successively the candles of two other candelabra in the salon, Fritz bowed and retired.

Five minutes elapsed, during which the cardinal, agitated by a strange emotion, gazed at the elegant furniture of this salon and at the eight pictures by the first masters which hung from the walls. The door opened, and the Comte de Fenix appeared on the threshold.

"Good evening, Monseigneur!" said he, simply.

"I am told that you expected me," exclaimed the cardinal, without replying to this salutation, — "that you expected me this evening. It is impossible!"

"I beg your pardon, Monseigneur, but I did expect you," replied the count. "Perhaps you doubt the truth of my words on seeing the poor reception I give you? But I have only very lately arrived in Paris, and can scarcely call myself installed here yet; your Eminence must therefore be good enough to excuse me."

"You expected me! But who could have told you that I was coming?"

"Yourself, Monseigneur."

"How so?"

"Did you not stop your carriage at the Barrière St. Denis?"

"Yes."

"Did you not summon your footman to the carriage-door, and give him the order, 'Rue St. Claude, in the Marais, by the Faubourg St. Denis and the boulevard,' — words which he repeated to the coachman?"

"Yes, certainly; did you see me, then, and hear me?"

"I saw and heard you, Monseigneur."

"Then you were there?"

"No, Monseigneur, I was not there."

"And where were you?"

"I was here."

"You saw me and heard me from here?"

"Yes, Monseigneur."

"Come, come!"

"Monseigneur forgets that I am a sorcerer."

"Ah, true; I did forget that! But, Monsieur, what am I to call you, — the Baron Balsamo, or the Comte de Fenix?"

"In my own house, my lord, I have no name: I am called the MASTER."

"Yes, that is the technical title. So then, Master, you expected me?"

"I did expect you."

"And your laboratory is heated?"

"My laboratory is always heated, Monseigneur."

"And you will permit me to enter it?"

"I shall have the honor of conducting your Eminence thither."

"And I will follow you, but only on one condition."

"What is that?"

"That you promise not to place me personally in contact with the devil. I am terribly afraid of his Majesty Lucifer."

"Oh, Monseigneur!"

"Yes, for in general you employ for such a purpose the greatest rogues, — discarded soldiers of the guards, or fencing-masters without pupils, who in order to play the part of Satan naturally, treat their dupes to sundry fillips and tweaks of the nose, after first putting out the lights."

"Monseigneur," said Balsamo, smiling, "my devils

never forget that they have the honor of dealing with princes, and ever bear in mind the Prince de Condé's speech to one of them who would not keep still, namely, that if he did not conduct himself more decently, he would so rub him down with an oaken towel that he would never need washing again."

"I am delighted to hear that you manage your imps so well. Let us proceed to the laboratory, then."

"Will your Eminence have the goodness to follow me?"

"Proceed!"

CHAPTER XIV.

GOLD.

THE Cardinal de Rohan and Balsamo went up a narrow staircase which ran parallel with the great staircase, and, like it, led to the apartments on the first floor. There, under an arch, appeared a door which Balsamo opened, and a very gloomy corridor was disclosed to the cardinal's view, who entered it resolutely. Balsamo closed the door behind them. At the noise which this door made in closing, the cardinal looked back with a slight feeling of trepidation.

"Monseigneur," said Balsamo, "we have now arrived. We have but one more door to open and close; but let me warn you not to be alarmed at the sound it will make, for it is of iron."

The cardinal, who had started at the sound of the first door, was glad to be thus warned in time, for the grating noise of the hinges and lock might have given a shock to nerves even less susceptible than his. They descended three steps and entered the laboratory. It was a large room, with the beams and joists of the ceiling left uncovered, and containing a huge lamp with a shade, several books, and a great number of appliances for use in chemistry and physics.

After a few seconds the cardinal noticed that he found difficulty in breathing. "What is the meaning of this?" said he. "The air is stifling here, Master; the perspiration pours from my forehead? What noise is that?"

"Here is the explanation of it, Monseigneur," said Balsamo, drawing back a large curtain of asbestos cloth, and disclosing to view an immense brick furnace, in the centre of which two holes glared in the darkness like the gleaming eyes of a panther. This furnace was situated in the middle of another room, twice as large as the first, which the prince had not perceived, hidden as it was by the asbestos curtain.

"Ah, ha!" cried the prince, retreating two or three steps, "that looks a little alarming."

"It is a furnace, Monseigneur."

"Yes, but this furnace of yours has a very diabolical appearance. What are you cooking in it?"

"What your Eminence asked from me."

"What I asked from you?"

"Yes. I think your Eminence said you wished for a specimen of my handiwork. I had not intended beginning the operation till to-morrow evening, as you were not to visit me till the day following; but your Eminence having changed your intention, as soon as I saw you coming to the Rue St. Claude I kindled the furnace fires and made the combination; so that now the charge is boiling, and in ten minutes you will have your gold. Permit me to open the ventilator to start a current of air."

"What! those crucibles on the furnace —"

"Will in ten minutes give us gold as pure as that of the sequins of Venice, or the florins of Tuscany."

"I should like to see it, — that is, if it may be seen."

"Certainly, your Eminence. But you must use some necessary precautions."

"What precautions?"

"Cover your face with this mask of asbestos with glass eyes; otherwise your sight might be injured by the glowing heat."

"*Peste!* I must take care of that. I attach a good deal of value to my eyes, and would not give them for the hundred thousand crowns which you have promised me."

"I should think so, Monseigneur; your Eminence has handsome eyes."

This compliment was by no means displeasing to the cardinal, who was not a little vain of his person. "Ha!" said he, putting on his mask, "so it seems we are to see gold?"

"I trust so, Monseigneur."

"Gold to the value of one hundred thousand crowns?"

"Yes, Monseigneur, perhaps even a little more; for I made a very abundant mixture."

"You are indeed a most generous sorcerer," said the prince, with a joyous palpitation of the heart.

"Less generous than your Eminence, who so kindly compliments me. In the mean time, Monseigneur, may I beg you to keep back a little while I take off the lid of the crucible?" And Balsamo, having put on a short shirt of asbestos, seized with a vigorous arm a pair of iron pincers, and raised the cover, now red hot, which revealed to view four crucibles of the same shape, some containing a mixture of a vermilion color, others a substance already whitening, though still somewhat purple and transparent.

"And that is gold!" said the prelate in a half-whisper, as if he feared to disturb the mysterious operation.

"Yes, Monseigneur. These four crucibles contain the substance in different stages, some of them having been subject to the process twelve, others only eleven hours. The mixture — and this is a secret which I reveal only to a friend of the hermetic science — is thrown into the matter at the moment of ebullition. But, as your Eminence may see, the first crucible is now at a white heat; it has reached the proper stage, and it is time to pour it out. Be good enough to keep back, Monseigneur."

The prince obeyed with the promptitude of a soldier at the command of his officer, and Balsamo, laying aside the pincers already heated by contact with the crucibles, rolled forward to the furnace a sort of movable anvil in which were hollowed eight cylindrical moulds of equal capacity.

"What is this, my dear sorcerer?" asked the prince.

"This, Monseigneur, contains the equal and uniform moulds in which your ingots are to be cast."

"Ah, ha!" exclaimed the cardinal, and he redoubled his attention.

Balsamo spread over the floor a thick layer of white tow as a protection against accidents; then, placing himself between the furnace and the anvil, he opened a huge book, and, wand in hand, repeated a solemn incantation. This ended, he seized an enormous pair of tongs intended for grasping the weighty crucibles.

"The gold will be excellent, Monseigneur," said he, — "of the finest quality."

"What! Are you going to lift off that flaming pot?"

"Which weighs fifty pounds? Yes, Monseigneur; few founders, I may say it without boasting, possess my muscles or my dexterity. Fear nothing, therefore."

"But if the crucible were to break?"

"Yes, that happened with me once, Monseigneur, — in the year 1399. I was making an experiment with Nicolas Flamel, in his house in the Rue des Ecrivains, near the church of St. Jacques-la-Boucherie. Poor Flamel was near losing his life, and I lost eighteen pounds of a substance more precious than gold."

"What the devil is that you are saying, Master?"

"The truth."

"Do you mean to say that you pursued the great work in 1399 with Nicolas Flamel?"

"Precisely so, Monseigneur. We found out the secret together, about fifty or sixty years before, when experimenting with Pierre le Bon in the town of Pola. He did not shut up the crucible quickly enough, and I lost the use of my right eye for nearly twelve years in consequence of the evaporation."

"Pierre le Bon?"

"He who composed the famous work, 'Margarita Pretiosa,'—a work with which, probably, you are acquainted."

"Yes, and which bears the date of 1330."

"Precisely so, Monseigneur."

"And you knew Pierre le Bon and Flamel?"

"I was the pupil of the one and the teacher of the other."

And while the terrified prelate asked himself whether the personage at his side was not the devil in person, instead of one of his satellites, Balsamo plunged his long tongs into the furnace. His grasp was quick and sure. He seized the crucible about four inches from the top, satisfied himself, by raising it up a little, that his hold was firm; then, by a vigorous effort which strained every muscle in his frame, he heaved up the terrible pot from the glowing furnace. The handle of the tongs turned glowing red immediately; then, rippling over the fused matter within, were seen white furrows, like lightning streaking a black sulphureous cloud; then the edges of the crucible turned a brownish red, while the conical base appeared still rose-colored and silvery in the shadow of the furnace; then the metal, on the surface of which had formed a violet-colored scum, crusted here and there with gold, hissed over the mouth of the crucible, and fell flashing into the dark mould, around the top of which the golden wave, angry and foaming, seemed by its shudderings to insult the vile metal with which it was forced into contact.

"Now for the second," said Balsamo, seizing another crucible; and another mould was filled by the same exercise of strength and dexterity as the first. The perspiration poured from the operator's forehead; and the cardinal, standing back in the shade, crossed himself.

In fact, the scene was one of wild and majestic horror. Balsamo, his features lighted by the reddish glare of the glowing metal, resembled one of the damned of Michael Angelo or Dante, writhing in the depths of their flaming pits; while over all brooded the feeling of the mysterious and unknown.

Balsamo took no breathing time between the two operations; time pressed. "There will be a slight loss," said he, after having filled the second mould. "I have allowed the mixture to boil the hundredth part of a minute too long."

"The hundredth part of a minute!" exclaimed the cardinal, no longer seeking to conceal his stupefaction.

"It is enormous in alchemy," replied Balsamo, quietly; "but in the mean time, your Eminence, here are two crucibles emptied, and two moulds filled with one hundred pounds' weight of pure gold;" and seizing the first mould with his powerful tongs, he plunged it into water, which hissed and bubbled around it for some time. Then he opened it, and took out a lump of solid gold in the form of a sugar-loaf flattened at each end.

"We shall have to wait some time for the other crucibles," said Balsamo. "Will your Eminence in the mean time be seated, or would you prefer to breathe for a few moments a cooler atmosphere than this?"

"And that is really gold?" asked the cardinal, without replying to the operator's question.

Balsamo smiled. The cardinal was his. "Do you doubt it, Monseigneur?"

"Why you know, science is so often mistaken"

"Prince, your words do not express your whole meaning," said Balsamo. "You think that I am deceiving you — intentionally. Monseigneur, I should sink very low in my own opinion could I act such a part; for my ambition in that case would not extend beyond the walls of my cabinet, which you would leave filled with wonder, only to be undeceived on taking your ingot to the nearest goldsmith. Come, come, Monseigneur, do not think so meanly of me; and be assured that if I wished to deceive you, I should do it more adroitly, and with a higher aim. However, your Eminence knows how to test gold?"

"Certainly, — by the touchstone."

"You have doubtless had occasion, Monseigneur, to make the experiment yourself, were it only on Spanish doubloons, which are much esteemed in play, because they are of the purest gold, but which, for that very reason, are frequently counterfeited."

"In fact, I have done so before now."

"Well, Monseigneur, here are the stone and the acid."

"No, I am satisfied."

"Monseigneur, do me the favor to assure yourself that these ingots are not only gold, but gold without alloy."

The cardinal appeared unwilling to give this evidence of his incredulity, and yet it was evident that he was not convinced. Balsamo himself tested the ingots, and showed the result of the experiment to his guest.

"Twenty-eight carats," said he; "and now I may pour out the two others."

Ten minutes afterward the two hundred pounds of gold,

in four ingots, were lying side by side on the tow, heated by their contact.

"Your Eminence came here in a carriage, did you not? At least, you were in a carriage when I saw you."

"Yes."

"If your Eminence will order it to the door, my servant will put the ingots into it."

"One hundred thousand crowns!" murmured the cardinal, as he took off his mask to feast his eyes on the gold lying at his feet.

"And as for this gold, your Eminence can tell whence it comes, having seen it made?"

"Oh, yes; I shall testify — "

"Oh, no!" said Balsamo, hastily; "alchemists are not much in favor in France! Testify nothing, Monseigneur. If instead of making gold I made theories, then indeed I should have no objection."

"Then what can I do for you?" said the prince, lifting an ingot of fifty pounds with difficulty in his delicate hands.

Balsamo looked at him steadily, and began to laugh irreverently.

"What is there so very ludicrous in what I have said?" asked the cardinal.

"Your Eminence offers me your services, I think!"

"Certainly."

"Would it not be much more to the purpose were I to offer mine to you?"

The cardinal's brow darkened. "You have obliged me, Monsieur," said he, "and I am ready to acknowledge it; but if my gratitude is to be a heavier burden than I imagined, I shall not accept the obligation. There are still, thank God, usurers enough in Paris from whom I can procure, half on some pledge and half on my bond, one hundred thousand crowns by day after to-morrow. My episcopal ring alone is worth forty thousand francs." And the prelate held out his hand, as white as a woman's, on which shone a diamond as large as a nut.

"Prince," said Balsamo, bowing, "it is impossible that you can for a moment imagine that I meant to offend you." Then, as if speaking to himself, he proceeded: " It is singular that the truth should always produce this effect on those who bear the title of prince."

"What is the meaning of that?"

"Your Eminence proposes to serve me; now I ask you, Monseigneur, of what nature are those services which your Eminence proposes to render me?"

"Why, in the first place, my credit at court."

"Monseigneur, you know too well that that credit is much shaken. In fact, I should almost prefer that of the Duc de Choiseul; and yet he has not perhaps a fortnight to hold his place. Take my word for it, Prince, as far as credit goes, mine is the best. There is good and sterling gold. Every time that your Eminence is in want of any, let me know the night before, and you shall have as much as you like. And with gold, Monseigneur, cannot all things be procured?"

"Not all," murmured the cardinal, sinking into the grade of a protégé, and no longer even making an effort to regain that of patron.

"Ah! true. I forgot that your Eminence desires something more than gold, — something more precious than all the riches of the earth. But in this, science cannot assist you; it is the province of magic. Monseigneur, say the word, and the alchemist is ready to become the magician."

"Thank you, Monsieur, but I want for nothing more; I desire nothing farther," said the cardinal, in a desponding voice.

Balsamo approached him.

"Monseigneur," said he, "a prince, young, handsome, ardent, rich, and bearing the name of Rohan, ought not to make such a reply to a magician."

"Why not, Monsieur?"

"Because the magician reads his heart, and knows the contrary."

"I wish for nothing; I desire nothing," repeated the cardinal, almost terrified.

"I should have thought, on the contrary, that your Eminence's wishes were such as you dared not avow, even to yourself, since they are those of a — king!"

"Monsieur," said the cardinal, with a start, "you allude, I presume, to a subject which you introduced before, when I saw you at St. Denis?"

"Yes, Monseigneur."

"Monsieur, you were mistaken then, and you are equally mistaken now."

"Do you forget, Monseigneur, that I can read the thoughts at this moment in your heart as clearly as, a short time ago, I saw your carriage enter the city, drive along the boulevard, and stop beneath the trees about fifty paces from my house?"

"Then explain yourself; tell me what you mean."

"Monseigneur, the princes of your family have always cherished a high and daring passion; you have not degenerated from your race in that respect."

"I do not know what you mean, Count," stammered the prince.

"On the contrary, you understand me perfectly. I could have touched many chords which vibrate in your heart, but why do so uselessly? I have touched the one which it was necessary to touch, and it vibrates deeply, I am certain."

The cardinal raised his head, and with a last effort at

defiance met the clear and penetrating glance of Balsamo. Balsamo smiled with such an expression of superiority that the cardinal cast down his eyes.

"Oh! you are right, Monseigneur, you are right; do not look at me, for then I read too plainly what passes in your heart, — that heart which, like a mirror, gives back the form of the objects reflected in it."

"Silence, Comte de Fenix, silence!" said the cardinal, completely subdued.

"Yes, you are right; it is better to be silent, for the moment has not yet come to let such a passion be seen."

"Not yet, did you say?"

"Not yet."

"That love, then, has a future?"

"Why not?"

"And can you tell me, then, if this love be not the love of a madman, as it often seems to myself, and as it ever will seem, until I have a proof to the contrary?"

"You ask much, Monseigneur. I can tell you nothing without being placed in contact with the person who inspires your love, — or at least with something belonging to her person."

"What would be necessary?"

"A ringlet, however small, of her beautiful golden hair, for example."

"Yes, you are a man profoundly skilled in the human heart; you read it as I should read an open book."

"Alas! that is just what your great-grand-uncle, the Chevalier Louis de Rohan, said to me when I bade him farewell on the platform of the Bastille, at the foot of the scaffold which he ascended so courageously."

"He said that to you, — that you were profoundly skilled in the human heart?"

"Yes, and that I could read it; for I had forewarned

him that the Chevalier de Preault would betray him. He would not believe me, and the Chevalier de Preault did betray him."

"But what a singular analogy you draw between my ancestor and myself!" said the cardinal, turning pale in spite of himself.

"I did so merely to remind you of the necessity of being prudent, Monseigneur, in obtaining a tress of hair whose curling locks are surmounted by a crown."

"No matter how obtained, you shall have the tress, Monsieur."

"It is well. In the mean time, here is your gold, Monseigneur; I hope you no longer doubt that it is really gold?"

"Give me a pen and paper."

"What for, Monseigneur?"

"To give you a receipt for the hundred thousand crowns which you are so good as to lend me."

"A receipt to me, Monseigneur? For what purpose?"

"I borrow often, my dear Count; but I tell you beforehand, I never take gifts."

"As you please, Prince."

The cardinal took a pen from the table, and wrote a receipt for the money in an enormous, illegible hand, and in a style of orthography which would shock a poor curate's housekeeper of the present day.

"Is that right?" he asked, as he handed it to Balsamo.

"Perfectly right," replied the count, putting it in his pocket without even looking at it.

"You have not read it, Monsieur."

"I have the word of your Eminence; and the word of a Rohan is better than any pledge."

"Comte de Fenix," said the cardinal, with a slight inclination very significant from a man of his rank, "you are an honest man; and if I cannot make you my debtor, I am at least fortunate in being yours."

Balsamo bowed in his turn, and rang a bell, in answer to which Fritz appeared. The count spoke a few words to him in German. He stooped, and like a child carrying a basket of oranges, — a little embarrassed, to be sure, but by no means oppressed with the burden, — he carried off the four ingots wrapped up in tow.

"Why, that fellow is a Hercules!" said the cardinal.

"He is tolerably strong indeed, Monseigneur; but since he has been in my service I give him every day three drops of an elixir compounded by my learned friend, the doctor Althotas. So, you see, the rogue profits by it; in a year he will be able to carry a hundredweight with one hand."

"Wonderful, incomprehensible!" murmured the cardinal; "I shall never be able to resist speaking of all this."

"Oh, speak of it by all means!" replied Balsamo, laughing; "but remember that by so doing you bind yourself to come in person and extinguish the flame of the fagots, if by chance the parliament should take it into their heads to burn me alive in the Place de Grève." And having escorted his illustrious visitor to the outer gate, Balsamo took leave of him with a respectful bow.

"But I do not see your servant," said the cardinal.

"He has gone to carry the gold to your carriage, Monseigneur."

"He knows, then, where it is?"

"Under the fourth tree to the right, on the boulevard; that was what I said to him in German, Monseigneur."

The cardinal raised his hands in astonishment, and disappeared in the darkness.

Balsamo waited for Fritz's return, and then entered the house, closing all the doors carefully behind him.

CHAPTER XV.

THE ELIXIR OF LIFE.

BALSAMO, being now alone, proceeded to listen at Lorenza's door. She was still sunk in a soft and gentle sleep. He half opened a wicket in the door, and contemplated her for some time in a sweet and tender revery. Then, shutting the wicket, he crossed the apartment which we have described, and which separated Lorenza's apartment from the laboratory, and hastened to extinguish the fire in the furnace by throwing open an immense conduit, which allowed the heat to escape into the chimney, and at the same time gave passage to the water of a reservoir on the roof.

Then, carefully placing the cardinal's receipt in a black morocco case, — "The word of a Rohan is good," he murmured, "but for myself alone; and it is well that the brethren yonder should know how I employ their gold."

As these words died away on his lips, three short, quick taps on the ceiling made him raise his head. "Oh, oh!" said he, "there is Althotas calling me."

Then, while he continued ventilating the laboratory, and arranging everything in order, the taps were repeated louder than before. "So, he is getting impatient; it is a good sign."

Balsamo took a long iron rod and knocked on the ceiling in answer. He then proceeded to move an iron ring fixed in the wall; and by means of a spring which was disclosed to view, a trap-door was detached from the ceiling and descended to the floor of the laboratory. Balsamo placed himself in the centre of this machine, which by means of another spring gently rose with its burden, with as much ease as in the opera the gods and goddesses are carried up to Elysium, and the pupil found himself in the presence of the master.

The new dwelling of the old alchemist was about eight or nine feet high and sixteen in diameter; it was lighted from the top like a well, and hermetically closed on the four sides. This apartment, as the reader may observe, was a palace when compared with his habitation in the vehicle.

The old man was seated in his armchair on wheels, within the curvature of a marble table formed like a horseshoe, and heaped up with a whole world, or rather a whole chaos, of plants, phials, tools, books, instruments, and papers covered with cabalistic characters. He was so absorbed that he did not raise his head when Balsamo appeared. The light of an astral lamp, suspended from the culminating point of the window in the roof, fell on his bald, shining head. He was turning to and fro in his fingers a small white bottle, the transparency of which he was examining, as a good housekeeper tries the eggs which she buys at market. Balsamo gazed on him at first in silence; then after a moment's pause, "Well," said he, "have you anything new?"

"Yes, yes; come hither, Acharat. You see me enchanted, — transported with joy! I have found, I have found — "

"What?"

"*Pardieu!* what I sought."

"Gold?"

"Gold indeed! I am surprised at you!"

"The diamond?"

"Gold, diamonds? The man raves! A fine discovery, forsooth, — a thing to rejoice over, on my soul, if I had found that!"

"Then what you have found is your elixir?"

"Yes, my son, it is my elixir; that is to say, life, — what do I say? The eternity of life!"

"Oh!" said Balsamo, in a dejected voice (for he looked on this pursuit as mere insanity), "so it is that dream which occupies you still?"

But Althotas, without listening, continued to gaze delightedly at his phial. "At last," said he, "the combination is complete: the elixir of Aristæus, twenty grams; balm of Mercury, fifteen grams; precipitate of gold, fifteen grams; essence of the cedar of Lebanon, twenty-five grams."

"But it seems to me that, with the exception of the elixir of Aristæus, this is precisely your last combination, Master?"

"Yes; but I had not then discovered one more ingredient which binds all the others, and without which all the rest are as nothing."

"And have you discovered it now?"

"Yes."

"Can you procure it?"

"I should think so!"

"What is it?"

"We must add to the several ingredients already combined in this phial, the three last drops of the arterial blood of an infant."

"Well, but where will you procure this infant?" said Balsamo, horror-struck.

"I trust to you for that."

"To me? You are mad, Master!"

"Mad! And why?" asked the old man, unmoved at

this charge, and licking with delight a drop of the fluid which had escaped from the cork of the phial and was trickling down the side.

"Why, for that purpose you must kill the child."

"Of course we must kill him; and the handsomer he is, the better."

"Impossible," said Balsamo, shrugging his shoulders; "in this country children are not taken in that way to be killed."

"Bah!" cried the old man, with hideous naïveté, "and what do they do with them, then?"

"They rear them, of course."

"Oh! then the world is changed. It is only three years ago since we were offered as many infants as we chose for four charges of powder and half a bottle of eau-de-vie."

"Was that in Congo, Master?"

"Well, yes, that was in Congo! It is quite the same to me whether the child be black or white. Those who were offered to us, I remember, were sweet, playful, curly-headed little things."

"Ah! yes," said Balsamo; "but unfortunately, my dear Master, we are not in Congo."

"Oh! we are not in Congo?" said Althotas. "And where are we, then?"

"In Paris."

"In Paris? Well, if we were to embark from Marseilles, we could be in Congo in six weeks."

"Yes, no doubt; but I am obliged to remain in France."

"You are obliged to remain in France? And why so?"

"Because I have business here."

"You have business in France?"

"Yes; important business."

The old man burst into a prolonged and ghastly laugh. "Business!" said he, "business in France! True, I forgot; you have your clubs to organize!"

"Yes, Master."

"Conspiracies to set on foot?"

"Yes, Master."

"And you call that business?" and the aged man again began to laugh, with an air of mockery and sarcasm. Balsamo remained silent, collecting his forces for the storm which was brewing, and which he saw was approaching.

"Well, and how is this business of yours getting on?" said the old man, turning with difficulty in his chair, and fixing his large gray eyes on his pupil.

Balsamo felt his glance pierce him like a ray of light. "How far have I advanced?" he asked.

"Yes."

"I have thrown the first stone, and the waters are troubled."

"Troubled? And what slime have you stirred up?— eh?"

"The best, — the slime of philosophy."

"Oh! so you are setting to work with your Utopias, your baseless visions, your fogs and mists! Fools! You discuss the existence or non-existence of God, instead of trying, like me, to make gods of yourselves. And who are these famous philosophers with whom you are connected? Let me hear."

"I have already gained over the greatest poet and the greatest atheist of the age. He is soon expected in France, whence he has been in a manner exiled, and he is to be made a freemason at the lodge which I have established in the old monastery of the Jesuits, in the Rue Pot-de-Fer."

"What is his name?"

"Voltaire."

"I never heard of him. Well, who else is with you?"

"I am very soon to have a conference with the man who has done more to overturn established ideas than any other in this age, — the man who wrote 'Le Contrat Social.'"

"What is his name?"

"Rousseau."

"I never heard of him."

"Very probably, since you read only Alphonso the Tenth, Raymond Lulle, Peter of Toledo, and Albertus Magnus."

"They are the only men who really lived, because all their lives they were occupied by that great question, to be, or not to be."

"There are two ways of living, Master."

"I know only one, for my part, — it is that of existence. But let us return to your philosophers. You called them, I think —"

"Voltaire and Rousseau."

"Good. I shall remember those names. And you propose by means of these men —"

"To make myself master of the present, and to undermine the future."

"The people in this country, then, are very stupid, since they can be led by ideas!"

"On the contrary, it is because they have too much mind that ideas have more power over them than facts. Besides, I have an auxiliary more powerful than all the philosophers on earth."

"What is that?"

"Love of change. It is now some sixteen hundred

years since monarchy was established in France, and the people are tired of it."

"So that you think they will overthrow it?"

"I am sure of it."

"And you would help them to begin the work?"

"Aye, with all my strength!"

"Fool!"

"How so?"

"What will you gain by the overthrow of this monarchy?"

"I? Nothing. But the people will gain happiness."

"Come, as I am satisfied with what I have done to-day, I am willing to lose my time in trying to follow you. Explain first how you are to attain to this happiness, and afterwards what happiness is."

"How I am to attain to it?"

"Yes, to this universal happiness of yours, or to the overthrow of the monarchy, which in your eyes seems to be the same thing."

"Well, there exists at this moment a ministry which is the last rampart of the monarchy, — intelligent, industrious, courageous, and which might perhaps maintain this tottering and worn-out monarchy for twenty years longer; but they will assist me to overturn it."

"Who? Your philosophers?"

"No. The philosophers support it, on the contrary."

"What! Your philosophers support a ministry which supports a monarchy to which they themselves are hostile? What fools these philosophers of yours are!"

"It is because the prime minister is himself a philosopher."

"So! I understand; they mean to govern in the person of this minister. They are not fools, then, they are egotists."

"I do not wish to discuss what they are," exclaimed

Balsamo, who began to get impatient. "All I know is that, this ministry overturned, every one will cry havoc, and let slip the dogs of war on their successors. First, there will be against them the philosophers, then the parliament. The philosophers will blame, the parliament will blame; the ministry will persecute the philosophers, and will dissolve the parliament. Then mind and matter will combine, and organize a silent league, — an opposition obstinate, tenacious, incessant, which will attack, undermine, destroy. Instead of parliaments, judges will be appointed; these judges, nominated by the king, will move heaven and earth in defence of royalty. They will be accused, and with truth, of venality, of connivance, of injustice. The nation will arise, and then the monarchy will have against it the philosophers, — that is, mind; the parliaments, — that is, the middle class; the people, — that is, the lever which Archimedes sought, and with which he could have raised the world."

"Well, when you have raised the world, you can only let it fall back again into its old place."

"Yes; but in falling back it will crush the monarchy to atoms."

"And when the monarchy is crushed to atoms — to adopt your false metaphors and inflated language — what will arise on its ruins?"

"Liberty!"

"Ah! the French will then be free?"

"They cannot fail to be so."

"All free?"

"All.

"There will then be in France thirty millions of free men?"

"Yes."

"And among those thirty millions of free men, has it

never occurred to you that there might be one, with a little more brains than the rest, who some fine morning will seize on the liberty of the twenty-nine millions nine hundred and ninety-nine thousand nine hundred and ninety-nine, in order that he might have a little more liberty himself? You remember that dog we had at Medina, who ate up what was intended for all the other dogs?"

"Yes; but you may remember also, that one day the others combined together and strangled him."

"Because they were dogs; in such a case men would have done nothing."

"Then you place man's intelligence below that of a dog, Master?"

"Certainly. All the examples sustain me."

"What examples?"

"I think you may recall among the ancients a certain Cæsar Augustus, and among the moderns a certain Oliver Cromwell, who bit rather deeply into the Roman cake and the English cake, without any great resistance having been offered by those from whom they snatched it."

"Well, and supposing that the man of whom you speak should arise, — he will be mortal, he will die; and before dying he will have done good even to those whom he may have oppressed; for he will have changed the nature of the aristocracy. Being obliged to lean for support on something, he will choose what is strongest, — the people. Instead of an equality which degrades, he will establish an equality which elevates. For equality has no fixed range; it adapts itself to the level of him who makes it. Now, in elevating the people in the social scale, he will have introduced a principle unknown until his time. A revolution will make the French free; a protectorate under another Cæsar Augustus or another Oliver Cromwell will make them equal."

Althotas wheeled round in his armchair. "Oh, the stupidity of man!" he cried. "Busy yourself for twenty years in educating a child; teach him all that you know, — that at thirty he may come and tell you, 'Men will be equal!'"

"Certainly, men will be equal, — equal before the law."

"And before death, fool?— before death, that law of laws, will they be equal, when one shall die at three days old, and another at a hundred years? Equal? Men equal so long as they have not conquered death? Oh, the fool, the double fool!" And Althotas threw himself back in his chair to laugh at his ease, while Balsamo, grave and sad, sat with his head leaning on his hand.

The old man at length turned a look of pity on him. "Am I," said he, "the equal of the workman who munches his coarse bread; of the sucking babe; of the drivelling old man sunk in second childhood? Wretched sophist that you are! Men can be equal only when they are immortal; for when immortal they will be gods, and gods alone are on an equality with one another."

"Immortal!" murmured Balsamo. "Immortal!—'t is a chimera."

"A chimera? Yes, a chimera like steam; a chimera like the electric fluid; a chimera like everything which is sought, — not yet discovered, but to be discovered. Rake up the dust of bygone worlds; lay bare one after another the superincumbent strata, each of which represents a social state now passed away; and in these human strata, in this detritus of kingdoms, in these slimy deposits of time, into which modern investigation has pierced like an iron ploughshare, — what do you read? Is it not that men have, in all ages, sought what I seek, under the various names of the highest good, human happiness, perfection? When did they not seek it? They sought it in the days of Homer, when men lived two hundred years; they sought it in the days of the patriarchs, when they lived eight centuries. They did not find that highest good, that well-being, that perfection; for if they had, this decrepit world would now be fresh, youthful, roseate as the morning dawn. Instead of that we have suffering, death, decay. Is suffering good? Is death lovely? Is decay fair to look upon?"

Here the old man was interrupted by his short, dry cough, and Balsamo had a moment to reply. "You acknowledge," said he, "that no one has yet discovered that elixir of life which you seek. I tell you that no one will ever discover it. Submit to God."

"Fool! No one has discovered it, therefore no one will discover it! By that mode of reasoning we should never have made any discoveries. But do you think that all discoveries are new things, inventions? No, they are forgotten things found again. Why should things, once discovered, be forgotten? Because life is too short for the discoverer to draw from his discovery all the deductions which belong to it. Twenty times has man been on the point of grasping the elixir of life. Do you think that the Styx was merely a dream of Homer's? Do you think that Achilles, almost immortal, because vulnerable in his heel alone, was a fable? No; Achilles was the pupil of Chiron, as you are my pupil. That word Chiron means either best or worst. Chiron was a sage whom they have depicted as a Centaur, because by his learning he had endowed man with the strength and swiftness of the horse. Well, like me, he had almost found the elixir of immortality. Perhaps, like me, he wanted only those three drops of blood which you refuse me. The want of those three drops of blood rendered Achilles vulnerable in his heel; death found a passage, — it entered. Yes, I repeat it, Chiron, the universal man, is only another Althotas, prevented by another Acharat from completing the work which would have saved humanity by arresting the operation of the Divine curse. Well, what have you to say to that?"

"I say," replied Balsamo, visibly shaken, "that I have my task, and you have yours; let each fulfil his own at his own personal risk and danger. I will not second your by a crime."

"By a crime?"

"Yes; and by such a crime as would raise a whole people with cries of indignation in pursuit of you, — a crime which would cause you to hang on one of those infamous gibbets from which your science has not secured the best men, any more than the worst."

Althotas struck the marble table with his dry and fleshless hands. "Come!" said he, "be not a humanitarian idiot, — the worst race of idiots which exists in the world! Let us converse a little on these laws of yours, — these brutal and absurd laws, written by animals of your species who shudder at a drop of blood shed for a wise purpose, but gloat over torrents of the vital fluid shed on scaffolds, before the ramparts of cities, or on those plains which they call fields of battle! Your laws, ignorant and selfish, sacrificing the man of the future to the man of the present, and which have taken for their motto, 'Live to-day; for tomorrow we die!' — let us speak of them, I say."

"Say what you have to say; I am listening," said Balsamo, becoming more and more gloomy.

"Have you a pencil? I wish you to make a little calculation."

"I can calculate without pen or pencil. Proceed with what you have to say."

"What was this project of yours? Oh! I remember. You are to overturn a ministry, dissolve the parliament, establish venal judges, cause a national bankruptcy, stir up rebellion, kindle a revolution, overturn the monarchy, raise up a protectorate, and hurl down the protector. The revolution is to bring freedom, the protectorship equality. Then, the French being free and equal, your task will be accomplished? Is not that it?"

"Yes; do you look on the thing as impossible?"

"I do not believe in impossibility. You see I play fairly with you."

"Well, what then?"

"In the first place, France is not England, where what you wish to do has already been done, — plagiarist that you are! France is not an isolated land, where ministers may be dismissed, parliaments dissolved, iniquitous judges established, bankruptcy brought about, revolt fomented, revolution kindled, the monarchy overturned, a protectorship established, and the protector then overthrown, without other nations interfering a little in these movements. France is incorporated in Europe as the liver in the frame of man. It has roots in all nations; its fibres extend through every people. Try to tear up the liver of this great machine, which is called the European continent, and for twenty, thirty, forty years perhaps, the whole body will quiver. But I will take the lowest number, — I will say twenty years. Is that too much, O sage philosopher?"

"No, it is not too much," said Balsamo; "it is not even enough."

"However, I am satisfied with it, — twenty years of war, of a bloody, mortal, incessant strife. Let me see, — I put down that at two hundred thousand dead each year. That is not too high a calculation, considering that there will be fighting at the same time in Germany, Italy, Spain, and Heaven knows where else! Two hundred thousand men a year in twenty years make four millions. Allowing each man seventeen pounds of blood, which is nearly the natural quantity, that will make — seventeen multiplied by four — let me see — that will make sixty-eight millions of pounds of blood shed for the attainment of your object. I, for my part, ask but three drops! Say, now, which of us is mad? which of us is the savage? which of us the cannibal? Well, you do not answer!"

"Yes, Master, I do answer, that three drops of blood would be nothing, were you sure of success."

"And you, who would shed sixty-eight millions of pounds, are you sure of success? Speak! If you be sure, lay your hand on your heart and say, 'Master, for these four millions of dead I guarantee the happiness of the human race!'"

"Master," said Balsamo, evading a direct reply, "in the name of Heaven seek for some other means than this!"

"Ah, you dare not answer me! You dare not answer me!" exclaimed Althotas, triumphantly.

"You are deceived, Master, about the efficacy of the means; it is impossible!"

"Aye? So you give advice, so you contradict me, so you give me the lie, do you?" said Althotas, rolling his gray eyes beneath his white and shaggy eyebrows with an expression of concentrated anger.

"No, Master; but I cannot help reflecting on the difficulties in your way, — I, who am brought every day into contact with the world in opposition to men, who have to struggle against princes, and who do not live, like you, secluded in a corner, indifferent to all that takes place around you, and careless whether your actions are forbidden or authorized by the laws, — a pure abstraction, in short, of the savant and the scholar. I, in short, who see the difficulties, warn you of them, that is all."

"You could easily set aside all those difficulties if you chose."

"Say rather if I believed that you were in the right."

"You do not believe it, then?"

"No," said Balsamo.

"You are only tempting me?" cried Althotas.

"No, I merely express my doubts."

"Well, come, do you believe in death?"

"I believe in what is. Now, death *is*."

Althotas shrugged his shoulders. "Death, then, *is*," he said; "that is one point which you will not contest?"

"No, it is incontestable."

"Death is omnipresent, invincible too, is it not?" added the old man, with a smile which made his disciple shudder.

"Oh, yes, Master, omnipresent, and, above all, invincible!"

"And when you see a corpse, the cold sweat bedews your forehead, regret pierces your heart?"

"No, the cold sweat does not bedew my forehead, because I am familiar with every form of human misery; grief does not pierce my heart, because I attach little value to life. I only say, in the presence of a corpse, 'Death, death! thou art as powerful as God! Thou reignest as a sovereign, O death, and none can prevail against thee!'"

Althotas listened to Balsamo in silence, giving no other sign of impatience than that of turning a scalpel eagerly in his fingers; but when the pupil had ended his painful and solemn invocation, the Master looked around him with a smile, and his piercing eyes, which seemed to penetrate Nature's most hidden secrets, rested on a poor black dog which lay trembling in a corner of the room on a little heap of straw. It was the last of three animals of the same species which Althotas had demanded for his experiments, and which Balsamo had procured for him.

"Take that dog," said Althotas, "and place it on the table."

Balsamo obeyed. The creature, which seemed to have a presentiment of its fate, and which had no doubt already been in the hands of the experimenter, began to tremble, struggle, and howl, as soon as it felt the contact of the marble table.

"And so," said Althotas, "you believe in life, do you not, since you believe in death?"

"Certainly."

"There is a dog which appears to me quite alive. What do you think?"

"He is alive, assuredly, because he howls, struggles, is terrified."

"How ugly black dogs are! By the by, remember on the first opportunity to get me some white ones."

"I will endeavor to do so."

"Well, you say this one is alive? Bark, my little fellow, bark!" said the old man, with his frightful laugh; "we must convince my Lord Acharat that you are alive." And he touched the dog on a certain muscle, which made him bark, or rather howl, immediately.

"Very well; now bring forward the air-pump, and put the dog under the receiver. But I forgot to ask you in which death you have the firmest belief."

"I do not know what you mean, Master; death is death."

"Very just; that is my opinion also. Then, since death is death, make a vacuum, Acharat."

Balsamo turned a handle, and the air which was

enclosed with the dog in the receiver rushed out by means of a tube with a sharp, whistling sound. The little dog seemed at first restless, then looked around, snuffed uneasily, raised its head, breathed noisily and hurriedly, and at last sank down, — suffocated, swollen, senseless.

"Now, the dog is dead of apoplexy, is he not?" said Althotas, — "a very good kind of death, as it does not cause much suffering."

"Yes."

"Is he really dead?"

"Certainly he is."

"You do not seem quite convinced, Acharat."

"Yes, I assure you I am."

"Oh, you know my resources, do you not? You suppose that I have discovered the art of insufflation, do you not? — that other achievement, which consists in restoring life by making the vital air circulate in a body which has not been wounded, as in a bladder which has not been pierced?"

"No, I suppose nothing. I simply believe that the dog is dead."

"However, for greater security we will kill him twice. Lift up the receiver, Acharat."

Acharat raised the glass apparatus. The dog did not stir; his eyelids were closed, and his heart had ceased to beat.

"Take this scalpel, and without wounding the larynx, divide the vertebral column."

"I do so only to satisfy you."

"And also to put an end to the poor animal in case it should not be quite dead," replied Althotas, smiling with that kind of obstinate pertinacity peculiar to the aged.

Balsamo made an incision with the keen blade, which divided the vertebral column about two inches below the brain, and opened a large, bloody wound. The animal, or rather the dead body of the animal, remained motionless.

"Ha! by my faith, he was quite dead," said Althotas. "See! not a fibre moves, not a muscle stirs, not one atom of his flesh recoils at this second attack."

"I will acknowledge all that as often as you like," said Balsamo, impatiently.

"Then you are certain that you behold an animal inert, cold, forever incapable of motion? Nothing can prevail against death, you say? No power can restore life, or even the semblance of life, to this poor creature?"

"No power, except that of God."

"Yes, but God turns not aside from his established laws. When God kills, he has a reason for doing so, since he is supreme wisdom; some benefit is to result from it. An assassin — I forget his name — said that, and it was well said. Nature has an interest in death. So you see before you a dog as dead as it is possible to be; Nature has reclaimed her rights over him."

Althotas fixed his piercing eye on Balsamo, who, wearied by the old man's rambling talk, only bowed in reply.

"Well," continued Althotas, "what would you say if this dog opened his eye and looked at you!"

"I should be very much surprised, Master," replied Balsamo, smiling.

"You would be surprised? Ha! I am delighted to hear it." On uttering these words, with his dreary, hollow laugh, the old man drew near the dog a machine composed of plates of metal separated by dampers of cloths; this apparatus was standing in an acidulated liquid; the two extremities, or poles, as they are called, projected from the trough.

"Which eye do you wish him to open, Acharat?" asked the old man.

"The right."

He placed the two poles of the machine nearly together, separated from each other by a small piece of silk, and fixed them on a muscle in the neck. Instantly the right eye of the dog opened and looked steadily at Balsamo, who recoiled with horror.

"Shall we now pass to the jaws?" said Althotas.

Balsamo made no reply; he was overpowered with astonishment.

Another muscle was touched; and the eye having closed, the jaws opened, showing the sharp white teeth, and at their roots the gums red, and quivering apparently with life.

"This is, in truth, strange!" murmured Balsamo, unable to conceal his agitation.

"You see that death is not so powerful after all," said Althotas, triumphing at the discomfiture of his pupil, "since a poor old man like me, who must soon be its prey, can turn it — the inexorable — from its path." Then, with a sharp, ringing laugh, he suddenly added: "Take care, Acharat! here is a dead dog which just now tried to bite you, and is now about to run at you. Take care!"

And in fact the dog, with its neck laid open, its mouth gaping, and eye quivering, rose suddenly on its four legs, and staggered for a moment, its head hanging down hideously. Balsamo felt his hair stand on end, and he recoiled to the wall of the apartment, uncertain whether to fly or remain.

"Come, come, I do not wish to kill you with fright in trying to instruct you," said Althotas, pushing aside the dead body and the machine. "Enough of experiments like that."

Immediately the body, ceasing to be in contact with the battery, fell down, stiff and motionless as before.

"Could you have believed that of death, Acharat? Did you think it so kindly disposed?"

"It is strange, in truth, — very strange!" replied Balsamo, drawing nearer.

"You see, my child, that we may arrive at what I seek, for the first step toward it is made. What is it to prolong life, when we have already succeeded in annulling death?"

"But we must not assume that yet," objected Balsamo; "for the life which you have just restored is only factitious."

"With time we shall discover the real life. Have you not read in the Roman poets that Cassidæus restored life to dead bodies?"

"In the poets, — yes."

"Do not forget, my friend, that the Romans called poets *vates*."

"But I have still an objection to offer."

"Let me hear it! Let me hear it!"

"If your elixir of life were made, and if you caused this dog to swallow some of it, he would live eternally?"

"Without doubt."

"But suppose he fell into the hands of an experimenter like you, who cut his throat, — what then?"

"Good! good!" cried the old man, joyfully, and rubbing his hands together; "this is what I expected from you."

"Well, if you expected it, reply to it."

"I ask nothing better."

"Will your elixir prevent a chimney from falling on a man's head, a pistol-ball from going through his heart, a horse from giving him a kick that shall destroy him?"

Althotas looked at Balsamo with the eye of a bravo who perceives that his adversary has exposed himself to his blow.

"No, no, no!" said he; "you are a real logician, my dear Acharat. No, I cannot prevent the effects of the chimney, or of the ball, or of the horse, while there are houses, firearms, and horses."

"However, you can bring the dead to life!"

"Why, yes, for a moment, — not for an indefinite period. In order to do that, I must first discover the spot where the soul is lodged, and that may be rather tedious; but I can prevent the soul from leaving the body by a wound."

"How so?"

"By causing the wound to close up."

"Even if an artery be divided?"

"Certainly."

"Ah! I should like to see that done."

"Very well, look!" and before Balsamo could prevent him, the old man opened a vein in his left arm with a lancet. There was so little blood in his body, and it circulated so slowly, that it was some time before it issued from the wound; but at last it did flow abundantly.

"Great God!" exclaimed Balsamo.

"Well, what is the matter?" said Althotas.

"You have wounded yourself seriously."

"That is because you are like Saint Thomas, and must see and touch before you will believe." He then took a little phial which he had placed near him, and poured a few drops of its contents on the wound. "Look!" said he.

At the touch of this magic fluid the blood ceased to flow, the flesh contracted, closing up the vein, and the wound became merely like the prick of a pin, — an opening too small for the blood to pass through.

This time Balsamo gazed at the old man in amazement.

"That is another of my discoveries, Acharat. What do you think of it?"

"Oh, Master, you are the most learned of men!"

"Yes, acknowledge that if I have not conquered death, I have at least dealt it a blow from which it will not readily recover. The bones of the human body are easily broken: I will render them, my son, as hard as steel. It has blood, which when it is shed carries life along with it: I will prevent the blood from leaving the body. The flesh is soft, and can be pierced without difficulty: I will make it invulnerable as that of the paladins of the Middle Ages, which blunted the edge of swords and axes. To do all that requires only an Althotas who shall live three hundred years. Well, give me what I ask, and I will live one thousand! Oh, my dear Acharat, all depends on you! Give me back my youth, give me back the vigor of my body, give me back the freshness of my ideas, and you shall see whether I fear the sword, the ball, the tottering wall, or the stupid beast which bites or kicks. In my fourth youth, Acharat,—that is, before I have lived to the age of four men,—I tell you I shall have renewed the face of the world; I shall have made for myself and for a regenerated race of men a new world, without falling chimneys, without swords, without musket-balls, without kicking horses; for men will then understand that it is better to live to help and love one another than to tear each other to pieces and to destroy each other."

"It is true, Master; or at least it is possible."

"Well, bring me the child, then."

"Give me time to reflect on the matter, and reflect on it yourself."

Althotas darted on his disciple a glance of sovereign scorn. "Go," said he, "go! I will yet convince you that I am right. And in truth the blood of man is not so precious an ingredient that a substitute for it may not be found. Go! I will seek, — I shall find. Go! I need you not."

Balsamo struck the trap-door with his foot, and descended into the lower apartment, mute, melancholy, and wholly subdued by the genius of this man, who compelled him to believe in impossibilities by accomplishing them before his eyes.

CHAPTER XVI.

INQUIRIES.

THIS night, so long and so fertile in events, during which we have been borne about, as in the cloud of the mythological deities, from St. Denis to Muette, from Muette to the Rue Coq-Heron, from the Rue Coq-Heron to the Rue Plastrière, and from thence to the Rue St. Claude, had been employed by Madame Dubarry in efforts to bend the king's mind to her new political views. She insisted in particular on the danger there would be in allowing the Choiseuls to gain ground with the dauphiness.

The king replied to this, with a shrug, that the dauphiness was a child and the Duc de Choiseul was an elderly minister, and that consequently there was no danger, seeing that he could not amuse her, and she would not understand him. Then, enchanted with this *bon mot*, the king had cut short the discussion.

But if the king was enchanted, the countess was far from being so, as she thought she perceived symptoms of his Majesty's throwing off her yoke.

Louis XV. was unstable in his affections. His greatest happiness consisted in his making his mistresses jealous, providing always that their jealousy did not assume the form of obstinate quarrels or prolonged sulkiness. Madame Dubarry was jealous, — at first through vanity, and then through fear. It had cost her too much pains to attain her present elevated position, and it was too far removed from her point of departure, for her to dare, like

Madame de Pompadour, to tolerate other favorites near the king. Madame Dubarry, then, being jealous, was determined to probe to the bottom this sudden change in the king's manner.

The king replied to her in these memorable words, in which there was not one particle of truth: "I am thinking very seriously about the happiness of my daughter-in-law; I really do not know whether the dauphin will make her happy or not."

"Why not, Sire?"

"Because Louis at Compiègne, St. Denis, and Muette, seemed to me much more occupied with other women than with his wife."

"In truth, Sire, if your Majesty had not told me this yourself, I should not have believed it; for the dauphiness is lovely."

"She is rather thin."

"She is so young."

"Oh! as for that, look at Mademoiselle de Taverney; she is of the same age as the archduchess."

"Well, Sire?"

"Well, she is a faultless beauty."

A flash from the countess's eye warned the king of his mistake. "And you yourself, dear Countess," he added, quickly, "you yourself, at sixteen, were as round as one of our friend Boucher's shepherdesses, I am sure."

This little bit of adulation smoothed matters in some degree, but the blow had taken effect. Madame Dubarry therefore assumed the offensive. "Ah!" said she, bridling, "so she is very handsome, this Mademoiselle de Taverney?"

"Handsome! How should I know?" replied the king.

"What? You praise her, and yet you do not know, you say, whether she is handsome or not?"

"I know that she is not thin, that is all."

"Then you have seen her, and looked rather narrowly at her?"

"Ah! my dear Countess, you push me rather closely. You know that I am short-sighted; a mass strikes me, but devil take details! In looking at the dauphiness, I saw bones, and nothing more."

"And in looking at Mademoiselle de Taverney you saw masses, to use your own expression; for the dauphiness is an aristocratic beauty, Mademoiselle de Taverney a vulgar one."

"Oh, ho!" said the king, "by this mode of reckoning, Jeanne, you will never be an aristocratic beauty! Come, you must be jesting, I think."

"Very good; a compliment!" thought the countess to herself. "Unfortunately, this compliment serves only to cover another compliment which is not intended for me." Then aloud, "On my honor," said she, "I shall be very glad if her Royal Highness the dauphiness chooses for her ladies of honor those that are a little attractive; a court of old women is frightful."

"My dear creature, you need not tell that to me. I said the same thing to the dauphin yesterday; but our newly fledged husband seems quite indifferent about the matter."

"And suppose, for a beginning, she were to take this Mademoiselle de Taverney?"

"I think she has already chosen her," replied Louis.

"Ah! you know that, Sire?"

"At least, I fancy I heard some one say so."

"She has no fortune, I hear."

"No, but she is of an old family. The Taverneys Maison Rouge are of ancient descent, and have served the State honorably."

"Who patronizes them?"

"I have no idea. But I think they are beggars, as you say."

"In that case it cannot be the Duc de Choiseul; otherwise they would actually burst with pensions."

"Countess, Countess, I beseech you, no politics!"

"Do you call it politics to say that the Choiseuls are robbing you?"

"Certainly," said the king, rising.

An hour afterward, the king arrived at the great Trianon, delighted at having awakened the countess's jealousy, but repeating to himself, in a half-whisper, as the Duc de Richelieu might have done at thirty, "Really, jealous women are very tiresome!"

No sooner had his Majesty left Madame Dubarry than she also rose and passed into her boudoir, where Chon awaited her, impatient to hear the news.

"Well!" said she, "your star has been in the ascendant these last few days, — presented to the dauphiness the day before yesterday, invited to her table yesterday!"

"A great triumph, truly!"

"Why do you speak in that tone? Are you aware that at this moment a hundred carriages are hastening to Luciennes, that their occupants may obtain a smile from you?"

"I am sorry to hear it."

"Why so?"

"Because they are losing their time. Neither the carriages nor their owners shall have a smile from me this morning."

"Ah! this is a cloudy morning, then, Countess?"

"Yes, very cloudy! My chocolate, quick, — my chocolate!"

Chon rang the bell, and Zamore appeared.

"My chocolate!" said the countess.

Zamore retired, walking very slowly and with a majestic strut.

"The wretch intends that I should die of hunger!" cried the countess. "A hundred blows of the whip if you do not run."

"Me not run,— me governor," said Zamore, majestically.

"Ah! you governor?" exclaimed the countess, seizing a little riding-whip with a silver handle, which she used for keeping peace among the spaniels and monkeys. "Governor, indeed! Wait, Governor, and you shall see!"

At this spectacle Zamore took to flight, slamming the doors behind him and uttering loud cries.

"Really, Jeanne, you are perfectly ferocious to-day," said Chon.

"I am at liberty to be so if I please, am I not?"

"Oh, very well; but in that case you must permit me to leave you, my dear!"

"Why so?"

"I am afraid of being devoured."

Three taps were heard at the door.

"Well, who is knocking now?" said the countess, impatiently.

"Whoever he is, he will get a warm reception," muttered Chon.

"Oh! I should advise you to give me a bad reception," said Jean, throwing open the door with an air of dignity.

"Well, and what would happen if you were ill received? For, after all, the thing is possible."

"It would happen," said Jean, "that I should never come back."

"Well?"

"And that you would lose a great deal more than I should by receiving me badly."

"Impertinent fellow!"

"Ah! I am impertinent, because I do not flatter. What is the matter with her this morning, Chon, my beauty?"

"Don't speak to me about her, Jean. She is perfectly insufferable. Oh! here is the chocolate."

"Oh, well, never mind her, then! How do you do, chocolate? I am very glad to see you, my dear chocolate!" continued Jean, taking the tray from the servant, placing it on a little table in the corner, and seating himself before it. "Come, Chon, come!" said he; "those who are too proud to speak shall not have any."

"You are quite delightful, you two!" said the countess, seeing that Chon by a sign gave Jean to understand that he might breakfast alone. "You pretend to be sensitive, and yet you do not see that I am suffering."

"What is the matter, then?" said Chon, approaching her.

"No!" exclaimed the countess, pettishly. "Neither of them bestows a thought on what torments me."

"And what does torment you?" asked Jean, coolly buttering his bread.

"Do you want money?" asked Chon.

"Oh! as for money, the king will want before I shall."

"I wish you would lend me a thousand louis-d'or, then," said Jean; "I need them very much."

"A thousand fillips on your great red nose!"

"The king has positively decided on keeping that abominable Choiseul, then?" asked Chon.

"Great news that! You know very well that the Choiseuls are immovable."

"Then his Majesty the king has fallen in love with the dauphiness."

"Now you are coming nearer it. But look at that beast stuffing himself with chocolate! He would not move his little finger to save me from destruction. Oh, those two creatures will be the death of me!"

Jean, without paying the least attention to the storm which was raging behind him, cut a second slice, buttered it carefully, and poured out another cup of chocolate.

"What! The king is really in love?" cried Chon, clasping her hands and turning pale.

Madame Dubarry nodded, as much as to say, "You have hit it."

"Oh, if it be so, we are lost!" continued Chon; "and will you suffer that, Jeanne? But to whom has he taken a fancy?"

"Ask your brother there, who is purple with chocolate, and who looks as if he were just going to burst. He will tell you, for he knows, or at least he suspects."

Jean raised his head.

"Did you speak to me?" said he.

"Yes, most obliging brother, most useful ally!" said Jeanne, "I was asking you the name of the person who has attracted the king."

The Viscount's mouth was so full that it was with great difficulty that he sputtered out, "Mademoiselle de Taverney."

"Mademoiselle de Taverney! Oh, mercy on us!" cried Chon.

"He knows it, the wretch!" shrieked the countess, throwing herself back in her chair, and clasping her hands, — "he knows it, and he eats!"

"Oh!" said Chon, visibly deserting from her brother's camp for that of her sister.

"I wonder," cried the countess, "what prevents me from tearing out his two great ugly eyes! Look at them, all swollen with sleep, the lazy idler! He has just got up, my dear — just got up!"

"You are mistaken," said Jean; "I have not been in bed at all."

"And what were you doing, then, glutton?"

"Why, faith, I have been running up and down all night and all the morning too."

"I told you so. Oh! who will render me the greatest service? Who will tell me what that girl has become, and where she is?"

"Where she is?" asked Jean.

"Yes."

"Where should she be but in Paris?"

"In Paris? But where in Paris?"

"Rue Coq-Héron."

"Who told you so?"

"The coachman who drove her; I waited for him at the stables and questioned him."

"He told you—"

"That he had just driven the Taverney family to a little hôtel in the Rue Coq-Héron, situated in a garden adjoining the Hôtel d'Armenonville."

"Oh, Jean, Jean!" cried the countess, "this reconciles me to you, my dear. But now we want the particulars,— how she lives; whom she sees; what she does; whether she receives letters. These are things we must find out."

"Well, you shall know all that."

"But how?"

"Ah! how? Try to find out for yourself. I have found out a great deal for my share."

"Oh!" said Chon, "there might be lodgings to let in the Rue Coq-Héron."

"An excellent idea!" exclaimed the countess. "You must hasten to the Rue Coq-Héron, Jean, and hire a house. We will conceal some one there who can see every one that goes in or comes out. Quick! Order the carriage."

"It is useless; there is neither house nor lodging to be let in that street."

"How do you know?"

"I have inquired, *parbleu;* but there are apartments to let—"

"Where?"

"In the Rue Plastrière."

"And where is the Rue Plastrière?"

"It is a street where there are houses overlooking the gardens of the Rue Coq-Héron."

"Well! quick, quick!" said the countess; "let us hire an apartment in the Rue Plastrière."

"It is already hired," said Jean.

"Admirable man!" cried the countess; "kiss me, Jean."

Jean wiped his mouth, kissed Madame Dubarry on both cheeks, and then made a ceremonious bow of thanks for the honor that had been done him.

"Was it not luck?" said he.

"But I hope no one recognized you?"

"Who the devil should recognize me in a street like that?"

"And what have you engaged?"

"A little apartment in an obscure, out-of-the-way house."

"But they must have asked for whom you wanted it?"

"Certainly they did."

"And what did you say?"

"That it was for a young widow; are you a widow, Chon?"

"Of course I am!" said Chon.

"Excellent!" said the countess. "Then it is Chon

who will be installed in the apartment; she will watch, she will spy. But not a moment must be lost."

"Therefore I will set off at once," said Chon. "The carriage, the carriage!"

"The carriage!" repeated Madame Dubarry, ringing loud enough to have awakened the whole household of the Sleeping Beauty in the Wood.

Jean and the countess well knew what they had to dread from Andrée's presence. She had, even on her first appearance, attracted the king's attention; therefore she was dangerous.

"This girl," said the countess, "is not a true provincial if she has not brought some rustic lover with her from her dovecot at Taverney; let us but discover the swain, and patch up a marriage at once. Nothing would cool the king like a marriage between country lovers."

"Oh, the devil! I am not quite so sure of that," said Jean. "You know better than any one, Countess, that a young married woman is a very dainty morsel for his most Christian Majesty; while a girl with a lover would be less attractive to him. But the carriage is ready."

Chon sprang into the carriage after having embraced her sister and pressed Jean's hand.

"But why not take Jean with you?" asked the countess.

"No, no; I will go my own way," replied Jean. "Wait for me in the Rue Plastrière; I shall be your first visitor in your new domicile."

Chon drove off. Jean seated himself at his table again, and poured out a third cup of chocolate.

Chon called first at the family residence, and changed her dress, studying as much as possible to assume the costume and appearance of a tradesman's wife. Then, when she was satisfied with her labors, she threw over her aristocratic shoulders a light black-silk mantle, ordered a sedan-chair to the door, and about half an hour afterward she and Sylvie were mounting the steep, narrow staircase leading up to the fourth story of a house in the Rue Plastrière; for in a fourth story was situated that lodging so fortunately procured by the viscount.

When she reached the landing of the second story, Chon turned, for she heard some one following her. It was the old proprietress of the house, who lived on the first-floor, and who, hearing a noise, had come out to see what caused it, and was rather puzzled at seeing two women, so young and pretty, enter her abode. She looked up with a scowling face, to meet the gaze of two smiling countenances. "Stop, ladies, stop!" she cried; "what do you want here?"

"The lodging which my brother was to engage for us, Madame," said Chon, assuming the serious air of a widow. "Have you not seen him, or can we have made a mistake in the house?"

"Oh, no!" replied the old proprietress, "you are quite right; it is on the fourth story. Poor young creature, — a widow at your age!"

"Alas, alas!" sighed Chon, raising her eyes to heaven.

"But do not grieve; you will be very pleasantly situated in the Rue Plastrière. It is a charming street; you will hear no noise, and your apartment looks into the gardens."

"That is just what I wished, Madame."

"And besides, by going into the corridor, you can see into the street when any procession is passing, or when the learned dogs are exhibited."

"Thank you; that will be a great relief to me," sighed Chon, and she continued to ascend.

The old proprietress followed her with her eyes until

she reached the fourth story. Then Chon, after shutting the door, hurried to the window which looked on the garden. Jean had made no mistake; almost immediately below the window of the apartment which he had engaged was the garden pavilion which the coachman had described to him. Soon all doubts were removed, — a young girl came forward to the window of the pavilion and seated herself before a little embroidery frame. It was Andrée.

CHAPTER XVII.

THE APARTMENT IN THE RUE PLASTRIÈRE.

Chon had not scrutinized the young girl many moments before Vicomte Jean, ascending the stairs four at a time, like a lawyer's clerk, appeared on the threshold of the pretended widow's apartment. "Well?" said he, inquiringly.

"Is it you, Jean? In truth, you frighten me."

"Well, what do you say to it?"

"Why, that I shall be admirably situated here for seeing all that happens; unluckily, I shall not be able to hear everything."

"Ah, faith! you want too much. By the by, I have another piece of news for you."

"What is it?"

"Wonderful!"

"Pooh!"

"Incomparable!"

"What a bore the man is with his exclamations!"

"The philosopher —"

"Well, what of the philosopher?"

"It is said, 'The wise man is for all events prepared.' Now, I am a wise man, but I was not prepared for this."

"I should like to know when you will finish. Perhaps this girl is in the way. In that case, Mademoiselle Sylvie, step into the next room."

"Oh! there is no occasion whatever. That charming girl is not in the way; quite the contrary. Remain,

Sylvie, remain;" and the viscount chucked the handsome waiting-maid's chin, whose brow began already to darken at the idea that something was about to be said which she was not to hear.

"Let her stay, then; but speak."

"Why, I have done nothing else since I have been here."

"And said nothing. So hold your tongue, and let me watch, — that will be more to the purpose."

"Don't be out of temper! As I was saying, then, I was passing the fountain —"

"Positively, you never said a word about it."

"Why, there you interrupt me again."

"No."

"I was passing the fountain, then, and bargaining for some old furniture for this frightful lodging, when all at once I felt a stream of water splashing my stockings."

"How very interesting all this is!"

"Only wait; you are in too great a hurry, my dear. Well, I looked, and I saw — guess what? I will give you a hundred guesses."

"Do go on."

"I saw a young gentleman obstructing the jet of the fountain with a piece of bread, and by means of this obstacle causing the water to diverge and to spirt upon me."

"I can't tell you how much your story interests me," said Chon, shrugging her shoulders.

"Only wait. I swore lustily on feeling myself splashed; the bread-soaker turned round, and I saw —"

"You saw?"

"My philosopher, — or rather, our philosopher."

"Who, then, — Gilbert?"

"Himself, — bareheaded, his waistcoat open, stockings

dangling about his heels, shoes unbuckled,— in complete undress, in short."

"Gilbert! And what did he say?"

"I recognized him at once, and he recognized me. I advanced; he retreated. I stretched out my arm; he stretched his legs, and off he scampered like a greyhound among the carriages and the water-porters."

"You lost sight of him, then?"

"*Parbleu!* I should say so. You surely don't suppose that I would start off and run too?"

"True; it was impossible, I admit. And so we have lost him."

"Ah, what a pity!" ejaculated Mademoiselle Sylvie.

"Oh, most certainly!" said Jean. "I owe him a sound thrashing, and if I had once laid hands upon him he should have lost nothing for waiting, I promise you; but he guessed my kind intentions toward him, and made good use of his legs. No matter, he is in Paris,— that is the essential point; and in Paris, if you are not on very bad terms with the lieutenant of police, you may find whatever you seek."

"We must find him."

"And when we have got him we will keep him fasting."

"He must be shut up," said Mademoiselle Sylvie; "only this time a safer place must be chosen for the purpose."

"And Sylvie will carry his bread and water to that safe place, will you not, Sylvie?" said the viscount.

"It is no subject for jesting, brother," said Chon. "That lad saw the affair of the post-horses; and if he had motives for bearing us a grudge, we might have reason to fear him."

"And therefore," replied Jean, "I made up my mind,

while ascending your stairs, to call on Monsieur de Sartines and inform him of my discovery. Monsieur de Sartines will reply that a man bare-headed, his stockings about his heels, his shoes unbuckled, soaking his bread at a fountain, must live near the spot where he has been seen in such a plight; and he will then engage to find him for us."

"What can he do here without money?"

"Do errands."

"He? A philosopher of that wild breed? Oh, no!"

"He has perhaps discovered a relative," said Sylvie,— "some old devotee, who gives him the crusts that are too stale for her lapdog."

"Enough, enough, Sylvie! Put the house-linen into that old chest, and come you, brother, to our observatory."

Accordingly, the pair approached the window with the greatest caution. Andrée had abandoned her embroidery, but still sat in the armchair, with her limbs carelessly thrust out; stretching out her hand to a book lying on another chair within her reach, she opened it, and was soon absorbed in what the spectators supposed must be a most interesting subject, for she remained motionless from the moment that she began to read.

"Oh, the studious creature!" said Mademoiselle Chon; "what can she be reading there?"

"First indispensable article of furniture," replied the viscount, taking from his pocket an opera-glass, which he drew out and pointed at Andrée, resting it upon the angle of the window to steady it.

Chon watched his movements with impatience. "Well, let us see; is the creature really handsome?" she asked.

"Admirable! She is an exquisite girl! What arms, what hands, what eyes! Lips too tempting for Saint Anthony! Feet, oh, divine feet! and the ankle,— what an ankle under that silk stocking!"

"Oh! I should advise you to fall in love with her,— that would complete the affair," said Chon, peevishly.

"Well, after all, that would be no bad idea either, especially if she would grant me a little love in return; that would somewhat cheer our poor countess."

"Come, hand me that glass, and a truce to your gabble, if that is possible! Yes, in truth the girl is handsome, and it is impossible that she should not have a lover. She is not reading — look! the book is slipping out of her hand. There! it drops. Stay — I told you, Jean, she was not reading; she is lost in thought."

"Or sleep."

"With her eyes open? Lovely eyes, upon my word!"

"At any rate," said Jean, "if she has a lover we shall have a good view of him here."

"Yes, if he comes in the day-time; but if he should come at night?"

"The deuce! I did not think of that, and yet it is the first thing that I ought to have thought of, — which proves how very simple I am."

"Yes; simple as a lawyer."

"However, now that I am forewarned, I will devise something."

"What an excellent glass this is!" said Chon. "I can almost read the characters in the book."

Chon had leaned forward out of the window, urged by curiosity; but she drew back her head more quickly than she had advanced it.

"Well, what is the matter?" asked the viscount.

Chon grasped his arm. "Look cautiously, brother," said she; "look! Who is that person leaning out of yonder garret-window on the left? Take care not to be seen!"

"Oh, ho!" cried Dubarry, in a low tone, "it is my crust-soaker, God forgive me!"

"He is going to throw himself out!"

"No; he has fast hold of the parapet."

"But what is he looking at with those piercing eyes, with that wild eagerness?"

"He is watching somebody." The viscount struck his forehead. "I have it!" he exclaimed.

"What?"

"*Pardieu!* he is watching the girl!"

"Mademoiselle de Taverney?"

"Yes, yes; that's the swain of the dovecot. She comes to Paris, — he hastens hither too; she takes lodgings in the Rue Coq-Héron, — he sneaks away from us to go and live in the Rue Plastrière. He is looking at her, and she is musing."

"Upon my word, it is true," said Chon. "Observe that look, how intently fixed, — that lurid fire of his eyes; he is distractedly in love."

"Sister," said Jean, "let us not give ourselves any further trouble to watch the lady; he will do our business."

"Yes, — to his own advantage."

"No; to ours. Now let me go and see that dear Sartines. *Pardieu!* we have a chance. But take care, Chon, not to let the philosopher see you; you know how quickly he decamps!"

CHAPTER XVIII.

PLAN OF CAMPAIGN.

MONSIEUR DE SARTINES had returned home at three in the morning, extremely fatigued, but at the same time highly pleased with the entertainment which he had provided, on the spur of the moment, for the king and Madame Dubarry. Rekindled by the arrival of the dauphiness, the popular enthusiasm had greeted his Majesty with shouts of *Vive le Roi!* greatly diminished in volume, however, since that famous illness at Metz, during which all France had been seen in the churches or on pilgrimage, to obtain the restoration to health of the young Louis XV., — called at that time the "well-beloved." On the other hand, Madame Dubarry, who scarcely ever failed to be insulted in public by certain exclamations, had, contrary to her expectation, been graciously received by several rows of spectators judiciously placed in front; so that the pleased monarch had smiled graciously on Monsieur de Sartines, and the lieutenant of police reckoned upon a handsome acknowledgment. In consequence, he thought that he might lie till noon, which he had not done for a very long time: and on rising he had taken advantage of this holiday, which he gave himself, to try on some dozen or two of new wigs, while listening to the reports of the night. At the sixth wig, and when he was about a third through the reports, the Vicomte Jean Dubarry was announced.

"Good!" thought Monsieur de Sartines, "here come my thanks. But who knows? Women are so capricious. Show Monsieur le Vicomte into the drawing-room."

Jean, already fatigued with his forenoon's work, seated himself in an armchair; and the lieutenant of police, who speedily joined him, felt convinced that there would be nothing unpleasant in this interview. Jean appeared in fact in the highest spirits. The two gentlemen shook hands.

"Well, Viscount," said Monsieur de Sartines, "what brings you here so early?"

"In the first place," replied Jean, who was accustomed above all things to flatter the self-love of those whose good offices he needed, "in the first place I was anxious to congratulate you on the capital arrangements of your fête yesterday."

"Ah! many thanks. Is it officially?"

"Officially as regards Luciennes."

"That is all I want. Is it not there that the sun rises?"

"And retires to rest occasionally;" and Dubarry burst into a loud and rather vulgar laugh, which imparted to his appearance a semblance of good-nature which was sometimes lacking. "But," said he, "besides the compliments which I have to pay you, I have come to solicit a service also."

"Two, if they are possible."

"Not so fast; I hope to hear you say so by and by. When a thing is lost in Paris, is there any hope of finding it again?"

"If it is either worth nothing, or worth a great deal, there is."

"What I am seeking is of no great value," said Jean, shaking his head.

"And what are you in search of?"

"I am in search of a lad about eighteen years old."

Monsieur de Sartines extended his hand to a paper, took

a pencil, and wrote. "Eighteen years old; what is your lad's name?"

"Gilbert."

"What does he do?"

"As little as he can, I suppose."

"Where does he come from?"

"From Lorraine."

"With whom was he?"

"In the service of the Taverneys."

"They brought him with them?"

"No, my sister Chon picked him up on the highroad, perishing with hunger; she took him into her carriage and brought him to Luciennes, and there—"

"Well, and there?"

"I am afraid the rogue has abused the hospitality he met with."

"Has he stolen anything?"

"I do not say that. But, in short, he absconded in a strange way."

"And you would now like to get him back?"

"Yes."

"Have you any idea where he can be?"

"I met him yesterday at the fountain which forms the corner of the Rue Plastrière, and have every reason to think that he lives in the street. In fact, I believe, if necessary, that I can point out the house."

"Well, but if you know the house, nothing is easier than to have him seized there. What do you wish to do with him when you have caught him? Have him shut up at Charenton?—at Bicêtre?"

"Not precisely that."

"Oh! whatever you please, my dear fellow. Don't stand on ceremony."

"No, on the contrary, this lad pleased my sister, and

she would have liked to keep him about her, as he is intelligent. If one could get him back for her by fair means, it would be more desirable."

"We must try. You have not made any inquiry in the Rue Plastrière to learn with whom he is?"

"Oh, no! You must understand that I did not wish to attract attention, for fear of losing the advantage I had gained. He had already perceived me, and scampered off as if the devil were at his heels; and if he had known that I was aware of his retreat, he would perhaps have decamped."

"Very likely. Rue Plastrière, you say? At the end, the middle, or the beginning of the street?"

"About one third down."

"Rest satisfied; I will send a clever fellow thither for you."

"Ah! my dear lieutenant, a man, let him be ever so clever, will always talk a little."

"No, our people never talk."

"The young one is cunning as a fox."

"Ah! I comprehend. Pardon me for not having seen your drift sooner. You wish me to go myself? In fact, you are right; it will be better, for there are perhaps difficulties in the way which you are not aware of."

Jean, though persuaded that the magistrate was desirous to assume a little consequence, was not disposed to diminish in the slightest degree the importance of his part. He even added, "It is precisely on account of these difficulties which you anticipate that I am desirous to have your personal assistance."

Monsieur de Sartines rang for his valet-de-chambre. "Let the horses be harnessed," said he.

"I have a carriage," said Jean.

"Thank you, but I prefer my own. Mine is without

arms, and holds a middle place between a hackney-coach and a chariot. It is freshly painted every month, and for that reason is scarcely to be recognized. In the mean time, while they are harnessing, permit me to try on my new wigs."

"Oh! by all means," said Jean.

Monsieur de Sartines summoned his wig-maker. He was an artist, and brought his client a veritable collection of wigs; they were of all forms, of all colors, of all dimensions, and of all denominations. Monsieur de Sartines occasionally changed his dress three or four times a day for his tours of inspection, and he was most particular with regard to the regularity of his costume. While the magistrate was trying on his twenty-fourth wig, a servant came to tell him that the carriage was ready.

"You will know the house again?" said Monsieur de Sartines to Jean, when they were in the carriage.

"Certainly; I see it from here."

"Have you examined the entrance?"

"That was the first thing I looked to."

"And what is the approach to it?"

"An alley."

"Ah! an alley, — one third down the street, you say?"

"Yes, with a private door."

"With a private door? The devil! Do you know on what floor your runaway lives?"

"In the attics. But you will see it directly; I perceive the fountain."

"At a foot-pace, coachman," said Monsieur de Sartines.

The coachman moderated his speed; Monsieur de Sartines drew up the window.

"Stop," said Jean; "it is that dingy-looking house."

"Ah, precisely!" exclaimed Monsieur de Sartines, clasping his hands; "that is just what I feared.

"What! Are you afraid of something?"

"Alas! yes."

"And what are you afraid of?"

"You are unlucky."

"Explain yourself."

"Why, that dingy house where your runaway lives is the house of Monsieur Rousseau, of Geneva."

"Rousseau, the author?"

"Yes."

"Well, and how does that concern you?"

"How does that concern me? Ah! it is plain enough that you are not lieutenant of police, and that you have nothing to do with philosophers."

"Pooh, pooh! Gilbert at Monsieur Rousseau's? What an improbable story!"

"Have you not said that your youth is a philosopher?"

"Yes."

"Well, 'birds of a feather, you know."

"And supposing that he is at Monsieur Rousseau's?"

"Yes, let us suppose that."

"What will be the consequence?"

"That you will not have him, *pardieu!*"

"Why not?"

"Because Monsieur Rousseau is a man who is much to be dreaded."

"Why not shut him up in the Bastille, then?"

"I proposed it the other day to the king, but he dared not."

"What! dared not?"

"No, no, — he wanted to leave the responsibility of his arrest to me; and by my faith, I was not bolder than the king."

"Indeed!"

"It is as I tell you. We have to look twice, I assure

you, before we bring all those philosophers about our ears. *Peste!* Take a person away from Monsieur Rousseau's? No, my dear friend, it will not do."

"In truth, my dear magistrate, you appear to be strangely timorous. Is not the king the king? Are you not his lieutenant of police?"

"And in truth, you citizens are charming fellows. When you have said, 'Is not the king the king?' you fancy that you have said all that is necessary. Well, listen to me, my dear viscount. I would rather arrest you at Madame Dubarry's than remove your Monsieur Gilbert from Monsieur Rousseau's."

"Really! Many thanks for the preference."

"Yes, upon my honor; there would be less outcry. You have no idea what delicate skins those literary men have; they cry out at the slightest scratch, as if you were breaking them upon the wheel."

"But let us not conjure up phantoms; look you, is it quite certain that Monsieur Rousseau has harbored our fugitive? This house has four floors. Does it belong to him, and does he live alone in it?"

"Monsieur Rousseau is not worth a farthing, and, consequently, has no house in Paris; there are probably from fifteen to twenty other inmates besides himself in yonder barrack. But take this for a rule of conduct: whenever ill-luck appears at all probable, reckon upon it; whenever good-luck, never reckon upon that. There are always ninety-nine chances for the ill, and one for the good. But wait a moment. As I suspected what would happen, I have brought my notes with me."

"What notes?"

"My notes respecting Monsieur Rousseau. Do you suppose that he can take a step without our knowing whither he goes?"

" Ha, indeed! Then he is really dangerous?"

" No; but he makes us uneasy. Such a madman may at any time break an arm or a leg, and people would say it was we who had broken it."

" A good thing if he would break his neck some day."

" God forbid!"

" Permit me to tell you that this is quite incomprehensible to me."

" The people stone this honest Genevese from time to time, but they allow no one else to do so; and if the smallest pebble were flung at him by us, they would stone us in return."

" Excuse me, but in truth I know not what to make of all these doings."

" And so we must use the most minute precautions. Now, let us test the only chance which is left us, — namely, that he does not lodge with Monsieur Rousseau. Keep yourself out of sight, at the back of the carriage."

Jean obeyed, and Monsieur de Sartines ordered the coachman to walk the horses a few paces to and fro in the street. He then opened his portfolio and took some papers out of it. " Let me see," said he, " if your youth is with Monsieur Rousseau. Since what day do you suppose him to have been there?"

" Since the sixteenth."

" ' 17*th*. — Monsieur Rousseau was seen herborizing at six o'clock in the morning in the wood of Meudon; he was alone.' "

" He was alone!"

" Let us proceed. ' At two o'clock in the afternoon he was herborizing again, but with a young man.' "

" Ah, ha!" cried Jean.

" ' With a young man,' " repeated Monsieur de Sartines : " do you understand?"

"That's he, *mordieu!* that's he!"

"'The young man is mean-looking—'"

"That's he!"

"'He is eating.'"

"That's he!"

"'The two individuals pick up plants, and dry them in a tin box.'"

"The devil! the devil!" exclaimed Dubarry.

"That is not all; listen further. 'In the evening he took the young man home; at midnight the young man had not left the house.'"

"Well?"

"'18*th*.—The young man has not left the house, and appears to be installed at Monsieur Rousseau's.'"

"I have still a gleam of hope."

"You are decidedly an optimist! No matter, tell me your hope."

"It is that he has some relative in the house."

"Come! we must satisfy you, or utterly destroy your hopes. Halt, coachman!"

Monsieur de Sartines alighted. He had not taken ten steps before he met a man in gray clothes and of very equivocal aspect. This man, on perceiving the illustrious magistrate, took off his hat and replaced it, without appearing to attach further importance to his salutation, although respect and attachment had been expressed in his look. Monsieur de Sartines made a sign; the man approached, received some whispered instructions, and disappeared in Rousseau's alley. The lieutenant of police returned to his carriage. Five minutes after, the man in gray made his appearance again, and approached the door.

"I will turn my head to the right," said Dubarry, "that I may not be seen."

Monsieur de Sartines smiled, received the communication of his agent, and dismissed him.

"Well?" inquired Dubarry.

"Well, the chance was against you, as I apprehended; it is with Rousseau that your Gilbert lodges. You must give him up, depend upon it."

"Give him up?"

"Yes. You would not, for a whim, raise all the philosophers in Paris against us, would you?"

"Oh, heavens! and what will my sister Jeanne say?"

"Is she so much attached to Gilbert?" asked Monsieur de Sartines.

"Indeed she is."

"Well, in that case you must resort to gentle means, — coax Monsieur Rousseau; and instead of suffering Gilbert to be taken from him only by force, he will give him up voluntarily."

"As well set us to tame a bear."

"It is perhaps not so difficult a task as you imagine; do not despair. He is fond of pretty faces; that of the countess is very handsome, and Mademoiselle Chon's is not unpleasing. Let me see, — the countess will make a sacrifice for her whim?"

"She will make a hundred."

"Would she consent to fall in love with Rousseau?"

"If it were absolutely necessary."

"It will perhaps be useful; but to bring the parties together, we shall need a third person. Are you acquainted with any one who knows Rousseau?"

"Monsieur de Conti."

"Won't do; he distrusts princes. We want a nobody, — a scholar, a poet."

"We never see people of that sort."

"Have I not met Monsieur de Jussieu at the countess's?"

"The botanist?"

"Yes."

"Faith! I believe so; he comes to Trianon, and the countess lets him ravage her flower-beds."

"That is your man; Jussieu is a friend of mine too."

"Then the thing is done."

"Almost."

"I shall get back my Gilbert, then?"

Monsieur de Sartines mused for a moment. "I begin to think you will," said he, "and without violence, without noise. Rousseau will deliver him up to you bound hand and foot."

"Do you think so?"

"I am sure of it."

"And what must be done to bring this about?"

"The merest trifle. You have, no doubt, a piece of vacant ground toward Meudon or Marly?"

"Oh! no want of that. I know ten such between Luciennes and Bougival."

"Well, get built upon it — what shall I call the thing? — a trap for philosophers."

"Excuse me, what do you say?"

"I said, a trap for philosophers."

"*Pardieu!* and how is that built?"

"I will give you a plan of it, rest satisfied. And now, let us be off; we begin to be noticed. To the hotel, coachman."

CHAPTER XIX.

MONSIEUR DE LA VAUGUYON.

THE important events of history are to the novelist what gigantic mountains are to the traveller. He surveys them, he skirts their base, he salutes them as he passes; but he does not climb them. In like manner we shall survey, skirt, and salute that august ceremony, the marriage of the dauphiness at Versailles. The Gazette de France is the only chronicle that ought to be consulted in such a case. It is not, in fact, in the splendor of the Versailles of Louis XV., in the description of the court-dresses, the liveries, the pontifical ornaments, that our particular history — that modest follower who takes a by-path leading along the highroad of the history of France — would find anything to pick up. Let us leave the ceremony to be performed amid the brilliant sunshine of a fine day in May; let us leave the illustrious spectators to retire in silence, or rehearsing and commenting on the marvels of the exhibition which they have just witnessed; and let us return to our own events and personages, which also have, historically speaking, a certain value.

The king, weary of the ceremonies, and especially of the dinner, — which had been of tedious duration, in imitation of that given on the marriage of the great dauphin, son of Louis XIV., — retired to his apartments at nine o'clock, and dismissed everybody, except Monsieur de la Vauguyon, tutor of his children.

This duke, a great friend of the Jesuits, whom he hoped to restore to favor through the influence of Madame Dubarry, saw a part of his task as tutor brought to a conclusion by the marriage of Monsieur le Duc de Berry. It was not the most difficult part, for he had yet to finish the education of Monsieur le Comte de Provence and of Monsieur le Comte d'Artois, — the former at this time fifteen years old, and the latter thirteen. Monsieur le Comte de Provence was sly and undisciplined; Monsieur le Comte d'Artois, thoughtless and ungovernable; and since the dauphin, besides possessing good qualities which made him a desirable pupil, was dauphin, — that is, the person in France next in importance to the king, — Monsieur de la Vauguyon would lose much in losing over such a spirit the influence which a woman was perhaps about to obtain.

Since the king had invited him to remain, Monsieur de la Vauguyon thought that the king comprehended this loss, and wished to recompense him. Ordinarily on the completion of an education the tutor receives a gratuity. This led Monsieur le Duc de la Vauguyon to make a great show of his emotion. During the whole dinner he had held his handkerchief to his eyes to show how much he felt the loss of his pupil. At the end of the dessert he had sobbed; but on finding himself alone, he became more calm. At the call of the king he again wiped the tears from his eyes.

"Come, my poor La Vauguyon," said the king, establishing himself comfortably on a lounge, "come, let us talk."

"I am at your Majesty's orders," replied the duke.

"Sit down there, my dear friend; you must be tired."

"I sit down, Sire?"

"Yes, without ceremony; take that seat." And Louis XV. pointed to a low seat placed in such a way that the light fell directly upon the face of the tutor, and left that of the king in shadow.

"Well, my dear Duke," said the king, "here is an education finished."

"Yes, Sire;" and Vauguyon sighed.

"A fine education, on my word," continued Louis XV.

"Your Majesty is too good."

"And which does you great credit, Duke."

"Your Majesty overwhelms me."

"Monsieur le Dauphin is, I suppose, one of the most learned princes in Europe?"

"I think so, Sire."

"Good historian?"

"Very good."

"Perfect geographer?"

"Sire, Monsieur le Dauphin draws better maps than any engineer."

"What skill has he in horology?"

"It is prodigious, Sire."

"For six months all my clocks have been running one behind another, like the four wheels of a carriage, without coming together. Well, he alone regulates them."

"That enters into mechanics, Sire; and I must confess that I am good for nothing there."

"Yes, but mathematics, — navigation?"

"Oh, Sire, those are the sciences to the study of which I have always urged Monsieur le Dauphin."

"And he is very strong in them. The other evening I heard him talking with Monsieur de la Peyrouse about stream-cables, shrouds, and brigantine sails."

"All marine terms, — yes, Sire."

"He talks navigation like Jean Bart."

"He does, indeed, know a great deal about it."

"It is you to whom he owes all this."

"Your Majesty rewards me beyond my deserts in attributing to me in the slightest degree the advantages which Monsieur le Dauphin has derived from study."

"The truth is, Duke, I think that Monsieur le Dauphin will be really a good king, a good administrator, a good family man — By the way, Monsieur le Duc," repeated the king, dwelling on these words, "will he be a good family man?"

"Indeed, Sire," replied Monsieur de la Vauguyon, innocently, "I presume that this virtue, like all the others, must be implanted in his heart."

"You do not understand me, Duke," said Louis XV.; "I ask if he will make a good family man?"

"Sire, I confess I do not understand your Majesty. In what sense do you use that term?"

"Why, in the sense, in the sense — You must have read your Bible, Monsieur le Duc?"

"Certainly, Sire. I have read it."

"Well, you know about the patriarchs, don't you?"

"Of course?"

"Will he be a good patriarch?"

Monsieur de la Vauguyon looked at the king as if he had spoken Hebrew; and twirling his hat in his hands, he replied, "Sire, a great king is all that he wishes to be."

"Pardon, Monsieur le Duc," insisted the king, "I see that we do not understand each other very well."

"Sire, I am nevertheless doing my best."

"Well," said the king, "I am going to speak more clearly. Come, you know the dauphin as if he were your own child, do you not?"

"Oh, certainly, Sire!"

"His tastes?"

"Yes."

"His passions?"

"Oh! as to passions, Sire, that is another thing; if Monseigneur had had any, I should have extirpated them radically. But I have not had that trouble, fortunately; Monseigneur has no passions."

"You said 'fortunately'?"

"Sire, is it not a good thing?"

"Then he has none?"

"Passions? No, Sire."

"Not one?"

"Not one, I assure you."

"Well, that is just what I feared. The dauphin will be a very good king, a very good administrator, but he will never be a good patriarch."

"Alas! Sire, you never told me to educate Monsieur le Dauphin for a patriarch."

"It was my mistake. I ought to have considered that he would some time marry. But although he has no passions, you do not entirely give him up?"

"I do not understand your Majesty."

"I mean that you do not consider him forever incapable of them?"

"Sire, I am afraid."

"Of what are you afraid?"

"In truth," said the poor duke, mournfully, "your Majesty tortures me."

"Monsieur de la Vauguyon," cried the king, who was becoming impatient, "I ask you plainly if, passion or no passion, Monsieur le Duc de Berry will be a good husband. I set aside the qualification of father of a family, and I abandon the patriarch."

"Well, Sire, that is something that I cannot tell your Majesty."

"What! it is something that you cannot tell me?"

"Certainly, for I do not know."

"You do not know," cried Louis XV., with an expression of astonishment which made Monsieur de la Vauguyon's wig tremble.

"Sire, Monsieur le Duc de Berry lived under your Majesty's roof in the innocence of a studious child."

"But, Monsieur, that child studies no longer; he is married."

"Sire, I was the tutor of Monseigneur — "

"Exactly, Monsieur! You should have taught him, then, all that he ought to know;" and Louis XV. threw himself back in his chair, shrugging his shoulders. "I suspected it," he added, with a sigh.

"*Mon Dieu*, Sire — "

"You know the history of France, do you not, Monsieur de la Vauguyon?"

"Sire, I have always thought so, and shall continue to think so, — at least until your Majesty has told me to the contrary."

"Well, then, you ought to know what happened to me the night of my marriage."

"No, Sire, I do not know it."

"Ah! do you know nothing?"

"If your Majesty would tell me this thing which is unknown to me?"

"Listen! and may this be a lesson to you as regards my two other grandsons."

"I listen, Sire."

"I also had been brought up as you have brought up the dauphin, under the roof of my grandfather. I had for tutor Monsieur de Villeroy, a noble man, — indeed, a *very* noble man, like you, Duke. Oh, if he had only left me oftener in the society of my uncle the regent! But no; in the innocence of study, as you call it, Duke, I neglected the study of innocence. However, I married; and when a king marries, Monsieur le Duc, it is a serious thing for the world."

"Oh, yes, Sire; I begin to understand!"

"Indeed, that is fortunate! I will go on, then. Monsieur le Cardinal examined me upon my inclinations toward the patriarchate. I had none; and was, besides, of such purity that there was danger of the kingdom of France falling into the female line. Fortunately, Monsieur le Cardinal consulted Monsieur de Richelieu; it was a delicate matter, but Monsieur de Richelieu was a master-spirit in such a case. He had a luminous idea. There was a Mlle. Lemaure, or Lemoure, who made admirable pictures; they ordered of her a series of scenes, — you understand?"

"No, Sire."

"How shall I say it? — rural scenes."

"Like the pictures of Teniers, then?"

"Better than that, — primitive."

"Primitive?"

"Natural. I think I have found the word at last; do you understand now?"

"What!" cried Monsieur de la Vauguyon, turning red, "they dared to present to your Majesty —"

"And who talks of presenting anything to me, Duke?"

"But in order that your Majesty should see —"

"It was necessary that my Majesty should look, that is all."

"Well?"

"Well, I looked."

"And — ?"

"And as man is essentially an imitator, I imitated."

"Certainly, Sire, the device was ingenious, excellent; although dangerous for a young man."

The king looked at the Duc de la Vauguyon with a smile almost cynical.

"Let us leave the danger for to-day," said he, "and consider what remains for us to do."

"Ah!"

"Do you know what it is?"

"No, Sire; and I shall be happy to be informed by your Majesty."

"Well, this is it: you will go and find Monsieur le Dauphin, who is receiving the last congratulations of the men, while Madame la Dauphine receives those of the women."

"Yes, Sire."

"Provide yourself with a candle, and take Monsieur le Dauphin aside."

"Yes, Sire."

"Show *your pupil*" — the king emphasized these words — "that his chamber is situated at the end of the new corridor."

"Of which no one has the key, Sire."

"Because I have kept it, Monsieur; I foresaw what would happen to-day. Here is the key."

Monsieur de la Vauguyon took it, trembling.

"I wish to say to you, Monsieur le Duc," continued the king, "that this gallery contains a score of pictures which I have had placed there."

"Ah, Sire, yes, yes!"

"Yes, Monsieur le Duc. Embrace your pupil, open for him the door of the corridor, put the candle in his hand wish him good-night, and say to him that he is to spend twenty minutes in going to the door of his chamber, — one minute for each picture."

"Ah, Sire, I understand!"

"That is well. I wish you good-night, Monsieur de la Vauguyon."

"Your Majesty has the goodness to pardon me?"

"Why, not too readily; for without my intervention you would have done fine things in my family."

The door closed upon the tutor. The king pulled the cord of his private bell, and Lebel appeared.

"My coffee," said the king. "By the way, Lebel."

"Sire?"

"When you have given me my coffee, follow Monsieur de la Vauguyon, who is going to pay his respects to Monsieur le Dauphin."

"I will go, Sire."

"But wait until I tell you what you are going for."

"True, Sire; but my eagerness to obey your Majesty is such —"

"Very well. Follow Monsieur de la Vauguyon."

"Yes, Sire."

"He is so troubled, so sad, that I fear the effect of his emotion on Monsieur le Dauphin."

"And what must I do, Sire, if he is affected?"

"Nothing; come and tell me, that is all."

Lebel put down the coffee before the king, who drank it slowly. Then the historical valet-de-chambre went out. A quarter of an hour after, he reappeared.

"Well, Lebel?" demanded the king.

"Sire, Monsieur de la Vauguyon was at the entrance to the new corridor, holding Monseigneur by the arm."

"Well, what then?"

"He did not seem very much affected; on the contrary, he rolled his little eyes quite briskly."

"Good! Well?"

"He took a key from his pocket, gave it to Monsieur le Dauphin, who opened the door and stepped into the corridor."

"Then?"

"Then Monsieur le Duc put his candle in the hand of

Monseigneur, and said to him in a low tone, but not too low for me to hear: 'Monseigneur, the nuptial chamber is at the end of this gallery, the key of which I have just given you. The king wishes you to spend twenty minutes in getting to the chamber.' 'What!' said the prince, 'twenty minutes? But it will take barely twenty seconds!' 'Monseigneur,' replied Monsieur le la Vauguyon, 'my authority ends here. I have no more lessons to give you, but a final piece of advice: examine carefully the opposite walls of this gallery, and I promise your Highness that you will find your twenty minutes fully employed.'"

"Not bad."

"Then, Sire, Monsieur de la Vauguyon made a low bow, and it seemed as if his piercing glances would penetrate into the corridor; then he left Monseigneur at the door."

"And Monseigneur entered, I suppose?"

"There, Sire, see the light in the gallery! It has been moving about there for at least a quarter of an hour."

"Well, it ought to disappear," said the king, after watching the window for some moments. "I had twenty minutes given me, but I remember that at the end of five I was with my wife. Alas! if only it could be said of Monsieur le Dauphin as they said of the second Racine, 'He is the grandson of his grandfather!'"

CHAPTER XX.

THE WEDDING-NIGHT.

THE dauphin opened the door of the nuptial chamber, — or rather of the antechamber adjoining it.

The archduchess, in a long white robe, lay on the gilded bed, which was hardly depressed by the light weight of her frail and delicate body. Madame de Noailles was sitting by the bed. The ladies were standing in another part of the room, waiting attentively for the lady of honor to give them the order to retire. The latter, faithful to the law of etiquette, awaited quietly the coming of the dauphin.

But as if all the laws of etiquette and of ceremonial had been forced to yield to malicious circumstance, it happened that those who were to introduce Monsieur le Dauphin into the nuptial chamber, not knowing that the king Louis XV. had arranged that his Highness should arrive by the new corridor, were awaiting him in another antechamber. The chamber which Monsieur le Dauphin had entered was empty, and the door which opened into the bed-chamber being ajar, the dauphin could see and hear what was going on there. He stood looking and listening stealthily.

The voice of Madame la Dauphine rose pure and sweet, but trembling. "Where will Monsieur le Dauphin enter?" she asked.

"By this door, Madame," said the Duchesse de Noailles; and she pointed to a door opposite the one at which Monsieur le Dauphin was standing.

"And what do we hear through that window?" added the dauphiness; "it sounds like the noise of the sea."

"It comes from the crowd of spectators who are enjoying the illumination and waiting to see the fireworks."

"The illumination?" said the dauphiness, with a sad smile. "It has been of use to-night, for the sky is very dark; have you noticed it, Madame?"

Just then the dauphin, tired of waiting, opened the door softly, and asked if he might come in. Madame de Noailles uttered a cry, for she did not recognize the prince at first. The dauphiness, made very nervous by so much excitement, seized the arm of Madame de Noailles.

"It is I, Madame," said the dauphin; "have no fear."

"Why did you come by that door?" asked Madame de Noailles.

"Because," said King Louis XV., thrusting his cynical face through the half-open door, "Monsieur de la Vauguyon, true Jesuit that he is, knows Latin, mathematics, and geography too well, and other things not well enough."

At this unexpected appearance of the king, the dauphiness slipped from her bed and stood up, her long dressing-gown covering her from head to foot as closely as the *stola* worn by Roman women.

"She is certainly thin," muttered Louis XV. "Devil take Monsieur de Choiseul, who among all the archduchesses selects for me just this one."

"Your Majesty," said Madame de Noailles, "sees that, as far as I am concerned, etiquette has been strictly observed; it is Monseigneur le Dauphin who has disregarded it."

"I take the blame upon myself, since I caused the offence, — which I hope you will pardon, my dear Madame de Noailles."

"I do not understand your Majesty."

"We will go away together, Duchess, and I will explain. Come, now, let these children go to bed."

Madame la Dauphine moved away from the bed and seized the arm of Madame de Noailles with more terror even than before. "Oh! for mercy's sake, Madame," said she, "I shall die of shame."

"Sire," said Madame de Noailles, "Madame la Dauphine begs you to let her go to bed like a woman of the people."

"The devil! Is it you who ask that, Madame Etiquette?"

"Sire, I know that it is against the law of the ceremonial of France; but look at the archduchess."

Indeed Marie Antoinette, erect, pale, clinging to the back of a chair for support, looked like a statue of Fright, except for the chattering of her teeth and the cold perspiration on her brow.

"Oh! I do not wish to annoy the dauphiness," said Louis XV., a prince as much an enemy to ceremony as Louis XIV. was its ardent supporter. "Let us retire, Duchess. Besides, there are key-holes in the doors, and that will be much more comical."

The dauphin heard these last words of his grandfather and blushed. The dauphiness heard also, but she did not understand.

The king embraced his daughter-in-law and went out, taking with him the Duchesse de Noailles, and with that mocking smile on his face, so sad for those who are not in sympathy with him who laughs. The others who were present went out by another door.

The two young people were alone. For a moment there was silence. At last the young prince approached Marie Antoinette. His heart beat violently; he felt rushing to his breast, to his temples, to the arteries of his hands, the rebellious blood of youth and love. But he felt that his grandfather was behind the door, and the thought of that cynical gaze penetrating even into the nuptial room, increased his natural timidity and awkwardness. "Madame," said he, looking at the archduchess, "are you suffering? You are pale, and you seem to tremble."

"Monsieur," said she, "I will not conceal from you that I am strangely agitated; there must be a violent storm coming. A thunder-storm has a terrible influence over me."

"Ah! you think that we are threatened with a hurricane?" said the dauphin.

"Oh, I am sure of it; see, I am trembling all over!" and it seemed as if the body of the poor princess were trembling under electric shocks.

At this moment, as if to justify her premonitions, a furious gust of wind, one of those powerful blasts which raise the waves of the sea and lay bare the mountain sides, the first onset of the approaching tempest, filled the chateau with tumult, moans, and violent creakings. Leaves torn from the branches, branches torn from the trees, statues thrown from their foundation, a long and loud clamor of the hundred thousand spectators in the gardens, a dismal and continuous roar, penetrating the galleries and corridors of the chateau, — composed at this moment the wildest and most mournful harmony ever heard by human ears.

Then a sinister rattling succeeded the roaring; it was the panes of glass, which, broken in a thousand pieces, fell upon the marble of the stairs and cornices. The wind had torn from its fastening one of the window-blinds which beat against the wall like the gigantic wing of a bird of night. Wherever in the chateau the windows were open, the lights were extinguished by this gust of wind.

The dauphin approached the window, — probably to refasten the window-blind; but the dauphiness stopped him. "Oh, Monsieur! for mercy's sake," said she, "do not open that window; our candles will go out, and I shall perish with fear."

The dauphin stopped. Through the curtain which he had drawn aside, the tops of the trees could be seen, tossed and twisted as if the arm of some invisible giant were shaking their trunks in the darkness. All the illuminations were extinguished. Then in the heavens were seen great black clouds, whirling and rolling on like a charge of cavalry.

The dauphin turned pale and remained standing, one hand resting on the casement of the window. The dauphiness fell into a chair with a sigh.

"You are afraid, Madame?" asked the dauphin.

"Oh, yes! but your presence reassures me. Oh, what a tempest! what a tempest! All the illuminations are extinguished."

"Yes," said Louis; "the wind blows south-southwest, and that is the wind which gives warning of the fiercest hurricanes. If it continues, I don't see how they can have the fireworks."

"Oh, Monsieur, there will be no one in the gardens to see them in such weather as this."

"Ah, Madame, you do not know the French people; they must have fireworks, and these will be superb, — the engineer showed me the plan of them. See, I am not mistaken; there are the first rockets."

Like long, fiery serpents, the rockets shot up toward the sky, but at the same time, as if the storm had taken these burning jets as a challenge, one single flash of lightning, which seemed to rend the heavens, wound in and out among the fireworks, mingling its bluish flame with the red fire of the rockets.

"Truly," said the archduchess, "it is wicked for man to struggle thus with God."

These preliminary rockets had preceded the firing of the other pieces but a few seconds; the engineer saw that he must make haste, and he lighted the first pieces, which were greeted with shouts of joy.

Then, as if there were really a struggle between earth and heaven; as if, as the archduchess had said, man had committed a sin against his God, — the noise of the angry storm rose above that of the people, all the windows of heaven opening at once; torrents of rain poured down from the highest clouds. The wind had extinguished the illuminations, the rain put out the fireworks.

"Ah, what a misfortune!" said the dauphin; "the fireworks are a failure."

"Yes, Monsieur," replied Marie Antoinette, sadly; "is not everything a failure since my arrival in France?"

"How is that, Madame?"

"Did you observe Versailles?"

"Certainly, Madame. Do you not like Versailles?"

"Oh, yes! I should like Versailles if it had remained as your illustrious ancestor Louis XIV. left it. But in what a condition we find Versailles! Everywhere ruin and mourning. Oh, yes! the tempest agrees well with the festival they have given me. Does not a hurricane fittingly conceal from our people the wretchedness of our palace? Is not darkness welcome to hide these paths overgrown with grass, these dirty Tritons, these empty fountains, these mutilated statues? Oh, yes, yes! blow, south wind; moan, tempest; pile up, ye clouds; hide from every eye the strange reception which France has given to a daughter of the Cæsars on the day when she places her hand in that of its future king!"

The dauphin, visibly embarrassed, for he did not know what to reply to these reproaches, could not sympathize with this exalted melancholy, so foreign to his character, and in his turn heaved a deep sigh.

"I distress you," said Marie Antoinette. "Do not think, however, that it is my pride which speaks; oh, no, no, it is not! If they had shown me only the Trianon, so smiling, so umbrageous, so flowery, — where, alas! the storm has stripped the groves and muddied the waters, — I should have been contented with that charming nest. But ruins frighten me; they are repugnant to my youth. And yet what ruins this frightful tempest still will make!"

Another blast, yet more terrible than the first, shook the palace. The princess rose, terrified. "Oh, my God!" she cried, "tell me that there is no danger, that nothing can happen! I am dying of fright!"

"There is no danger, Madame. Versailles, built in terraces, cannot draw the lightning. If it should strike anywhere, it would strike the chapel, which has a sharp roof, or the little chateau, which rises into points. You know that points attract the electric fluid, while flat masses, on the contrary, repel it."

"No," cried Marie Antoinette, "I do not know, I do not know!"

Louis took the hand of the archduchess, which was trembling and cold. At that moment a flash of lightning inundated the chamber with its livid and purple light. Marie Antoinette uttered a cry and repulsed the dauphin.

"Why Madame," he asked, "what, then, is the matter?"

"Oh!" she said, "in the light of that flash you appeared to me pale, fainting, and bloody. I seemed to see a ghost."

"That is a reflection from the burning of sulphur," said the prince; "I could explain to you —"

A tremendous clap of thunder, whose echoes rolled with a prolonged roaring till they reached their culmination, and then gradually died away in the distance, cut short the scientific explanation which the young man so coolly offered to his royal spouse. "Come, Madame," he said, after a moment of silence, "take courage, I entreat you. Let us leave these fears to the vulgar. Physical agitation is one of the conditions of nature; there is nothing in it more surprising than in a calm. Only, the calm and the commotion succeed each other; the calm is troubled by the commotion, and the commotion is stilled by the calm. After all, Madame, it is only a storm, and a storm is among the most natural and most frequent phenomena of the creation. I don't know, then, why any one should be afraid of it."

"Oh! the tempest alone perhaps would not frighten me so; but this tempest, on the very day of our marriage, — does it not seem to you a fearful omen, when taken with those that have attended me since my arrival in France?"

"What are you saying, Madame?" cried the dauphin, moved in spite of himself by a superstitious terror, — "omens, do you say?"

"Yes, yes, — fearful, bloody omens."

"And what are these omens, Madame? I am generally believed to have a steady and cool mind; perhaps I shall have the good fortune to combat and defeat these omens which terrify you."

"Monsieur, I passed my first night in France at Strasburg. I was lodged in a large chamber lighted by torches. Now, by the light of those torches I saw a wall dripping with blood. Yet I had the courage to approach the panels and examine those red stains with more attention. Those walls were hung with a tapestry representing the Massacre of the Innocents. Despair, with its hopeless look, Murder with flaming eyes, the gleam of the axe and the sword, tears, cries of 'Mother!' sighs of agony, — seemed to break forth from that prophetic wall, which by force of gazing upon it I came to regard as living. Oh! frozen with terror, I could not sleep. Tell me, was not that a gloomy omen?"

"For a woman of antiquity, perhaps, Madame; but not for a princess of our age."

"Monsieur, this age is freighted with calamities, my mother has told me, as the sky which blazes above our heads is charged with sulphur, flame, and desolation. Oh! this is why I am so afraid; this is why every omen seems to me a warning."

"Madame, no danger menaces the throne to which we ascend; we live, we kings, in a region above the clouds. The thunder is at our feet, and when it falls upon the earth it is we who launch it."

"Alas! alas! that is not what has been predicted to me, Monsieur."

"And what has been predicted to you?"

"Something frightful, unspeakable."

"Some one has predicted to you?"

"Or rather, has made me see."

"See?"

"Yes, I have seen, — seen, I tell you; and that vision has so remained with me that there is not a day on which I do not tremble with thinking of it, not a night during which I do not see it again in my dreams."

"And cannot you tell what you have seen? Are you pledged to silence?"

"No, I am pledged to nothing."

"Speak, then, Madame."

"Listen! It was a thing impossible to describe. It was a machine raised above the ground like a scaffold; but to that scaffold were fitted the two uprights of a ladder, and between those two uprights glided a knife, a chopper, an axe. I saw that, and — strange thing! — I saw also my head beneath the knife. The knife fell between the two uprights, and separated my head from my body; the head fell and rolled on the ground. That is what I saw, Monsieur, that is what I saw."

"Pure hallucination, Madame," said the dauphin. "I am somewhat acquainted with all the instruments of punishment by whose aid death is inflicted, and that instrument is not in existence. You may, then, reassure yourself."

"Alas!" said Marie Antoinette, "I cannot banish that hateful thought; I do what I can, however."

"You will succeed, Madame," said the dauphin, approaching his wife. "From this moment you have near you an affectionate friend, a devoted protector."

"Alas!" repeated Marie Antoinette, closing her eyes and falling back in her chair.

The dauphin drew still nearer to the princess, and she could feel his breath upon her cheek. At that moment the door by which the dauphin had entered was gently opened, and the curious, eager gaze of Louis XV. pierced the shades of that vast chamber, hardly lighted by the two remaining candles.

The old king opened his mouth, no doubt to utter in a suppressed tone a word of encouragement to his grandson, when a crash that cannot be described resounded through the palace, this time accompanied by the lightning flash which had preceded the previous bursts of thunder. At the same time a column of white flame, crossed with green, darted before the window, breaking all the remaining panes of glass, and crushing a statue under the balcony; then, after a fearful noise, it returned to the sky and vanished like a meteor.

The two candles were extinguished by the wind that entered the chamber. The dauphin, frightened, tottering, dazzled, recoiled till he reached the wall, and remained leaning against it. The dauphiness, almost unconscious, fell upon the steps of her *prie-Dieu* and remained shrouded in mortal terror. Louis XV., trembling, thought that the earth was about to open under his feet, and followed by Lebel, hastened back to his deserted apartments.

Meanwhile the people of Versailles and Paris fled like a flock of frightened birds, scattered over the gardens, in the roads, in the woods, pursued in all directions by thick hail, which, beating down the flowers in the gardens, the foliage in the forest, the wheat and the barley in the fields, and slates and ornaments from the buildings, added ruin to desolation.

The dauphiness, resting her forehead on her hands, sobbed and prayed. The dauphin dully contemplated the water that entered the chamber through the broken windows and reflected on the floor the lightning-flashes that continued for several hours.

By morning, however, all the tumult was calmed, and the first rays of light, darting from between copper-colored clouds, displayed to view the ravages of the nocturnal hurricane. Versailles was no longer to be recognized. The ground had imbibed that deluge of water, the trees had absorbed that deluge of fire; everywhere were seas of muddy water, and trees broken, twisted, calcined, by that serpent with flaming coils called lightning.

As soon as it was light, Louis XV., whose terror was so great that he could not sleep, ordered Lebel, who had not left him during the night, to dress him. He then proceeded to the bridal-chamber, and pushing open the door, shuddered on perceiving the future queen of France reclining on a *prie-Dieu*, pale, and with eyes swollen and violet-colored, like those of the sublime Magdalen of Rubens. Her terror, caused by the hurricane, had at length been suspended by sleep, and the first dawn of morning which stole into the apartment tinged, with religious respect, her long white robe with an azure hue. At the farther end of the chamber, in an armchair pushed back to the wall, and surrounded by a pool of water, reposed the dauphin of France, pale as his young bride, and, like her, having the perspiration of nightmare on his brow. The nuptial bed was as the king had seen it on the preceding evening.

Louis XV. knit his brow; a grief such as he had not before experienced pierced like a hot iron that heart chilled by egotism, — still cold when he sought to warm it by debauchery, He shook his head, heaved a deep sigh, and returned to his apartments, more gloomy and more affrighted, perhaps, at that moment than he had been during the night.

CHAPTER XXI.

ANDRÉE DE TAVERNEY.

On the 30th of May, — that is, on the second day after that frightful night, that night fraught, as Marie Antoinette had said, with presages and warnings, — Paris celebrated in its turn the marriage festival of its future sovereign. The whole population poured, in consequence, toward the Place Louis XV., where were to be exhibited the fireworks, — that necessary accompaniment to every great public solemnity, which the Parisian accepts scoffingly, but which he cannot dispense with. The spot was judiciously chosen. Six hundred thousand spectators could move about there at their ease. Around the equestrian statue of Louis XV. had been erected a circular scaffolding, which by raising the fireworks ten or twelve feet above the ground, enabled all the spectators in the Place to see them distinctly. The Parisians arrived, according to custom, in groups, and spent some time in choosing the best places, — an inalienable privilege of the first-comers. Boys found trees, grave men posts, women the railings of fences and temporary stands, erected in the open air, as usual at all Parisian festivities, by adventurous speculators, whose fertile imagination allows them to change their mode of speculation every day. About seven o'clock, with the earliest of the spectators, arrived several parties of police.

The duty of watching over the safety of Paris was not performed by the French Guards, to whom the city authorities would not grant the gratuity of a thousand crowns demanded by their colonel, the Maréchal Duc de Biron. That regiment was both feared and liked by the people, by whom each member of the corps was regarded at once as a Cæsar and a Maudrin.

The French Guards, terrible on the field of battle, inexorable in the fulfilment of their functions, had in time of peace and out of service a frightful reputation for brutality and misconduct. On duty they were handsome, brave intractable, and their evolutions delighted women and awed husbands; but when dispersed among the crowd as individuals, they became the terror of those whose admiration they had won the day before, and severely persecuted the people whom they would have to protect on the morrow.

Now, the city, finding in its old grudge against these night-brawlers and sharpers a reason for not giving a thousand crowns to the French Guards, sent only its civil force, upon the specious pretext that in a family festivity, like that in preparation, the usual guardians of the family ought to be sufficient. The French Guards, on leave therefore, mingled among the groups mentioned above, and, as licentious as they would under other circumstances have been severe, they produced among the crowd, in their quality of soldier-citizens, all those little irregularities which they would have repressed with the butts of their muskets, with kicks and cuffs, nay, even with taking the offenders into custody, if their commander, their Cæsar Biron, had had a right to call them on that evening soldiers.

The shrieks of the women, the grumbling of the citizens, the complaints of the hucksters, whose cakes and gingerbread were eaten without being paid for, raised a sham tumult preparatory to the real commotion which could not fail to take place when six hundred thousand sight-loving persons should be assembled on that spot, and constituted so animated a scene that the Place Louis XV., about eight o'clock in the evening, presented much the appearance of one of Teniers' pictures on a large scale, and with French instead of Dutch merry-makers.

After the *gamins*, or street-boys, of Paris (at once the most impatient and the idlest in the known world) had taken or clambered up to their places; after the citizens and the populace had settled themselves in theirs, — the carriages of the nobility and the financiers arrived. No route had been marked out for them, and they therefore entered the Place at random by the Rue de la Madeleine and the Rue St. Honoré, setting down at the new buildings those who had received invitations for the windows and balconies of the governor's house, from which an excellent view could be obtained of the fireworks.

Those of the persons in carriages who had not invitations, left their equipages at the corner of the Place, and, preceded by their footmen, mingled in the crowd, already very dense, but in which there was still room for any one who knew how to conquer it. It was curious to observe with what sagacity those lovers of sights availed themselves, in their ambitious progress, of every inequality of ground. The very wide, but as yet unfinished, street which was to be called the Rue Royale, was intersected here and there by deep ditches, on the margins of which had been heaped the mould thrown out of them and other rubbish. Each of these little eminences had its group, looking like a loftier billow rising above the level of that human ocean.

From time to time this wave, propelled by other waves behind it, toppled over, amid the laughter of the multitude, not yet so crowded as to cause such falls to be attended with danger, or to prevent those who fell from scrambling to their feet again.

About half-past eight all eyes, hitherto wandering in different directions, began to converge toward the same point, and to fix themselves on the scaffolding which contained the fireworks. It was then that elbows, plied without ceasing, began seriously to maintain positions that had been gained, against the assaults of invaders incessantly reinforced.

These fireworks, designed by Ruggieri, were intended to rival (a rivalry, by the way, which the storm two evenings before had rendered easy) those executed at Versailles by Torre, the engineer. It was known in Paris that Versailles had derived little pleasure from the royal liberality, which had granted fifty thousand francs for their exhibition, since the very first discharges had been extinguished by the rain; and as the weather was fine on the evening of May 30, the Parisians reckoned upon a certain triumph over their neighbors of Versailles. Besides, Paris expected much more from the established popularity of Ruggieri than from the recent reputation of Torre.

Moreover, the plan of Ruggieri, less capricious and less vague than that of his colleague, outlined pyrotechnical intentions of a highly distinguished order. Allegory, which reigned supreme at that period, was aided by the most graceful architectural conceptions; the scaffolding represented the ancient temple of Hymen, which, with the French, rivals in ever-springing youth the temple of Glory. It was supported by a gigantic colonnade and surrounded by a parapet, at the angles of which dolphins, open-mouthed, awaited the signal to spout forth torrents of flames. Facing the dolphins rose majestically upon their urns the Loire, the Rhone, the Seine, and the Rhine, —that river which we persist in naturalizing and accounting French, in spite of all the world, and, if we may believe the modern lays of our friends the Germans, in spite even of itself, — all four — we mean the rivers — ready to pour forth, instead of water, blue, white, green, and rose-colored flames at the moment when the colonnade should be fired. Other parts of the works, which were to be discharged at the same time, were to form gigantic vases of flowers on the terrace of the temple of Hymen. Lastly, still upon this same palace destined to support so many different things, rose a luminous pyramid, terminated by a globe representing the earth. This globe, after emitting a rumbling noise like distant thunder, was to burst with a crash and to discharge a mass of colored girandoles.

As for the bouquet, — so important and indeed indispensable an accompaniment that no Parisian ever judges of fireworks but by the bouquet, — Ruggieri had separated it from the main body of the structure. It was placed toward the river, close to the statue, in a bastion crammed with spare pieces, so that the effect would be greatly improved by this additional elevation of six or eight yards, which would place the foot of the sheaf, as it were, upon a pedestal.

Such were the details which had engrossed the attention of all Paris for the last fortnight. The Parisians now watched with great admiration Ruggieri and his assistants passing like shades amid the lurid lights of their scaffolding, and pausing, with strange gestures, to fix their matches and to secure their priming.

The moment, therefore, that the lanterns were brought upon the terrace of the building — an appearance which indicated that the discharge was about to take place — there was a strong sensation in the crowd, and some rows of the least courageous recoiled, producing a long oscillation, which extended to the very extremities of the assembled multitude.

Carriages now continued to arrive in quick succession,

and began to encroach more and more upon the Place, — the horses resting their heads upon the shoulders of the outside spectators, who began to feel uneasy at the close vicinity of these dangerous neighbors. Presently a crowd, every moment increasing, collected behind the carriages, so that it was not possible to withdraw them from their position, even had their occupants desired to do so, imbedded as they were in this compact and tumultuous throng. Then might be seen — inspired by that audacity peculiar to the Parisians when in an encroaching mood, and which has no parallel except the long-suffering of the same people when encroached upon — French Guards, artisans, and lackeys climbing upon the roofs of these carriages, like shipwrecked mariners upon a rocky shore.

The illumination of the boulevards threw from a distance its ruddy glare upon the heads of the thousands of spectators, among whom the bayonet of a city official, flashing like lightning, appeared as rare as the ears of corn left standing in a field levelled by the reaper.

On either side of the new buildings, now the Hôtel Crillon and the Garde-Meuble of the Crown, the carriages of the invited guests — in the midst of which no precaution had been taken to leave a passage — had formed a triple rank which extended on one side from the boulevard to the Tuileries, and on the other from the boulevard to the Rue des Champs Elysées, turning like a serpent thrice doubled upon itself.

Along this triple row of carriages were seen wandering, like spectres on the banks of the Styx, such of the invited as were prevented by the carriages of those earlier on the ground from reaching the principal entrance. Stunned by the noise, and unwilling, especially the ladies, who were dressed in satin from head to foot, to step upon the dusty pavement, they were hustled to and fro by the waves of the populace, who jeered at them for their delicacy, and, seeking a passage between the wheels of the carriages and the feet of the horses, crept onward as well as they could to the place of their destination, — a goal as fervently desired as a haven of refuge by mariners in a storm.

One of these carriages arrived at about nine o'clock, — that is to say, a very few minutes before the time fixed for the discharge of the fireworks, — and attempted, in its turn, to find a passage to the governor's door; but the attempt, so warmly disputed for some time back, had at this moment become extremely hazardous, if not impracticable. A fourth row of carriages had begun to form, reinforcing the first three; and the mettled horses, tormented by the crowd, had become furious, lashing out right and left upon the slightest provocation, and already causing several accidents unnoticed amid the noise and bustle of the crowd.

Clinging to the springs of this carriage, which was attempting to force its way through the concourse, walked a youth, pushing aside all comers who endeavored to avail themselves of this means of locomotion, which he appeared desirous to monopolize. When the carriage stopped, the youth stepped aside, but without loosing his hold of the protecting spring, which he continued to grasp with one hand. He could thus overhear, through the open door, the animated conversation of the party in the vehicle.

A female head, attired in white and adorned with a few natural flowers, leaned forward out of the carriage-door. Immediately a voice exclaimed: "Come, Andrée, provincial that you are, you must not lean out in that manner, or, *mordieu!* you run a great risk of being kissed by the first bumpkin that passes. Don't you see that our carriage is swimming as it were in the middle of this mob, just as if it were in the middle of the river? We are in the water, my dear, and dirty water it is; let us not soil ourselves more than is necessary."

The young lady's head was drawn back into the carriage. "We cannot see anything from here, Monsieur," said she. "If our horses were to make a half-turn, we could see from the door of the carriage, and be almost as well off as if we were at the governor's window."

"Turn about a little, coachman," cried the baron.

"It is impossible, Monsieur le Baron; I should be obliged to crush ten persons."

"Well, *pardieu!* crush away."

"Oh, Monsieur!" exclaimed Andrée.

"Oh, father!" cried Philippe.

"Who is that baron that talks of crushing poor folk?" cried several threatening voices.

"*Parbleu!* it is I," said Taverney, leaning out, and exhibiting as he did so a broad red ribbon crossed over his breast.

At that time people still paid some respect to broad ribbons, — even to red ones. There was some grumbling, but on a descending scale.

"Wait, father, I will alight," said Philippe, "and see if there is any possibility of advancing."

"Take care, brother, or you will be killed. Hark to the neighing of the horses, which are fighting with one another!"

"Say rather the roaring," resumed the baron. "Stay! we will alight. Tell them to make way, Philippe, and let us pass."

"Ah, father!" said Philippe, "you are quite a stranger to the Paris of the present day. Such lordly airs might have passed current formerly, but nowadays they are but little heeded; and you have no wish to compromise your dignity, I am sure."

"Still, when these fellows know who I am —"

"My dear father," said Philippe, smiling, "were you the dauphin himself they would not stir an inch for you. At this moment, particularly, I should fear the consequences of such a step, for I see the fireworks are about to be lighted."

"Then we shall see nothing!" said Andrée, with vexation.

"It is your own fault, *pardieu!*" replied the baron; "you were upwards of two hours at your toilet."

"Brother," said Andrée, "could I not take your arm and place myself with you among the crowd?"

"Yes, yes, my sweet lady," exclaimed several voices, touched by her beauty; "yes, come along, — you are not very large, and we'll make room for you."

"Should you like to come, Andrée?" asked Philippe.

"Oh, yes!" said Andrée; and she sprang lightly from the carriage, without touching the steps..

"Very well," said the baron; "but I, who care not a straw about fireworks, will stay where I am."

"Yes, remain here," said Philippe; "we will not go far, my dear father."

In fact the mob, ever respectful when not irritated by any passion, ever paying homage to that sovereign goddess called Beauty, opened to make way for Andrée and her brother; and a good-natured citizen, who with his family occupied a stone bench, desired his wife and daughter to make room for Andrée between them. Philippe placed himself at his sister's feet, who leaned with one hand on his shoulder. Gilbert had followed them, and was stationed about four paces off, with his eyes riveted upon Andrée.

"Are you comfortably placed, Andrée?" asked Philippe.

"Excellently," replied the young girl.

"See what it is to be beautiful!" said the viscount, smiling.

"Yes, yes, beautiful! beautiful!" murmured Gilbert.

Andrée heard those words; but as they proceeded doubtless from the lips of one of the populace, she cared no more about them than an Indian god cares for the offering which a poor pariah lays at his feet.

CHAPTER XXII.

THE FIREWORKS.

ANDRÉE and her brother had scarcely settled themselves in their new position when the first rockets pierced the clouds, and a prodigious shout arose from the crowd, thenceforward alive only to the spectacle which was exhibiting in the centre of the Place.

The opening of the exhibition was magnificent, and in every respect worthy of the high reputation of Ruggieri. The decorations of the temple were lighted up one after another, and soon presented a sheet of flame. The air rang with plaudits; but these plaudits were soon succeeded by frantic cheers when the gaping mouths of the dolphins and the urns of the rivers began to spout forth streams of fire of different colors, which crossed and intermingled with each other.

Andrée, transported with astonishment at this sight, which has not its equal in the world, — that of a population of seven hundred thousand souls frantic with delight in front of a palace in flames — did not even attempt to conceal her feelings.

Three paces distant from her, hidden by the herculean shoulders of a porter who held his child aloft over his head, stood Gilbert, gazing at Andrée for her own sake, and at the fireworks because she was looking at them. Gilbert's view of Andrée was in profile; every rocket lighted up that lovely face and made him tremble with delight. It seemed to him that the whole crowd shared in his admiration of the heavenly creature whom he adored. Andrée had never before seen Paris, or a crowd, or the splendors of a public rejoicing; and her mind was stunned by the multiplicity of novel sensations which beset it at once.

Suddenly a bright light burst forth and darted in a diagonal line toward the river. It was a bomb, which exploded with a crash, scattering the many-colored fires which Andrée admired.

"Look, Philippe; how beautiful that is!" said she.

"Good heavens!" exclaimed her brother, anxiously, without replying; "that last rocket took a wrong direction! It must have deviated from its course; instead of describing a parabola, it went almost horizontally."

Philippe had scarcely finished this expression of an uneasiness which began to be manifested in the agitation of the crowd, when a hurricane of flame burst from the bastion upon which were placed the bouquet and the spare fireworks. A crash equal to that of a hundred peals of thunder, crossing in all directions, bellowed through the Place; and as if the fire had included a discharge of grapeshot, it put to rout the nearest spectators, who for a moment felt the unexpected flame scorch their faces.

"The bouquet already? the bouquet already?" cried the more distant of the crowd. "Not yet,—it is too early!"

"Already?" repeated Andrée. "Ah, yes; it is too early!"

"No," said Philippe, "no, it is not the bouquet; it is an accident, which in a moment will agitate this prodigious crowd, now so calm, like the ocean in a storm. Come, Andrée, let us return to our carriage,—come."

"Oh! let me stay a little longer, Philippe,—it is so beautiful!"

"Andrée, we have not a moment to lose; follow me! It is the misfortune which I feared, — a stray rocket has set fire to the bastion. Hark! they are already crushing one another yonder. Don't you hear their cries? Those are not cries of joy, but shrieks of distress. Quick! quick! to the carriage. Gentlemen, gentlemen, allow us to pass!" And Philippe, throwing his arm round his sister's waist, drew her toward the place where he had left his father, who, uneasy, and dreading, from the noise which he heard, a danger, of the nature of which he could form no conception, but whose presence was obvious to him, put his head out of the carriage-door and looked about for his children.

It was already too late, and the prediction of Philippe was verified. The bouquet, composed of fifteen thousand pieces, exploded, flying in all directions, and pursuing the spectators like those fiery darts which are flung at the bulls in the arena to provoke them to fight.

The spectators, at first astonished, then terrified, recoiled by mere force of instinct with resistless impetus, communicating the same movement to myriads of spectators in the rear, who, breathless and suffocated, pressed backward in their turn on those behind them. The scaffolding took fire; children shrieked; screaming women, almost stifled, raised them in their arms; and the police, thinking to silence the screamers and to restore order by violence, struck right and left at random. All these terrors combined made the storm-tossed ocean of which Philippe had spoken fall like a water-spout on that corner of the Place where he was; and instead of rejoining the baron's carriage, as he had designed, the youth was hurried away by the mighty and irresistible current of which no description could convey any idea, — for individual strength, increased tenfold by terror and anxiety, was again augmented a hundredfold by the added force of combination.

At the moment when Philippe drew Andrée away, Gilbert had resigned himself to the movement which bore them along; but he had not gone above twenty paces before a band of fugitives, turning to the left into the Rue de la Madeleine, surrounded Gilbert and swept him away, foaming with rage on finding himself separated from Andrée.

Andrée, clinging fast to Philippe's arm, was inclosed in a group which was striving to get out of the way of a carriage dragged along by a pair of furious horses. Philippe saw it approaching swiftly and threateningly; the horses' eyes seemed to emit flame, and they snorted foam from their nostrils. He made superhuman efforts to escape them, but in vain. He saw the crowd open behind him; he perceived the foaming heads of the two ungovernable animals; he saw them rear, like the two marble horses which guard the entrance of the Tuileries; and, like the slave who is striving to subdue them, — letting go Andrée's arm, and pushing her as far as he could out of the way of danger, — he sprang up to seize the rein of the horse that was next to him. The animal reared a second time; Andrée saw her brother sink back, fall, and disappear from her sight. She shrieked, extended her arms, was hustled to and fro in the crowd, and in a moment found herself helpless, tottering, borne along like a feather by the wind, and just as incapable of resisting the force that was hurrying her away.

The stunning cries, — far more terrible than those of the battlefield, — the neighing of horses, the frightful noise of wheels, grinding now the pavement, now the bodies of the slain; the lurid flames of the scaffolds which were on fire, the sinister gleaming of swords drawn by some of the infuriated soldiers; and over all this ensanguined chaos, the bronze statue, tinged by the ruddy reflections, and seeming to preside over the carnage, — were more than was needed to disturb Andrée's reason and paralyze her strength. Besides, the power of a Titan would have been impotent in such a struggle, — a struggle for life and limb, of one against all. Andrée uttered a piercing shriek; a soldier, opening himself a passage through the crowd, was striking the people with his sword, and the weapon flashed over her head. She clasped her hands, like a shipwrecked mariner when the last wave is passing over him, and exclaiming, "Oh, my God!" sank to the ground. Whoever fell in that scene might give himself up for lost!

But that terrible, that despairing shriek was heard and answered. Gilbert, carried to a distance from Andrée, had by dint of struggling once more approached her. Bending beneath the same wave which had engulfed Andrée, he raised himself again, made a frantic leap at the sword which had unwittingly threatened her, grasped the throat of the soldier who was going to strike, and hurled him to the ground. Beside the soldier lay a female form dressed in white; he raised her up and bore her off as though he had been a giant.

When he felt that lovely form, that corpse, perhaps, pressed to his heart, a gleam of pride lighted up his countenance; his force and courage rose with the circumstances, — he felt himself a hero! He flung himself and his burden into a stream of people, whose resistless flow would certainly have levelled a wall encountered in its course. Supported by this group, which lifted him up and bore him along with his lovely burden, he walked, or rather rolled onward, for some minutes. All at once the torrent stopped, as if broken by some opposing obstacle. Gilbert's feet touched the ground, and not till then was he sensible of the weight of Andrée. He looked up, to ascertain what the obstacle might be, and perceived that he was within a few steps of the Garde-Meuble. That mass of stone had broken the mass of flesh.

During that momentary and anxious halt he had time to look at Andrée, overcome by a sleep heavy as that of death. Her heart had ceased to beat, her eyes were closed, and her face was of a violet tinge, like a white rose that is fading. Gilbert thought that she was dead. He cried out in despair, and pressed his lips to her dress, to her hand; then, emboldened by her insensibility, he covered with kisses that cold face, those eyes swollen beneath their sealed lids. He blushed, wept, raved, strove to transfuse his soul into the bosom of Andrée, feeling astonished that his kisses, which might have warmed a marble statue, had no effect upon that inanimate form. All at once Gilbert felt her heart beat under his hand. "She is saved!" he exclaimed, at the same time perceiving the swart and blood-stained mob dispersing, and hearing the imprecations, the shrieks, the sighs, the agony of the victims. "She is saved; and it is I who have saved her!"

The poor fellow, who stood leaning with his back against the wall and his eyes turned toward the bridge, had not looked to his right. In front of the carriages, which, long detained by the crowd, but now hemmed in less closely, began once more to move, and soon came on galloping as if coachman and horses had been seized with a general frenzy, fled twenty thousand unfortunate creatures, mutilated, wounded, bruised one against the other. Instinctively they fled close to the walls, against which the nearest of them were crushed. This mass swept away, or suffocated, all those who, having taken up their position near the Garde-Meuble, imagined that they had escaped the wreck. Another shower of blows, of living and dead bodies, rained on Gilbert. He found one of the recesses formed by the iron gates, and stationed himself there. The weight of the fugitives made the wall crack.

Gilbert, nearly stifled, perceived that he was near losing his hold; but with a last desperate effort, mustering all his strength, he encompassed Andrée's body with his arms, resting his head on the bosom of the young girl. One would have supposed that he meant to suffocate her whom he was protecting.

"Farewell," murmured he, biting, rather than kissing, her dress, "farewell!" And he raised his eyes to heaven, as if directing a last supplicating glance to it for assistance. Then a strange sight met his eyes.

Mounted on a post, holding with his right hand by a ring let into the wall, while with his left hand he seemed to be rallying an army of fugitives, was a man who, looking at the furious sea raging at his feet, sometimes dropped a word, sometimes made a gesture. At that word, at that gesture, some individual among the crowd might be seen to pause, struggle, and by a violent effort strive to reach the man. Others who had already reached him seemed to recognize the new-comers as brothers, and assisted to drag them out of the crowd, raising, supporting, and drawing them toward themselves. In this manner, by acting together, this knot had, like the pier of a bridge which divides and resists the water, succeeded in dividing the crowd and holding in check the flying masses.

Every moment fresh stragglers, seeming to rise out of the ground at those strange words and singular gestures, swelled the retinue of this man. Gilbert raised himself by a last effort; he felt that *there* was safety, for *there* was calmness and power. A last dying gleam from the burning scaffold, leaping up only to expire, fell upon his face. Gilbert uttered a cry of amazement. "Oh, let me die!"

he murmured; "let me die, but she must live! That man can save her." Then, with a sublime forgetfulness of self, raising the young girl in both his arms, he exclaimed, " Baron de Balsamo, save Mademoiselle Andrée de Taverney!"

Balsamo heard that voice which cried to him, like that in the Bible, from the depths; he beheld a white figure raised above the devouring waves. He leaped from his post to the ground, crying, "This way!" His party overturned all that obstructed their course, and seizing Andrée, still supported in Gilbert's sinking arms, he lifted her up, and, impelled by a movement of that crowd which he had ceased to repress, he bore her off without once turning to look behind.

Gilbert endeavored to utter a last word. Perhaps, after imploring the protection of this strange man for Andrée, he might have solicited it for himself; but he had only strength to press his lips to the drooping arm of the young girl, and to snatch, with a wild and despairing grasp, a portion of her dress. After that last kiss, after that final farewell, the young man had nothing left to live for; he made no further struggle, but closing his eyes, sank dying upon a heap of dead.

CHAPTER XXIII.

THE FIELD OF THE DEAD.

GREAT storms are always succeeded by calms, fearful in their very stillness, but healing in their effects.

It was about two o'clock in the morning. The moon, shining through large white clouds which hovered over Paris, showed in strong relief by her wan and sickly light the inequalities of this sad spot, and the pits and holes in which so many of the fleeing crowd had found an untimely grave.

Here and there in the moonlight, which was obscured from time to time by the large white floating clouds we have mentioned, might be seen on the margin of the slopes and in the ditches heaps of corpses with disordered attire, stiffened limbs, livid and discolored faces, and hands stretched out in an attitude of terror or of prayer.

In the centre of the Place a heavy, tainted smoke, emitted from the burning embers of the timber, contributed to give to the Place Louis XV. the appearance of a battlefield.

Over this bloody and desolate plain flitted, with rapid and mysterious steps, shadowy figures, who stopped, looked stealthily round, bent down, and then fled. They were the robbers of the slain, attracted to their prey like vultures to the decaying carrion. They had not been able to rob the living, and they came to despoil the dead. Surprised at seeing themselves anticipated by their fellow-robbers, they might be seen escaping sullenly and fearfully at the sight of the tardy bayonets which menaced them.

But the robber and the lazy watchman were not the only persons moving among the long ranks of the dead. There were some there who, furnished with lanterns, might have been taken for curious lookers-on. Sad lookers-on, alas! for they were parents and anxious friends, whose children, brothers, friends, or lovers had not returned home. They had come from great distances, for the dreadful news had already spread over Paris like a hurricane, scattering dismay and horror, and their anxiety had quickly led them into active search. It was a sight perhaps more dreadful to behold than the catastrophe itself. Every expression was portrayed on these pale faces, from the despair of those who discovered the corpse of the beloved one, to the gloomy uncertainty of those who had found nothing, and who cast an anxious and longing glance toward the river which flowed onward with a monotonous murmur. It was reported that many corpses had already been thrown into the river by the provostry of Paris, who wished to conceal the fearful number of deaths their guilty imprudence had occasioned.

Then, when they had satiated their eyes with this fruitless spectacle, and, standing ankle deep in the Seine, had watched with anguished hearts its dark waters flow past unburdened with the loved bodies of those whom they sought, they proceeded, lantern in hand, to explore the neighboring streets, where it was said many of the wounded had dragged themselves, to seek for help, or at least to flee from the scene of their sufferings.

When unfortunately they found among the dead the object of their search — the lost and wept-for friend — then cries succeeded to their heart-rending surprise, and their sobs, rising from some new point of the bloody scene, were responded to by other sobs.

At times the Place resounded with sudden noises. A lantern would fall and be broken; the living had fallen senseless on the dead, to embrace him for the last time.

There are yet other noises in this vast cemetery. Sometimes one of the wounded, whose limbs have been broken by the fall, whose breast has been pierced by the sword, or crushed by the weight of the crowd, utters a hoarse cry, or groans forth a prayer; and then those who hope to find in the sufferer a friend hastily approach, but retire when they do not recognize him.

In the mean time, at the extremity of the Place, near the garden, a field-hospital is formed by the kindness and charity of the people. A young surgeon, known as such by the profusion of instruments which surround him, has the wounded men and women brought to him; he bandages their wounds, and while he tends them, he speaks to them in words which express hatred for the cause rather than pity for the effect. To his two robust assistants, who pass the sufferers in bloody review before him, he cries repeatedly: "The women of the people, the men of the people, first! They can be easily recognized; they are almost always more severely wounded, certainly always less richly dressed."

At these words, repeated after each dressing with a shrill monotony, a young man who, torch in hand, is seeking among the dead, has twice already raised his head. From a large wound which furrows his forehead a few drops of crimson blood are falling. One of his arms is supported by his coat, which he has buttoned over it; and his countenance, covered with perspiration, betrays deep and absorbing emotion. At these words of the surgeon, which he has heard, as we have said, for the second time, he raises his head, and looking sadly on the mutilated limbs which the operator seems almost to gloat over: "Oh, Monsieur," said he, "why do you make a choice among the victims?"

"Because," replied the surgeon, raising his head at this interruption, "because no one will care for the poor if I do not think of them, and the rich are always well looked after. Lower your lantern, and search upon the ground: you will find a hundred poor people for one rich or noble. In this catastrophe, with a good fortune which will in the end weary even Providence, the noble and the rich have paid only the tribute they generally pay,—one in a thousand."

The young man raised his torch to a level with his bleeding forehead. "Then I am that one," said he, without anger, — "I, a gentleman, lost among so many others in the crowd, wounded in the forehead by a horse's hoof, and my left arm broken by falling into a pit. You say that the noble and the rich are sought after and cared for; you see plainly, however, that my wounds are not yet dressed."

"You have your hôtel, your physician. Return home, since you can walk."

"I do not ask for your care, Monsieur; I seek my sister, a beautiful young girl of sixteen, — killed probably, alas! though she is not of the people. She wore a white dress, and a chain with a cross round her neck. Though she has her hôtel and her physician, answer me, for pity's sake, Monsieur, have you seen her whom I seek?"

"Monsieur," said the young surgeon, with a feverish vehemence which showed that the ideas he expressed had long boiled within his breast, "Monsieur, humanity is my guide. It is to her service I devote myself; and when I leave the noble on their bed of death to assist the suffering people, I obey the true laws of humanity, who is my goddess. All this day's misfortunes have been caused by you. They arose from your abuses, from your usurpations. Therefore, bear the consequences. No, Monsieur, I have not seen your sister."

And after this harsh apostrophe, the operator returned to his task. A poor woman had just been brought to him, whose two legs had been fractured by a carriage.

"See!" he exclaimed, calling after Philippe, who was rushing away, "see, do the poor bring their carriages to the public festivals to break the legs of the rich?"

Philippe, who belonged to that class of the young nobility from which sprang the Lafayettes and Lameths, had often professed the same maxims which terrified him in the mouth of this young man, and their application recoiled upon him like a judgment. His heart bursting with grief, he left the neighborhood of the hospital and continued his sad search. He had not proceeded many steps when, carried away by his grief, he could not repress a heart-rending cry of, "Andrée! Andrée!"

At that moment there passed by him, walking with hasty steps, a man already advanced in years, wearing a gray cloth coat and milled stockings, his right hand resting on a stick, while with the left he held one of those lanterns made of a candle enclosed in oiled paper. Hearing Philippe's cry of grief, he understood his suffering, and murmured: "Poor young man!" But as the young man seemed to have come for the same purpose as himself, he passed on. Then suddenly, as if he reproached himself for having passed unheeding by so much suffering without attempting to console it, "Monsieur," said he, "pardon me for mingling my grief with yours; but those who are struck by the same blow should lean on one another for support. Besides, you may be useful to me. You have already sought for a considerable time, I see, as your light is nearly extinguished, and you must therefore be acquainted with the most fatal localities of the Place."

"Oh, yes, Monsieur, I know them!"

"Well, I also seek some one."

"Then look first in the great ditch; you will find more than fifty corpses there."

"Fifty! Just Heaven! So many victims killed at a fête!"

"So many! Monsieur, I have already looked at a thousand faces, and have not yet found my sister."

"Your sister?"

"It was yonder, in that direction, that she was. I lost her near a bench. I have found the place since, but no trace of her was visible. I am about to resume the search, beginning with the bastion."

"In what direction did the crowd move, Monsieur?"

"Toward the new buildings; toward the Rue de la Madeleine."

"Then it must have been in this direction?"

"Yes, and I therefore searched on this side first; but there were terrible eddies. Besides, although the tide flowed as I have said, a poor bewildered woman soon loses her senses in such a scene; she knows not whither she goes, and endeavors to escape in any direction."

"Monsieur, it is not probable that she would struggle against the current. I am about to search the streets on this side; come with me, and both working together, perhaps we shall succeed."

"And whom do you seek? Your son?" asked Philippe, timidly.

"No, Monsieur, but a child whom I had almost adopted."

"And you allowed him to come alone?"

"Oh! he is a young man eighteen or nineteen years old. He is master of his own actions; and as he wished to come, I could not hinder him. Besides, we were far from expecting this horrible catastrophe! But your light is going out."

"Yes, Monsieur."

"Come with me; I will light you."

"Thank you, you are very good; but I fear I shall incommode you."

"Oh! do not fear, since I must search at any rate. The poor child generally came home very punctually," continued the old man, proceeding in the direction of the streets; "but this evening I felt a sort of foreboding. I waited for him; it was already eleven o'clock when my wife heard of the misfortunes of this fête from a neighbor. I waited two hours longer, still hoping that he would return. Then, as he did not appear, I thought it would be base and cowardly in me to sleep without having news of him."

"Then we are going toward the houses?" asked the young man.

"Yes; you said the crowd must have rushed in this direction, and it certainly has done so. The unfortunate boy had doubtless been carried this way also! He is from the provinces, and is alike ignorant of the usages and of the localities of this great town. Probably this was the first time he had ever been in the Place Louis XV."

"Alas! my sister also is from the provinces, Monsieur."

"What a fearful sight!" said the old man, turning away from a group of corpses heaped together.

"Yet it is there we must look," replied the young man, resolutely holding his light over the mound of dead bodies.

"Oh! I shudder to look at it, for, simple man that I

am, the sight of destruction causes in me an unconquerable horror."

"I had the same horror; but this evening I have served my apprenticeship! Hold, here is a young man of about eighteen years; he has been suffocated, for I see no wounds. Is it he whom you seek?"

The old man made an effort, and held his lantern close to the body. "No, Monsieur," said he, "no; my child is younger, has black hair and a pale complexion."

"Alas! all are pale to-night," replied Philippe.

"Oh! see," said the old man, "here we are, at the foot of the Garde-Meuble. Look at these tokens of the struggle. This blood upon the walls, these shreds of garments upon the iron bars, these torn dresses on the points of the railing!"

"It was here; it was certainly here," murmured Philippe.

"What sufferings!"

"Ah! my God!"

"What?"

"Something white under these corpses! My sister wore a white dress. Lend me your lamp, Monsieur, I beseech you."

In fact, Philippe had seen and snatched a shred of white cloth. He let go his hold, having but one hand, to take the lamp.

"It is a fragment of a woman's dress, held firmly in a young man's hand," he cried, — "of a white dress like my sister's. Oh! Andrée! Andrée!" And the young man uttered heart-rending sobs.

The old man now approached. "It is he!" he exclaimed, opening his arms.

This exclamation attracted the young man's attention. "Gilbert!" exclaimed Philippe in his turn.

"You know Gilbert, Monsieur?"

"Is it Gilbert whom you seek?"

These two questions were uttered simultaneously. The old man seized Gilbert's hand, — it was as cold as death. Philippe opened the young man's coat, pushed aside the shirt, and placed his hand upon his heart. "Poor Gilbert!" said he.

"My dear child!" sobbed the old man.

"He breathes, he lives! He lives, I tell you!" exclaimed Philippe.

"Oh! do you think so?"

"I am certain of it; his heart beats."

"It is true," replied the old man. "Help! help! There is a surgeon yonder."

"Oh! let us succor him ourselves, Monsieur; just now I asked that man for help, and he refused me."

"He must help my child!" cried the old man, indignantly. "Assist me, Monsieur, to carry Gilbert to him."

"I have only one arm, but it is at your service, Monsieur," replied Philippe.

"And I, old as I am, feel strong again! Come!"

The old man seized Gilbert by the shoulders; the young man took his two feet under his right arm, and in this manner they advanced toward the group in the midst of which the surgeon was operating.

"Help, help!" cried the old man.

"The men of the people first!" replied the surgeon, faithful to his maxim, and sure, each time he replied thus, of exciting a murmur of applause among the group which surrounded him.

"It is a man of the people whom I am bringing," replied the old man with vehemence, but beginning to share in the general admiration which the firm and resolute tone of the young operator excited.

"After the women, then," said the surgeon; "men have more strength to support pain than women."

"A simple bleeding will suffice, Monsieur," replied the old man.

"Oh! is it you again, my young nobleman?" said the surgeon, perceiving Philippe before noticing the old man.

Philippe did not reply. The old man thought that these words were addressed to him. "I am not a nobleman," said he, "I am a man of the people; my name is Jean-Jacques Rousseau."

The doctor gave a cry of astonishment, and making an imperative gesture, "Give place," said he, "to the man of nature! Make room for the emancipator of the human race! Place for the citizen of Geneva!"

"Thanks, Monsieur," said Rousseau, "thanks!"

"Has any accident happened to you?" asked the young doctor.

"Not to me, but to this poor child. See!"

"Ah! you too," cried the physician, "you too, like myself, represent the cause of humanity."

Rousseau, deeply moved by this unexpected triumph, could only stammer forth some almost unintelligible words. Philippe, dumb with astonishment at finding himself in the presence of the philosopher whom he admired so highly, remained standing apart. Those who stood around assisted Rousseau to lay the unconscious Gilbert upon the table.

It was at this moment that the old man glanced at the person whose assistance he was imploring. He was a young man of about Gilbert's age, but his features presented no appearance of youth. His sallow complexion was withered, like that of an old man; his heavy and drooping eyelids covered an eye like a serpent's, and his mouth was distorted like that of an epileptic in a fit.

His sleeves turned back to the elbow, his arms covered with blood, surrounded by lifeless and bleeding limbs, he seemed more like an executioner at work, and glorying in his task, than a physician accomplishing his sad and holy mission.

Nevertheless, Rousseau's name had so much influence over him as to cause him to lay aside for an instant his customary rudeness; he gently opened Gilbert's sleeve, tied a band of linen round his arm, and opened the vein. The blood flowed at first drop by drop; but after some moments the pure and generous current of youth spouted forth freely.

"Ha! we shall save him," said the operator. "But he will require great care; his chest has been rudely pressed."

"I have now to thank you, Monsieur," said Rousseau, "and praise you, not for the exclusive preference you show for the poor, but for your care and kindness toward them. All men are brothers."

"Even the noble, even the aristocrats, even the rich?" asked the surgeon, his piercing eyes flashing beneath his heavy eyelids.

"Even the noble, the aristocrats, the rich, when they suffer," said Rousseau.

"Monsieur," said the operator, "excuse me. I am from Baudry, near Neufchâtel; I am a Switzer like yourself, and therefore somewhat democratic."

"A countryman," cried Rousseau, "a native of Switzerland? Your name, Monsieur, if you please?"

"An obscure name, Monsieur, — the name of a retiring man who devotes his life to study, waiting till he may, like yourself, devote it to the good of humanity. My name is Jean-Paul Marat."

"Thanks, Monsieur Marat," said Rousseau. "But while enlightening the people as to their rights, do not excite them to vengeance; for if they should ever revenge themselves, you will perhaps yourself be terrified at their reprisals."

Marat smiled a fearful smile. "Oh! if that day should happen during my life!" said he; "if I could only have the happiness to see that day!"

Rousseau heard these words, and alarmed at the tone in which they were uttered, as a traveller trembles at the first mutterings of the far-distant thunder, he took Gilbert in his arms and attempted to carry him away.

"Two volunteers to help Monsieur Rousseau! Two men of the people!" cried the surgeon.

"Here! here! here!" cried twenty voices at once.

Rousseau had only to choose; he selected two vigorous porters, who took the youth up in their arms. As he was leaving the Place, he passed Philippe. "Here, Monsieur," said he, "I have no more use for the lantern; take it."

"Thank you, Monsieur," said Philippe; "thank you." He seized the lantern; and while Rousseau once more took the way to the Rue Plastrière, he continued his search.

"Poor young man!" murmured Rousseau, turning back, and seeing Philippe disappear in the blocked-up and encumbered streets. He proceeded on his way shuddering, for he still heard the shrill voice of the surgeon echoing over the field of blood, and crying: "The men of the people! None but the men of the people! Woe to the noble, to the rich, to the aristocrats!"

CHAPTER XXIV.

THE RETURN.

WHILE the countless catastrophes we have mentioned were rapidly succeeding each other, Monsieur de Taverney escaped all these dangers as if by a miracle. Unable to oppose any physical resistance to the devouring force which swept away everything in its passage, but at the same time calm and collected, he had succeeded in maintaining his position in the centre of a group which was rolling onward toward the Rue de la Madeleine. This group, crushed against the parapet walls of the Place, ground against the angles of the Garde-Meuble, had left on either side a long trail of wounded and dead; but, decimated as it was, it had yet succeeded in reaching a place of safety. When this was accomplished, the handful of men and women remaining, dispersed themselves over the boulevards with cries of joy. Monsieur de Taverney found himself, like his companions, completely out of danger.

What we are about to say would be difficult to believe, had we not already so frankly sketched the character of the baron. During the whole of this fearful passage, Monsieur de Taverney — may God forgive him! — had absolutely thought only of himself. Besides that he was not of a very affectionate disposition, he was a man of action; and in the great crises of life such characters always put into practice Cæsar's maxim, "Age quod agis." We shall not say, therefore, that Monsieur de Taverney was utterly selfish; we shall merely admit that he was absent-minded. But once upon the pavement of the boulevards, once more master of his actions, sensible of having escaped from death to life, satisfied, in short, of his safety, the baron uttered a loud cry of satisfaction, which was followed by another cry. That other cry was not so loud as the first, but it was a cry of grief. "My daughter!" said he, "my daughter!" and he remained motionless, his hands fell by his side, his eyes were fixed and glassy, while he searched his memory for all the particulars of that separation.

"Poor dear man!" murmured some compassionate women.

A group had collected around the baron, ready to pity, but above all to question. But Monsieur de Taverney had no popular instincts; he felt ill at ease in the centre of this compassionate group, and making a successful effort, he broke through them, and, we say it to his praise, made a few steps toward the Place Louis XV. But these few steps were the unreflecting movement of paternal love, which is never entirely extinguished in the heart of man. Reason immediately came to the baron's aid and arrested his steps.

We will follow, with the reader's permission, the course of the baron's reasoning. First, the impossibility of returning to the Place Louis XV. occurred to him. In it there was only confusion and death, and the crowds which were still rushing from it would render any attempt to pass through them as futile as for the swimmer to seek to ascend the Fall of the Rhine at Schaffhausen. Besides, even if the divine arm should enable him to reach the Place, how could he hope to find one woman among a hundred thousand women? And why should he expose himself again, and fruitlessly, to a death from which he had so miraculously escaped?

Then came hope, — that light which ever gilds the clouds of the darkest night. Was not Andrée near Philippe, resting on his arm, protected by his manly strength and his brotherly heart? That he, the baron, a feeble and tottering old man, should have been carried away, was very natural; but that Philippe, with his ardent, vigorous, hopeful nature, — Philippe, with his arm of iron, — Philippe, responsible for his sister's safety, should be so, was impossible. Philippe had struggled, and must have conquered.

The baron, like all selfish men, endowed Philippe with those qualities which his selfishness denied to himself, but which nevertheless he sought in others, — strength, generosity, and valor. For one selfish man regards all other selfish men as rivals and enemies, who rob him of those advantages which he believes he has the right to reap from society.

Monsieur de Taverney, being thus reassured by the force of his own arguments, concluded that Philippe, naturally, must have saved his sister; that he had perhaps lost some time in seeking his father to save him also, but that probably, nay certainly, he had taken the way to the Rue Coq-Héron, to bring back Andrée, who must be somewhat dazed by all that tumult. He therefore wheeled round, and descending the Rue des Capucines, he gained the Place des Conquêtes, or Louis le Grand, now called the Place des Victoires.

But scarcely had the baron arrived within twenty paces of the hôtel, when Nicole, placed as sentinel on the threshold, where she was chattering with some companions, exclaimed: "And Monsieur Philippe? and Mademoiselle Andrée? What has become of them?" For all Paris was already informed by the earliest fugitives of the catastrophe, which their terror had even exaggerated.

"Oh, heavens!" cried the baron, a little agitated, "have they not returned, Nicole?"

"No, no, Monsieur, they have not been seen."

"They most probably have been obliged to make a détour," replied the baron, trembling more and more in proportion as the calculations of his logic were demolished; and he remained standing in the street, waiting in his turn, with Nicole, who was sobbing, and La Brie who raised his clasped hands to heaven.

"Ah, here is Monsieur Philippe!" exclaimed Nicole, in a tone of indescribable terror, for Philippe was alone.

And in the darkness of the night Philippe was seen running toward them, breathless and despairing. "Is my sister here?" he cried, while yet at a distance, as soon as he could see the group assembled at the door of the hôtel.

"Oh, my God!" exclaimed the baron, pale and trembling.

"Andrée! Andrée!" cried the young man, approaching nearer and nearer, "where is Andrée?"

"We have not seen her; she is not here, Monsieur Philippe. Oh, heavens! my dear young lady!" cried Nicole, bursting into tears.

"And yet you have returned?" said the baron, in a tone of anger, which must seem to the reader the more unjust that we have already made him acquainted with the secrets of his logic.

Philippe, instead of replying, approached and showed his bleeding face and his arm, broken and hanging at his side like a withered branch.

"Alas! alas!" sighed the old man, "Andrée! my poor Andrée!" and he sank back upon the stone bench beside the door.

"I will find her, living or dead!" exclaimed Philippe,

gloomily. And he again started off with feverish activity. Without slackening his pace, he secured his left arm in the opening of his vest, for this useless limb would have fettered his movements in the crowd, and if he had had a hatchet at that moment, he would have struck it off. It was then that he met on that fatal field of the dead, Rousseau, Gilbert, and the fierce and gloomy operator, who, covered with blood, seemed rather an infernal demon presiding over the massacre than a beneficent genius appearing to succor and to help. During a great portion of the night Philippe wandered over the Place Louis XV., unable to tear himself away from the walls of the Garde-Meuble, near which Gilbert had been found, and incessantly gazing at the piece of white muslin which the young man had held firmly grasped in his hand.

But when the first light of day appeared, worn-out, ready to sink among the heaps of corpses scarcely paler than himself, seized with a strange giddiness, and hoping, as his father had hoped, that Andrée might have returned or been carried back to the house, Philippe bent his steps once more toward the Rue Coq-Héron. While still at a distance he saw the same group he had left there; and understanding at once that Andrée had not returned, he stopped. The baron, on his side, had recognized his son.

"Well?" he cried.

"What! has my sister not returned?" asked the young man.

"Alas!" cried, with one voice, the baron, Nicole, and La Brie.

"Nothing, — no news; no information; no hope?"

"Nothing?"

Philippe fell upon the stone bench of the hôtel; the baron uttered a savage exclamation.

At this very moment a carriage appeared at the end of

the street; it approached slowly, and stopped in front of the hôtel. A woman's head was seen through the door, leaning over, as if she had fainted. Philippe, roused by this sight, hastened toward the vehicle. The door of the coach opened, and a man alighted, bearing the senseless form of Andrée in his arms.

"Dead, dead! They bring us her corpse!" cried Philippe, falling on his knees.

"Dead!" stammered the baron, "oh, Monsieur, is she indeed dead?"

"I think not, gentlemen," calmly replied the man who carried Andrée. "Mademoiselle de Taverney, I hope, is only in a swoon."

"Oh, the sorcerer, the sorcerer!" cried the baron.

"The Comte de Balsamo!" murmured Philippe.

"Myself, Monsieur, and truly happy in having recognized Mademoiselle de Taverney in the frightful mêlée."

"Where were you, Monsieur?" asked Philippe.

"Near the Garde-Meuble."

"Yes," said Philippe. Then his expression of joy changing suddenly to one of gloomy distrust, "You bring her back very late, Count," said he.

"Monsieur," replied Balsamo, without embarrassment, "you may easily comprehend the difficulties of my situation. I did not know your sister's address, and I had no resource but to take her to the Marquise de Savigny's, a friend of mine who lives near the royal stables. Then this honest fellow whom you see, and who assisted me to rescue the young lady — Come hither, Comtois." Balsamo accompanied these last words by a sign, and a man in the royal livery alighted from the coach. "Then," continued Balsamo, "this worthy fellow, who belongs to the royal stables, recognized the young lady, having one evening driven her from Muette to your hôtel. Mademoiselle owes this lucky recognition to her marvellous beauty. I made him accompany me in the coach, and I have the honor to restore Mademoiselle de Taverney to you with all the respect due to her, and less injured than you think;" and as he concluded, he gave the young girl into the care of her father and Nicole.

For the first time the baron felt a tear trembling on his eyelids; and though no doubt inwardly surprised at this mark of feeling, he permitted it to roll unheeded down his wrinkled cheeks. Philippe held out to Balsamo his only free hand. "Monsieur," he said, "you know my name and my address. Give me an opportunity of showing my gratitude for the service you have rendered us."

"I have only fulfilled a duty," replied Balsamo. "Do I not owe you hospitality?" And bowing low, he made a few steps to retire, without replying to the baron's invitation to enter. But returning, — "Pardon me," said he, "but I omitted to give you the exact address of the Marquise de Savigny. She lives in the Rue St. Honoré, near the Feuillants. I thought it necessary to give you this information, in case Mademoiselle de Taverney should think proper to call on her."

There was in this precision of details, in this accumulation of proofs, a delicacy which touched Philippe deeply, and affected even the baron.

"Monsieur," said the baron, "my daughter owes her life to you."

"I know it, Monsieur, and I feel proud and happy at the thought," replied Balsamo; and this time, followed by Comtois, who refused Philippe's proffered purse, he entered the carriage, which drove off rapidly.

Almost at the same moment, and as if Balsamo's departure had put an end to her swoon, Andrée opened her eyes; but she remained for some moments mute, bewildered, and with a wild and staring look.

"Oh, heavens!" murmured Philippe, "has Providence only half restored her to us? Has her reason fled?"

Andrée seemed to comprehend these words, and shook her head; but she remained silent, and as if under the influence of a sort of ecstasy. She was still standing, and one of her arms was extended in the direction of the street by which Balsamo had disappeared.

"Come, come!" said the baron, "it is time to put an end to all this. Assist Andrée into the house, Philippe."

The young man supported Andrée with his uninjured arm, Nicole sustained her on the other side; and walking on, but after the manner of a sleeping person, she entered the hôtel and gained her apartments. There, for the first time, the power of speech returned.

"Philippe! My father!" said she.

"She recognizes us! she knows us again!" exclaimed Philippe.

"Of course I know you again; but, O heavens! what has happened?" And Andrée closed her eyes, not now in a swoon, but in a calm and peaceful slumber. Nicole, left alone with her young mistress, undressed her and put her in bed.

When Philippe returned to his apartments he found there a physician, whom the thoughtful La Brie had run to summon as soon as the anxiety on Andrée's account had subsided. The doctor examined Philippe's arm. It was not broken, but only dislocated; and a skilful compression replaced the shoulder in the socket from which it had been moved. After the operation Philippe, who was still uneasy on his sister's account, conducted the doctor to her bedside. The doctor felt her pulse, listened to her breathing, and smiled. "Your sister sleeps as calmly as an infant," said he. "Let her sleep, Chevalier; there is nothing to do."

As for the baron, sufficiently reassured on his children's account, he had long been sound asleep.

CHAPTER XXV.

MONSIEUR DE JUSSIEU.

WE must again transport the reader to the house in the Rue Plastrière to which Monsieur de Sartines had sent his agent; and there on the morning of the 31st of May we shall once more find Gilbert, stretched upon a mattress in Thérèse's room, and standing around him Thérèse and Rousseau, with several of their neighbors, contemplating this single result of the terrible event, at the horror of which all Paris still shuddered.

Gilbert, pale and bleeding, opened his eyes; and as soon as he regained his consciousness, he endeavored to raise himself, and looked round as if he were still in the Place Louis XV. A profound anxiety, then a great joy were pictured in his features; then came a second cloud, effacing the joy.

"Are you suffering, my dear child?" inquired Rousseau, taking his hand affectionately.

"Oh! who, then, has saved me?" asked Gilbert. "Who thought of me, lonely and friendless that I am?"

"What saved you, my child, was the happy chance that you were not yet dead. He who thought of you is He who thinks of all."

"No matter; it was very imprudent," grumbled Thérèse, "to go into such a crowd."

"Yes, yes, it was very imprudent," repeated all the neighbors, with one voice.

"Why, ladies," interrupted Rousseau, "there is no imprudence when there is no manifest danger; and there is no manifest danger in going to see fireworks. When danger arrives under such circumstances, you do not call the sufferer imprudent, but unfortunate. Any of us present would have done the same."

Gilbert looked round, and seeing himself in Rousseau's apartment, endeavored to speak; but the effort was too much for him, the blood gushed from his mouth and nostrils, and he sank back insensible. Rousseau had been warned by the surgeon of the Place Louis XV., and was therefore not alarmed. He had expected that result, and had placed the invalid on a temporary mattress without sheets. "Now," said he to Thérèse, "you will be able to put the poor lad to bed."

"Where?"

"Why, here, in my bed."

Gilbert heard these words. Extreme weakness alone prevented his replying immediately; but he made a violent effort, and opening his eyes he said, slowly and painfully, "No, no; upstairs."

"You wish to return to your own room?"

"Yes, yes, if you please;" and he expressed with his eyes, rather than with his tongue, this wish, dictated by a recollection still more powerful than pain, and which with him seemed to survive even his consciousness.

Rousseau, whose own sensibility was so extreme, doubtless understood him, for he added: "It is well, my child; we will carry you up. He does not wish to inconvenience us," said he to Thérèse, who had warmly applauded the resolution. It was therefore decided that Gilbert should be instantly installed in the attic he preferred.

Toward the middle of the day Rousseau came to pass by the bedside of his disciple the hours he usually spent in collecting his favorite plants; and the young man, feeling a little better, related to him, in a low and almost inaudible voice, the details of the catastrophe. But he did not mention the real reason why he went to see the fireworks. Curiosity alone, he said, led him to the Place Louis XV. Rousseau could not suspect anything further, unless he had been a sorcerer, and he therefore expressed no surprise at Gilbert's story, but contented himself with the questions he had already put, and only recommended patience. He did not speak of the fragment of muslin which had been found in Gilbert's hand, and of which Philippe had taken possession. This conversation, which on both sides bordered so narrowly on the real feelings of each, was no less attractive on that account; and they were still deeply absorbed in it, when suddenly Thérèse's step was heard upon the landing.

"Jacques!" said she; "Jacques!"

"Well, what is it?"

"Some prince coming to visit me in my turn," said Gilbert, with a feeble smile.

"Jacques!" cried Thérèse, advancing and still calling.

"Well! What do you want with me?"

Thérèse entered. "Monsieur de Jussieu is below," said she; "he heard that you were in the crowd during that night, and he has come to see if you have been hurt."

"The good Jussieu!" said Rousseau. "Excellent man, like all those who, from taste or from necessity, commune with Nature, the source of all good. Be calm; do not move, Gilbert; I will return."

"Yes, thank you," said the young man.

Rousseau left the room; but scarcely had he gone, when Gilbert, raising himself as well as he could, dragged himself toward the skylight from which Andrée's window could be seen. It was a most painful effort for a young man without strength, almost without the power of thought, to raise himself upon the stool, lift the sash of the skylight, and prop himself upon the edge of the roof. Gilbert nevertheless succeeded in effecting this; but once there, his eyes swam, his hand shook, the blood rushed to his head, and he fell heavily upon the floor. At that moment the door of the garret was opened, and Rousseau entered, followed by Jussieu, to whom he was paying great civility.

"Take care, my dear philosopher; stoop a little here," said Rousseau. "There is a step there, — we are not entering a palace."

"Thank you; I have good eyes and stout limbs," replied the learned botanist.

"Here is some one come to visit you, my little Gilbert," said Rousseau, looking toward the bed. "Oh, good heavens! where is he? He has got up, the unfortunate lad!" and Rousseau, seeing the window open, began to vent his displeasure in affectionate grumblings.

Gilbert raised himself with difficulty, and said, in an almost inaudible voice, "I wanted air."

It was impossible to scold him, for suffering was plainly depicted in his pale and altered features.

"In fact," interrupted Monsieur de Jussieu, "it is very warm here. Come, young man, let me feel your pulse; I am also a doctor."

"And better than many regular physicians," said Rousseau; "for you are a healer of the mind as well as of the body."

"It is too much honor," murmured Gilbert, feebly, endeavoring to shroud himself from view on his humble pallet.

"Monsieur de Jussieu insisted on visiting you," said Rousseau, "and I accepted his offer. Well, dear Doctor, what do you think of his chest?"

The skilful anatomist felt the bones, and sounded the cavity by an attentive auscultation. "The vital parts are uninjured," said he. "But who has pressed you in his arms with so much force?"

"Alas! Monsieur, it was Death!" said Gilbert.

Rousseau looked at the young man with astonishment.

"Oh! you are bruised, my child, greatly bruised," said Monsieur de Jussieu; "but tonics, air, leisure, will make all that disappear."

"No leisure; I cannot afford it," said the young man, looking at Rousseau.

"What does he mean?" asked Jussieu.

"Gilbert is a determined worker, my dear Monsieur," replied Rousseau.

"That may be; but he cannot possibly work for a day or two yet."

"To obtain a livelihood," said Gilbert, "one must work every day; for every day one eats."

"Oh! you will not consume much food, and your medicine will not cost much."

"However little they cost, Monsieur," said Gilbert, "I never receive alms."

"You are mad," said Rousseau, "and you exaggerate. I tell you that you must be governed by Monsieur de Jussieu's orders, who will be your doctor in spite of you. Would you believe it?" continued he, addressing Monsieur de Jussieu, "he had begged me not to send for a physician."

"Why?"

"Because it would have cost me money, and he is proud."

"But," replied Monsieur de Jussieu, gazing at Gilbert's fine, expressive features with growing interest, "no matter how proud he is, he cannot accomplish impossibilities.

Do you think yourself capable of working, when you fell down with the mere exertion of going to the window?"

"It is true," sighed Gilbert, "I am weak; I know it."

"Well, then, take repose, and, above all, mentally. You are the guest of a man whom all men obey, except his guest."

Rousseau, delighted at this delicate compliment from so great a man, took his hand and pressed it.

"And then," continued Monsieur de Jussieu, "you will become an object of particular care to the king and the princes."

"I!" exclaimed Gilbert.

"You, a poor victim of that unfortunate evening. The dauphin, when he heard the news, uttered cries of grief; and the dauphiness, who was going to Marly, remained at Trianon to be nearer the unfortunate sufferers."

"Ah, really?" said Rousseau.

"Yes, my dear philosopher; and nothing is spoken of but the letter written by the dauphin to Monsieur de Sartines."

"I have not heard of it."

"It is at once simple and touching. The dauphin receives a monthly pension of two thousand crowns. This morning his month's income had not been paid. The prince walked to and fro quite alarmed, asked for the treasurer several times, and as soon as the latter brought him the money, sent it instantly to Paris with two charming lines to Monsieur de Sartines, who has just shown them to me."

"Ah! then you have seen Monsieur de Sartines today?" said Rousseau, with a kind of uneasiness, or rather distrust.

"Yes; I have just left him," replied Monsieur de Jussieu, rather embarrassed. "I had to ask him for some seeds. So that," added he, quickly, "the dauphiness remained at Versailles to tend her sick and wounded."

"Her sick and wounded?" asked Rousseau.

"Yes; Monsieur Gilbert is not the only one who has suffered. This time the people have contributed only a portion of the victims of the catastrophe; it is said that there are among the wounded many belonging to noble families."

Gilbert listened with inexpressible eagerness and anxiety. It seemed to him that every moment the name of Andrée would be pronounced by the illustrious naturalist. Monsieur de Jussieu rose.

"So our consultation is over?" said Rousseau.

"And henceforward our science will be useless with regard to this young invalid; air, moderate exercise, the woods— Ah! by the by, I was forgetting—"

"What?"

"Next Sunday I am to make a botanical excursion to the forest of Marly; will you accompany me, my illustrious colleague?"

"Oh!" replied Rousseau, "say rather your unworthy admirer."

"*Parbleu!* that will be a fine opportunity for giving our invalid an airing. Bring him."

"So far?"

"The distance is nothing; besides, I shall go in my carriage as far as Bougival, and I can take you with me. We will go by the Princess's Road to Luciennes, and from there proceed to Marly. Botanists stop every moment; our invalid will carry our camp-stools. You and I will gather samples; he will gather health."

"What an amiable man you are, my dear Jussieu!" said Rousseau.

"Never mind; it is for my own interest. You have

in hand, I know, a great work upon mosses, and I am feeling my way a little on the same subject; you will guide me."

"Oh!" exclaimed Rousseau, whose satisfaction was apparent in spite of himself.

"And when there," added the botanist, "we will have a little breakfast in the open air, and will enjoy the shade and the beautiful flowers. It is settled?"

"Oh, certainly!"

"For Sunday, then?"

"Delightful! It seems to me as if I were fifteen again. I revel beforehand in all the pleasure I have in prospect," replied Rousseau, with almost childish satisfaction.

"And you, my young friend, must get stronger on your legs in the mean time."

Gilbert stammered out some words of thanks, which Monsieur de Jussieu did not hear, and the two botanists left Gilbert alone with his thoughts, and especially with his fears.

CHAPTER XXVI.

LIFE RETURNS.

In the mean time, while Rousseau believed his invalid to be on the highroad to health, and while Thérèse informed all her neighbors that, thanks to the prescriptions of the learned doctor, Monsieur de Jussieu, Gilbert was entirely out of danger, — during this period of general confidence the young man ran into a worse danger than he had yet encountered through his obstinacy and his perpetual reveries.

Rousseau could not be so confident but that he entertained in his inmost thoughts a distrust solidly founded on philosophical reasonings. Knowing Gilbert to be in love, and having caught him in open rebellion to medical authority, he judged that he would again commit the same faults if he gave him too much liberty. Therefore, like a good father, he had locked the door of Gilbert's attic more carefully than ever, tacitly permitting him meanwhile to go to the window, but carefully preventing his crossing the threshold.

It may easily be imagined what rage this solicitude, which changed his garret into a prison, aroused in Gilbert's breast, and what hosts of projects crowded his teeming brain. To many minds constraint is fruitful in inventions. Gilbert now thought only of Andrée, of the happiness of seeing and watching over the progress of her convalescence, even from afar. But Andrée did not appear at the windows of the pavilion, and Gilbert, when he fixed his ardent and searching looks on the opposite apartments, or surveyed every nook and corner of the building, could see only Nicole carrying the invalid's draught on a porcelain plate, or Monsieur de Taverney walking in the garden and vigorously taking snuff, as if to clear and refresh his intellect. Still these details tranquillized him, for they betokened illness, but not death.

"There," thought he, "beyond that door, behind that blind, breathes, sighs, and suffers, she whom I adore, whom I idolize, — she, the very sight of whom would cause the perspiration to stand upon my forehead and make my limbs tremble; she to whose existence mine is forever riveted; she for whom alone I breathe and live!"

And then, leaning forward out of his window, — so that the inquisitive Chon thought, twenty times in an hour, that he would throw himself out, — Gilbert, with his practised eye, took the measure of the partitions, of the floors, of the depth of the pavilion, and constructed an exact plan of them in his brain. There Monsieur de Taverney slept; there must be the kitchen; there Philippe's apartments; there the cabinet occupied by Nicole; and, last of all, there must be Andrée's chamber, — the sanctuary at the door of which he would have given his life to remain for one day kneeling.

This sanctuary, according to Gilbert's plan, was a large apartment on the ground-floor, guarded by an antechamber, from which opened a small cabinet with a glass door, which should be Nicole's sleeping-chamber.

"Oh!" exclaimed the excited youth, in his fits of jealous fury, "how happy are the beings who are privileged to walk in the garden on which my window and that of the stairway look! How happy those thoughtless mortals who tread the gravel of the parterre! For there, during the silence of night, may be heard Mademoiselle Andrée's plaints and sighs."

Between the formation of a wish and its accomplishment there is a wide gulf; but fertile imaginations can throw a bridge across. They can find the real in the impossible; they know how to cross the broadest rivers and scale the highest mountains.

For the first few days Gilbert contented himself with wishing. Then he reflected that these much-envied, happy beings were simple mortals, endowed, as he was, with limbs to tread the soil of the garden, and with arms to open the doors. Then by degrees he pictured to himself the happiness there would be in secretly gliding into this forbidden house, — in pressing his ears against the Venetian blinds, through which the sounds from the interior were, as it were, filtered. With Gilbert, wishing did not long suffice; the fulfilment must be immediate.

Besides, his strength returned rapidly: youth is fruitful and rich. At the end of three days, his veins still throbbing with feverish excitement, Gilbert felt himself as strong as he had ever been in his life. He calculated that as Rousseau had locked him in, one of the greatest difficulties — that of obtaining an entrance into the hôtel of the Taverneys by the street-door — was placed out of the question; for as the entrance door opened upon the Rue Coq-Héron, and as Gilbert was locked up in the Rue Plastrière, he could not of course reach any street, and had therefore no need to open any doors. There remained the windows. That of his garret looked down upon a perpendicular wall of forty-eight feet in height. No one, unless he were drunk or mad, would attempt to descend it. "Oh! those doors are happy inventions after all," thought he, clenching his hands; "and yet Monsieur Rousseau, a philosopher, locks them!"

To break the padlock! That would be easily done; but when done, adieu to the hospitable roof which had sheltered him.

To escape from Luciennes, from the Rue Plastrière, from Taverney, — always to escape, — would be to render himself unable to look any one in the face without fearing to meet the reproach of ingratitude.

"No!" thought Gilbert, "Monsieur Rousseau shall know nothing of it." Leaning out of his window, he continued: "With my hands and my legs, those instruments granted to free men by Nature, I will creep along the tiles, and, keeping in the gutter — which is narrow indeed, but straight, and therefore the direct road from one end to the other — I shall arrive, if I get on so far, at the skylight parallel to this. Now, that skylight belongs to the stairs. If I do not arrive, I shall fall into the garden; that will make a noise, — people will hasten from the pavilion, will raise me up, will recognize me, and I shall die nobly, poetically, pitied! That will be glorious!

"If I arrive, as everything leads me to believe I shall, I will creep in through the skylight over the stairs, and descend bare-footed to the first story, the window of which also opens in the garden, at fifteen feet from the ground. I jump. Alas, my strength, my activity are gone! It is true that there is a trellis to assist me. Yes, but this trellis, with its rotten framework, will break; I shall tumble down, not killed nobly and poetically, but whitened with plaster, my clothes torn, ashamed, and looking as if I had come to rob the orchard! Odious thought! Monsieur de Taverney will order the porter to flog me, or La Brie to pull my ears.

"No! I have here twenty strings, which, twisted together, will make a rope, according to Monsieur Rousseau's saying, that many straws make a sheaf. I will borrow all these strings from Madame Thérèse for one night; I will make knots in them; and when I have reached the window on the first-floor, I will tie the rope to the little balcony, or even to the lead, and slip down into the garden."

When Gilbert had inspected the spout, separated and measured the cords, and calculated the height by his eye, he felt himself strong and determined. He twisted the pieces of twine together and made a tolerably strong rope of them, then tried its strength by hanging to a beam in his garret, and, happy to find that he had spat blood only once during his efforts, he decided upon undertaking the nocturnal expedition.

The better to hoodwink Monsieur Jacques and Thérèse, he counterfeited illness, and kept his bed until two o'clock, at which time Rousseau went out for his after-dinner walk, from which he usually did not return till the evening. When Rousseau paid a visit to his attic before setting out, Gilbert announced to him his wish to sleep until the next morning; to which Rousseau replied that as he had made an engagement to take supper away from home that evening, he was happy to find Gilbert inclined to rest. With these mutual explanations they separated.

When Rousseau had gone, Gilbert brought out his cords again, and this time he twisted them permanently. He again examined the spout and the tiles; then placed himself at the window to keep watch on the garden until evening.

CHAPTER XXVII.

THE AERIAL JOURNEY.

GILBERT was now prepared for his entrance into the enemy's camp, — for thus he mentally termed Monsieur de Taverney's grounds, — and from his window was exploring the garden with the care and attention of a skilful strategist who is about to give battle, when in that calm and silent mansion an incident occurred which attracted the philosopher's attention.

A stone flew over the garden wall and struck at an angle at the side of the house. Gilbert, who had already learned that there can be no effect without a cause, determined, having seen the effect, to discover the cause. But although he leaned out as far as possible, he could not discover the person in the street who had thrown the stone. However, he immediately comprehended that this manœuvre had reference to an event which just then took place, — one of the outside shutters of the ground-floor opened cautiously, and through the opening appeared Nicole's head.

On seeing Nicole, Gilbert made a plunge back into his garret, but without losing sight of the alert young girl. The latter, after throwing a stealthy glance at all the windows, particularly at those of the pavilion, emerged from her hiding-place and ran toward the garden, as if going to the trellis where some lace was drying in the sun. It was on the path which led toward the trellis that the stone had fallen, and neither Nicole nor Gilbert lost sight of it.

Gilbert saw her kick this stone — which for the moment became of such great importance — before her several times; and she continued this manœuvre until she reached the flower-border in which the trellis stood. Once there, Nicole raised her hands to take down the lace, let fall some of it, and in picking it up again seized the stone.

As yet Gilbert could understand nothing of this movement; but seeing Nicole pick up the stone as a greedy school-boy picks up a nut, and unroll a slip of paper which was tied round it, he at once guessed the degree of importance which was attached to this aerolite. It was, in fact, neither more nor less than a note which Nicole had found rolled round the stone. The cunning girl quickly unfolded it, read it, and put it into her pocket, and then immediately discovered that there was no more occasion for looking at the lace; it was dry.

Meanwhile Gilbert shook his head, saying to himself, with the blind selfishness of men who entertain a bad opinion of women, that Nicole was in reality a viciously inclined person, and that he (Gilbert) had performed an act of sound and moral policy in breaking off so suddenly and so boldly with a girl who had letters thrown to her over the wall. In reasoning thus, Gilbert, who had just before pondered so wisely on causes and effects, condemned an effect of which perhaps he was the cause.

Nicole ran back to the house, and soon reappeared, this time with her hand in her pocket. She drew from it a key, which Gilbert saw glitter in her hand for a moment; and then the young girl slipped this key under a little door which served to admit the gardener, and which was situated at the end of the wall opposite the street, and parallel to the great door which was generally used.

"Good!" said Gilbert; "I understand, — a love-letter

and a rendezvous. Nicole loses no time; she has already a new lover." And he frowned with the disappointment of a man who thinks that his loss should cause an irreparable void in the heart of the woman he abandons, and who to his great astonishment finds this void completely filled. "This may spoil all my projects," he continued, seeking a factitious cause for his ill-humor. "No matter," he resumed, after a moment's silence, "I shall not be sorry to know the happy mortal who succeeds me in Mademoiselle Nicole's good graces."

But Gilbert on certain subjects had a very discerning judgment. He calculated that the discovery which he had made, and which Nicole was far from suspecting, would give him an advantage over her which might be of use to him, since he knew her secret, with such details as she could not deny, while she scarcely suspected his; and even if she did, there existed no facts which could give a color to her suspicions. He promised himself, therefore, to take advantage of the discovery whenever he should find occasion.

During all these goings and comings, the anxiously expected night had come on. The only thing which Gilbert now feared was the return of Rousseau, who might surprise him on the roof or on the staircase, or might come up and find his room empty. In the latter case the anger of the philosopher of Geneva would be terrible; but Gilbert hoped to avert the blow by means of the following note, which he left upon his little table, addressed to the philosopher: —

MY DEAR AND ILLUSTRIOUS PROTECTOR, — Do not think ill of me if, notwithstanding your recommendations, and even against your order, I have dared to leave my apartment. I shall soon return, unless some accident, similar to that which has already happened to me, should again take place; but at the risk of a similar, or even a worse, accident, I must leave my room for two hours.

"I do not know what I shall say when I return," thought Gilbert; "but at least Monsieur Rousseau will not be uneasy or angry."

The evening was dark. A suffocating heat prevailed, as it often does during the first warm days of spring. The sky was cloudy, and at half-past eight the most practised eye could have distinguished nothing at the bottom of the dark gulf into which Gilbert peered.

It was then, for the first time, that the young man perceived that he breathed with difficulty, and that sudden perspirations bedewed his forehead and breast, — unmistakable signs of a weak and unhinged system. Prudence counselled him not to undertake, in his present condition, an expedition for which strength and steadiness in all his members were peculiarly necessary, not only to ensure success, but even for the preservation of his life; but Gilbert did not listen to what his physical instincts counselled. His moral will spoke more loudly; and to it, as ever, the young man vowed obedience.

The moment had come. Gilbert rolled his rope several times round his neck, and began, with beating heart, to scale the skylight; then, firmly grasping the casement, he made the first step in the gutter toward the skylight on the right, which was, as we have said, that of the stairway, and about four yards distant from his own.

His feet in a groove of lead, at the utmost only eight inches wide, which, though it was supported here and there by holdfasts of iron, yet, owing to the pliability of the lead, yielded to his steps; his hands resting against the tiles, which could be only a point of support for his equilibrium, but no help in case of falling, since the fingers could take no hold of them, — such was Gilbert's position during this aerial passage, which lasted two minutes; that is to say, two eternities.

But Gilbert determined not to be afraid; and such was the power of will in this young man that he was not afraid. He recollected to have heard a rope-dancer say, that to walk safely on narrow ways one ought never to look downward, but about ten feet in advance, and never think of the abyss beneath but as an eagle might, — that is, with the conviction of being able to float over it at pleasure. Besides, Gilbert had already put these precepts in practice in several visits he had paid to Nicole, — that Nicole who was now so bold that she could find her profit in keys and doors instead of in roofs and chimneys.

In this manner he had often traversed the sluices of the mill at Taverney, and the naked beams of the roof of an old barn. He arrived, therefore, at the goal without a shudder; and once arrived there, he glided through the skylight, and with a thrill of joy alighted on the staircase. But on reaching the landing-place he stopped short. Voices were heard on the lower stories: they were those of Thérèse and certain neighbors of hers, who were speaking of Rousseau's genius, of the merit of his books, and of the harmony of his music.

The neighbors had read "La Nouvelle Héloïse," and confessed frankly that they found the book improper. In reply to this criticism Madame Thérèse observed that they did not understand the philosophical part of that excellent book. To this the neighbors had nothing to reply, except to confess their incompetence to give an opinion on such a subject.

This edifying conversation was held from one landing-place to another; and the fire of discussion, ardent as it was, was less so than that of the stoves on which the savory suppers of these ladies were cooking. Gilbert was listening to the arguments, therefore, and enjoying the smell of the viands, when his name, pronounced in the midst of the tumult, caused him to start rather unpleasantly.

"After my supper," said Thérèse, "I must go and see if that dear child does not want something in his attic."

This "dear child" gave Gilbert less pleasure than the promise of the visit gave him alarm. Luckily, he remembered that Thérèse, when she supped alone, chatted a long time with her bottle, that the meat seemed savory, and that "after supper" meant — ten o'clock. It was now only quarter of nine. Besides, it was probable that after supper the course of ideas in Thérèse's brain would take a change, and that she would then think of anything else rather than of the "dear child."

But time was slipping by, to the great vexation of Gilbert, when suddenly one of the joints of meat pertaining to the coterie began to burn. The cry of the alarmed cook was heard, which put an end to all conversation, for every one hurried to the theatre of the catastrophe.

Gilbert profited by this culinary panic among the ladies to glide down the stairs like a shadow. Arrived at the first story, he found that the window-frame was sufficiently strong to hold his rope, and attaching it by a slip-knot, he mounted the window-sill and began to descend. He was still suspended between the window and the ground, when a rapid step sounded in the garden beneath him. He had sufficient time, before the step reached him, to turn himself round, and holding fast by the knots, he watched to see who this untimely visitor was.

The intruder was a man, and as he proceeded from the direction of the little door, Gilbert did not doubt for a moment that it was the happy mortal whom Nicole was expecting. He fixed all his attention therefore upon this other invader, who had thus arrested him in the midst of his perilous descent. By his walk, by a glance at his profile, seen beneath his three-cornered hat, and by the particular mode in which this hat was placed over the corner of his attentive ear, Gilbert thought he recognized the famous Beausire, that officer whose acquaintance Nicole had made in Taverney.

Almost immediately Gilbert saw Nicole open the door of the pavilion, hasten into the garden, leaving the door open, and light and active as a bird, direct her steps toward the greenhouse, — that is to say, the place toward which Monsieur Beausire was already advancing. This was most certainly not their first rendezvous, since neither one nor the other betrayed the least hesitation as to the place of meeting.

"Now I can finish my descent," thought Gilbert; "for if Nicole has appointed this hour for meeting her lover, it must be because she is certain of being undisturbed. Andrée must be alone, then, — alone!"

In fact, no noise was heard in the house, and only a faint light gleamed from the windows of the ground-floor. Gilbert alighted upon the ground without any accident, and, unwilling to cross the garden, he glided gently along the wall till he came to a clump of trees, crossed it in a stooping posture, and without being seen, arrived at the door which Nicole had left open. There, sheltered by an immense aristolochia, which was trained over the door and hung down in large festoons, he observed that the outer apartment, which was a spacious antechamber, was, as he had supposed, entirely empty. This antechamber communicated with the interior of the house by means of two doors, one open, the other closed. Gilbert conjectured that the open door was that belonging to Nicole's chamber. He softly entered this room, stretching out his hands before him for fear of accident, for the room was entirely without light; but at the end of a sort of corridor was seen a glass door whose framework was clearly designed against the light of the adjoining apartment. On the inner side of this glass door was drawn a muslin curtain.

As Gilbert advanced along the corridor he heard a feeble voice speaking in the lighted apartment; it was Andrée's, and every drop of Gilbert's blood rushed to his heart. Another voice replied to hers; it was Philippe's. The young man was anxiously inquiring after his sister's health.

Gilbert, now on his guard, proceeded a few steps farther, and placed himself behind one of those truncated columns, surmounted by a bust, which at that period formed the usual ornament of double doors. Thus concealed, he strained his eyes and ears to the utmost stretch, — so happy that his heart melted with joy, so fearful that the same heart shrank together till it seemed to become only a minute point in his breast. He listened and gazed.

CHAPTER XXVIII.

BROTHER AND SISTER.

GILBERT, as we have said, gazed and listened. He saw Andrée stretched on a reclining-chair, her face turned toward the glass door, that is to say, directly toward him. This door was slightly ajar.

A small lamp with a deep shade was placed upon an adjoining table covered with books, indicating the only species of recreation permitted to the invalid, and lighted only the lower part of Mademoiselle de Taverney's face. Sometimes, however, when she leaned back, so as to rest against the pillow of the lounge, the light overspread her marble forehead, which was veiled in a lace cap. Philippe was sitting on the end of the lounge with his back toward Gilbert; his arm was still in a sling, and all exercise of it was forbidden.

It was the first time that Andrée had been up, and the first time also that Philippe had left his room. Therefore they had not seen each other since that terrible night; but each knew that the other was recovering, and hastening toward convalescence. They had been together only for a few moments, and were conversing without restraint; for they supposed that even if any one should interrupt them, they would be warned by the noise of the bell attached to the door which Nicole had left open. Gilbert saw and heard all, therefore; for through this open door he could seize every word of their conversation.

"So now," Philippe was saying, just as Gilbert took his place behind a curtain hung loosely before the door of a dressing-room,— "so now you breathe more easily, my poor sister?"

"Yes, more easily, but still with a slight pain."

"And your strength?"

"Returns but slowly; nevertheless, I have been able to walk to the window two or three times to-day. How sweet the fresh air is, how lovely the flowers! It seems to me that, surrounded with air and flowers, it is impossible to die."

"But still you are very weak, are you not, Andrée?"

"Oh yes, the shock was terrible! I walk with difficulty, and am obliged to lean on the tables and the projecting points of the wainscoting. Without this support my limbs bend under me, and I feel as if I should every moment fall."

"Courage, Andrée! The fresh air and the beautiful flowers you spoke of just now will cure you, and in a week you will be able to pay a visit to the dauphiness, who, I am informed, so kindly sends to inquire about you."

"Yes, I hope so, Philippe; for the dauphiness in truth seems very good to me." And Andrée, leaning back, put her hand upon her chest and closed her lovely eyes. Gilbert made a step forward with outstretched arms.

"You are in pain, my sister?" asked Philippe, taking her hand.

"Yes, at times I have slight spasms, and sometimes the blood mounts to my head, and my temples throb; sometimes again I feel quite giddy, and my heart sinks within me."

"Oh!" said Philippe, thoughtfully, "that is not surprising; you have met with a dreadful trial, and your escape was almost miraculous."

"Miraculous is in truth the proper term, brother."

"But speaking of your miraculous escape, Andrée," said Philippe, approaching closer to his sister, to give more emphasis to the question, "do you know I have never yet had an opportunity of speaking to you of this catastrophe?"

Andrée blushed and seemed uneasy; but Philippe did not remark this change of color, or at least did not appear to remark it.

"I thought, however," said the young girl, "that the person who restored me to you gave all the explanations you could wish; my father, at least, told me he was quite satisfied."

"Of course, my dear Andrée; and this man, so far as I could judge, behaved with extreme delicacy in the whole affair; but still some parts of his tale seemed to me, not suspicious, indeed, but — obscure; that is the proper term."

"How so, and what do you mean, brother?" asked Andrée, with the frankness of innocence.

"For instance," said Philippe, "there is one point which did not at first strike me, but which has since seemed to me to bear a very strange aspect."

"What is that?" asked Andrée.

"Why, the very manner in which you were saved. Can you describe it to me?"

The young girl seemed to make an effort over herself. "Oh! Philippe," said she, "I have almost forgotten, I was in such terror."

"No matter, my dear Andrée; tell me all you remember."

"Well, you know, brother, we were separated at about twenty paces from the Garde-Meuble. I saw you dragged away toward the garden of the Tuileries, while I was drawn toward the Rue Royale. For an instant I could still see you making fruitless attempts to rejoin me. I stretched out my arms toward you, crying, Philippe! Philippe! when all at once I was, as it were, seized by a whirlwind, which raised me aloft and bore me in the direction of the railings. I felt the living tide carrying me toward the wall against which it would break; I heard the cries of those who were crushed against the railings; I understood that my turn would come to be crushed and killed; I could almost calculate the number of seconds I had yet to live, when, half-dead and almost frantic, raising my hands and eyes to heaven in a last prayer, I met the burning glance of a man who seemed to govern the crowd, and whom the crowd seemed to obey."

"And this man was the Comte Joseph Balsamo?"

"Yes; he whom I had already seen at Taverney; he who, even there, had inspired me with such a strange terror; he, in short, who seems to be endowed with some supernatural power, who has fascinated my sight with his eyes, my ears with his voice, who has made my whole being tremble by the mere touch of his finger on my shoulder."

"Proceed, proceed, Andrée," said Philippe, his features and voice becoming gloomier as she spoke.

"Well, this man seemed to tower aloft above the catastrophe, as if human suffering could not reach him. I read in his eyes that he wished to save me,— that he had the power to do so. Then something extraordinary took place within me. Bruised, powerless, half-dead as I was, I felt myself raised toward this man as if some unknown, mysterious, invincible power lifted me up to him. I felt as if some strong arm, by a mighty effort, was drawing me out of the gulf of mangled flesh in which so many unhappy victims were suffocating, and was restoring me to air, to life. Oh, Philippe!" continued Andrée, with a sort of exaltation, "I feel certain it was that man's look which attracted me to him. I reached his hand; I was saved!"

"Alas!" murmured Gilbert, "she had eyes only for him; and I — I — who was dying at her feet — she did not see me." He wiped his brow, bathed in perspiration.

"That is how the affair happened, then?" asked Philippe.

"Yes; up to the moment when I felt myself out of danger. Then, whether all my force had been exhausted in the last effort I had made, or whether the terror I had experienced had exceeded the measure of my strength, I do not know, but I fainted."

"And at what time do you think you fainted?"

"About ten minutes after we were separated, brother."

"Yes," pursued Philippe, "that was about midnight. How then did it happen that you did not return till three o'clock? Forgive me this catechizing, which may seem ridiculous to you, dear Andrée, but I have a good reason for it."

"Thanks, Philippe!" said Andrée, pressing her brother's hand. "Three days ago I could not have replied to you as I have now done; but to-day — what I am saying may seem strange to you — my mental vision is stronger; it seems to me as if some will stronger than my own ordered me to remember, and I do remember."

"Speak, then, speak, dear Andrée; I am waiting impatiently. Did this man carry you away in his arms?"

"In his arms?" said Andrée, blushing; "I do not well recollect. All I know is, that he drew me out of the crowd. But the touch of his hand caused me the same feeling as at Taverney, and scarcely had he touched me when I fainted again, or rather, I sank to sleep; for fainting is generally preceded by a painful feeling, and on this occasion I felt only the pleasing sensation attendant on sleep."

"In truth, Andrée, what you tell me seems so strange that if any other related these things I should not believe them. But proceed," continued he, in a voice which betrayed more emotion than he was willing to show. As for Gilbert, he devoured Andrée's every word, for he knew that, so far at least, every word was true.

"When I regained my consciousness," continued the young girl, "I was in a splendidly furnished saloon. A waiting-maid and a lady were standing beside me; but they did not seem at all uneasy, for when I awoke they were smiling kindly."

"Do you know at what time this was, Andrée?"

"The half-hour after midnight was just striking."

"Oh!" said the young man, breathing freely, "that is well. Go on, Andrée; go on."

"I thanked the ladies for the attentions they lavished on me; but knowing how uneasy you would be, I begged them to send me home immediately. Then they told me that the count had returned to the scene of the catastrophe to assist the wounded, but that he would return with a carriage and convey me himself to our hôtel. In fact, at about two o'clock I heard a carriage roll along the street; then the same sensation which I had formerly felt on the approach of that man overpowered me; I fell back trembling and almost senseless upon a sofa. The door opened. In the midst of my confusion I could still recognize the man who had saved me; then for a second time I lost all consciousness. They must then have carried me down, placed me in the carriage, and brought me here. That is all I can remember, brother."

Philippe calculated the time, and saw that his sister must have been brought directly from the Rue des

Écuries-du-Louvre to the Rue Coq-Héron, as she had been from the Place Louis XV. to the Rue des Écuries-du-Louvre; and, joyfully pressing her hand, he said in a frank, cheerful voice : " Thanks, my dear sister, thanks; all the calculations correspond exactly. I will call upon the Marquise de Savigny and thank her in person. In the mean time one word more upon a subject of secondary importance."

" Speak."

" Do you remember seeing among the crowd any face which you knew?"

" No, none."

" The little Gilbert's, for example?"

" In fact," said Andrée, endeavoring to recall her thoughts, " I do remember to have seen him. At the moment when we were separated, he was about ten paces from me."

" She saw me!" murmured Gilbert.

" Because, while searching for you, Andrée, I found the poor lad."

" Among the dead?" asked Andrée, with that peculiar shade of interest which the great testify for their dependents.

" No, he was only wounded; he was rescued, and I hope he will recover."

" Oh! I am glad to hear it," said Andrée; " and what injury had he received?"

" His chest was greatly bruised."

" Yes, yes, against thine, Andrée!" murmured Gilbert.

"But," continued Philippe, " the strangest circumstance of all, and the one which induced me to speak of the lad, was that I found in his hand, clenched and stiffened by pain, a fragment of your dress."

" That is strange indeed."

"Did you not see him at the last moment?"

"At the last moment, Philippe, I saw so many faces frightful through terror, pain, selfishness, love, pity, avarice, and indifference that I seem to have spent a year in hell. Among all these faces, which had the effect upon me of a procession of the damned passing in review before me, it may be that I saw the good little fellow, but I cannot recall him."

"And yet the piece of stuff torn from your dress?— and it was your dress, Andrée, for Nicole has identified it."

"Did you tell the girl for what purpose you questioned her?" asked Andrée; for she remembered the singular explanation she had had at Taverney with her waiting-maid in relation to this same Gilbert.

"Oh, no! But the fragment was in his hand. How can you explain that?"

"Oh! very easily," said Andrée, with a calmness which contrasted strangely with the fearful beating of Gilbert's heart; "if he was near me when I felt myself raised aloft, as it were, by this man's look, he probably clung to me to profit by the help I was receiving, in the same manner as a drowning man clings to the belt of the swimmer."

"Oh!" said Gilbert, with a feeling of angry contempt at this idea of the young girl, "oh, what an ignoble interpretation of my devotion! How these nobles judge us sons of the people! Monsieur Rousseau is right,—we are worth more than they; our hearts are purer, and our arms stronger."

As he once more settled himself to listen to the conversation of the brother and sister, which he had for a moment lost during this soliloquy, he heard a noise behind him. "My God!" he murmured, "some one in the ante-room!" And hearing the step approach the corridor, he drew back into the dressing-room, letting the curtain fall before him.

"Well! Is that madcap Nicole not here?" said the Baron de Taverney's voice as he entered his daughter's apartment, touching Gilbert with the flaps of his coat as he passed.

"I daresay she is in the garden," said Andrée, with a tranquillity which showed that she had no suspicion of the presence of a third person; "good evening, father."

Philippe rose respectfully; the baron motioned him to remain where he was, and taking an armchair, sat down near his children.

"Ah! my children," said the baron, "it is a long journey from the Rue Coq-Héron to Versailles when, instead of going in a good court carriage, you have only a fiacre drawn by one horse. However, I saw the dauphiness."

"Ah!" said Andrée, "then you have just arrived from Versailles, father?"

"Yes; the princess did me the honor to send for me, having heard of the accident which had happened to my daughter."

"Andrée is much better, father," said Philippe.

"I am aware of it, and I told her Royal Highness so, who was kind enough to promise that as soon as your sister is completely restored, she will summon her to the little Trianon, which she has fixed upon for her residence, and which she is now having decorated according to her taste."

"I — I at court!" said Andrée, timidly.

"It is not the court, my child. The dauphiness has quiet and unobtrusive habits, and the dauphin hates show and noise. They will live in complete retirement at Trianon. However, from what I know of her Highness the dauphiness's disposition, her little family parties will turn out in the end much better than Beds of Justice and meetings of States-General. The princess has a decided character, and the dauphin, I am told, is learned."

"Oh, it will always be the court! Do not deceive yourself, sister," said Philippe, mournfully.

"The court!" said Gilbert to himself, with an emotion of concentrated rage and despair. "The court! that is a summit which I cannot reach, — a gulf into which I cannot dash myself. In that case, farewell, Andrée! Lost, — lost to me forever!"

"But, father," replied Andrée, "we have neither the fortune which would warrant our choosing such a residence, nor the education necessary for those who move in its lofty circle. What shall I, a poor girl, do among those brilliant ladies whose dazzling splendor I on one occasion witnessed, whose minds I thought so empty, but at the same time so sparkling? Alas! my brother, we are too obscure to mingle among so many dazzling lights."

The baron knit his brow. "Still the same absurd ideas!" said he. "In truth, I cannot understand the pains which my family take to depreciate everything which they inherit from me or which relates to me. Obscure! Really, Mademoiselle, you are mad. Obscure, — a Taverney Maison Rouge obscure! And who will shine, pray, if you do not! Fortune? — *pardieu!* we know what the fortunes of the court are; the sun of royalty fills them, the same sun makes them blow, — it is the great vivifier of nature. I have ruined myself at court, and now I shall grow rich again at court, that's all. Has the king no more money to bestow upon his faithful servants? And do you really think I should blush at the offer of a regiment to the heir of my family; at the grant of a dowry to you, Andrée; at a nice little appanage conferred on myself, or at finding a handsome pension under my napkin some day at dinner? No, no; fools alone have prejudices. I have none. Besides, it is only my own property which is given back to me. Do not, therefore, entertain these foolish scruples. There remains only one of your objections, — your education, of which you spoke just now. But, Mademoiselle, remember that no young lady of the court has been educated as you have been. Nay, more; you have, besides the education usually given to the daughters of the nobility, the solid acquirements more generally confined to the families of lawyers or financiers. You are a musician, and you draw landscapes, with sheep and cows, which Berghem would not disown. Now, the dauphiness dotes on cows, on sheep, and on Berghem. You are beautiful; the king cannot fail to notice it. You can converse; that will charm the Comte d'Artois and the Comte de Provence. You will not only be well received, therefore, but adored. Yes, yes," continued the baron, rubbing his hands, and chuckling in so strange a manner that Philippe gazed at his father, doubting if such a laugh could proceed from human lips, "adored! I have said the word."

Andrée cast down her eyes, and Philippe, taking her hand, said: "Our father is right, Andrée; you are all that he has said. None can be more worthy to enter Versailles than you."

"But I shall be separated from you," replied Andrée.

"By no means, by no means," interrupted the baron; "Versailles is large, my dear."

"Yes, but Trianon is little," replied Andrée, haughty and rather unmanageable when she was opposed.

"Trianon will always be large enough to provide a chamber for Monsieur de Taverney. A man such as I am always finds room," added he, with a modesty which meant, — "always knows how to make room for himself."

Andrée, not much comforted by this promised proximity of her father, turned to Philippe.

"My sister," said the latter, "you will certainly not belong to what is called the court. Instead of placing you in a convent and paying your dowry, the dauphiness, who wishes to distinguish you, will keep you near herself in some employment. Etiquette is not so rigid now as in the time of Louis XIV. Offices are more easily fused together and separated. You may occupy the post of reader or companion to the dauphiness; she will draw with you, she will always keep you near her; probably you will never appear in public, but you will enjoy her immediate protection, and consequently will inspire envy. That is what you fear, is it not?"

"Yes, brother."

"However," said the baron, "we shall not grieve for such a trifle as one or two envious persons. Get better quickly, therefore, Andrée, and I shall have the pleasure of taking you to Trianon myself; it is the dauphiness's command."

"Very well, father, I will go."

"By the way, Philippe, have you any money?" asked the baron.

"If you want any, Monsieur," replied the young man, "I have not enough to offer you; if, on the contrary, you are offering any to me, I shall answer you that I have enough for myself."

"True, you are a philosopher," said the baron, laughing sarcastically. "Are you a philosopher also, Andrée, who have nothing to ask from me? or is there something you wish for?"

"I am afraid of embarrassing you, father."

"Oh! we are not at Taverney now. The king has sent me five hundred louis-d'or, — on account, his Majesty said. Think of your wardrobe, Andrée."

"Thank you, my dear father," said the young girl, joyously.

"There, there," said the baron; "see the extremes! Only a minute ago she wanted nothing; now she would ruin the Emperor of China. But no matter, ask; fine dresses will become you well, Andrée." Then, giving her a very affectionate kiss, the baron opened the door of an apartment which separated his own from his daughter's chamber, and left the room, saying, "That cursed Nicole is not here to light my way."

"Shall I ring for her, father?"

"No, I have La Brie, who is sleeping in some armchair or other; good-night, my children."

Philippe now rose in his turn.

"Good-night, brother," said Andrée. "I am dreadfully tired. It is the first time I have spoken so much since my accident. Good-night, dear Philippe." And she gave her hand to the young man, who kissed it with brotherly affection, but at the same time with a sort of respect with which his sister always inspired him, and retired, touching, as he passed, the door behind which Gilbert was concealed.

"Shall I call Nicole?" asked he, as he left the room.

"No, no," said Andrée "I can undress alone; adieu, Philippe!"

CHAPTER XXIX.

WHAT GILBERT HAD FORESEEN.

WHEN Andrée was alone she rose from the chair, and a shudder passed through Gilbert's frame. The young girl stood upright, and with her hands, white as alabaster, she took the hairpins one by one from her headdress, while the light robe which covered her slipped from her shoulders and showed her snowy, graceful neck and her arms, which, raised carelessly above her head, displayed to advantage her exquisite throat and her bosom palpitating under the cambric.

Gilbert, on his knees, breathless, intoxicated, felt the blood rush furiously to his heart and forehead. Fiery waves circulated in his veins, a cloud of flame descended over his sight, and there was a strange, feverish buzzing in his ears. His state of mind bordered on madness. He was on the point of crossing the threshold of Andrée's door and crying: "Yes, thou art beautiful, thou art indeed beautiful! But be not so proud of thy beauty, for thou owest it to me; I saved thy life!"

All at once a knot in her waistband embarrassed the young girl; she became impatient, stamped with her foot, and sat down weak and trembling on her bed, as if this slight obstacle had overcome her strength. Then, bending toward the cord of the bell, she pulled it impatiently.

This noise recalled Gilbert to his senses. Nicole had left the door open to hear, therefore she would come. "Farewell, my dream!" he murmured. "Farewell, happiness! henceforth only a baseless vision, — henceforth only a remembrance, ever burning in my imagination, ever present to my heart!"

Gilbert endeavored to rush from the pavilion; but the baron on entering had closed the doors of the corridor after him. Gilbert had not anticipated this obstacle, and was delayed some seconds opening the doors. Just as he entered Nicole's apartment, Nicole reached the pavilion. The young man heard the gravel of the garden walk grinding under her steps. He had only time to conceal himself in the shade, in order to let the young girl pass him; for after crossing the antechamber, the door of which she locked, she flew along the corridor as light as a bird.

Gilbert gained the antechamber, and attempted to escape into the garden; but Nicole, while running on and crying, "I am coming, Mademoiselle, I am coming! I am just closing the door!" had closed it indeed, and not only closed it and double-locked it, but in her confusion had put the key into her pocket.

Gilbert tried in vain to open the door. Then he had recourse to the windows; but they were barred, and after five minutes' investigation he saw that it was impossible to escape. He crouched in a corner, fortifying himself with the firm resolve to make Nicole open the door for him.

As for the latter, when she had given the plausible excuse for her absence that she had gone to close the windows of the greenhouse, lest the night air should injure her young lady's flowers, she finished undressing Andrée and assisted her to bed.

There was a tremulousness in Nicole's voice, an unsteadiness in her hands, and an eagerness in all her attentions, which were very unusual, and indicated some extraordinary emotion. But from the calm and lofty sphere in which Andrée's thoughts revolved, she rarely looked down upon the lower earth, and when she did so, the inferior beings whom she saw seemed like atoms in her eyes. She therefore perceived nothing. Meanwhile Gilbert was boiling with impatience, since he found his retreat cut off. He now longed only for liberty.

Andrée dismissed Nicole after a short chat, in which the latter exhibited all the wheedling manner of a remorseful waiting-maid. Before withdrawing, she turned back her mistress's coverlet, lowered the light, and sweetened the warm drink which was standing in a silver goblet upon an alabaster night-lamp; she then wished her mistress good-night in her sweetest voice, and left the room on tip-toe. As she came out, she closed the glass door. Then, humming gayly, as if her mind was entirely tranquil, she crossed the antechamber, and advanced toward the door leading into the garden.

Gilbert understood Nicole's intention; and for a moment he asked himself if he should not, instead of making himself known, slip out suddenly, taking advantage of the opportunity to escape when the door should be opened. But in that case he would be seen without being recognized, and would be taken for a robber. Nicole would cry for help, he would not have time to reach the cord; and even if he should reach it, he would be seen in his aerial flight, his retreat discovered, and himself made the object of the Taverneys' displeasure, which could not fail to be deep and lasting, considering the feeling evinced toward him by the head of the family. True, he might expose Nicole, and procure her dismissal; but of what use would that be to him? He would in that case have done evil without reaping any corresponding advantage, — in short, from pure revenge; and Gilbert was not so feeble-minded as to feel satisfied when he was revenged. Useless revenge was to him worse than a bad action, — it was folly.

As Nicole approached the door where Gilbert was in waiting, he suddenly emerged from the shadow in which he was concealed, and appeared to the young girl in the full rays of the moonlight, which was streaming through the window. Nicole was on the point of crying out; but she took Gilbert for another, and after the first emotion of terror was past, "You here!" she said. "What imprudence!"

"Yes, it is I," replied Gilbert, in a whisper; "but do not cry out for me more than you would for another."

This time Nicole recognized her interlocutor. "Gilbert!" she exclaimed; "my God!"

"I requested you not to cry out," said the young man, coldly.

"But what are you doing here, Monsieur?" exclaimed Nicole, angrily.

"Come," said Gilbert, as coolly as before, "a moment ago you called me imprudent; and now you are more imprudent than I."

"I think I am only too kind to you in asking what you are doing here," said Nicole; "for I know very well."

"What am I doing, then?"

"You came to see Mademoiselle Andrée."

"Mademoiselle Andrée?" said Gilbert, as calmly as before.

"Yes, you are in love with her; but, fortunately, she does not love you."

"Really?"

"But you had better take care, Monsieur Gilbert," said Nicole, threateningly.

"Oh, I must take care!"

"Yes."

"Of what?"

"Take care that I do not inform on you."

"You, Nicole?"

"Yes, I; take care that I don't get you dismissed from the house."

"Try," said Gilbert, smiling.

"You defy me?"

"Yes, absolutely defy you."

"What will happen, then, if I tell Mademoiselle, Monsieur Philippe, and the baron that I have found you here?"

"It will happen as you have said, — not that I shall be dismissed; I am, thank God, dismissed already, — but that I shall be tracked and hunted like a wild beast. She who will be dismissed will be Nicole."

"How Nicole?"

"Certainly, — Nicole, who has stones thrown to her over the walls."

"Take care, Monsieur Gilbert!" said Nicole, in a threatening tone, "a piece of Mademoiselle's dress was found in your hand upon the Place Louis XV."

"You think so?"

"Monsieur Philippe told his father so. He suspects nothing as yet; but if he gets a hint or two, perhaps he will suspect in the end."

"And who will give him the hint?"

"I will."

"Take care, Nicole! One might suspect also that when you seem to be drying lace, you are picking up the stones that are thrown over the wall!"

"It is false!" cried Nicole. Then, retracting her denial, she continued: "At all events, it is not a crime to receive a letter, — not like stealing in here while Mademoiselle is undressing. Ah! what will you say to that, Monsieur Gilbert?"

"I shall say, Mademoiselle Nicole, that it is also a crime for such a well-conducted young lady as you are to slip keys under the doors of gardens."

Nicole trembled.

"I shall say," continued Gilbert, "that if I, who am known to Monsieur de Taverney, to Monsieur Philippe, to Mademoiselle Andrée, have committed a crime in entering here, in my anxiety concerning the health of my former masters, and particularly of Mademoiselle Andrée, whom I endeavored so strenuously to save on the evening of the fireworks that a piece of her dress remained in my hand, — I shall say that if I have committed this pardonable crime, you have committed the unpardonable one of introducing a stranger into your master's house, and are now going to meet him a second time, in the greenhouse, where you have already spent an hour in his company —"

"Gilbert! Gilbert!"

"Oh! how virtuous we are, all of a sudden, Mademoiselle Nicole! You deem it very wicked that I should be found here, while —"

"Gilbert!"

"Yes, go and tell Mademoiselle that I love her. I shall say that it is you whom I love; and she will believe me, for you were foolish enough to tell her so at Taverney."

"Gilbert, my friend!"

"And you will be dismissed, Nicole; and instead of going to Trianon, and entering the household of the dauphiness with Mademoiselle; instead of coquetting with the fine lords and rich gentlemen, as you will not fail to do if you remain with the family, — instead of all this, you will be sent to enjoy the society of your admirer,

Monsieur Beausire, a soldier! Oh, what a direful fall! What a noble ambition Mademoiselle Nicole's is, — to be the mistress of a guardsman!" And Gilbert began to hum, in a low voice, with a most malicious accent, —

"In the Garde Française
I had a faithful lover—"

"In mercy, Monsieur Gilbert," said Nicole, "do not look at me in that ill-natured manner. Your eyes pierce me, even in the darkness. Do not laugh either, — your laugh terrifies me."

"Then open the door," said Gilbert, imperatively; "open the door for me, Nicole, and not another word of all this."

Nicole opened the door with so violent a nervous trembling that her shoulders and head shook like those of an old woman. Gilbert tranquilly went out first, and seeing that the young girl was leading him toward the door of the garden, he said: "No, no; you have your own way of admitting visitors, I have my own way of departure. Go to the greenhouse, to Monsieur Beausire, who must be waiting impatiently for you, and remain with him ten minutes longer than you ought to. I will grant you this recompense for your discretion."

"Ten minutes, and why ten minutes?" asked Nicole, trembling.

"Because I need ten minutes for my disappearance. Go, Nicole, go; and like Lot's wife, whose story I told you at Taverney when you gave me a rendezvous among the haystacks, do not turn round, else something worse will happen to you than to be changed into a pillar of salt. Go, beautiful siren, go; I have nothing else to say to you."

Nicole, subdued, alarmed, conquered, by the coolness

and presence of mind shown by Gilbert, who held her future in his hands, turned with drooping head toward the greenhouse, where Beausire was already uneasy at her prolonged absence.

Gilbert, observing the same precautions as before to avoid discovery, once more reached the wall, seized his rope, and assisted by the vine and trellis-work, gained the first story in safety, and quickly ascended the stairs. As luck would have it, he met no one on his way up; the neighbors were already gone to bed, and Thérèse was still at supper.

Gilbert was too much excited by his victory over Nicole to entertain the least fear of missing his foot in the leaden gutter. He felt as if he could have walked on the edge of a sharpened razor, had the razor been a league long. He regained his attic in safety, therefore, closed the window, seized the note, which no one had touched, and tore it in pieces. Then he stretched himself with a delicious feeling of languor upon his bed.

Half an hour afterward Thérèse kept her word, and came to the door to inquire how he was. Gilbert thanked her, in a voice interrupted by terrific yawns, as if he were dying of sleep. He was eager to be alone, quite alone, in darkness and silence, to collect his thoughts and analyze the varied emotions of this ever-memorable day. Soon, indeed, everything faded from his mind; the baron, Philippe, Nicole, Beausire, disappeared from view, to give place to the vision of Andrée at her toilet, her arms raised above her head, and detaching the pins from her long and flowing hair.

CHAPTER XXX.

THE BOTANISTS.

The events which we have just related happened on Friday evening; the excursion to which Rousseau looked forward with so much pleasure was to take place, therefore, two days later.

Gilbert, indifferent to everything since he had heard that Andrée was so soon to depart for Trianon, had spent the entire day leaning on his window-sill. During this day the window of Andrée's room remained open, and once or twice the young girl had approached it, as if to breathe the fresh air. She was pale and weak; but it seemed to Gilbert as if he would wish for nothing more than that Andrée should always inhabit that pavilion, that he should always have his attic, and that once or twice every day Andrée should come to the window as he had seen her that day.

The long-looked-for Sunday at last arrived. Rousseau had made his preparations the day before; his shoes were carefully blacked, and his gray coat, at once light and warm, was taken from the chest, — to the great annoyance of Thérèse, who thought a blouse or a linen frock quite good enough for such an expedition. But Rousseau had completed his toilet without replying to her complaint. Not only his own clothes, but Gilbert's also, had been examined with the greatest care, and the latter's had even been supplemented by a pair of irreproachable stockings and by new shoes, which Rousseau had presented him with as an agreeable surprise.

The herbal also was put in good condition. Rousseau had not forgotten his collection of mosses, which was to play a part in the proceedings of the day. Impatient as a child, he went more than twenty times to the window to see if the carriage that was passing was not Monsieur de Jussieu's. At last he perceived a highly varnished chariot, a pair of splendid horses with rich harness, and an immense, powdered footman standing at his door. He ran instantly to Thérèse, exclaiming: "Here he is! here he is!" and he called to Gilbert: "Quick, quick; the carriage is waiting."

"Well," said Thérèse, sharply, "if you are so fond of riding in a coach, why do you not work, in order to have one of your own, like Monsieur de Voltaire?"

"Be quiet!" grumbled Rousseau.

"*Dame!* you always say you have as much talent as he."

"I do not say so, hark you!" cried Rousseau, in a rage; "I say — I say nothing!" and all his joy fled, as it invariably did at the mention of that hated name.

Happily, Monsieur de Jussieu entered. He was pomatumed, powdered, fresh as the spring. His dress consisted of a splendid coat of ribbed Indian satin of a light gray color, a vest of pale lilac silk, white silk stockings of extraordinary fineness, and bright gold buckles. On entering Rousseau's apartment he filled the room with a delightful perfume, which Thérèse inhaled without concealing her admiration.

"How fine you are!" said Rousseau, looking askance at Thérèse, and comparing his modest dress and clumsy equipment with the elegant toilet of Monsieur de Jussieu.

"Oh! I am afraid of the heat," said the elegant botanist.

"But the wood is damp. If we botanize in the marshes your silk stockings — "

"Oh! we can choose the driest places."

"And the aquatic mosses, — must we give them up for to-day?"

"Do not be uneasy about that, my dear colleague."

"One would think you were going to a ball, or to pay your respects to ladies."

"Why should we not honor Dame Nature with a pair of silk stockings?" replied Monsieur de Jussieu, rather embarrassed; "does she not deserve that we should dress ourselves for her?"

Rousseau said no more; from the moment that Monsieur de Jussieu invoked Nature, he agreed with him that it was impossible to honor her too highly. As for Gilbert, notwithstanding his stoicism he gazed at Monsieur de Jussieu with envious eyes. Since he had observed so many young exquisites improving their natural advantages with dress, he had seen the utility, from a frivolous point of view, of elegance, and he had whispered to himself that this silk, this lace, this linen, would add a charm to his youth; and that if Andrée saw him dressed like Monsieur de Jussieu instead of as he was, she would then deign to look at him.

The carriage rolled off at the utmost speed of two fine Danish horses; and an hour after their departure the botanists alighted at Bougival, and turned to the left by the Chestnut Walk.

This walk, which at present is so surpassingly beautiful, was then at least quite as much so; for the portion of the rising ground which our explorers had to traverse, already planted by Louis XIV., had been the object of constant care since the king had taken a fancy to Marly.

The chestnut-trees, with their rough bark, their gigantic

branches, and their fantastic forms, sometimes presenting in their knotty circumvolutions the appearance of a huge boa twining itself round the trunk, sometimes that of a bull prostrate upon the butcher's block and vomiting a stream of black and clotted blood; the moss-covered apple-trees and the colossal walnuts, whose foliage was already assuming the dark-blue shade of summer; the solitude, the picturesque simplicity and grandeur of the landscape, which with its old, shadowy trees, stood out in bold relief against the clear blue sky, — all this, clothed with that simple and touching charm which Nature ever lends to her productions, plunged Rousseau into a state of ecstasy impossible to be described.

Gilbert was calm, but moody; his whole being was absorbed in this one thought: "Andrée leaves the garden pavilion and goes to Trianon."

Upon the summit of the little hill, which the three botanists were climbing on foot, was seen the square tower of Luciennes. The sight of this building, from which he had fled, changed the current of Gilbert's thoughts, and recalled rather unpleasant recollections, unmingled, however, with fear. From his position in the rear of the party he saw two protectors before him; and thinking himself in safety, he gazed at Luciennes as a shipwrecked sailor from the shore looks upon the sand-bank upon which his vessel has struck.

Rousseau, spade in hand, began to fix his looks on the ground; Monsieur de Jussieu did the same, but with this difference, — that the former was searching for plants, while the latter was only endeavoring to keep his stockings from the damp.

"What a splendid *lepopodium!*" exclaimed Rousseau.

"Charming," replied Monsieur de Jussieu; "but let us pass on, if you have no objection."

"Ah! the *Lyrimachia fenella*,— it is ready to pluck; look!"

"Pluck it, then, if it gives you pleasure."

"Ah! we are not botanizing, then?"

"Yes, yes; but I think we shall do better upon that height yonder."

"As you please; let us go, then."

"What time is it?" asked Monsieur de Jussieu; "in my hurry I forgot my watch."

Rousseau pulled a very large silver watch from his pocket. "Nine o'clock," said he.

"Have you any objection to our resting a little while?" continued Monsieur de Jussieu.

"Oh! what a wretched walker you are," said Rousseau. "You see what it is to botanize in fine shoes and silk stockings."

"Perhaps I am hungry."

"Well, then, let us breakfast; the village is about a quarter of a league from here."

"Oh, no! we need not go so far."

"How so? Have you our breakfast in your carriage?"

"Look yonder,— into that thicket!" said Monsieur de Jussieu, pointing with his hand toward the place he wished to indicate.

Rousseau stood upon tiptoe, and shaded his eyes with his hand. "I can see nothing," said he.

"What! Do you not see that little rustic roof?"

"No."

"Surmounted by a weather-cock, and the walls thatched with red and white straw,— a sort of rustic cottage, in short?"

"Yes, I see it now,— a little house recently built."

"A kiosk, that is it."

"Well?"

"Well, we shall find there the little luncheon I promised you."

"Very good," said Rousseau. "Are you hungry, Gilbert?"

Gilbert, who had not paid any attention to this debate, and was employed in mechanically knocking off the heads of the wild-flowers, replied: "Whatever is agreeable to you, Monsieur."

"Come, then, if you please," said Monsieur de Jussieu; "besides, nothing need prevent our gathering flowers on the way."

"Oh!" said Rousseau, "your nephew is a more ardent botanist than you. I spent a day with him botanizing in the woods of Montmorency, with a select party. He finds well, he gathers well, he explains well."

"Oh! he is young; he has his name to make yet."

"Has he not yours already made? Oh! comrade, comrade, you botanize like an amateur."

"Come, do not be angry, my dear philosopher. Hold! here is the beautiful *Plantago monanthos*. Did you find anything like that at your Montmorency?"

"No, indeed," said Rousseau, quite delighted; "I have often searched for it in vain. Upon the faith of a naturalist, it is magnificent."

"Oh, the beautiful pavilion!" said Gilbert, who had passed from the rear-guard of the party into the van.

"Gilbert is hungry," replied Monsieur de Jussieu.

"Oh, Monsieur, I beg your pardon! I can wait patiently until you are ready."

"Let us continue our task a little longer," said Rousseau, "inasmuch as botanizing after a meal is bad for digestion; and besides, the eye is then heavy, and the back stiff. But what is this pavilion called?"

"The Trap," answered Monsieur de Jussieu, remembering the name invented by Monsieur de Sartines.

"What a singular name!"

"Oh! the country, you know, is the place for indulging all sorts of caprices."

"To whom do those beautiful grounds belong?"

"I do not exactly know."

"You must know the proprietor, however, since you are going to breakfast there," said Rousseau, pricking up his ears with a slight shade of suspicion.

"Not at all — or rather, I know every one here, including the gamekeepers, who have often seen me in their enclosures, and who always touch their hats, and sometimes offer me a hare or a string of woodcocks as a present from their masters. The people on this and the neighboring estates let me do here just as if I were on my own grounds. I do not know exactly whether this summerhouse belongs to Madame de Mirepoix or to Madame d'Egmont, or — in short, I do not know to whom it belongs. But the most important point, my dear philosopher, I am sure you will agree with me, is that we shall find there bread, fruit, and pastry."

The good-natured tone in which Monsieur de Jussieu spoke, dispelled the cloud of suspicion which had already begun to darken Rousseau's brow. The philosopher wiped his feet on the grass, rubbed the mould off his hands, and preceded by Monsieur de Jussieu, entered the mossy walk which wound gracefully beneath the chestnut-trees leading up to the hermitage. Gilbert, who had again taken up his position in the rear, closed the march, dreaming of Andrée and of the means of seeing her when she should be at Trianon.

CHAPTER XXXI.

THE TRAP FOR PHILOSOPHERS.

ON the summit of the hill, which the three botanists were ascending with some difficulty, stood one of those little rustic retreats, with gnarled and knotty pillars, pointed gables, and windows festooned with ivy and clematis, which are the genuine offspring of English architecture, or to speak more correctly, of English gardening, which imitates nature, or rather invents a species of nature for itself, thus giving a certain air of originality to its creations. The English have invented blue roses, and their greatest ambition has always been toward the antithesis of all received ideas. Some day they will invent black lilies.

This summer-house, which was large enough to contain a table and six chairs, was floored with tiles and carpeted with handsome matting. The walls were covered with little mosaics of flint picked up on the river's bank, mingled with foreign shells of the most delicate tints, gathered from the shores of the Indian Ocean.

The ceiling was in relief, and was composed of fir-cones and knotty excrescences of bark, arranged so as to imitate hideous profiles of fauns or savage animals, who seemed suspended over the heads of the visitors. The windows were each stained with some different shade, so that, according as the spectator looked out of the violet, the red, or the blue glass, the woods of Vesinet seemed tinted by a stormy sky, bathed in the burning rays of an August sun, or sleeping beneath the cold and frosty atmosphere of December. The visitor had only to consult his taste, that is to say, choose his window, and look out.

This sight pleased Gilbert greatly, and he amused himself with looking through the differently tinted windows at the rich valley which lies stretched beneath the feet of a spectator situated on the hill of Luciennes, and at the noble Seine winding in the midst.

A sight nearly as interesting, however, at least in Monsieur de Jussieu's opinion, was the tempting breakfast spread in the centre of the summer-house, upon a table formed of gnarled and fantastic woodwork, on which the bark had been allowed to remain.

The exquisite cream for which Marly is celebrated, the luscious apricots and plums of Luciennes, the crisp sausages of Nanterre smoking upon a porcelain dish,— without any appearance of a servant bringing them,— strawberries peeping from a graceful little basket lined with vine-leaves, and beside the fresh and glistening pats of butter rolls of homely peasant bread, with its rich brown crust, so dear to the pampered appetite of the inhabitant of towns,— all this drew an exclamation of admiration from Rousseau, who, philosopher as he was, was not the less an unaffected gourmand; for his appetite was as keen as his taste was simple.

"What folly!" said he to Monsieur de Jussieu, "bread and fruit would have been sufficient; and even then, as true botanists and industrious explorers, we ought to have eaten the bread and munched the plums without ceasing our search among the grass or along the hedgerows. Do you remember, Gilbert, our luncheon at Plessis-Piquet?"

"Yes, Monsieur,—the bread and cherries which appeared to me so delicious."

"Yes, that is how true lovers of Nature should breakfast."

"But, my dear master," interrupted Monsieur de Jussieu, "if you reproach me with extravagance, you are wrong; a more modest meal was never—"

"Oh!" cried the philosopher, "you do your table injustice, Seigneur Lucullus."

"My table?— by no means," said Jussieu.

"Who are our hosts, then?" resumed Rousseau, with a smile which evinced at once good humor and constraint, — "sprites?"

"Or fairies!" said Monsieur de Jussieu, rising, and glancing stealthily toward the door.

"Fairies?" exclaimed Rousseau, gayly, — "a thousand blessings on them for their hospitality! I am hungry. Come, Gilbert, fall to;" and he cut a very respectable slice from the brown loaf, passing the bread and the knife to his disciple. Then, while taking a huge bite, he picked out some plums from the dish.

Gilbert hesitated.

"Come, come!" said Rousseau. "The fairies will be offended by your stiffness, and will imagine you are dissatisfied with their banquet."

"Or that it is unworthy of you, gentlemen," uttered a silvery voice from the door of the pavilion, where two young and lovely women appeared arm in arm, smiling, and making signs to Monsieur de Jussieu to moderate his obeisances.

Rousseau turned, holding the half-tasted bread in his right hand, and the remains of a plum in his left; and beholding these two goddesses, — at least such they seemed to him by their youth and beauty, — he remained stupefied with astonishment, bowing mechanically, and retreating toward the wall of the summer-house.

"Oh, Countess!" said Monsieur de Jussieu, "you here? What a delightful surprise!"

"Good-day, my dear botanist," said one of the ladies, with a grace and condescension quite regal.

"Allow me to present Monsieur Rousseau to you," said Jussieu, taking the philosopher by the hand which held the brown bread.

Gilbert also had seen and recognized the ladies. He opened his eyes to their utmost width, and, pale as death, looked out of the window of the summer-house, with the idea of throwing himself from it.

"Good-day, my little philosopher," said the other lady to the almost lifeless Gilbert, patting his cheek with her rosy fingers.

Rousseau saw and heard; he was almost choking with rage. His disciple knew these goddesses, and was known to them. Gilbert was almost fainting.

"Do you not know Madame la Comtesse, Monsieur Rousseau?" asked Jussieu.

"No," he replied, thunderstruck; "it is the first time, I think —"

"Madame Dubarry," continued Monsieur de Jussieu.

Rousseau started up as if he stood on a red-hot ploughshare. "Madame Dubarry!" he exclaimed.

"Myself, Monsieur," said the young lady, with surpassing grace, "who is most happy to have received in her house and to have been favored with a near view of one of the most illustrious thinkers of the age."

"Madame Dubarry!" continued Rousseau, without remarking that his astonishment was becoming a grave offence against good-breeding. "She! and doubtless this pavilion is hers, and doubtless it is she who has provided this breakfast."

"You have conjectured rightly, my dear philosopher,

— she and her sister," continued Jussieu, ill at ease in presence of this threatening storm.

"Her sister, who knows Gilbert!"

"Intimately, Monsieur," replied Chon, with that saucy boldness which respected neither royal whims nor philosophers' fancies.

Gilbert looked as if he wished the earth would open and swallow him, so fiercely did Rousseau's eye rest upon him.

"Intimately?" repeated Rousseau; "Gilbert knew Madame intimately, and I was not told of it? But in that case I was betrayed, I was sported with!"

Mademoiselle Chon and her sister looked at each other with a malicious smile. Monsieur de Jussieu in his agitation tore a Malines ruffle which was worth at least forty louis-d'or.

Gilbert clasped his hands as if to entreat Chon to be silent, or Monsieur Rousseau to speak more graciously to him. But, on the contrary, it was Rousseau who was silent, and Chon who spoke.

"Yes," said she, "Gilbert and I are old friends; he was a guest of mine. Were you not, little one? What! are you already ungrateful for the dainties of Luciennes and Versailles?"

This was the final blow; Rousseau's arms fell stiff and motionless. "Oh!" said he, looking askance at the young man, "that was the way, was it, you little scoundrel?"

"Monsieur Rousseau!" murmured Gilbert.

"Why, one would think you were weeping for the little tap I gave your cheek," continued Chon. "Well, I always feared you were ungrateful."

"Mademoiselle!" entreated Gilbert.

"Little one," said Madame Dubarry, "return to

Luciennes; your bonbons and Zamore await you, and though you left it in rather a strange manner, you will be well received."

"Thank you, Madame!" said Gilbert dryly; "when I leave a place it is because I do not like it."

"And why refuse the favor that is offered to you?" interrupted Rousseau, bitterly. "You have tasted of wealth, my dear Gilbert, and you had better return to it."

"But, Monsieur, when I swear to you —"

"Go, go! I do not like those who blow hot and cold with the same breath."

"But you will not listen to me, Monsieur Rousseau!"

"Well?"

"I ran away from Luciennes, where I was kept locked up."

"A trap, — I know the malice of men!"

"But since I preferred you to them, since I accepted you as my host, my protector, my master —"

"Hypocrisy!"

"But, Monsieur Rousseau, if I wished for riches, I should accept the offer these ladies have made me."

"Monsieur Gilbert, I have been often deceived, but never twice by the same person. You are free; go where you please."

"But where in the world shall I go?" cried Gilbert, plunged in an abyss of despair; for he saw his window, and the neighborhood of Andrée, and his love, lost to him forever. His pride was hurt at being suspected of treachery; and the idea that his self-denial, his long and arduous struggle against the indolence and the passions natural to his age, was misconstrued and despised, stung him to the quick.

"Where?" said Rousseau. "Why, in the first place,

to this lady, of course. Where could you find a lovelier or more worthy protector?"

"Oh, my God, my God!" cried Gilbert, burying his head in his hands.

"Do not be afraid," said Monsieur de Jussieu, deeply wounded, as a man of the world, by Rousseau's strange sally against the ladies; "you will be taken care of, and whatever you may lose in one way, will be amply made good to you."

"You see," said Rousseau, bitterly, "there is Monsieur de Jussieu, a learned man, a lover of Nature, — one of your accomplices," added he, with a grin which was meant for a smile, "who promises you assistance and fortune; and you may be sure that what Monsieur de Jussieu promises he can perform."

As he spoke, Rousseau, no longer master of himself, bowed to the ladies with a most majestic air, did the same to Monsieur de Jussieu, to the latter's consternation, and then, with a tragic air and without even looking at Gilbert, he left the pavilion.

"Oh! what an ugly animal a philosopher is!" said Chon, coolly, looking after the Genevese, who walked, or rather stumbled, down the path.

"Ask what you wish," said Monsieur de Jussieu to Gilbert, who still kept his face buried in his hands.

"Yes, ask, Monsieur Gilbert," added the countess, smiling on the abandoned disciple.

The latter raised his pale face, pushed back the hair which perspiration and tears had matted over his forehead, and said with a firm voice: "Since you are kind enough to offer me an employment, I would wish to be an assistant-gardener at Trianon."

Chon and the countess looked at each other, and the former, with her tiny little foot, touched her sister's with a triumphant glance. The countess made a sign with her head that she understood.

"Is that practicable, Monsieur de Jussieu?" asked the countess; "I should wish it very much."

"If you wish it, Madame," replied he, "it is done."

Gilbert bowed, and put his hand upon his heart, which now bounded with joy as a few moments before it had been overwhelmed with grief.

CHAPTER XXXII.

THE APOLOGUE.

In that little cabinet at Luciennes where we have seen the Vicomte Jean Dubarry imbibe so much chocolate, to the great annoyance of the countess, the Maréchal de Richelieu was lunching with Madame Dubarry, who, while amusing herself with pulling Zamore's ears, carelessly reclined upon a couch of brocaded satin, while the old courtier uttered sighs of admiration at each new position the charming creature assumed. "Oh, Countess!" said he, smirking like an old woman, "your hair is falling down; look, there is a ringlet drooping on your neck. Ah! your slipper is falling off, Countess."

"Bah! my dear Duke, never mind," said she, absently, and pulling a handful of hair from Zamore's head while she lay back at full length on the couch, more lovely and fascinating than Venus on her shell.

Zamore, entirely insensible to these graceful attitudes, bellowed with anger. The countess endeavored to quiet him by taking a handful of sugar-plums from the table and filling his pockets with them. But Zamore was sulky, turned his pocket inside out, and emptied his sugar-plums upon the carpet.

"Oh, the little scoundrel!" continued the countess, stretching out her tiny foot till it came in contact with the fantastic hose of the little negro.

"Oh, have mercy!" cried the old marshal; "upon my faith, you will kill him!"

"Why cannot I kill everything which displeases me to-day?" said the countess. "I feel merciless!"

"Oh!" said the duke, "then perhaps I displease you."

"Oh, no! quite the contrary; you are an old friend, and I adore you. But the fact is, I believe I am going mad."

"Can it be that those whom you have made mad have smitten you with their complaint?"

"Take care! you provoke me horribly with your gallant speeches, of which you do not believe one word."

"Countess, Countess! I begin to think you are not mad, but ungrateful."

"No, I am neither mad nor ungrateful; I am —"

"Well, confess! What are you?"

"I am angry, Duke."

"Really?"

"Are you surprised at that?"

"Not in the least, Countess; upon my honor, you have reason to be so."

"Ah! that is what annoys me in you, Marshal."

"Then there is something in my conduct which annoys you, Countess?"

"Yes."

"And what is this something, if you please? I am rather old to begin to correct my faults, and yet there is no effort I would not make for you."

"Well, it is that you do not even know what is the cause of my anger, Marshal."

"Oh! but I do."

"You know what vexes me?"

"Of course I do! Zamore has broken the Chinese fountain."

An imperceptible smile played around the young

countess's mouth; but Zamore, who felt himself guilty, drooped his head humbly, as if the skies were pregnant with clouds of blows and kicks.

"Oh, yes!" said the Countess, with a sigh, "yes, Duke, you are right, — that is it; and in truth you are a very deep politician."

"I have always been told so, Madame," replied Monsieur de Richelieu, with an air of profound modesty.

"Oh! I can see that without being told, Duke. Have you not guessed the cause of my annoyance immediately, without looking to the right or left? It is superb."

"Superb indeed; but still that is not all."

"Indeed!"

"No, I divine something else."

"And what do you divine?"

"That you expected his Majesty last evening."

"Where?"

"Here."

"Well, what then?"

"And that his Majesty did not come."

The countess reddened, and raised herself slightly upon her elbow.

"Oh!" said she.

"And meantime," said the duke, "I have come from Paris."

"Well, what does that prove?"

"*Pardieu!* that I could not, of course, know what took place at Versailles; and yet — "

"My dear Duke, you are full of mystery to-day. When a person begins, he should finish, or else he should not have commenced."

"You speak quite at your ease, Countess. Allow me, at least, to take breath. Where was I?"

"You were at — 'and yet.'"

"Oh, yes! true; and yet I not only know that his Majesty did not come, but also why he did not come."

"Duke, I have always thought you a sorcerer; but the proof was lacking."

"Well, that proof I will now give you."

The countess, who attached much more interest to this conversation than she wished to let appear, relinquished her hold of Zamore's head, in whose hair her long taper fingers had been carelessly playing.

"Give it, Duke, give it!" said she.

"Before the governor?" asked the duke.

"Vanish, Zamore!" said the countess to the negro boy, who, mad with delight, made only one bound from the boudoir to the antechamber.

"An excellent step," murmured Richelieu; "then I must tell you all, Countess?"

"What! did that monkey Zamore embarrass you, Duke?"

"To tell the truth, Countess, any one can embarrass me."

"Yes, I can understand that; but is Zamore any one?"

"Zamore is neither blind, deaf, nor dumb; therefore he is some one. I distinguish by the title of some one every person who is my equal in the hearing, seeing, and speaking faculties, every person who can see what I do, hear and repeat what I say, — every person, in short, who might betray me. This theory established, I proceed."

"Yes, yes, Duke, pray proceed; you will gratify me exceedingly."

"Gratify! I think not, Countess; but no matter, I must on. Well, the king was at Trianon yesterday."

" little or the great Trianon."

" ие little. The dauphiness was leaning on his arm."

"Ah!"

"And the dauphiness, who is charming, as you know —"

"Alas!"

"Coaxed him so much, with dear papa here, and dear papa there, that his Majesty, who has a heart of gold, could not resist her. So, after the walk came supper, and after supper amusing games; so that, in short —"

"In short," said Madame Dubarry, pale with impatience, "in short, the king did not come to Luciennes, — that is what you would say?"

"Exactly."

"Oh! it is easily explained; his Majesty found there all that he loves."

"Ah! by no means, and you are far from believing one word of what you say; all that pleases him he found, no doubt."

"Take care, Duke, that is much worse; to sup, chat, and play is all that he wants. And with whom did he play?"

"With Monsieur de Choiseul."

The countess made an angry gesture.

"Shall I not pursue the subject further, Countess?" asked Richelieu.

"On the contrary, Monsieur, speak on."

"You are as courageous, Madame, as you are witty; let me therefore take the bull by the horns, as the Spaniards say."

"Madame de Choiseul would not forgive you for that proverb, Duke."

"It is, however, not applied to her husband. I must tell you, then, Madame, that Monsieur de Choiseul, since I must name him, held the cards; and with so much good fortune, so much address —"

"That he won."

"By no means, — that he lost, and that his Majesty

won a thousand louis-d'or at piquet, — a game on which his Majesty prides himself very much, seeing that he plays it very badly."

"Oh, that Choiseul, that Choiseul!" murmured Madame Dubarry. "But Madame de Grammont was of the party also, was she not?"

"That is to say, Countess, she was paying her respects before her departure."

"The duchess!"

"Yes; she is very foolish, I think."

"Why so?"

"Finding that no one persecutes her, she pouts; finding that no one exiles her, she exiles herself."

"Where to?"

"To the provinces."

"She is going to plot."

"*Parbleu!* what else would you expect her to do? Well, as she was about to set out, she very naturally wished to take leave of the dauphiness, who besides is very fond of her. That is why she was at Trianon."

"The great?"

"Of course. The little Trianon is not yet furnished."

"Ah! her Highness the Dauphiness, by surrounding herself with all these Choiseuls, shows plainly which party she intends to embrace."

"No, Countess, do not let us exaggerate; to-morrow the duchess will have departed."

"And the king was amused where I was absent!" cried the countess, with indignation not unmixed with terror.

"Yes; it is incredible, Countess, but still it is so. Well, what do you conclude from it?"

"That you are well informed, Duke."

"Is that all?"

"No."

"Finish, then."

"I gather from it that we shall all be lost if we do not rescue the king from the clutches of these Choiseuls, either with his consent or without it."

"Alas!"

"I say we," resumed the countess, — "but do not fear, Duke; I speak only of our own family."

"And your friends, Countess; permit me to claim that title. So then —"

"Then you are one of my friends?"

"I think I have said so, Madame."

"That is not enough."

"I think I have proved it."

"That is better. And you will assist me?"

"With all my power, Countess; but —"

"But what?"

"I cannot conceal from you that the task is difficult."

"Are these Choiseuls positively not to be rooted out, then?"

"They are firmly planted, at least."

"Then, whatever our friend La Fontaine may say, neither wind nor storm can prevail against this oak?"

"The minister is a lofty genius."

"Bah! you speak like an encyclopedist!"

"Am I not a member of the Académie?"

"Oh! you are slightly so."

"True, you are right; my secretary is the member, not I. But, nevertheless, I maintain my opinion."

"That Monsieur de Choiseul is a genius?"

"Eh! yes."

"But may I ask in what does this mighty genius shine?"

"In this, Madame, that he has made such a piece of work with the parliament and the English that the king cannot do without him."

"The parliament? Why, he excites it against his Majesty."

"Of course; therein lies his cleverness."

"He provokes the English to war."

"Of course. Peace would ruin him."

"That is not genius, Duke."

"What is it then, Countess?"

"It is high treason."

"When high treason is successful, Countess, it is genius, and genius of a lofty description."

"But by that mode of reasoning I know some one who is as great a genius as Monsieur de Choiseul."

"Bah!"

"As regards the parliament, at least."

"You puzzle me, Countess."

"Do you not know him, Duke? He belongs to your own family."

"Can I have a man of genius in my family? Do you speak of my uncle, the cardinal duke, Madame?"

"No; I mean the Duc d'Aiguillon, your nephew."

"Ah! Monsieur d'Aiguillon. Yes, true, it was he who set that affair of La Chalotais moving. 'Pon honor, he is a brave youth. Yes, true; that was a tough piece of work. Countess, there is a man whom a woman of spirit should attach to her interests."

"Are you aware, Duke," said the countess, "that I do not know your nephew?"

"Indeed, Madame, you don't know him?"

"No; I have never seen him."

"Poor fellow! In fact, I now remember that since you came to court he has always been at Brittany. Let him look to himself when he first sees you; he has not latterly been accustomed to the sun."

"What does he do among all those black gowns, — a nobleman of spirit like him?"

"He revolutionizes them, not being able to do better. You understand, Countess, every one takes his pleasure where he can find it, and there is not much pleasure to be had in Brittany. Ah! he is an active man. *Peste!* what a servant the king might have in him, if he wished. Parliament would not be insolent to him. Oh! he is a true Richelieu. Permit me, therefore, Countess — "

"What?"

"To present him to you on his first appearance."

"Does he intend to visit Paris soon?"

"Oh! Madame, who knows? Perhaps he will have to remain in Brittany another lustre, as that scoundrel Voltaire says; perhaps he is on his way hither; perhaps two hundred leagues off; perhaps at the barrier."

And while he spoke, the marshal studied the lady's features, to see what effect his last words produced. But after having reflected for a moment, she said: "Let us return to the point where we left off."

"Wherever you please, Countess."

"Where were we?"

"At the moment when his Majesty was enjoying himself so much at Trianon in the company of Monsieur de Choiseul."

"And when we were speaking of getting rid of this Choiseul, Duke."

"That is to say, when you were speaking of getting rid of him, Countess."

"Oh! I am so anxious that he should go," said the favorite, "that I think I shall die if he remains. Will you not assist me a little, my dear Duke?"

"Oh!" said Richelieu, bridling; "in politics that is called an overture."

"Take it as you will, call it what you please, but answer categorically."

"Oh, what a long, ugly adverb in such a pretty little mouth!"

"Do you call that answering, Duke?"

"No, not exactly; I call that preparing my answer."

"Is it prepared?"

"Wait a little."

"You hesitate, Duke?"

"Oh, no!"

"Well, I am listening."

"What do you think of apologues, Countess?"

"Why, that they are very antiquated."

"Bah! the sun is antiquated also, and yet we have not invented any better means of light."

"Well, let me hear your apologue, then; but let it be clear."

"As crystal. Let us suppose, then, Countess — You know one always supposes something in an apologue."

"How tiresome you are, Duke."

"You do not believe one word of what you say, Countess, for you never listened to me more attentively."

"I was wrong, then; go on."

"Suppose, then, that you were walking in your beautiful garden at Luciennes, and that you saw a magnificent plum, — one of those Queen Claudes which you are so fond of, because their vermilion and purple tints resemble your own."

"Go on, flatterer."

"Well, I was saying, suppose you saw one of these plums at the extremity of one of the loftiest branches of the tree, what would you do, Countess?"

"I would shake the tree, to be sure!"

"Yes, but in vain, for the tree is large and massive, and not to be rooted out, as you said just now; and you would soon perceive that, without even succeeding in shaking it, you would tear your charming little hands against its rough bark. And then you would say, reclining your head to one side in that adorable manner which belongs only to you and the flowers, 'Oh, how I wish I had that plum upon the ground!' and then you would get angry."

"That is all very natural, Duke."

"I shall certainly not be the person to contradict you."

"Go on, my dear Duke; your apologue is exceedingly interesting."

"All at once, when turning your little head from side to side, you perceive your friend the Duc de Richelieu, who is walking behind you, thinking."

"Of what?"

"What a question! *Pardieu!* of you. You say to him with your heavenly voice, 'Oh, Duke, Duke!'"

"Well?"

"'You are a man; you are strong; you took Mahon. Shake this devil of a plum-tree for me, that I may have that provoking plum!' Is not that it, Countess?"

"Exactly, Duke; I repeated that to myself while you were saying it aloud. But what did you reply?"

"Reply? Oh, I replied, 'How you run on, Countess! Certainly nothing could give me greater pleasure; but only see how firm the tree is, how knotty the branches! I have a sort of affection for my hands as well as you have for yours, though mine are fifty years older than yours.'"

"Ah!" said the countess, suddenly, "yes, yes; I comprehend."

"Then finish the apologue. What did you say to me?"

"I said, 'My little Marshal, do not look with indifferent eyes upon this plum, which you look at indifferently only because it is not for you. Wish for it along with me, my dear Marshal; covet it along with me. And if you shake the tree properly, if the plum falls, then we will eat it together.'"

"Bravo!" exclaimed the duke, clapping his hands.

"Is that it?"

"Faith, Countess, there is no one like you for finishing an apologue. By mine horns, as my deceased father used to say, it is right well tricked out!"

"You will shake the tree, Duke?"

"With two hands and three hearts, Countess."

"And the plum was really a Queen Claude?"

"I am not quite sure of that, Countess."

"What was it, then?"

"Do you know, it seemed much more like a portfolio dangling from the tree."

"Then we will divide the portfolio."

"Oh, no! for me alone. Do not envy me the morocco, Countess. There will fall so many beautiful things from the tree along with the portfolio, when I shake it, that you will not know how to choose."

"Then, Marshal, it is a settled affair?"

"I am to have Monsieur de Choiseul's place?"

"If the king consents."

"Does not the king do all you wish?"

"You see plainly he does not, since he will not send this Choiseul away."

"Oh! I trust that the king will gladly recall his old companion."

"And you ask nothing for the Duc d'Aiguillon?"

"No, faith; the rascal can ask for himself."

"Besides, you will be there. And now it is my turn to ask."

"That is but just."

"What will you give me?"

"Whatever you wish."

"I want everything."

"That is reasonable."

"And shall I have it?"

"What a question! But will you be satisfied at least, and ask me for nothing further?"

"Only that, and something more."

"Speak."

"You know Monsieur de Taverney?"

"He is a friend of forty years' standing."

"He has a son?"

"And a daughter. Well?"

"That is all."

"How! all?"

"Yes; the other demand I have to make shall be made in proper time and place. In the mean time, we understand each other, Duke?"

"Yes, Countess."

"Our compact is signed."

"Nay, more, it is sworn."

"Then shake the tree for me."

"Oh, rest satisfied! I have the means."

"What are they?"

"My nephew."

"What else?"

"The Jesuits."

"Oh! ho!"

"I have a very nice little plan already formed."

"May I know it?"

"Alas! Countess —"

"Well, you are right."

"You know, secrecy—"

"Is half the battle. I complete your thought for you."

"You are charming."

"But I wish to shake the tree also."

"Oh! very well, shake away, Countess; it can do no harm."

"But when will you begin to undermine, Duke?" asked the countess.

"To-morrow. And when do you begin to shake?"

A loud noise of carriages was heard in the courtyard, and almost immediately cries of "Long live the king!" rose on the air.

"I?" said the countess, glancing at the window, "I will begin immediately."

"Bravo!"

"Retire by the little staircase, Duke, and wait in the courtyard. You shall have my answer in an hour."

CHAPTER XXXIII.

THE EXPEDIENT OF HIS MAJESTY LOUIS XV.

LOUIS XV. was not so easy tempered that one could talk politics with him every day; for in truth, politics were his aversion, and when he was in a bad temper he always avoided that subject with this argument, which admitted of no reply: "Bah! the machine will last as long as I shall."

When circumstances were favorable, it was necessary to take advantage of them; but it rarely happened that the king did not regain the advantage which a moment of good-humor had caused him to lose. Madame Dubarry knew her king well, and like fishermen well skilled in the dangers of the sea, she never attempted to start in bad weather. Now, the present visit of his Majesty to Luciennes was one of the best opportunities possible. The king had done wrong the previous day, and knew beforehand that he should receive a scolding; he would therefore be an easy prey.

But however confiding the game for which the hunter lies in wait, it has always a certain instinct which must be taken into account. But this instinct is set at nought if the sportsman knows how to thwart it. The countess managed the royal game she had in view and which she wished to capture, in the following manner.

We have said that she was in a most becoming morning-dress, like those in which Boucher represents his shepherdesses. Only she had no rouge on, for Louis XV. had an antipathy to rouge. The moment his Majesty was announced she seized her pot of rouge and began to rub her cheeks vigorously. The king saw what the countess was doing from the anteroom. "Fie!" said he, as he entered, "how she daubs herself!"

"Ah! good-day, Sire," said the countess, without interrupting her occupation even when the king kissed her on the neck.

"You did not expect me, it seems, Countess?" asked the king.

"Why do you think so, Sire?"

"Because you soil your face in that manner."

"On the contrary, Sire, I was certain that I should have the honor of receiving your Majesty in the course of the day."

"Ah! how you say that, Countess!"

"Indeed?"

"Yes, you are as serious as Monsieur Rousseau when he is listening to his own music."

"That is because I have serious things to say to your Majesty."

"Ah, good! I see what is coming, Countess."

"Really?"

"Yes, — reproaches."

"I reproach you, Sire? — and why, if you please?"

"Because I did not come yesterday."

"Oh, Sire, do me the justice not to imagine that I pretend to monopolize your Majesty."

"My little Jeanne, you are getting angry."

"Oh! no, Sire, I am angry already."

"But hear me, Countess; I assure you I have not ceased thinking of you."

"Pshaw!"

"And the evening seemed interminable to me."

"But once more, Sire, I am not speaking of that at all. Your Majesty may spend your evenings where you please, without consulting any one."

"Quite a family party, Madame; only my own family."

"Sire, I have not even inquired."

"Why not?"

"What! you know it would be very unbecoming for me to do so."

"Well," said the king, "if you are not displeased with me about that, what is it, then? We must be just in this world."

"I have no complaint to make against you, Sire."

"But since you are angry—"

"Yes, I am angry, Sire, that is true; but it is at being made a make-shift."

"You a make-shift? Good heavens!"

"Yes, I! The Comtesse Dubarry, the beautiful Jeanne, the charming Jeannette, the fascinating Jeanneton, as your Majesty calls me, — I am a make-shift!"

"But how?"

"Because I have my king, my lover, only when Madame de Choiseul and Madame de Grammont do not want him."

"Oh! oh! Countess—"

"My faith! I speak right out what is in my heart. Hold, Sire. They tell me that Madame de Grammont has often watched for your entrance to your bedchamber. Well, I will take a course just contrary to that of the noble duchess, — I will watch for the coming out; and the first Choiseul or Grammont that falls into my hands — so much the worse, by my faith!"

"Countess, Countess!"

"Oh! what can you expect? I am an uneducated

woman. I am the mistress of Blaise,—the beautiful Bourbonnaise, you know."

"Countess, the Choiseuls will avenge themselves."

"What matter, if they avenge themselves for my vengeance?"

"They will despise you."

"You are right. Well, I have an excellent plan, which I shall carry into execution at once."

"And that is?" asked the king, uneasily.

"Simply to go away."

The king shrugged his shoulders.

"Ah! you do not believe me, Sire?"

"No, indeed!"

"That is because you do not take the trouble to reason; you confound me with others."

"How so?"

"Madame de Châteauroux wanted to be a goddess; Madame de Pompadour aimed at being a queen; others wished to be rich, powerful, or to humiliate the ladies of the court by the weight of their favors. I have none of these defects."

"That is true."

"But yet I have many good qualities."

"That is also true."

"You do not think a word of what you say."

"Oh, Countess! no one knows your worth better than I do."

"Well, but listen. What I am going to say will not alter your conviction."

"Speak."

"In the first place, I am rich, and independent of every one."

"Do you wish to make me regret that, Countess?"

"Then I have not the least ambition for all that flatters

these ladies, the least desire for what they aim at; my only wish is to love sincerely him whom I have chosen, whether he be a soldier or a king. When I love him no longer, I care for nothing else."

"Let me trust you care a little for me yet, Countess."

"I have not finished, Sire."

"Proceed, Madame."

"I am pretty, I am young, and may reasonably hope for ten years more of beauty; and the moment I cease to be your Majesty's favorite, I shall be the happiest and most honored woman in the world. You smile, Sire. I am sorry to tell you it is because you do not reflect. When you had had enough, and your people too much, of your other favorites, you sent them away, and your people blessed you and execrated the disgraced favorite more than ever; but I will not wait until I am sent away. I will leave the place, and make it known publicly that I have left it. I will give a hundred thousand francs to the poor; I will retire to a convent for a week; and in less than a month my portrait will be hung up in all the churches as that of a repentant Magdalen."

"Oh, Countess! you do not speak seriously?" said the king.

"Look at me, Sire, and see whether I am serious or not. I swear to you that I never was more serious in my life."

"Then you will commit this folly, Jeanne? But do you not see that by so doing you place yourself at the mercy of my whim, Madame la Comtesse?"

"No, Sire; to do so would be to say, 'Choose between this and that;' whereas I say, 'Adieu, Sire!'—nothing more."

The king turned pale, but this time with anger. "If you forget yourself so far, Madame, take care."

"Of what, Sire?"

"I will send you to the Bastille, and you will find the Bastille rather more tiresome than a convent."

"Oh, Sire!" said the countess, clasping her hands, "if you would but do me that favor, it would delight me!"

"Delight you? How so?"

"Yes, indeed. My secret ambition has always been to be popular, like Monsieur de la Chalotais, or Monsieur de Voltaire. I only want the Bastille for that. A little of the Bastille, and I shall be the happiest of women. I can then write memoirs of myself, of your ministers, of your daughters, of yourself, and transmit the virtues of Louis the Well-Beloved to the remotest posterity. Give me the *lettre-de-cachet*, Sire. Here, I will provide the pen and ink." And she pushed a pen and an inkstand which were upon the work-table toward the king.

The king, thus braved, reflected a moment, then, rising, "Very well, Madame," said he: "adieu."

"My horses!" cried the countess. "Adieu, Sire."

The king made a step toward the door.

"Chon!" said the countess.

Chon entered.

"My trunks, my travelling equipage, and post-horses," said she. "Quick! lose no time!"

"Post-horses!" said Chon, startled. "Good heavens! what is the matter?"

"We must leave this as quickly as possible, my dear, else the king will send us to the Bastille. There is no time to be lost. Make haste, Chon, make haste!"

This reproach stung Louis to the heart. He approached the countess and took her hand. "Forgive my warmth, Countess," said he.

"In truth, Sire, I am surprised you did not threaten me with the gibbet."

"Oh, Countess!"

"Of course. Thieves are always hanged."

"Thieves?"

"Yes; do I not steal the Comtesse de Grammont's place?"

"Countess!"

"Certainly! that is my crime, Sire."

"Be just, Countess; you irritated me."

"And how?"

The king took her hands. "We were both wrong. Let us forgive each other."

"Are you serious in your wish for a reconciliation, Sire?"

"On my honor."

"Go, Chon."

"Without ordering anything?" asked Chon.

"No, order what I told you."

"Countess!"

"But let them wait for fresh orders."

"Ah!"

Chon left the room.

"Then you wish me to remain?" said the countess.

"Above all things."

"Reflect on what you say, Sire."

The king reflected, but he could not retract; besides, he wanted to see how far the requirements of the victor would go.

"Speak," said he.

"Immediately. Mark, Sire! I was going away without asking anything."

"I observed it."

"But if I remain, I shall ask for something."

"Well, what is it? It is only necessary to know what it is."

"Ah! you know very well."

"No."

"Yes, for you make a grimace."

"Monsieur de Choiseul's dismissal, is it?"

"Exactly."

"It is impossible, Countess."

"My horses, then."

"But, ill-natured creature that you are —"

"Sign my *lettre-de-cachet* for the Bastille, or the letter which dismisses the minister."

"There is a middle course," said the king.

"Thanks for your clemency, Sire; it seems I shall be permitted to go without being arrested."

"Countess, you are a woman."

"Fortunately I am."

"And you talk politics like an angry, rebellious woman. I have no grounds for dismissing Monsieur de Choiseul."

"I understand he is the idol of the parliament; he encourages them in their revolt."

"But there must be some pretext."

"A pretext is the reason of the weak."

"Countess, Monsieur de Choiseul is an honest man, and honest men are rare."

"Honest! he sells you to the gentlemen of the black robe, who swallow up all the gold in the kingdom."

"No exaggeration, Countess."

"Half, then."

"Good heavens!" cried Louis XV., with vexation.

"Yes, I know," cried the countess, "I am very foolish. What are parliaments, Choiseuls, governments, to me? What is the king to me, when I am only his make-shift?"

"Again!"

"Always, Sire."

"Give me two hours to consider, Countess."

"Ten minutes, Sire. I will retire into my apartment;

slip your answer under the door. There are pen, ink, and paper. If in ten minutes you have not replied, and replied as I wish, adieu; think no more of me, — I shall have gone. Otherwise, — "

" Otherwise ? "

"Pull at the bobbin, and the latch will fly up."

Louis XV. kissed the hands of the countess, who, like the Parthian, threw back her most fascinating smile on him as she left the room. The king made no opposition to her withdrawal, and the countess entered the adjoining chamber and shut the door. Five minutes afterward a folded paper grazed the silken mat and the rich carpet beneath the door. The countess eagerly devoured the contents of the letter, hastily wrote some words with a pencil on a scrap of paper, and opening the window, threw the paper to Monsieur de Richelieu, who was walking in the little courtyard under an awning, in great trepidation lest he should be seen, and keeping himself out of view as much as possible.

The marshal unfolded the paper, read it, and in spite of his sixty-five years hastily ran to the large courtyard and jumped into his carriage. "Coachman," said he, "to Versailles, as quick as possible!"

The paper which was thrown to Monsieur de Richelieu from the window contained only these words: "I have shaken the tree; the portfolio has fallen!"

CHAPTER XXXIV.

HOW KING LOUIS XV. TRANSACTED BUSINESS.

THE next day there was a great commotion at Versailles. Whenever two courtiers met, there was nothing but mysterious signs and significant shakes of the hand, or else folded arms and upward looks expressive of grief and surprise.

Monsieur de Richelieu, with a number of his partisans, was in the king's antechamber at Trianon at about ten o'clock. The Count Jean, all bedizened with lace and quite dazzling, conversed with the old marshal, and conversed gayly, if his joyous face could be trusted as evidence.

At about eleven o'clock the king passed quickly through the gallery and entered the council-chamber, without speaking to any one.

At about five minutes past eleven Monsieur de Choiseul alighted from his carriage and crossed the gallery with his portfolio under his arm. As he passed through the throng, there was a hurried movement among the courtiers, who all turned round as if talking among themselves, in order to avoid bowing to the minister. The duke paid no attention to this manœuvre; he entered the closet where the king was turning over some papers while sipping his chocolate.

"Good morning, Duke," said the king, familiarly; "are we feeling well this morning?"

"Sire, Monsieur de Choiseul is quite well, but the minister is very ill, and comes to request that your Majesty, since you have not yet spoken, will accept his resignation. I thank the king for permitting me to take the initiative in this matter; it is a last favor, for which I am deeply grateful."

"What, Duke! — your resignation? What does that mean?"

"Sire, your Majesty yesterday signed for Madame Dubarry an order which deposes me. This news is already spread all over Paris and Versailles. The evil is done; nevertheless, I was unwilling to leave your Majesty's service without receiving a formal order with the permission. For, nominated officially, I can consider myself dismissed only by an official act."

"What, Duke!" exclaimed the king, laughing, — for the severe and lofty attitude of Monsieur de Choiseul made him almost tremble, — "did you, a man of genius, and skilled in official forms, did you believe that?"

"But, Sire," said the surprised minister, "you have signed — "

"What?"

"A letter, in the possession of Madame Dubarry."

"Ah, Duke! have you never felt the want of peace? You are most fortunate! Madame de Choiseul must indeed be a model."

The duke, offended by the comparison, frowned. "Your Majesty," said he, "has too much firmness of character, and above all, too much tact and discretion, to mix up affairs of state with what you deign to call household matters."

"Choiseul, I must tell you how that affair happened; it is very amusing. You are aware that you are very much feared in that quarter."

"Rather say hated, Sire."

"Hated, if you will. Well, this madcap countess left me no alternative but to send her to the Bastille or to thank you for your services."

"Well, Sire?"

"Well, Duke, you must confess that it would have been a pity to lose the sight which Versailles presents this morning. I have been amused since yesterday with seeing the couriers depart in all directions, and watching the faces brighten up or lengthen. Since yesterday Cotillon III. is queen of France. It is exceedingly amusing."

"But the end of all this, Sire?"

"The end, my dear Duke," said the king, seriously, "the end will always be the same. You know me; I always seem to yield, but I never yield. Let the women swallow the honored morsel I throw them now and then, as to another Cerberus; but let us live quietly, uninterruptedly, always together. And since we are on the chapter of explanations, keep this one for yourself. Whatever report you may hear, whatever letter you may receive from me, do not absent yourself from Versailles. As long as I continue to say to you what I now do, Duke, we shall be good friends."

The king extended his hand to his minister, who bowed over it, without gratitude and without anger.

"And now, my dear Duke, let us to business."

"At your Majesty's pleasure," replied the minister, opening his portfolio.

"Well, tell me something of these fireworks, to begin with."

"Ah! that was a great disaster, Sire."

"Whose fault was it?"

"Monsieur Bignon's, the provost of the merchants."

"Did the people cry out very much?"

"Oh, very much!"

"Then perhaps we had better dismiss this Monsieur Bignon."

"One of the members of parliament was nearly killed in the mêlée, and his colleagues took up the matter warmly. But the advocate-general, Séguier, made a very eloquent speech to prove that this misfortune was the work of fate alone. His speech was applauded, and so the affair is over for the present."

"So much the better! Let us pass to the parliament, Duke. Ah! we are reproached in that quarter."

"I am blamed, Sire, for not supporting Monsieur d'Aiguillon against Monsieur de la Chalotais. But who blames me? The very people who carried your Majesty's letter about with all the demonstrations of joy. Remember, Sire, that Monsieur d'Aiguillon overstepped the bounds of his authority in Brittany, that the Jesuits were really exiled, and that Monsieur de la Chalotais was right. Your Majesty has publicly acknowledged the innocence of the attorney-general. The king cannot thus be made to stultify himself. To his minister that is nothing, but to his people —!"

"In the mean time the parliament feels itself strong?"

"And it is strong. How can it be otherwise? The members are reprimanded, imprisoned, persecuted, and then declared innocent! I do not accuse Monsieur d'Aiguillon of having initiated this affair of Chalotais, but I can never forgive him for having been on the wrong side of it."

"Oh, come, Duke! the evil is done; think of the remedy. How can we bridle those insolent fellows?"

"Let the intrigues of the chancellor cease, let Monsieur d'Aiguillon have no more support, and the anger of the parliament will at once subside."

"But that would be to yield, Duke."

"Then your Majesty is represented by Monsieur d'Aiguillon, and not by me?"

This was a home-thrust, and the king felt it. "You know," said he, "I do not like to affront my servants, even when they have been in the wrong. But no more of this unfortunate business; time will decide who is right. Let us speak of foreign affairs. I am told we shall have a war?"

"Sire, if there be war, it will be a just and necessary war."

"With the English — the devil!"

"Does your Majesty fear the English?"

"Oh! upon the sea — "

"Your Majesty may rest tranquil. My cousin the Duc de Praslin, your minister of marine, will tell you that he has sixty-four men-of-war, not including those which are on the stocks. Besides, there are materials sufficient to construct twelve more in a year. Then there are fifty first-rate frigates, — a respectable force with which to meet a naval war. For a Continental war we have more than all that, — we have the remembrance of Fontenoi."

"Very well; but why must I fight the English, my dear Duke? A much less skilful minister than you, the Abbé Dubois, always avoided a war with England."

"I daresay, Sire. The Abbé Dubois received from the English six hundred thousand francs a month."

"Oh, Duke!"

"I have the proof, Sire."

"Well, be it so. But where are the grounds for war?"

"England covets all the Indies; I have been obliged to give the most stringent and hostile orders to your officers there. The first collision will call forth demands for redress from England; my official advice is that we do not listen to them. Your Majesty's Government must make itself respected by force, as it formerly was through corruption."

"Oh, let us be patient! Who will know what happens in India? It is so far from here!"

The duke bit his lips. "There is a *casus belli* nearer home, Sire," said he.

"Another! What is that?"

"The Spaniards claim the Malouine and Falkland Islands. The port of Egmont was arbitrarily occupied by the English; the Spaniards drove them from it by main force. The English are enraged; they threaten the Spaniards with instant war if they do not give them satisfaction."

"Well! but if the Spaniards are in the wrong, let them unravel the knot themselves."

"And the family compact, Sire? Why did you insist on the signing of this compact, which allies so closely all the Bourbons in Europe against English encroachment?"

The king hung his head.

"Do not be uneasy, Sire," continued Choiseul; "you have a formidable army, an imposing fleet, and sufficient money. I can raise enough without making the people cry out. If we have a war, it will be an additional glory to your Majesty's reign, and it will furnish the pretext and excuse for several aggrandizements which I have in view."

"But in that case, Duke, we must have peace in the interior; let there not be war everywhere."

"But the interior is quiet, Sire," replied the duke, affecting not to understand.

"No, no! you see plainly it is not. You love me, and serve me well. Others say they love me, and their conduct does not at all resemble yours. Let there be concord between all shades of opinion; let me live happily, my dear Duke."

"It is not my fault, Sire, if your happiness is not complete."

"That is the way to speak. Well, come, then, and dine with me to-day."

"At Versailles, Sire?"

"No; at Luciennes."

"I regret exceedingly, Sire, that I cannot; but my family is in great alarm on account of the reports which were spread yesterday. They think I am in disgrace with your Majesty, and I cannot let so many loving hearts suffer."

"And do those of whom I speak not suffer, Duke? Remember how happily we three used to live together in the time of the poor Marchioness."

The duke drooped his head, his eyes dimmed, and he uttered a half-suppressed sigh. "Madame de Pompadour was extremely jealous of your Majesty's glory," he said, "and had lofty political ideas. I confess that her character sympathized strongly with my own. Often, Sire, I was joined with her in the great enterprises she undertook. Yes, we understood each other."

"But she meddled with politics, Duke, and every one blamed her for it."

"True!"

"This other, on the contrary, is mild as a lamb; she has never yet asked me for a single *lettre-de-cachet*, even against the pamphleteers and sonnet-writers. Well, they reproach her as if she followed in the other's footsteps. Oh, Duke, it is enough to disgust one with progress! Come, will you make your peace at Luciennes?"

"Sire, deign to assure the Comtesse Dubarry that I esteem her as a charming woman, and well worthy of the king's love; but —"

"Ah! a but, Duke —"

"But," continued Monsieur de Choiseul, "my conviction is that if your Majesty is necessary for the welfare of France, a good minister is of more importance to your Majesty in the present juncture than a charming mistress."

"Let us speak no more of it, Duke, and let us remain good friends. But calm Madame de Grammont, and let her not lay any more plots against the Countess; the women will embroil us."

"Madame de Grammont, Sire, is too anxious to please your Majesty; that is her failing."

"But she displeases me by annoying the Countess, Duke."

"Well, Madame de Grammont is going, Sire; we shall see her no more. That will be an enemy the less."

"I did not mean that; you go too far. But my head burns, Duke; we have worked this morning like Louis XIV. and Colbert, — quite in the style of the *grand siècle*, as the philosophers say. By the way, Duke, are you a philosopher?"

"I am your Majesty's humble servant," replied Monsieur de Choiseul.

"You charm me; you are an invaluable man. Give me your arm, — I am quite giddy."

The duke hastened to offer his arm to his Majesty. He understood that the folding-doors would be thrown open, that the whole court was in the gallery, and that he would be seen in this triumphant position. After having suffered so much, he was not sorry to make his enemies suffer in their turn. The usher, in fact, now opened the doors and announced the king in the gallery.

Louis XV. crossed the gallery leaning heavily on Monsieur de Choiseul's arm, talking and smiling, without remarking, or seeming to remark, how pale Jean Dubarry was, and how red Monsieur de Richelieu. But Monsieur de Choiseul saw these shades of expression very well. With elastic step, lofty head, and sparkling eyes, he passed before the courtiers, who now approached as eagerly as they had before kept away.

"There," said the king, at the end of the gallery, "wait for me; I will take you with me to Trianon. Remember what I have told you."

"I have treasured it up in my heart," replied the minister, well knowing what a sting this cutting sentence would inflict on his enemies.

The king once more entered his apartments.

Monsieur de Richelieu broke the file, and hastened to press the minister's hand between his meagre fingers, exclaiming, "I have known for a long time that a Choiseul bears a charmed life."

"Thank you!" said the duke, who knew how the land lay.

"But this absurd report?" continued the marshal.

"The report made his Majesty laugh," said Choiseul.

"I heard something of a letter —"

"A little joke of the king's," replied the minister, glancing, while he spoke, at Jean, who lost countenance.

"Wonderful, wonderful!" repeated the marshal, turning to the viscount as soon as the Duc de Choiseul was out of sight.

The king descended the staircase, calling the duke, who eagerly followed him.

"We have been tricked," said the marshal to Jean.

"Where are they going?"

"To the little Trianon, to amuse themselves at our expense."

"Hell and furies!" exclaimed Jean. "Ah, pardon me, Marshal!"

"It is now my turn," said the latter. "We shall see if my plans are more successful than those of the countess."

CHAPTER XXXV.

THE LITTLE TRIANON.

WHEN Louis XIV. had built Versailles, and had felt the inconvenience of grandeur, when he saw the immense salons full of guards, the ante-rooms thronged with courtiers, the corridors and entresols crowded with footmen, pages, and officers, he said to himself that Versailles was indeed what Louis XIV. had planned, and what Mansard, Le Brun, and Le Nôtre had executed, — a sojourn for a god, but not a habitation for a man. Then the Grand Monarque, who deigned to be a man in his leisure moments, built Trianon, that he might breathe more freely and enjoy a little retirement. But the sword of Achilles, which had fatigued even Achilles himself, was an insupportable burden to his puny successor.

Trianon, the miniature replica of Versailles, seemed yet too pompous to Louis XV., who caused the little Trianon, a pavilion of sixty feet square, to be built by the architect Gabriel.

To the left of this building was erected an oblong square structure without character and without ornament; this was the dwelling of the servants and officers of the household. It contained about ten lodgings for masters, and had accommodation for fifty servants. This building still remains entire, and is composed of a ground-floor, a first story, and attics. This ground-floor is protected by a paved moat, which separates it from the plantation; and all the windows in it, as well as those of the first-floor, are grated. On the side next Trianon the windows admit light to a long corridor, like that of a convent.

Eight or nine doors opening from the corridor give entrance to the different suites of apartments, each consisting of an ante-room and two closets, one to the left, the other to the right, and of one, and sometimes two, rooms in the basement, looking upon the inner court of the building. Over the basement are the kitchens, and in the attics the chambers of the domestics. Such is the little Trianon.

Add to this a chapel about forty yards from the chateau, which we shall not describe, because there is no necessity for our doing so, and because it is too small to deserve our notice.

The topography of the establishment is therefore as follows: a chateau looking with its large eyes upon the park and wood in front, and on the left looking toward the offices, which present only barred windows, — the windows of the corridors or of the kitchens, masked by a thick trellis.

The path leading from the great Trianon, the established residence of Louis XIV., to the little, was through a kitchen-garden which connected the two residences by means of a wooden bridge. It was through this kitchen and fruit garden, which La Quintinie had designed and planted, that Louis XV. conducted Monsieur de Choiseul to the little Trianon after the laborious council we have just mentioned. He wished to show him the improvements he had made in the new abode of the dauphin and dauphiness.

Monsieur de Choiseul admired everything and commented upon everything with the sagacity of a courtier. He listened while the king told him that the little Trianon became every day more beautiful, more charming to live in; and the minister added that it would serve as his Majesty's private residence.

"The dauphiness," said the king, "is rather timid yet, like all young Germans; she speaks French well, but she is afraid of a slight accent, which to French ears betrays the Austrian. At Trianon she will see only friends, and will speak only when she wishes."

"The result will be that she will speak well. I have already had the honor to remark," said Monsieur de Choiseul, "that her Royal Highness is accomplished, and needs nothing to make her perfect."

On the way the two travellers found the dauphin standing motionless upon a lawn, measuring the sun's altitude. Monsieur de Choiseul bent low; but as the dauphin did not speak to him, he did not speak to the dauphin.

The king said, loud enough to be heard by his grandson, "Louis is a finished scholar, but he is wrong thus to run his head against the sciences; his wife will suffer for it."

"By no means, Sire," replied a low, soft voice issuing from a thicket; and the king saw the dauphiness running toward him. She had been talking to a man provided with papers, compasses, and chalk.

"Sire," said the princess, "Monsieur Mique, my architect."

"Ah!" exclaimed the king, "then you, too, are bitten by that mania, Madame?"

"Sire, it runs in the family."

"You are going to build?"

"I am going to improve this great park, in which every one gets wearied."

"Oh, oh! my dear daughter, you speak too loud; the dauphin might hear you."

"It is a matter agreed upon between us, my father," replied the princess.

"To be wearied?"

"No; but to try to amuse ourselves."

"And so your Highness is going to build?" asked Monsieur de Choiseul.

"I intend making a garden of this park, Monsieur le Duc."

"Ah! poor Le Nôtre!" said the king.

"Le Nôtre was a great man, Sire, for what was in vogue then; but for what I love—"

"What do you love, Madame?"

"Nature."

"Ah! like the philosophers."

"Or like the English."

"Good! Say that before Choiseul, and you will have a declaration of war immediately. He will let loose upon you the sixty-four ships and forty frigates of his cousin, Monsieur de Praslin."

"Sire," said the dauphiness, "I am going to have a natural garden laid out here by Monsieur Robert, who is the cleverest man in the world in that particular branch of horticulture."

"And what do you call a natural garden?" asked the king. "I thought that trees and flowers and even fruit such as I gathered as I came along, were natural objects."

"Sire, you may walk a hundred years in your grounds, and you will see nothing but straight alleys, or thickets cut off at an angle of forty-five degrees, as the dauphin says, or pieces of water wedded to lawns, which in their turn are wedded to perspectives, parterres, or terraces."

"Well, that is ugly, is it?"

"It is not natural."

"There is a little girl who loves Nature!" said the

king, with a jovial rather than a joyous air. "Well, come; what will you make of my Trianon?"

"Rivers, cascades, bridges, grottos, rocks, woods, ravines, houses, mountains, fields."

"For dolls?" said the king.

"Alas! Sire, for kings such as we shall be," replied the princess, without remarking the blush which overspread her grandfather's face, and without perceiving that she foretold a sad truth for herself.

"Then you will destroy; but what will you build?"

"I shall preserve the present buildings."

"Ah! your people may consider themselves fortunate that you do not intend to lodge them in these woods and rivers you speak of, like Hurons, Esquimaux, and Greenlanders. They would live a natural life there, and Monsieur Rousseau would call them children of Nature. Do that, my child, and the encyclopedists will adore you."

"Sire, my servants would be too cold in such lodgings."

"Where will you lodge them, then, if you destroy all? Not in the palace; there is scarcely room for you two there."

"Sire, I will keep the offices as they are;" and the dauphiness pointed to the windows of the corridor which we have described.

"What do I see there?" said the king, shading his eyes with his hand.

"A woman, Sire," said Monsieur de Choiseul.

"A young lady whom I have taken into my household," replied the dauphiness.

"Mademoiselle de Taverney," said Choiseul, with his piercing glance.

"Ah!" said the king; "so you have the Taverneys here?"

"Only Mademoiselle de Taverney, Sire."

"A charming girl! What do you make of her."

"My reader."

"Very good," said the king, without taking his eye from the window through which Mademoiselle de Taverney, still pale from her illness, was looking very innocently, and without in the least suspecting that she was observed.

"How pale she is," said Monsieur de Choiseul.

"She was nearly killed on the 30th of May. Monsieur le Duc."

"Indeed?. Poor girl!" said the king. "That Monsieur Bignon deserves to be disgraced."

"She is quite well again?" said Monsieur de Choiseul, hastily.

"Thank God, yes, Monsieur le Duc!"

"Ah!" said the king, "she has fled."

"She has perhaps recognized your Majesty; she is very timid."

"Has she been with you long?"

"Since yesterday, Sire; I sent for her when I installed myself here."

"What a melancholy abode for a young girl!" said Louis. "That devil of a Gabriel was very clumsy. He did not remember that the trees, as they grew, would conceal and darken that building."

"But I assure you, Sire, that the apartments are very tolerable."

"That is impossible," said Louis XV.

"Will your Majesty deign to convince yourself?" said the dauphiness, anxious to do the honors of her palace.

"Very well. Will you come, Choiseul?"

"Sire, it is two o'clock. I have a parliamentary meeting at half-past two. I have only time to return to Versailles."

"Well, Duke, go; and give those black-gowns a shake for me. Dauphiness, show me these little apartments, if you please; I have a great liking for interiors."

"Come, Monsieur Mique," said the dauphiness to her architect, "you will have an opportunity of profiting by the opinion of his Majesty, who understands everything so well."

The king walked first, the dauphiness followed. They mounted the little flight of steps which led to the chapel, avoiding the entrance of the courtyard, which was at one side. The door of the chapel is on the left; the staircase, narrow and unpretending, which leads to the corridor, on the right.

"Who lives here?" asked Louis XV.

"No one yet, Sire."

"There is a key in the door of the first suite of apartments."

"Ah, yes, true! Mademoiselle de Taverney enters it to-day."

"Here?" said the king, pointing to the door.

"Yes, Sire."

"And is she there at present? If so, let us not enter."

"Sire, she has just gone down; I saw her walking under the veranda of the court-yard."

"Then show me her apartments as an example."

"As you please," replied the dauphiness; and she introduced the king into the principal apartment, which was preceded by an ante-room and two closets.

Some articles of furniture which were already arranged, several books, a pianoforte, and, above all, an enormous bouquet of the most beautiful flowers, which Mademoiselle de Taverney had placed in a Chinese vase, attracted the king's attention. "Ah!" said he, "what beautiful flowers! And yet you wish to change the garden! Who the devil supplies your people with flowers like these? Do they keep some for you?"

"It is in truth a beautiful bouquet."

"The gardener takes good care of Mademoiselle de Taverney. Who is your gardener here?"

"I do not know, Sire. Monsieur de Jussieu undertook to procure them for me."

The king gave a curious glance around the apartments, looked again at the exterior, peeped into the courtyard, and went away. His Majesty crossed the park and returned to the great Trianon, where his equipages were already in waiting for a hunt which was to take place after dinner, in carriages, from three till six o'clock.

The dauphin was still measuring the sun's altitude.

CHAPTER XXXVI.

THE CONSPIRACY IS RENEWED.

WHILE the king, in order to reassure Monsieur de Choiseul and not to lose any time himself, was walking thus in the Trianon till the chase should begin, Luciennes was the centre of a reunion of frightened conspirators, who had flown swiftly to Madame Dubarry, like birds who have smelt the sportsman's powder.

Jean and the Maréchal de Richelieu, after having looked at each other ill-humoredly for some time, were the first to take flight. The others were the usual herd of favorites, whom the certain disgrace of the Choiseuls had allured, whom the duke's return to favor had alarmed, and who, no longer finding the minister there to fawn upon, had returned mechanically to Luciennes, to see if the tree was yet strong enough for them to cling to as before.

Madame Dubarry was taking a siesta after the fatigues of her diplomacy and the deceptive triumph which had crowned it, when Richelieu's carriage rolled into the court with the noise and swiftness of a whirlwind.

"Mistress Dubarry is asleep," said Zamore, without moving.

Jean sent Zamore rolling on the carpet with a scientific kick, inflicted upon the most highly ornamented portion of his governor's uniform. Zamore screamed, and Chon hastened to inquire the cause. "You are beating that little fellow again, you brute!" said she.

"And I will exterminate you," continued Jean, with kindling eyes, "if you do not immediately awaken the Countess."

But there was no need to awaken the countess; at Zamore's cries, at the growling tones of Jean's voice, she had suspected some misfortune, and hastened into the room, wrapped in a dressing-gown.

"What is the matter?" she exclaimed, alarmed at seeing Jean stretched at full length upon the sofa to calm the agitation of his bile, and at finding that the marshal did not even kiss her hand.

"The matter, the matter?" said Jean. "*Parbleu!* what is always the matter, — the Choiseuls!"

"What do you mean?"

"Yes, thousand thunders! — firmer than ever."

"What are you saying?"

"The Comte Dubarry is right," continued Richelieu; "Monsieur the Duc de Choiseul is firmer than ever."

The countess drew the king's letter from her bosom. "And this?" said she, smiling.

"Have you read it aright, Countess?" asked the marshal.

"Why, I fancy I can read, Duke," replied Madame Dubarry.

"I do not doubt it, Madame. Will you allow me to read it also?"

"Oh, certainly! Read."

The duke took the paper, unfolded it slowly, and read: —

To-morrow I will thank Monsieur de Choiseul for his services. I promise it positively.   LOUIS.

"Is that clear?" said the countess.

"Perfectly clear," replied the marshal, with a grimace.

"Well, what?" said Jean.

"Well, it is to-morrow that we shall be victorious, and nothing is lost as yet."

"What! to-morrow? The king signed that for me yesterday; therefore 'to-morrow' is to-day."

"Pardon me, Madame!" said the duke; "as there is no date to the note, to-morrow will always be the day after you wish to see Monsieur de Choiseul dismissed. In the Rue de la Grange-Batalière, about one hundred paces from my house, there is a tavern, on the signboard of which is written in red characters, 'Credit given here to-morrow.' To-morrow, — that is, never."

"The king mocks us!" said Jean, furiously.

"Impossible," said the alarmed countess; "impossible! Such a trick would be unworthy —"

"Ah, Madame, his Majesty is so merry!" said Richelieu.

"He shall pay for this, Duke," said the countess, in a tone of anger.

"After all, Countess, we must not be angry with the king. We cannot accuse his Majesty of cheating or tricking us, for the king has performed what he promised."

"Oh!" said Jean, with a more than vulgar shrug of his shoulders.

"What did he promise?" cried the countess. "To thank Choiseul for his services?"

"And that is precisely what he has done, Madame. I heard his Majesty myself thank the Duke for his services. The word has two meanings: in diplomacy, each takes the one he prefers. You have chosen yours, the king has chosen his. Therefore there is no more question of to-morrow. It is indeed to-day, according to your opinion, that the king should have kept his promise; and he has done so. I who speak to you heard him thank Choiseul."

"Duke, this is no time for jesting, I think."

"Do you think I am jesting, Countess? Ask Comte Jean."

"No, *pardieu!*" said Jean, "it is no laughing matter. This morning Choiseul was embraced, flattered, feasted by the king; and even now he is walking arm in arm with him at Trianon."

"Arm in arm!" exclaimed Chon, who had slipped into the room, and who raised her snowy arms like a second Niobe in despair.

"Yes, I have been tricked," said the countess; "but we shall see. Chon, countermand my carriage for the chase. I will not go."

"Good!" said Jean.

"One moment," cried Richelieu. "No hurry, no pouting! Ah, forgive me, Countess, for daring to advise you! I entreat you to pardon me!"

"Go on, Duke; do not apologize. I think I am losing my senses. See how I am placed! I did not wish to meddle with politics, and the first time I touch upon them self-love launches me so far. You were saying —"

"That pouting now would not be prudent. The position is difficult, Countess. If the king is so decidedly in favor of these Choiseuls, if the dauphiness has so much influence over him, if he thus openly breaks a lance with you, you must —"

"Well, what?"

"You must be even more amiable than usual, Countess. I know it is impossible; but in a position like ours, the impossible becomes necessary. Attempt the impossible, then."

The countess reflected.

"For, in short," said the duke, "if the king should adopt German manners —"

"If he should become virtuous!" exclaimed Jean, horrified.

"Who knows, Countess?" said Richelieu; "novelty is so attractive."

"Oh, as for that," replied the Countess, with a nod of incredulity, "I do not believe it!"

"More extraordinary things have happened, Countess. You know the proverb of the devil turning hermit. So you must not pout."

"But I am suffocating with rage."

"*Parbleu!* Countess, I can believe you; but suffocate before us, breathe freely before the enemy. Do not let the king — that is to say, Monsieur de Choiseul — perceive your anger."

"And shall I go to the chase?"

"It would be most politic."

"And you, Duke?"

"Oh! I? If I should have to crawl on all-fours, I shall go."

"Come in my carriage, then!" cried the countess, to see what face her ally would put on.

"Oh, Countess!" replied the duke, smirking to hide his vexation, "it is such an honor—"

"That you refuse?"

"I? God forbid!"

"Take care; you will compromise yourself."

"I have no wish to compromise myself."

"He confesses it,—he dares to confess it!" cried Madame Dubarry.

"Countess, Countess! Monsieur de Choiseul will never forgive me."

"Are you already on such good terms with Monsieur de Choiseul?"

"Countess, Countess! I shall get into disgrace with the dauphiness."

"Would you rather we should each continue the war

separately, without sharing the spoil? There is still time. You are not compromised, and you may yet withdraw from the partnership."

"You misunderstand me, Countess," said the duke, kissing her hands. "Did I hesitate on the day of your presentation to send you a dress, a hairdresser, and a carriage? Well, I shall not hesitate any more to-day. Oh! I am bolder than you imagine, Countess."

"Then it is agreed. We will go to this hunt together; and that will serve me as a pretext for not seeing or speaking to any one."

"Not even to the king?"

"Oh! on the contrary, I will give him such sweet words that he will be in despair."

"Bravo! that is good tactics."

"But you, Jean, what are you doing there? Do endeavor to rise from those cushions; you are burying yourself alive, my good friend."

"You want to know what I am doing, do you? Well, I am thinking —"

"Of what?"

"I am thinking that all the ballad-writers of the town and of the department are setting us to all possible tunes; that the 'Nouvelles à la Main' is cutting us up like meat for pies; that the 'Gazetier Cuirassé' is piercing us for want of a cuirass; that the 'Journal des Observateurs' observes us even to the marrow of our bones; that, in short, to-morrow we shall be in so pitiable a state that even a Choiseul might pity us."

"And what is the result of your reflections?" asked the duke.

"Why, that I must hasten to Paris to buy a little lint and no inconsiderable quantity of ointment to put upon our wounds. Give me some money, my little sister."

"How much?" asked the countess.

"A trifle; two or three hundred louis."

"You see, Duke," said the countess, turning to Richelieu, "that I am already paying the expenses of the war."

"That is only the beginning of the campaign; and what you sow to-day, to-morrow you will reap."

The countess shrugged her shoulders slightly, rose, went to her chiffonniere, and opening it, took out a handful of bank-notes, which, without counting them, she handed to Jean, who, also without counting them, pocketed them with a deep sigh. Then rising, yawning, and stretching himself like a man overwhelmed with fatigue, he took a few steps across the room. "See," said he, pointing to the duke and the countess, "these people are going to amuse themselves at the chase, while I have to gallop to Paris. They will see gay cavaliers and lovely women, and I shall see nothing but the hideous faces of scribbling drudges. Certainly, I am the turnspit of the establishment."

"Mark me, Duke," said the countess, "he will never bestow a thought on us. Half my bank-notes will be squandered on some opera-girl, and the rest will disappear in a gambling-house. That is his errand to Paris, and yet he bemoans himself, the wretch! Leave my sight, Jean, you disgust me."

Jean emptied three plates of bonbons, stuffed the contents into his pockets, stole a Chinese figure with diamond eyes from the landing, and stalked off with a most majestic strut, pursued by the exclamations of the countess.

"What a delightful youth!" said Richelieu, in the tone of a parasite who praises a spoiled brat, while all the time he is inwardly devoting him to the infernal regions; "he is very dear to you, I suppose, Countess?"

"As you say, Duke, he has fixed all his happiness in me, and the speculation brings him three or four hundred thousand francs a year."

The clock struck.

"Half-past twelve, Countess," said the duke. "Luckily you are almost dressed. Show yourself a little to your courtiers, who might otherwise think there is an eclipse, and then let us to our carriage. You know how the chase is ordered?"

"His Majesty and I arranged it yesterday; they were to proceed to the forest of Marly, and take me up in passing."

"Oh! I am very sure the king has not changed the programme."

"In the mean time, Duke, let me hear your plan; it is your turn now."

"Madame, I wrote yesterday to my nephew, who, if I may believe my presentiments, is already on his way hither."

"Monsieur d'Aiguillon?"

"I should not be surprised if he crosses my letter on the road, and if he were here to-morrow or the day after at the latest."

"Then you count upon him?"

"Oh! Madame, he does not want for sense."

"No matter who it is, for we are at the last extremity. The king might perhaps submit, if he had not such a mortal antipathy to business."

"So that —"

"So that I fear he will never consent to give up Monsieur de Choiseul."

"Shall I speak frankly to you, Countess?"

"Certainly."

"Well! I think so too. The king will find a hundred

stratagems like that of yesterday; his Majesty has so much wit! And then, on your side, Countess, you will never risk losing his love by an unheard-of obstinacy."

"Perhaps. I must reflect upon that."

"You see, Countess, Monsieur de Choiseul is there for an eternity; nothing but a miracle can dislodge him."

"Yes, a miracle," repeated Jeanne.

"And unfortunately we are not now in the age of miracles."

"Oh!" said Madame Dubarry, "I know some one who works miracles yet."

"You know a man who works miracles?"

"By my faith, yes!"

"And you have not told me?"

"I thought of it only just now, Duke."

"Do you think he could assist us in this affair?"

"I think he can do everything."

"Oh, indeed! And what miracle has he worked? Tell me that, Countess, so that I may judge of his skill by the example."

"Duke," said Madame Dubarry, approaching Richelieu and involuntarily lowering her voice, "he is a man who, ten years ago, met me upon the Place Louis XV., and told me I should be queen of France."

"Indeed! that is miraculous; and could he tell me, think you, that I shall die prime minister?"

"Don't you think so?"

"Oh, I don't doubt it in the least! What is his name?"

"His name will tell you nothing."

"Where is he?"

"Ah! that I don't know."

"He did not give you his address?"

"No; he was to come to me for his recompense."

"What did you promise him?"

"Whatever he should ask."

"And he has not come?"

"No."

"Countess, that is even more miraculous than his prediction. We must certainly have this man."

"But how shall we proceed?"

"His name, Countess, his name!"

"He has two."

"Proceed according to order, — the first?"

"The Comte de Fenix."

"What! the man you pointed out to me on the day of your presentation?"

"Yes; the Prussian officer."

"Oh! I have no longer any faith in him. All the sorcerers I have ever known had names ending in *i* or *o*."

"That exactly suits, Duke; for his second name is Joseph Balsamo."

"But have you no way of finding him?"

"I shall task my brain, Duke. I think I know some one who knows him."

"Good! But make haste, Countess. It is now a quarter to one."

"I am ready. My carriage, there!"

Ten minutes afterward Madame Dubarry and Monsieur de Richelieu were seated side by side, and driving rapidly on their way to the hunting party.

CHAPTER XXXVII.

THE SORCERER CHASE.

A LONG train of carriages filled the avenues of the forest of Marly, where the king was hunting. It was what was called the afternoon chase. In the latter part of his life Louis XV. neither shot at nor rode after the game; he was content with watching the progress of the chase.

Those of our readers who have read Plutarch will perhaps remember that cook of Mark Antony's who put a boar on the spit every hour, so that among the six or seven boars which were roasting, there might always be one ready whenever Mark Antony wished to dine. The reason of this was that Mark Antony, as governor of Asia Minor, was overwhelmed with business. He was the dispenser of justice, and as the Cilicians are great thieves (the fact is confirmed by Juvenal), Mark Antony had abundance of work on his hands. He had therefore always five or six roasts in various degrees of progress on the spit, waiting for the moment when his functions as judge would permit him to snatch a hasty morsel.

Louis XV. acted in a similar manner. For the afternoon chase there were three or four stags started at different hours; and accordingly as the king felt disposed he chose a nearer or more distant "view halloo." On this day his Majesty had signified his intention of hunting until four o'clock. A stag was therefore chosen, which had been started at noon, and which might consequently be expected to run until that hour.

Madame Dubarry intended to follow the king as faithfully as the king intended to follow the stag. But hunters propose, and fate disposes. A combination of circumstances frustrated this happy project of Madame Dubarry's, and the countess found in fate an adversary almost as capricious as herself.

While the countess, talking politics with Monsieur de Richelieu, drove rapidly after the king, who in his turn drove rapidly after the stag, and while the duke and she returned in part the bows which greeted them as they passed, they suddenly perceived, about fifty paces from the road, beneath a magnificent canopy of verdure, an open carriage turned upside down, while the two black horses which should have drawn it were peaceably munching, the one the bark of a beech-tree, the other the moss growing at his feet.

Madame Dubarry's horses, a magnificent pair presented to her by the king, had distanced — as we say nowadays — all the other carriages, and were the first to arrive in sight of the broken carriage.

"Ha, an accident!" said the countess, calmly.

"Faith, yes!" said the Duc de Richelieu, with equal coolness, for sensibility is little in fashion at court; "the carriage is broken to pieces."

"Is that a corpse upon the grass?" asked the countess. "Look, Duke."

"I think not; it moves."

"Is it a man or a woman?"

"I don't know; I cannot see well."

"Ha! it bows to us."

"Then it cannot be dead;" and Richelieu at all hazards took off his hat. "But, Countess," said he, "it seems to me —"

"And to me also —"

"A long train of carriages filled the avenues of the forest."

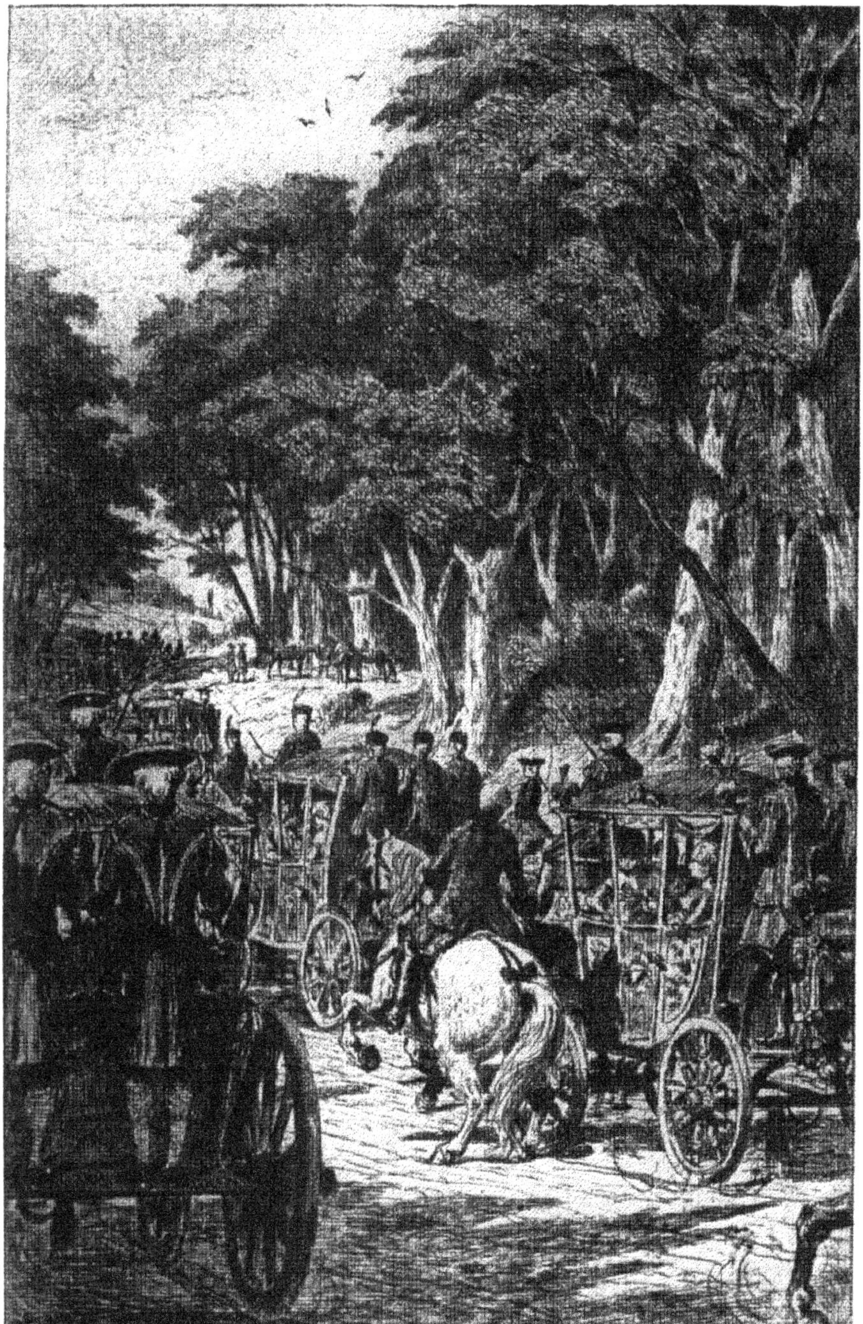

"That it is his Eminence Prince Louis."

"The Cardinal de Rohan in person!"

"What the devil is he doing there?" asked the duke.

"Let us go and see," replied the countess. "Champagne, drive on to the broken carriage."

The coachman immediately left the highroad and dashed in among the lofty trees.

"Faith, yes! it is Monseigneur le Cardinal," said Richelieu.

It was in truth his Eminence, who was lying stretched upon the grass, waiting until some of his friends should pass. Seeing Madame Dubarry approach, he rose. "A thousand compliments to the countess!" said he.

"What, Cardinal! is it you?"

"Myself, Madame."

"On foot?"

"No, sitting."

"Are you hurt?"

"Not in the least."

"And how in all the world do you happen to be in this condition?"

"Do not speak of it, Madame; that brute of a coachman, a rascal whom I imported from England, when I told him to cut across the wood in order to join the chase, turned so suddenly that he upset me and broke my best carriage."

"You must not complain, Cardinal," said the countess; "a French coachman would have broken your neck, or at least your ribs."

"Very possibly."

"Therefore be consoled."

"Oh! I am somewhat of a philosopher, Countess. But I shall have to wait, and that is fatal."

"How, Prince! to wait? A Rohan wait?"

"There is no alternative."

"Oh, no! I would rather alight and leave you my carriage."

"In truth, Madame, your kindness makes me ashamed."

"Come, jump in, Prince; jump in."

"No, thank you, Madame; I am waiting for Soubise, who is at the chase, and who cannot fail to pass in a few moments."

"But if he should have taken another road?"

"Oh! it is of no consequence."

"Monseigneur, I entreat you."

"No, thank you."

"But why not?"

"I am unwilling to incommode you."

"Cardinal, if you refuse to enter, I will order one of the footmen to carry my train, and I will roam through the woods like a dryad."

The cardinal smiled, and thinking that a longer resistance might be interpreted unfavorably by the countess, he consented to enter the carriage. The duke had already given up his place, and moved over to the seat in front. The cardinal entreated him to resume his former position, but the duke was inflexible. The countess's splendid horses soon made up for the time which had thus been lost.

"Pardon me, Monseigneur," said the countess, addressing the cardinal, "has your Eminence been reconciled to the chase?"

"Why do you ask?"

"Because this is the first time I have seen you join in that amusement."

"By no means, Countess. I had come to Versailles to have the honor of paying my respects to his Majesty, when I was told he was at the chase. I had to speak to him on some important business, and therefore followed, hoping to overtake him; but thanks to this cursed coachman, I shall not only lose his Majesty's ear, but also my assignation in town."

"You see, Madame," said the duke, laughing, "Monseigneur makes a free confession, — he has an assignation!"

"Which, I repeat, I shall fail to meet," replied the cardinal.

"Does a Rohan, a prince, a cardinal, ever fail in anything?" said the countess.

"It looks so now," said the prince, "unless a miracle comes to my assistance."

The duke and the countess looked at each other; this word recalled their recent conversation.

"Faith! Prince," said the countess, "speaking of miracles, I will confess frankly that I am very happy to meet a dignitary of the Church, that I may ask him if he believes in them."

"In what, Madame?"

"*Parbleu!* in miracles," said the duke.

"The Scriptures give them as an article of faith, Madame," said the cardinal, trying to look devout.

"Oh! I am not speaking of ancient miracles," replied the countess.

"And of what miracles do you speak, Madame?"

"Of modern miracles."

"Those indeed, I confess, are rather more rare," said the cardinal; "but still —"

"But still, what?"

"Faith! I have seen things which, if they were not miraculous, were at least very incredible."

"You have seen such things, Prince?"

"On my honor."

"But you know, Madame," said Richelieu, laughing, "that his Eminence is said to be in communication with spirits, which, perhaps, is not very orthodox."

"No, but which must be very convenient," said the countess. "And what have you seen, Prince?"

"I have sworn not to reveal it."

"Oh! that begins to look serious."

"It is a fact, Madame."

"But if you have promised to observe secrecy respecting the sorcery, perhaps you have not done so as regards the sorcerer?"

"No."

"Well, then, Prince, I must tell you that the duke and myself came out to-day with the intention of seeking some magician."

"Really?"

"Upon my honor."

"Take mine."

"I desire nothing better."

"He is at your disposal, Countess."

"And at mine also, Prince?"

"And at yours also, Duke."

"What is his name?"

"The Comte de Fenix."

The countess and the duke looked at each other and turned pale. "That is strange," said they together.

"Do you know him?" asked the prince.

"No. And you think him a sorcerer?"

"I am positive of it."

"You have spoken to him, then?"

"Of course."

"And you found him —"

"Perfect."

"On what occasion, may I ask?"

"Why —" the cardinal hesitated, — "on the occasion of his foretelling my fortune."

"Correctly?"

"He told me things of the other world."

"Has he no other name than the Comte de Fenix?"

"Yes; I have heard him called —"

"Speak Monseigneur," said the countess, impatiently.

"Joseph Balsamo, Madame."

The countess clasped her hands and looked at Richelieu. Richelieu rubbed the end of his nose and looked at the countess.

"Is the devil very black?" asked Madame Dubarry, suddenly.

"The devil, Countess? I have not seen him."

"What are you thinking of, Countess?" cried Richelieu. "*Pardieu!* that would be respectable company for a cardinal!"

"And did he tell you your fortune without showing you the devil?" asked the countess.

"Oh! certainly," said the cardinal; "they show the devil only to people of no consideration. We can dispense with him."

"But say what you will, Prince," continued Madame Dubarry, "there must be a little deviltry at the bottom of it."

"Faith! I think so."

"Blue fire, spectres, infernal caldrons which smell horribly while they boil, eh?"

"Oh, no! my sorcerer is most polite and well-bred; he is a very gallant man, and receives his visitors in good style."

"Will you not have your horoscope drawn by this man, Countess?" said Richelieu.

"I long to do so, I confess."

"Do so, then, Madame."

"But where does all this take place?" asked Madame Dubarry, hoping that the cardinal would give her the wished-for address.

"In a very handsome room, fashionably furnished."

The countess could scarcely conceal her impatience. "Very well," said she; "but the house?"

"A very fine house, though in a singular style of architecture."

The countess stamped with rage at being so ill understood. Richelieu came to her assistance. "But do you not see, Monseigneur," said he, "that madame is eager to know where your sorcerer lives?"

"Where he lives, you say? Oh! well," replied the cardinal, "eh! faith — wait a moment — no — yes — no. It is in the Marais, near the corner of the boulevard, Rue St. François, St. Anastasie — no. However, it is the name of some saint."

"But what saint? You must surely know them all."

"No, faith! I know very little about them," said the cardinal. "But stay — my fool of a footman must remember."

"Oh! very fortunately he got up behind," said the duke. "Stop, Champagne, stop!" and the duke pulled the cord which was attached to the coachman's little finger, who suddenly reined in the foaming horses, throwing them on their sinewy haunches.

"Olive," said the cardinal, "are you there, you scoundrel?"

"Yes, Monseigneur."

"Where did I stop one evening in the Marais, — a long time back?"

The lackey had overheard the whole conversation, but took care not to appear as if he had done so. "In the Marais?" said he, seeming to search his memory.

"Yes, near the boulevards."

"What day, Monseigneur?"

"One day when I was returning from St. Denis."

"From St. Denis?" said Olive, to give himself importance, and to make his hesitation seem more natural.

"Eh! yes, from St. Denis; the carriage, I think, waited for me in the boulevards."

"Oh, yes, Monseigneur," said Olive, "I remember now. A man came and threw a very heavy parcel into the carriage; I remember it perfectly."

"Very possibly," replied the cardinal; "but who asked you about that, you scoundrel?"

"What does your Eminence wish, then?"

"To know the name of the street."

"Rue St. Claude, Monseigneur."

"Claude, that is it!" cried the cardinal. "I would have laid any wager it was the name of a saint."

"Rue St. Claude!" repeated the countess, darting such an expressive glance at Richelieu that the marshal, fearing to let any one into his secrets, especially when they related to a conspiracy, interrupted Madame Dubarry by these words: "Ha! Countess, — the king!"

"Where?"

"Yonder."

"The king! the king!" exclaimed the countess. "To the left, Champagne, to the left, that his Majesty may not see us."

"And why, Countess?" asked the astonished cardinal. "I thought that, on the contrary, you were taking me to his Majesty."

"Oh, true! you wish to see the king, do you not?"

"I came for that alone, Madame."

"Very well! you shall be taken to the king —"

"But you?"

"Oh! we shall remain here."

"But, Countess —"

"No apologies, Prince, I entreat; every one to his own

business. The king is yonder, under those chestnut-trees; you have business with the king, — very well, the affair is easily arranged. Champagne!"

Champagne pulled up.

"Champagne, let us alight here, and you may take his Eminence to the king."

"What! alone, Countess?" exclaimed the cardinal.

"You wish to have an audience of his Majesty, Cardinal?"

"It is true."

"Well! you shall have him entirely to yourself."

"Ah! this kindness overwhelms me;" and the prelate gallantly kissed Madame Dubarry's hand. "But where will you remain yourself, Madame?" he inquired.

"Here, under these trees."

"The king will be looking for you."

"So much the better."

"He will be uneasy at not seeing you."

"And that will torment him, — just what I wish."

"Countess, you are adorable."

"That is precisely what the king says when I have tormented him. Champagne, when you have taken his Eminence to the king, you will return at full gallop."

"Yes, Madame."

"Adieu, Duke," said the cardinal."

"Au revoir, Monseigneur," replied the duke.

And the valet having let down the step, the duke alighted and handed out the countess, who leaped to the ground as lightly as a nun escaping from a convent, while the carriage rapidly bore his Eminence to the hillock from which his most Christian Majesty was seeking, with his short-sighted eyes, the naughty countess whom every one had seen but himself.

Madame Dubarry lost no time. She took the duke's

arm, and drawing him into the thicket,—"Do you know," said she, "it must have been Providence who sent that dear cardinal to us."

"To get rid of him for a moment,—I understand that," replied the duke.

"No, to put us on the trace of our man!"

"Then we are going to his house?"

"I think so; but—"

"What, Countess?"

"I am afraid, I confess it."

"Of whom?"

"Of the sorcerer. Oh, I am very superstitious!"

"The devil!"

"And you, do you believe in sorcerers?"

"I can't say I do not, Countess."

"My story of the prediction—"

"Is a startling fact. And I myself," said the old marshal, scratching his ear, "once met a certain sorcerer—"

"Bah!"

"— Who rendered me a very important service."

"What service, Duke?"

"He resuscitated me."

"He resuscitated you?"

"Certainly; I was dead,—no less."

"Oh! tell me the whole affair, Duke."

"Let us conceal ourselves, then."

"Duke, you are a dreadful coward."

"Oh, no! I am only prudent."

"Are we well placed here?"

"Yes, I think so."

"Well, the story, the story!"

"Well, I was at Vienna. It was when I was ambassador there. One evening, while I was standing under a lamp, I received a sword-thrust through my body. It was a husband's sword, — devilishly unwholesome. I fell. Some one picked me up; I was dead."

"What! you were dead?"

"Yes, or nearly so. A sorcerer passes, who asks who is the man whom they are carrying. He is told it is I; he stops the litter, pours three drops of some unknown liquid into the wound, three more between my lips, and the bleeding stops, respiration returns, my eyes open, and I am cured."

"It is a miracle from heaven, Duke."

"That is just what frightens me; for, on the contrary, I believe it is a miracle of the devil."

"True, Marshal; God would not have saved a dissipated rake like you. Honor to whom honor is due. And does your sorcerer still live?"

"I doubt it, unless he has found the elixir of life."

"Like you, Marshal?"

"Do you believe these stories, then?"

"I believe everything. He was old?"

"Methuselah in person."

"And his name?"

"Ah! a magnificent Greek name, — Althotas."

"What a terrible name, Marshal!"

"Is it not, Madame?"

"Duke, there is the carriage returning. Are we decided? Shall we go to Paris and visit the Rue St. Claude?"

"If you like. But the king is waiting for you."

"That would determine me, Duke, if I had not already determined. He has tormented me. Now, France, it is your turn to suffer."

"But he will think you are lost, — carried off."

"And so much the more, that I have been seen with you, Marshal."

"Stay, Countess! I will be frank with you; I am afraid."

"Of what?"

"I am afraid that you will tell all this to some one, and that I shall be laughed at."

"Then we shall both be laughed at together, since I go with you."

"That decides me, Countess. However, if you betray me, I shall say —"

"What will you say?"

"I shall say that you came with me *tête-à-tête*."

"No one will believe you, Duke."

"Ah, Countess, if the king were not there!"

"Champagne, Champagne! Here, behind this thicket, that we may not be seen. Germain, the door. That will do. Now to Paris, Rue St. Claude, in the Marais, and let the pavement smoke for it."

CHAPTER XXXVIII.

THE COURIER.

It was six o'clock in the evening. In that chamber in the Rue St. Claude into which we have already introduced our readers, Balsamo was seated beside Lorenza, now awake, and was endeavoring by persuasion to soften that rebellious spirit. But the young woman looked askance at him, as Dido looked at Æneas when he was about to leave her, she spoke only to reproach him, and moved her hand only to repulse him. She complained that she was a prisoner, a slave; that she could no longer breathe the fresh air, nor see the sun. She envied the fate of the poorest creatures, of the birds, of the flowers. She called Balsamo her tyrant. Then, passing from reproaches to rage, she tore into shreds the rich stuffs which her husband had given her to cheer, by this semblance of gayety, the solitude he imposed on her.

Balsamo, on the other hand, spoke gently to her, and looked at her lovingly. It was evident that this weak, irritable creature filled a large place in his heart, if not in his life.

"Lorenza," said he to her, "my beloved, why do you display this spirit of resistance and hostility? Why will you not live with me, who love you inexpressibly, as a gentle and devoted companion? You would then have nothing to wish for; you would be free to bloom in the sun like the flowers of which you spoke just now, — to stretch your wings like the birds whose fate you envy.

We would go everywhere together. You would not only see the sun which delights you so much, but the factitious sun of splendor and fashion, — those assemblies to which the women of this country resort. You would be happy according to your tastes, while rendering me happy in mine. Why will you refuse this happiness, Lorenza, — you who, with your beauty and riches, would make so many women envious?"

"Because I abhor you!" said the proud young woman.

Balsamo cast on Lorenza a glance expressive at once of anger and pity. "Live, then, as you condemn yourself to live," said he; "and since you are so proud, do not complain."

"I should not complain, if you would leave me alone; I should not complain, if you did not force me to speak to you. Do not come into my presence, or when you do enter my prison, do not speak to me, and I will do as the poor birds from the South do when they are imprisoned in cages, — they die, but they do not sing."

Balsamo made an effort to control himself.

"Come, Lorenza," said he, "a little more gentleness and resignation. Look into my heart, which loves you above all things. Do you wish for books?"

"No."

"Why not? Books would amuse you."

"I wish to weary myself to death."

Balsamo smiled, or rather endeavored to smile. "You are mad," said he; "you know very well that you cannot die while I am here to take care of you and to cure you when you fall ill."

"Oh!" cried Lorenza, "you will not cure me when you find me strangled with this scarf against the bars of my window."

Balsamo shuddered.

"Or when," continued she, furiously, "I have opened this knife and stabbed myself to the heart."

Balsamo, pale as death, and bathed in cold perspiration, gazed at Lorenza, and with a threatening voice, "No, Lorenza," said he, "you are right; I shall not cure you then, I shall bring you back to life."

Lorenza gave a cry of terror. She knew no bounds to Balsamo's power, and believed his threat. Balsamo was saved. While she was plunged in this new abyss of suffering, which she had not foreseen, and while her vacillating reason saw itself encircled by a never-ceasing round of torture, the sound of the signal-bell pulled by Fritz reached Balsamo's ear. It struck three times quickly, and at regular intervals.

"A courier," said he.

Then after a pause another ring was heard.

"And in haste," he said.

"Ah!" said Lorenza, "you are about to leave me, then!"

He took the young woman's cold hand in his. "Once more and for the last time, Lorenza," said he, "let us live on good terms with each other like brother and sister. Since destiny unites us to each other, let us make destiny a friend, and not an executioner."

Lorenza did not reply. Her eye, motionless and sad, seemed to seek some thought which she could not find, perhaps because she had sought it too long and too earnestly, — like those who, after having lived in darkness, gaze too ardently on the sun, and are blinded by excess of light. Balsamo took her hand and kissed it without her giving any sign of life. Then he advanced toward the chimney. Immediately Lorenza started from her torpor, and eagerly fixed her gaze upon him.

"Oh!" said he, "you wish to know how I leave this,

in order to leave it one day after me and flee from me as you threatened. And therefore you awake; therefore you look at me."

Then, passing his hand over his forehead, as if he imposed a painful constraint on himself, he stretched his hand toward Lorenza, and said in a commanding voice, looking at her as if he were darting a javelin against her head and breast: "Sleep!"

The word was scarcely uttered when Lorenza bent like a flower upon its stem; her head, for a single moment unsteady, drooped and rested against the cushion of the sofa; her hands, of an opaque and waxen whiteness, glided down her sides, rustling her silken dress. Balsamo, seeing her so beautiful, approached her and pressed his lips upon her lovely forehead.

Then Lorenza's features brightened, as if a breath from the God of Love himself had swept away the cloud which rested on her brow. Her lips opened tremulously, her eyes swam in voluptuous tears, and she sighed as the angels must have sighed when in earth's youthful prime they stooped to love the children of men. Balsamo looked upon her for a moment, as if unable to withdraw his gaze; then as the bell sounded anew, he turned toward the chimney, touched a spring, and disappeared behind the flowers.

Fritz was waiting for him in the salon with a man dressed in the closely fitting jacket of a courier, and wearing thick boots armed with long spurs. The commonplace and inexpressive features of this man showed him to be one of the people; but his eye had in it a spark of sacred fire which seemed to have been breathed into him by some superior intelligence. His left hand grasped a short and knotty whip, while with his right hand he made some signs to Balsamo, which the latter instantly recognized, and to which, without speaking, he replied by touching his forehead with his forefinger.

The postilion's hand moved upward to his breast, where it traced another sign, which an indifferent observer would not have remarked, so closely did it resemble the movement made in fastening a button. To this sign the Master replied by showing a ring which he wore upon his finger. Before this powerful signet the messenger bent his knee.

"Whence come you?" asked Balsamo.

"From Rouen, Master."

"What is your profession?"

"I am a courier in the service of the Duchesse de Grammont."

"Who placed you there?"

"The will of the Great Copt."

"What orders did you receive when you entered the service?"

"To have no secret from the Master."

"Whither are you going?"

"To Versailles."

"What are you carrying?"

"A letter."

"For whom?"

"For the minister."

"Give it me."

The courier took a letter from a leathern bag fastened upon his shoulders behind, and gave it to Balsamo.

"Shall I wait?" he asked.

"Yes."

"I wait."

"Fritz!"

The German appeared.

"Keep Sebastian concealed in the office."

"He knows my name," murmured the courier, with superstitious fear.

"He knows everything," said Fritz, drawing him away.

When Balsamo was once more alone, he looked at the unbroken, deeply cut seal of the letter, which the imploring glance of the messenger had entreated him to respect as much as possible. Then, slowly and pensively, he once more mounted toward Lorenza's apartment, and opened the door of communication.

Lorenza was still sleeping, but seemingly tired and enervated by inaction. He took her hand, which she closed convulsively, and then he placed the letter, sealed as it was, upon her heart.

"Do you see?" he asked.

"Yes I see," replied Lorenza.

"What is the object which I hold in my hand?"

"A letter."

"Can you read it?"

"I can."

"Do so, then."

With closed eyes and palpitating bosom, Lorenza repeated, word for word, the following lines, which Balsamo wrote down as she spoke:—

DEAR BROTHER,— As I had foreseen, my exile will be at least of some service to us. I have this morning seen the president of Rouen; he is for us, but timid. I urged him in your name; he has at last decided, and the remonstrance of his division will be in Versailles within a week. I am about setting off for Rennes to rouse Karadeuc and La Chalotais, who are sleeping on their post. Our agent from Caudebec was in Rouen. I have seen him. England will not stop midway; she is preparing a sharp notification for the cabinet of Versailles. X— asked me if he should produce it, and I authorized him to do so. You will receive the last pamphlets of Morande and Delille against the Dubarry. They are petards which might blow up a town. A sad report reached me, that there was disgrace in the air; but as you have not written to me, I laugh at it. Do not leave me in doubt, however, and reply courier for courier. Your message will find me at Caen, where I have some of our gentlemen to gain over. Adieu; I salute you.

Duchesse de Grammont.

After reading thus far Lorenza stopped.

"You see nothing more?" asked Balsamo.

"I see nothing."

"No postscript?"

"No."

Balsamo, whose brow had gradually smoothed as Lorenza read the letter, now took it from her. "A curious document," said he, "and one for which they would pay me well. Oh! how can any one write such things?" he continued. "Yes, it is always women who are the ruin of great men. This Choiseul could not have been overthrown by an army of enemies, or by a world of intrigues; and now the breath of a woman crushes while it caresses him. Yes, we all perish by the treachery or the weakness of women. If we have a heart, and in that heart a sensitive chord, we are lost."

And as he spoke Balsamo gazed with inexpressible tenderness at Lorenza, who shuddered under his glance. "Is it true, what I think?" said he.

"No, no, it is not true!" she replied, eagerly; "you see plainly that I love you too dearly to do you any hurt, like those women you spoke of, without sense and without heart."

Balsamo allowed himself to be embraced by the arms of his enchantress.. Suddenly a double ring of Fritz's bell sounded twice.

"Two visitors," said Balsamo.

A single violent ring completed the telegraphic message. Balsamo, disengaging himself from Lorenza's arms, hastened from the apartment, leaving the young girl still asleep. On his way he met the courier, who was waiting for orders. "Here is your letter," said he.

"What must I do with it?"

"Deliver it as addressed."

"Is that all?"

"Yes."

The courier looked at the envelope and at the seal, and seeing them intact, as when he had brought them, expressed his satisfaction, and disappeared in the darkness.

"What a pity not to keep such an autograph," said Balsamo, "and, above all, what a pity not to be able to forward it by a safe hand to the king."

Fritz now appeared.

"Who is there?" asked Balsamo.

"A man and a woman."

"Have they been here before?"

"No."

"Do you know them?"

"No."

"Is the woman young?"

"Young and handsome."

"The man?"

"From sixty to sixty-five years of age."

"Where are they?"

"In the salon."

Balsamo entered.

CHAPTER XXXIX.

THE EVOCATION.

THE countess had completely concealed her face in a hood. As she had found time in passing to call at the family residence, she had assumed the dress of a citizen's wife. She had come in a carriage with the marshal, who, even more timid than she, had donned a gray dress like that of a superior servant in a respectable household.

"Do you recognize me, Count?" said Madame Dubarry.

"Perfectly, Madame la Comtesse."

Richelieu had remained in the background.

"Deign to be seated, Madame, and you also, Monsieur."

"This is my intendant," said the countess.

"You err, Madame," said Balsamo, bowing; "the gentleman is the Maréchal Duc de Richelieu, whom I recognize easily, and who would be very ungrateful if he did not recognize me."

"How so?" asked the duke, quite confounded.

"Monsieur le Duc, a man owes a little gratitude, I think, to those who have saved his life."

"Ah, ah, Duke!" said the countess, laughing; "do you hear, Duke?"

"What! you saved my life, Count?" asked Richelieu, astonished.

"Yes, Monseigneur, — at Vienna, in the year 1725, when you were ambassador there."

"In 1725! But you were not born, then, my dear Monsieur."

Balsamo smiled. "It seems to me that I was, Monsieur le Duc," said he, "since I met you dying, or rather dead, upon a litter. You had just received a sword-thrust right through your body, and I poured three drops of my elixir upon the wound. There, hold! in the place where you are ruffling your Alençon lace, — rather fine for an intendant."

"But," interrupted the marshal, "you are scarcely thirty-five years of age, Count."

"There, Duke," cried the countess, laughing heartily, "there you are before the sorcerer! Do you believe now?"

"I am stupefied, Countess! But at that period," continued the duke, addressing Balsamo, "you called yourself —"

"Oh, Duke, we sorcerers change our names in each generation! Now, in 1725 names ending in *us, os*, or *as*, were the fashion; and I should not be surprised if at that time I had been seized with the whim of bartering my name for one taken from the Latin or Greek. This being disposed of, I am at your service, Madame la Comtesse, — at your service, Monsieur le Duc."

"Count, the Marshal and I have come to consult you."

"You do me too much honor. Madame, especially if this idea arose naturally in your minds."

"Oh, in the most natural manner in the world, Count! Your prediction still haunts my thoughts; only I fear it will not be realized."

"Never doubt what science says, Madame."

"Oh, oh!" said Richelieu; "but our crown is a hazardous game, Count. It is not here an affair of a wound which three drops of elixir can cure."

"No; but of a minister whom three words can ruin," replied Balsamo. "Well, have I rightly divined? Tell me."

"Perfectly," said the countess, trembling. "Really, Duke, what do you say to all this?"

"Oh, do not let such a trifle astonish you, Madame!" said Balsamo; "whoever sees Madame Dubarry and Richelieu uneasy, may divine the cause without magic."

"And so," added the marshal, "I shall adore you if you will point out to us the remedy."

"The remedy for your complaint?"

"Yes; we are ill of the Choiseul."

"And you wish to be cured?"

"Yes, great magician."

"Count, you will not leave us in our embarrassment!" said the countess; "your honor is engaged."

"My best services are at your command, Madame; but I first wish to know if the duke had not some definite plan formed when he came here?"

"I confess it, Monsieur le Comte! Really, it is delightful to have a sorcerer who may be addressed as 'Monsieur le Comte;' we do not need to change our modes of speech."

Balsamo smiled. "Come," said he, "let us be frank."

"'Pon honor, I wish for nothing else," replied the duke.

"You had some plan to submit to me?"

"That is true."

"Ah, deceiver!" said the countess, "you never spoke of that to me."

"I could speak of it only to the count, and that in the most secret corner of his ear," replied the marshal.

"Why, Duke?"

"Because you would have blushed, Countess, to the whites of your eyes."

"Oh, tell it now, Marshal, to satisfy my curiosity! I am rouged, so you will see nothing."

"Well," said Richelieu, "this is what I thought. Take

care, Countess, I am going to take a most extravagant flight!"

"Fly as high as you will, Duke, I am prepared."

"Oh! but I fear you will beat me when you hear what I am about to say."

"You are not accustomed to be beaten, Monsieur le Duc," said Balsamo to the old marshal, who was delighted with the compliment.

"Well," he replied, " here it is. With all deference to Madame, to his Majesty, how am I to express it?"

"How tiresome he is!" cried the countess.

"You will have it, then?"

"Yes, yes; a hundred times, yes!"

"Then I will venture. It is a sad thing to say, Count, but his Majesty is no longer amusable! The word is not mine, Countess; it is Madame de Maintenon's."

"There is nothing in that which hurts me, Duke," said Madame Dubarry.

"So much the better; then I shall feel at my ease. Well, the Count, who discovers such precious elixirs, must —"

"Find one which shall restore to the king the faculty of being amused."

"Exactly."

"Oh, Duke, that is mere child's play, — the *a b c* of our craft! Any charlatan can furnish you with a philter —"

"Whose virtue," continued the duke, "would be put to the account of Madame's merit?"

"Duke!" exclaimed the countess.

"Oh! I knew you would be angry, but you would have it."

"Monsieur le Duc," replied Balsamo, "you were right. Look! the countess blushes. But just now we agreed that it is not now a question of wounds or of love. A philter will not rid France of Monsieur de Choiseul. In fact, if the king loved Madame ten times more than he does, — and that is impossible, — Monsieur de Choiseul would still retain the same influence over his mind which Madame exerts over his heart."

"Very true," said the marshal; "but it was our only resource."

"You think so?"

"Certainly; find another."

"Oh! that would be easy."

"Easy! do you hear, Countess? These sorcerers stop at nothing."

"Why should I stop, when the only thing necessary is to prove to the king that Monsieur de Choiseul betrays him, — that is to say, regarding the matter from the king's point of view, you understand; for Monsieur de Choiseul has no thought of treachery in acting as he does."

"And what does he do?"

"You know as well as I do, Countess, — he supports the parliament in their revolt against the royal authority."

"Certainly; but we must know by what means."

"By the means of agents who encourage them by promising them impunity."

"Who are the agents? We must know that."

"Do you believe, for example, that Madame de Grammont is gone for any other purpose than to sustain the ardent and warm the timid?"

"Certainly; she left for no other reason," replied the countess.

"Yes; but the king thinks it a simple exile."

"It is true. How can you prove to him that in this departure there is anything more than he supposes?"

"By accusing Madame de Grammont."

"Ah! if there were nothing necessary but to accuse her, Count!" said the marshal.

"But, unfortunately, the accusation must be proved," added the countess.

"And if this accusation were proved, incontrovertibly proved, do you think Monsieur de Choiseul would still be minister?"

"Certainly not," said the countess.

"Nothing is necessary, then, but to discover the treachery of Monsieur de Choiseul," pursued Balsamo, with assurance, "and to display it clearly, precisely, and palpably before the eyes of his Majesty."

The marshal threw himself back upon an armchair and burst into peals of laughter. "Charming!" he exclaimed; "he stops at nothing! Discover Monsieur de Choiseul in the act of committing treason, — that is all; nothing more!"

Balsamo remained calm and unmoved, waiting until the marshal's mirth had subsided. Then he said: "Come, let us speak seriously; let us recapitulate."

"So be it."

"Is not Monsieur de Choiseul suspected of encouraging the revolt of the parliament?"

"Granted; but the proof?"

"Is not Monsieur de Choiseul supposed," continued Balsamo, "to be attempting to bring about a war with England, in order that he may become indispensable?"

"It is so believed; but the proof?"

"Is not Monsieur de Choiseul the declared enemy of the countess, and does he not seek, by all possible means, to drag her from the throne I promised her?"

"Ah! all this is very true," said the countess; "but once more I repeat, it must be proved. Oh that I could prove it!"

"What is necessary for that? A mere trifle."

The marshal gave a low whistle. "Yes, a mere trifle!" said he, sarcastically.

"A confidential letter, for example," said Balsamo.

"Yes; that is all, — a mere nothing."

"A letter from Madame de Grammont would do, would it not, Marshal?" continued the count.

"Sorcerer, my good sorcerer, find me such a letter!" cried Madame Dubarry. "I have been trying for five years; I have spent in that quest a hundred thousand francs a year, and have never succeeded."

"Because you never applied to me, Madame," said Balsamo.

"How so?" said the countess.

"Without doubt, if you had applied to me, I could have assisted you."

"Could you? Count, is it yet too late?"

The count smiled. "It is never too late," said he.

"Oh, my dear Count!" said Madame Dubarry, clasping her hands.

"You want a letter, then?"

"Yes."

"From Madame de Grammont?"

"If it is possible."

"Which shall compromise Monsieur de Choiseul on the three points which I have mentioned?"

"I would give — one of my eyes to have it."

"Oh, Countess, that would be too dear! — especially as I will give it to you for nothing;" and Balsamo drew a folded paper from his pocket.

"What is that?" asked the countess, devouring the paper with her eyes.

"Yes, what is that?" repeated the duke.

"The letter you wished for;" and the count, amid

the most profound silence, read the letter, with which our readers are already acquainted, to his two astonished auditors. As he read, the countess opened her eyes to their utmost width, and began to lose countenance.

"It is a forgery," said Richelieu, when the letter had been read. "The devil! we must take care."

"Monsieur, it is the simple and literal copy of a letter from the Duchesse de Grammont, which a courier, despatched this morning from Rouen, is now carrying to the Duc de Choiseul at Versailles."

"Oh, my God!" cried the marshal, "do you speak truly, Monsieur Balsamo?"

"I always speak the truth, Marshal."

"The duchess has written such a letter?"

"Yes, Marshal."

"She has been so imprudent?"

"It is incredible, I confess; but so it is."

The old duke looked at the countess, who had no longer the power to utter a word.

"Well," said she at last, "I am like the duke, I can scarcely believe — pardon me, Count — that Madame de Grammont, a woman of sense, should compromise her own position and that of her brother by a letter so strongly expressed. Besides, to know of such a letter, one must have read it —"

"And then," said the marshal, quickly, "if the Count had read this letter, he would have kept it; it is a precious treasure."

Balsamo gently shook his head. "Oh!" said he, "such a plan might suit those who have to break open letters in order to ascertain their contents; but not those who, like myself, can read through the envelopes. Fie upon you! Besides, what interest could I have in ruining Monsieur de Choiseul and Madame de Grammont? You come to consult me, — as friends, I presume, — and I answer you in the same manner. You wish me to render you a service; I do so. You do not mean, I suppose, to ask me my charge for the interview, as you would the fortune-tellers of the Quai de la Ferraille?"

"Oh, Count!" said Madame Dubarry.

"Well, I give you this advice, and you seem not to comprehend it. You express a wish to overthrow Monsieur de Choiseul, and you seek the means. I tell you one; you approve it. I put it into your hands, and — you do not believe it."

"Because — because — Count — I —"

"The letter exists, I tell you, for I have the copy."

"But who told you of its existence, Count?" cried Richelieu.

"Ah! that is a great word, — who told me? You wish to know in one moment as much as I know, — I the worker, the sage, the adept who has lived three thousand seven hundred years."

"Oh, oh!" said Richelieu, discouraged, "you are going to spoil the good opinion I had formed of you, Count."

"I do not ask you to believe me, Monsieur le Duc; it is not I who brought you hither from the chase."

"Duke, he is right," said the countess. "Monsieur de Balsamo, pray do not be impatient."

"He who has time never gets impatient, Madame."

"Will you be so good as to add another favor to those you have already conferred upon me, and tell me how these secrets are revealed to you."

"I will not hesitate, Madame," said Balsamo, as slowly as if he were searching for each word separately; "the revelation is made to me by a voice."

"By a voice!" cried the duke and the countess simultaneously, — "a voice which tells you everything?"

"Everything I wish to know, yes."

"Was it a voice that told you what Madame de Grammont had written to her brother?"

"I repeat, Madame, it is a voice which tells me."

"Miraculous!"

"But you do not believe it."

"Well, no, Count," said the duke; "how do you imagine I can believe such things?"

"Would you believe it if I told you what the courier who carries the letter to Monsieur de Choiseul is doing at this moment?"

"Certainly!" exclaimed the countess.

"I would believe it," cried the duke, "if I heard the voice; but messieurs the necromancers and magicians have the privilege of seeing and hearing the supernatural without witnesses."

Balsamo looked at Richelieu with a singular expression, which made a shudder pass through the veins of the countess, and even sent a slight chill to the heart of the sceptical egotist called the Duc de Richelieu. "Yes," said he, after a long silence, "alone, I see and hear supernatural objects and sounds; but when I am in the society of people of rank, — of your talent, Duke, and of your beauty, Countess, — I display my treasures and share them. Would it please you very much to hear the mysterious voice which speaks to me?"

"Yes," said the duke, clenching his hands tightly, that he might not tremble.

"Yes," stammered the countess, trembling.

"Well, Duke, — well, Countess, you shall hear it. What language shall it speak?"

"French, if you please," said the countess. "I know no other; any other would frighten me."

"And you, Duke?"

"As Madame says, French; for then I shall be able to repeat what the devil says, and to discover if he is well educated and speaks correctly the language of my friend Monsieur de Voltaire."

Balsamo, his head drooping on his breast, crossed over to the door leading into the little salon, which opened, as we are aware, on the stairs.

"Permit me," said he, "to conceal you here, in order not to expose you to the risk of discovery."

The countess turned pale, approached the duke, and took his arm. Balsamo, almost touching the door leading to the stairs, made a step toward that part of the house in which Lorenza was, and pronounced in a low voice the following words, in the Arabic tongue, which we translate: "My friend, do you hear me? If so, pull the cord of the bell twice."

Balsamo waited to see the effect of these words, and looked at the duke and countess, who opened their eyes and ears, — with the more eager curiosity that they could not understand what the count said. The bell sounded twice distinctly. The countess started from her sofa, and the duke wiped his forehead with his handkerchief.

"Since you hear me," continued Balsamo in the same language, "press the marble button which forms the right eye of the sculptured figure on the mantelpiece, the back will open; pass out by this opening, cross my room, descend the stairs, and enter the apartment adjoining the one in which I am."

A moment later a faint noise, like a scarcely audible breath, told Balsamo that his order had been understood and obeyed.

"What language is that," asked the duke, affecting assurance, — "the cabalistic language?"

"Yes, Duke; the language used for the summoning of spirits."

"You said we should understand it."

"What the voice said, but not what I say."

"Has the devil come yet?"

"Who spoke of the devil, Duke?"

"Whom do you evoke but the devil?"

"Every superior spirit, every supernatural being, can be evoked."

"And the superior spirit, the supernatural being —"

Balsamo extended his hand toward the tapestry which concealed the door of the next apartment.

"Is in direct communication with me, Monseigneur."

"I am afraid," said the countess; "are you, Duke?"

"Faith, Countess! I confess to you that I would almost as soon be at Mahon or at Philipsburg."

"Madame la Comtesse, and you, Monsieur le Duc, listen, since you wish to hear," said Balsamo, severely; and he turned toward the door.

CHAPTER XL.

THE VOICE.

There was a moment of solemn silence. Then Balsamo asked in French, "Are you there?"

"I am," replied a clear, silvery voice, which, penetrating through the hangings and the portières, seemed to those present rather like a metallic sound than a human voice.

"*Peste!* it is becoming interesting," said the duke; "and all without torches, magic, or Bengal lights."

"It is fearful," whispered the countess.

"Listen attentively to my questions," continued Balsamo.

"I listen with my whole being."

"First tell me how many persons are with me at this moment."

"Two."

"Of what sex?"

"A man and a woman."

"Read the man's name in my thoughts."

"The Duc de Richelieu."

"And the woman's?"

"Madame the Comtesse Dubarry."

"Ha!" said the duke, "this is becoming serious."

"I never saw anything like it," murmured the trembling countess.

"Good!" said Balsamo; "now read the first sentence of the letter I hold in my hand."

The voice obeyed. The duke and the countess looked at each other with astonishment bordering upon admiration.

"What has become of the letter I wrote at your dictation?"

"It is hastening on."

"In which direction?"

"Toward the East."

"Is it far?"

"Yes, very far."

"Who is carrying it?"

"A man dressed in a green vest, leathern cap, and large boots."

"On foot or on horseback?"

"On horseback."

"What kind of a horse?"

"A piebald horse."

"Where do you see him?"

There was a moment's silence.

"Look," said Balsamo, imperatively.

"On a wide road planted with trees."

"But on which road?"

"I do not know; all the roads are alike."

"What! does nothing indicate what road it is, — no post nor inscription?"

"Stay, stay! A carriage is passing near the man on horseback; it crosses his course, coming toward me."

"What kind of carriage?"

"A heavy carriage, full of abbés and soldiers."

"A stage coach," murmured Richelieu.

"Is there no inscription upon the carriage?" asked Balsamo.

"Yes," said the voice.

"Read it."

"'VERSAILLES' is written in yellow letters upon the carriage, but the word is nearly effaced."

"Leave the carriage, and follow the courier."

"I do not see him now."

"Why do you not see him?"

"Because the road turns."

"Turn the corner, and follow him."

"Oh! he is going as fast as he can urge on his horse; he looks at his watch."

"What do you see in front of the horse?"

"A long avenue, splendid buildings, a large town."

"Follow him still."

"I follow."

"Well?"

"The courier redoubles his blows, the animal is bathed in perspiration; its iron-shod hoofs strike the pavement so loudly that all the passers-by look round. Ah! the courier dashes into a long street which descends. He turns to the right. He slackens his horse's speed. He stops at the door of a large hôtel."

"Now you must follow him attentively, do you hear?"

The voice heaved a sigh.

"You are tired. I understand."

"Oh! crushed with weariness."

"Cease to be fatigued; I will it."

"Ah! thanks."

"Are you still fatigued?"

"No."

"Do you still see the courier?"

"Yes, yes; he ascends a large stone staircase. He is preceded by a valet in blue and gold livery. He crosses large salons full of splendid gilt ornaments. He stops at a small lighted cabinet. The valet opens the door and retires."

"What do you see?"

"The courier bows."

"To whom does he bow?"

"He bows to a man seated at a desk, with his back toward the door."

"How is the man dressed?"

"Oh! in full dress, as if he were going to a ball."

"Has he any decoration?"

"He wears a broad blue ribbon crosswise on his breast."

"His face?"

"I cannot see it. Ah!—"

"What?"

"He turns."

"What sort of features has he?"

"A keen glance, irregular features, beautiful teeth."

"What is his age?"

"From fifty to fifty-eight years."

"The duke!" whispered the countess to the marshal; "it is the duke!"

The marshal made a sign as if to say, "Yes, it is he; but listen."

"Well?" asked Balsamo.

"The courier gives a letter to the man with the blue ribbon—"

"You may say to the duke; he is a duke."

"The courier," repeated the obedient voice, "takes a letter from the leathern bag behind him and gives it to the duke. The duke breaks the seal and reads it attentively."

"Well?"

"He takes a pen and a sheet of paper and writes."

"He writes?" said Richelieu. "The devil! if we could only know what he writes!"

"Tell me what he writes," commanded Balsamo.

"I cannot."

"Because you are too far away. Enter the room. Are you there?"

"Yes."

"Look over his shoulder."

"I am doing so."

"Now read."

"The writing is bad, small, irregular."

"Read it; I will it."

The countess and Richelieu held their breaths.

"Read!" repeated Balsamo, more imperatively still.

"'My sister,'" said the voice, trembling and hesitating.

"It is the reply," said the countess and Richelieu in the same breath.

"'My sister,'" continued the voice, "'do not be uneasy. The crisis took place, it is true; it was a dangerous one,—that is true also; but it is over. I am anxiously awaiting to-morrow, for to-morrow it will be my turn to act on the offensive, and everything leads me to expect a decisive triumph. What you say of the parliament of Rouen, Milord X., and the petards, is all satisfactory. To-morrow, after my interview with the king, I shall add a postscript to my letter, and send it you by the same courier.'"

Balsamo, with his left hand extended, seemed to drag each word painfully from the voice, while with the right hand he hastily took down those lines which Monsieur de Choiseul was at the same time writing in his cabinet at Versailles.

"Is that all?" asked Balsamo.

"That is all."

"What is the duke doing now?"

"He folds the paper on which he has just written, and puts it into a small portfolio, which he takes from the pocket in the left side of his coat."

"You hear?" said Balsamo to the almost stupefied countess. "Well?"

"Then he sends away the courier."

"What does he say to him?"

"I heard only the end of the sentence."

"What was it?"

"'At one o'clock at the postern gate of Trianon.' The courier bows and retires."

"Yes," said Richelieu, "he makes an appointment to meet the courier when his audience is over, as he says in his letter."

Balsamo made a sign with his hand to command silence. "What is the duke doing now?" he asked.

"He rises. He holds in his hand the letter he has received. He goes straight toward his bed, enters the passage between it and the wall, and presses a spring which opens an iron box. He throws the letter into the box and closes it."

"Oh," cried the countess and the duke, turning pale, "this is magic, indeed!"

"Do you know now all that you wished to know, Madame?" asked Balsamo.

"Count," said Madame Dubarry, approaching him with terror, "you have rendered me a service which I would pay with ten years of my life, — or rather, which I can never pay. Ask what you wish."

"Oh, Madame, you know we already have an account!"

"Speak; say what you wish."

"The time has not yet come."

"Well, when it comes, if it were a million —"

Balsamo smiled.

"Oh, Countess," exclaimed the marshal, "you should rather ask the count for a million! Cannot a man who knows what he knows, and who sees what he sees, discover diamonds and gold in the bosom of the earth as easily as he discovers the thoughts in the heart of man?"

"Then, Count," said the countess, "I prostrate myself before you in my weakness."

"No, Countess. One day you will pay your debt to me; I shall give you the opportunity."

"Count," said Richelieu to Balsamo, "I am conquered, crushed. I believe."

"As Saint Thomas believed, Duke. I do not call that believing, but seeing."

"Call it what you will, I will make the *amende honorable;* and in future if I am asked about sorcerers I shall know what to say."

Balsamo smiled. "Madame," said he to the countess, "will you permit me to do one thing now?"

"Speak."

"My spirit is wearied. Let me restore it to liberty by a magic formula."

"Do so, Monsieur."

"Lorenza," said Balsamo in Arabic, "thanks! I love you. Return to your apartment by the same way you came, and wait for me. Go, my beloved."

"I am very tired," replied in Italian the voice, softer still than even during the evocation. "Hasten, Acharat."

"I come;" and the footsteps were heard retreating with the same rustling noise with which they had approached.

Then Balsamo, after a few moments' interval, during which he convinced himself of Lorenza's departure, bowed profoundly, but with majestic dignity, to his visitors, who returned to their carriage more like intoxicated persons than human beings gifted with reason, so much were they occupied by the crowd of tumultuous ideas which assailed them.

CHAPTER XLI.

DISGRACE.

THE next morning, as the great clock of Versailles struck eleven, King Louis XV. issued from his apartment, and crossing the adjoining gallery, called in a loud and stern voice, " Monsieur de la Vrillière."

The king was pale, and seemed agitated. The more he endeavored to hide his emotion, the more it was manifest in the embarrassment of his looks and the rigid tension of his usually impassive features.

A death-like stillness pervaded the long ranks of courtiers, among whom the Duc de Richelieu and Comte Jean Dubarry might be seen, both seemingly calm, and affecting indifference or ignorance as to what was going on.

The Duc de la Vrillière approached, and took a *lettre-de-cachet* from the king's hand.

" Is the Duc de Choiseul at Versailles? " asked the king.

" Yes, Sire. He returned from Paris yesterday, at two o'clock in the afternoon."

" Is he in his hôtel, or in the chateau? "

" In the chateau, Sire."

" Carry this order to him, Duke," said the king.

A shudder ran through the whole file of spectators, who bent down whispering, like ears of corn under the blast of a tornado. The king, frowning as if he wished to add terror to this scene, haughtily entered his cabinet, followed by the captain of the guard and the commandant of the Light Horse.

All eyes followed Monsieur de la Vrillière, who slowly crossed the courtyard and entered Monsieur de Choiseul's apartments, rather uneasy at the commission with which he was charged.

In the mean time loud and eager conversations, some threatening, some timid, burst forth on all sides around the old marshal, who pretended to be even more surprised than the others, but who, thanks to his cunning smile, deceived no one.

Monsieur de la Vrillière returned, and was immediately surrounded.

"Well?" cried every one.

"Well, it was an order of banishment."

"Of banishment?"

"Yes, in due form."

"Then you have read it, Duke?"

"I have."

"Really?"

"Judge for yourselves."

And the Duc de la Vrillière repeated the following lines, which he had treasured up with the retentive memory which marks the true courtier: —

MY COUSIN, — The displeasure which your conduct causes me obliges me to exile you to Chanteloup, whither you must repair in four and twenty hours from this time. I should have sent you farther, had it not been for the particular esteem I feel for Madame de Choiseul, in whose health I am much interested. Take care that your conduct does not force me to proceed to further measures.

A long murmur ran through the group which surrounded Monsieur de la Vrillière.

"And what did he reply to you, Monsieur de St. Florentin?" asked Richelieu, affecting not to give to the duke either his new name or his new title.

"He replied, 'Monsieur le Duc, I am satisfied that you find much pleasure in being the bearer of this letter.'"

"That was severe, my poor Duke," said Jean.

"What could you expect, Monsieur le Vicomte? A man does not receive such a tile on his head without crying out a little."

"Do you know what he will do?" asked Richelieu.

"Why, according to all probability he will obey."

"Ahem!" said the marshal.

"Here is the duke coming!" said Jean, who stood as sentinel at the window.

"Coming here?" exclaimed the Duc de la Vrillière.

"I said so, Monsieur de St. Florentin. He is crossing the courtyard," continued Jean.

"Alone?"

"Quite alone, — his portfolio under his arm."

"Oh, good heavens!" said Richelieu, "is yesterday's scene to be repeated?"

"Do not speak of it; I shudder at the thought," replied Jean.

He had scarcely spoken, when the Duc de Choiseul appeared at the entrance of the gallery, with head erect and confident look, alarming his enemies, or those who would declare themselves such on his disgrace, by his calm and piercing glance. As no one expected this step after what had happened, no one opposed his progress.

"Are you sure you read correctly, Duke?" asked Jean.

"Of course!"

"And he returns after such a letter as you have described?"

"Upon my honor, I cannot understand it."

"The king will send him to the Bastille."

"That would cause a fearful commotion."

"I should almost pity him."

"Look, he is going to the king! It is incredible."

In fact, without paying attention to the show of resistance which the astounded usher offered, Monsieur de Choiseul entered the king's cabinet. Louis, on seeing him, uttered an exclamation of astonishment.

The duke held his *lettre-de-cachet* in his hand, and showed it to the king almost smilingly. "Sire," said he, "as your Majesty had the goodness to forewarn me yesterday, I have indeed received a letter to-day."

"Yes, Monsieur," replied the king.

"And as your Majesty had the goodness yesterday to tell me not to look upon any letter as serious which was not ratified by the express words of the king, I have come to request an explanation."

"It will be very short, Monsieur le Duc," replied the king. "To-day the letter is valid."

"Valid?" said the duke. "So offensive a letter to so devoted a servant?"

"A devoted servant, Monsieur, does not make his master play a ridiculous part."

"Sire," replied the minister, haughtily, "I was born near the throne that I might comprehend its majesty."

"Monsieur," replied the king, in a severe voice, "I will not keep you in suspense. Yesterday evening you received a courier from Madame de Grammont in your cabinet at Versailles."

"It is true, Sire."

"He brought you a letter."

"Are a brother and sister forbidden to correspond?"

"Wait a moment, if you please. I know the contents of that letter."

"Oh, Sire!"

"Here it is; I took the trouble to copy it with my own

hand." And the king handed to the duke an exact copy of the letter he had received.

"Sire!"

"Do not deny it, Duke; you placed the letter in an iron coffer standing at your bedside."

The duke became pale as a ghost.

"That is not all," continued the king, pitilessly; "you have replied to Madame de Grammont's letter. I know the contents of that letter also. It is there in your portfolio, and wants only the postscript, which you are to add when you leave me. You see I am well informed, do you not?"

The duke wiped his forehead, on which the large drops of perspiration were standing, bowed without uttering a word, and left the cabinet tottering as if he had been struck with apoplexy. Had it not been for the fresh air which fanned his face, he must have fallen. But he was a man of strong will. When he reached the gallery he had regained his strength, and with head erect he passed the hedge of courtiers, and entered his apartments in order to burn divers papers and lock up others. A quarter of an hour afterward he left the chateau in his carriage.

Monsieur de Choiseul's disgrace was a thunderbolt which set all France in flames. The parliament, sustained in reality by the tolerance of the minister, proclaimed that the State had lost its firmest pillar. The nobility supported him as being one of themselves. The clergy felt themselves soothed by this man, whose personal dignity, often carried even to the extent of pride, gave a sacerdotal effect to his ministerial functions.

The encyclopedist, or the philosophical, party, who were very numerous and also very strong, because they were reinforced by all the enlightened, clever, and cavilling spirits of the age, cried out loudly when the government was taken from the hands of a minister who admired Voltaire, pensioned the "Encyclopédie," and preserved, by developing them in a more useful manner, the traditions of Madame de Pompadour, the female Mecænas of the writers for the "Mercure" and of philosophers in general.

The people had far better grounds for complaint than any of the other malecontents. They also complained, but without reasoning; and, as they always do, they hit the truth and laid bare the bleeding wound.

Monsieur de Choiseul, absolutely speaking, was a bad minister and a bad citizen; but relatively he was a paragon of virtue, of morality, and of patriotism. When the people, dying of hunger in the fields, heard of his Majesty's prodigality and of Madame Dubarry's ruinous whims; when open warnings were sent him, such as "L'homme aux Quarante Écus," or counsels like those in "Le Contrat Social," or, secretly, revelations like the "Nouvelles à la Main," and the "Idées Singulières d'un Bon Citoyen,"— then the people were terrified at the prospect of falling back into the impure hands of the favorite, "less respectable than a collier's wife," as Bauveau said, and into the hands of the favorite's favorites; and wearied with so much suffering, they were alarmed to behold the future looking even blacker than the past.

It was not that the people, who had antipathies, had any well-defined sympathies. They did not like the parliament, because they who ought to have been their natural protectors had always abandoned them for idle inquiries, questions of precedence, or selfish interests, and because, dazzled by the reflected light of the royal omnipotence, they imagined themselves something like an aristocracy, occupying an intermediate place between the nobility and the people.

The people disliked the nobility by instinct and by remembrance. They feared the sword as much as they hated the Church. Their position could not, therefore, be affected by the disgrace of Monsieur de Choiseul, but they heard the complaints of the nobility, of the clergy, of the parliament; and this noise, joined to their own murmurs, made an uproar which intoxicated them.

The consequence of these feelings was regret, and a sort of a quasi-popularity for the name of Choiseul. All Paris — the word in this case can be justified by the facts — accompanied the exile on his way to Chanteloup as far as the town gates. The people lined the road which the carriage was to take, while the members of the parliament and the court who could not be received by the duke stationed themselves in their carriages in advance of the crowd of people, that they might salute him as he passed and bid him adieu.

The procession was the densest at the Barrière d'Enfer, which is on the road to Touraine, at which place there was such a conflux of foot-passengers, horsemen, and carriages that the traffic was interrupted for several hours.

When the duke had crossed the barrier, he found himself escorted by more than a hundred carriages, which formed a sort of triumphal halo around him. Acclamations and sighs still followed him; but he had too much sense and penetration not to know that all this noise was not so much occasioned by regret for him personally, as by the fear of those persons unknown, who were to be lifted up by his downfall.

At a short distance from the barrier a post-chaise, driven at great speed along the crowded road, met the procession; and had it not been for the skill of the postilion, the horses, white with foam and dust, would have dashed against Monsieur de Choiseul's equipage. A head leaned forward from the carriage window, and Monsieur de Choiseul also leaned from his.

Monsieur d'Aiguillon bowed profoundly to the fallen minister whose heritage he had come to obtain. Monsieur de Choiseul threw himself back in the carriage: a single second had sufficed to wither the laurels which had crowned his disgrace.

But at the same moment, as a compensation, no doubt, a carriage drawn by eight horses and bearing the royal arms of France, which was seen advancing along the cross road from Sèvres to St. Cloud, and which, whether by accident or on account of the crowd, did not turn into the highroad, also crossed before Monsieur de Choiseul's carriage. The dauphiness, with her lady of honor, Madame de Noailles, was on the back seat of the carriage; on the front was Mademoiselle Andrée de Taverney. Monsieur de Choiseul, crimson with exultation and joy, bent forward out of the door and bowed profoundly.

"Adieu, Madame," said he, in a low voice.

"Au revoir, Monsieur de Choiseul," replied the dauphiness, with an imperial smile and a majestic contempt of all etiquette.

"Long live Monsieur de Choiseul!" cried a voice enthusiastically, after the dauphiness had spoken.

At the sound of the voice Mademoiselle Andrée turned round quickly.

"Make way! make way!" cried her Highness's grooms, forcing Gilbert, pale as death and eager to see, to range himself with the other people on the road.

It was indeed our hero, who in his philosophical enthusiasm had cried out, "Long live Monsieur de Choiseul!"

CHAPTER XLII.

THE DUC D'AIGUILLON.

WHILE melancholy visages and red eyes were the order of the day on the road from Paris to Chanteloup, Luciennes was radiant with blooming faces and charming smiles. It was because at Luciennes was enthroned, no longer a mere mortal, the most beautiful and most adorable of mortals, as the poets and courtiers declared, but a veritable divinity who governed France.

The evening after Monsieur de Choiseul's disgrace, therefore, the road leading to Luciennes was thronged with the same carriages which in the morning had rolled after the exiled minister. There were, besides, the partisans of the chancellor, and the votaries of corruption and self-interest; and altogether they made an imposing procession.

But Madame Dubarry had her police, and Jean knew, to a baron, the names of those who had strewn the last flowers over the expiring Choiseuls. He gave a list of these names to the countess, and those who bore them were pitilessly excluded; while the courage of others in braving public opinion was rewarded by the protecting smile and frank welcome of the goddess of the day. What joy and what congratulations echoed on all sides! Pressings of the hand, little smothered laughs, and enthusiastic applause, seemed to have become the habitual language of the inhabitants of Luciennes.

After the great throng of carriages and the general crowd followed the private receptions. Richelieu, the secret and modest hero, indeed, but yet the real hero of the day, saw the crowd of visitors and petitioners pass away, and remained the last in the countess's boudoir.

"It must be confessed," said the countess, "that the Comte de Balsamo, or de Fenix, whichever name you give him, Marshal, is one of the first men of the age. It would be a thousand pities if they still burned sorcerers."

"Certainly, Countess, he is a great man," replied Richelieu.

"And a very handsome man too; I have taken quite a fancy for him, Duke."

"You will make me jealous," said Richelieu, laughing, and eager besides to direct the conversation to a more serious subject. "The Comte de Fenix would make a dreadful minister of police."

"I was thinking of that," replied the countess; "only it is impossible."

"Why, Countess?"

"Because he would render colleagues impossible."

"How so?"

"Knowing everything, seeing all their play —"

Richelieu blushed beneath his rouge. "Countess," he replied, "if he were my colleague, I would wish him to see into mine always, and communicate the cards to you; for you would ever see the knave of hearts on his knees before the queen, and prostrate at the feet of the king."

"No one has more wit than you, my dear Duke," replied the countess. "But let us talk a little of our ministry. I think you mentioned that you had sent word to your nephew —"

"D'Aiguillon? He has arrived, Madame, and with what Roman augurs would have called the best conjunction of omens possible, — his carriage met Choiseul's leaving Paris."

"That is indeed a favorable omen," said the countess. "Then he is coming here?"

"Madame, I thought that if Monsieur d'Aiguillon was seen at Luciennes at such a time, it would give rise to unpleasant comment; I begged him, therefore, to remain in the village until I should send for him by your orders."

"Send for him immediately, then, Marshal, for we are alone, or very nearly so."

"The more willingly that we quite understand each other, — do we not, Countess?"

"Certainly, Duke. You prefer war to finance, do you not? Or do you wish for the marine?"

"I prefer war, Madame; I can be of most service in that department."

"True; I will speak of it to the king. You have no antipathies?"

"For whom?"

"For any colleagues his Majesty might present to you?"

"I am the least difficult man in the world to live with, Countess; but allow me to send for my nephew, since you are good enough to grant him the favor of an audience."

Richelieu approached the window and looked into the courtyard, now illumined by the last rays of the setting sun. He made a sign to one of his footmen, who was watching the window, and who darted off as soon as he received the signal.

Lights were now brought in.

Ten minutes after the footman had disappeared, a carriage rolled into the courtyard. The countess turned quickly toward the window. Richelieu saw the move ment, which seemed to him an excellent prognostic for Monsieur d'Aiguillon's affairs, and consequently for his own. "She likes the uncle," said he to himself, "and she is in a fair way to like the nephew. We shall be masters here." While he was in the enjoyment of these chimerical visions, a slight noise was heard at the door, and the confidential valet, throwing it open, announced the Duc d'Aiguillon.

The duke was a very handsome and graceful nobleman, richly, and at the same time elegantly and tastefully, dressed. Monsieur d'Aiguillon had passed the age of youth, but he was one of those men who, whether judged by their looks or by their minds, seem young until old age renders them infirm. The cares of government had traced no wrinkles on his brow; they had only enlarged the natural fold which seems to be the birthplace of great thoughts both in statesmen and in poets. His air and carriage were lofty and commanding, and his handsome features wore an expression at once of intelligence and melancholy, as if he knew that the hatred of ten millions of men weighed upon his head, but at the same time wished to prove that the weight was not beyond his strength.

Monsieur d'Aiguillon had the most beautiful hands in the world; they looked white and delicate even when buried in the softest folds of lace. A well-turned leg was prized very highly at that period, and the duke's was a model of manly elegance and aristocratic form. He combined the suavity of the poet with the nobility of the lord and the suppleness and ease of the dashing guardsman. He was thus a beau-idéal for the countess in the three several qualities which the instinct of this beautiful sensualist taught her to love.

By a remarkable coincidence, or rather by a chain of

circumstances skilfully contrived by Monsieur d'Aiguillon, these two objects of public animadversion, the favorite and the courtier, had never yet encountered one another at court, with all their respective attractions.

For the last three years Monsieur d'Aiguillon had managed to be very busy either in Brittany or in his cabinet, and had not once shown himself at court, knowing well that a favorable or unfavorable crisis must soon take place. In the first case it would be better to be comparatively unknown; in the second, to disappear without leaving any trace behind, and thus be able easily to emerge from the gulf under new auspices and in a new character. Another motive influenced his calculations, — a motive which is the mainspring of romance, but which nevertheless was the most powerful of all.

Before Madame Dubarry was a countess, and every evening touched the crown of France with her lips, she had been a lovely creature, smiling and adored; she had been loved, — a happiness she could no longer hope for, since she was feared.

Among the young, rich, powerful, and handsome men who had paid court to Jeanne Vaubernier, among the rhymers who had harnessed in verse the words *Lange* and *ange*, the Duc d'Aiguillon had formerly figured in the first rank; but either because the duke was not sufficiently ardent, or because Mademoiselle Lange was not so easily pleased as her detractors pretended, or because the sudden attachment of the king separated two hearts ready to unite, Monsieur d'Aiguillon reclaimed his verses, acrostics, bouquets, and perfumes, and Mademoiselle Lange closed her door in the Rue des Petits-Champs. The duke hastened to Brittany, suppressing his sighs; Mademoiselle Lange wafted all hers toward Versailles, to the Baron de Gonesse, — that is, the king of France.

D'Aiguillon's sudden disappearance had at first troubled Madame Dubarry very little, for she feared the remembrances of the past; but when subsequently she observed the continued silence of her former admirer, she at first had been annoyed, then astonished, and being in a good position for judging of men, she had concluded by thinking him a man of tact and discretion. For the countess this was a great distinction; but it was not all, and the time might come when she would think D'Aiguillon a man of heart.

We have seen that the marshal, in all his conversations with Madame Dubarry, had never touched upon the subject of his nephew's acquaintance with Mademoiselle Lange. This silence on the part of a man accustomed, as the old duke was, to say the most difficult things in the world, had much surprised, and even alarmed, the countess. She therefore impatiently awaited Monsieur d'Aiguillon's arrival, to know how to conduct herself, and to ascertain whether the marshal had been discreet, or merely ignorant.

The duke entered, respectful, but with an air of freedom, and sufficiently confident in himself to draw a distinction in his salutation between the reigning sultana and the court lady. By this discriminating tact he instantly gained a protectress quite disposed to find good perfect, and perfection wonderful.

Monsieur d'Aiguillon then took his uncle's hand, and the latter, advancing toward the countess, said in his most insinuating voice: "The Duc d'Aiguillon, Madame. It is not so much my nephew as one of your most ardent servants whom I have the honor to present to you."

The countess glanced at the duke as the marshal spoke, and looked at him as women can look, — that is to say, with eyes which nothing escapes. But she saw only two heads bowing respectfully before her, and two faces serene and calm after the salutation.

"I know, Marshal, that you love the duke," said the countess. "You are my friend. I shall request Monsieur d'Aiguillon, therefore, in deference to his uncle, to imitate him in all that will be agreeable to me."

"That is the conduct I have already marked out for myself, Madame," said D'Aiguillon, with another bow.

"You have suffered much in Brittany?" asked the countess.

"Yes, Madame; and it is not yet over," replied D'Aiguillon.

"I believe it is, Monsieur; besides, here is Monsieur de Richelieu, who will be a powerful aid to you."

D'Aiguillon looked at Richelieu as if surprised.

"Ah!" said the countess, "I see that the marshal has not yet had time to have any conversation with you. That is very natural, as you have just arrived from a journey. Well, you must have a thousand things to say to each other, and I will therefore leave you, Marshal, for the present. Monsieur le Duc, consider yourself at home here."

So saying, the countess retired; but she did not go far away. Behind the boudoir opened a large cabinet filled with all sorts of fantastic baubles, with which the king was accustomed to amuse himself when he came to Luciennes. He preferred this cabinet to the boudoir, because in it one could hear all that was said in the next room. Madame Dubarry, therefore, was certain to hear the whole conversation between the duke and his nephew, and she counted upon forming from it a correct and final opinion of the latter.

But Richelieu was not duped; he knew most of the secrets of every royal and ministerial residence. To listen when people were speaking of him was one of his devices; to speak while others were overhearing him was one of his ruses. He determined, therefore, still animated by the favorable reception of D'Aiguillon, to proceed in the same vein, and to reveal to the favorite, under cover of her supposed absence, a plan of secret happiness and great power, complicated with intrigues, — a double allurement, which a pretty woman, and especially a woman of the court, rarely can resist. He desired the duke to be seated, and said to him, "You see, Duke, I am installed here?"

"Yes, Monsieur, I see it."

"I have had the good-fortune to gain the favor of this charming woman, who is looked upon as a queen here, and who is one in reality."

D'Aiguillon bowed.

"I must tell you, Duke," continued Richelieu, "what I could not say in the open street, — that Madame Dubarry has promised me a portfolio."

"Ah!" said D'Aiguillon, "that is only your desert, Monsieur."

"I do not know whether I deserve it or not; but I am to have it, — rather late in the day, it is true. Then, situated as I shall be, I shall endeavor to advance your interests, D'Aiguillon."

"Thank you, Monsieur le Duc; you are a kind relative, and have often proved it."

"You have nothing in view, D'Aiguillon?"

"Absolutely nothing, except to escape being degraded from my title of duke and peer, as the parliament demand."

"Have you supporters anywhere?"

"Not one."

"You would have fallen, then, but for this new turn in public affairs?"

"At full length, Monsieur le Duc."

"Ah! you talk like a philosopher. The devil! for that reason I speak to you roughly, my poor D'Aiguillon, — more like a minister than an uncle."

"Uncle, your goodness penetrates me with gratitude."

"When I sent for you in such a hurry you may be sure it was because I wished you to play an important part here. Let me see. Have you reflected on the part Monsieur de Choiseul played for ten years?"

"Yes; certainly his was an enviable position."

"Enviable! Yes, enviable, when with Madame de Pompadour he governed the king and exiled the Jesuits; but very sad when, having quarrelled with Madame Dubarry, who is worth a hundred Pompadours, he was dismissed from office in twenty-four hours. You do not reply."

"I am listening, Monsieur, and endeavoring to discover your meaning."

"You like Monsieur de Choiseul's first part best, do you not?"

"Certainly."

"Well, my dear Duke, I have decided upon playing this part."

D'Aiguillon turned abruptly toward his uncle. "Do you speak seriously?" said he.

"Yes. Why not?"

"You will be Madame Dubarry's lover?"

"Ah, the devil! you go too fast. But I see you understand me. Yes, Choiseul was very lucky; he governed the king, and governed his mistress. It is said that he was a lover of Madame de Pompadour, — in fact, why not? Well, no, I cannot act the lover; your cold smile tells me that plainly! You, with your young eyes, look at my furrowed brow, my bending knees, and my withered hands, which were once so beautiful. Instead of saying, when I was speaking of Choiseul's part, that I would play it, I should have said we will play it."

"Uncle!"

"No, she cannot love me, I know it; nevertheless,— I may confess it to you without fear, for she will never learn it, — I could have loved this woman beyond everything — but —"

D'Aiguillon frowned.

"But," continued Richelieu, "this part, which my age renders impossible for me, I will divide."

"Ah, ah!" said D'Aiguillon.

"Some one of my family," continued Richelieu, "will love Madame Dubarry. *Parbleu!* a glorious chance,— such an accomplished woman!" and Richelieu, in saying these words, raised his voice. "You know it cannot be Fronsac, — a degenerate wretch, a fool, a coward, a rogue, a gambler. Duke, will you be the man?"

"I?" cried D'Aiguillon; "are you mad, Uncle?"

"Mad! What! you are not already on your knees before him who gives you this advice? What! you do not bound with joy; you do not burn with gratitude? You are not already out of your senses with delight at the manner in which she received you? You are not yet mad with love? Go, go!" cried the old marshal; "since the days of Alcibiades there has been but one Richelieu in the world, and I see there will be no more after him."

"Uncle," replied the duke, with much agitation, either feigned, and in that case it was admirably counterfeited, or real, for the proposition was sudden, "I perceive all the advantage you would gain by the position of which you speak; you would govern with the authority of Monsieur de Choiseul, and I should be the lover who would establish that authority. The plan is worthy of the cleverest man in France; but you have forgotten one thing in projecting it."

"What!" cried Richelieu, uneasily, "is it possible you do not love Madame Dubarry? Is that it? Fool! triple fool! wretch! is that it?"

"Ah, no! it is not that, my dear uncle," cried D'Aiguillon, as if he knew that not one of his words was lost; "Madame Dubarry, whom I scarcely know, seems to me the most beautiful and the most charming of women. I should, on the contrary, love Madame Dubarry madly, — I should love her only too well; that is not the question."

"What is it, then?"

"This, Monsieur le Duc. Madame Dubarry will never love me, and the first condition of such an alliance is love. How do you imagine that the beautiful countess could distinguish among all the gentlemen of this brilliant court — surrounded as she is by the homage of so much youth and beauty — how could she distinguish one who has no merit, who is already no longer young, who is overwhelmed with sorrows, and who hides himself from all eyes because he feels that he will soon disappear forever? Uncle, if I had known Madame Dubarry in the period of my youth and beauty, when women admired in me all that is lovable in a man, then she might have given me a place in her memory. That would have been much. But now there is nothing, — neither past, nor present, nor future. No, Uncle, we must renounce this chimera. You have pierced my heart by presenting it to me in such bright and glowing colors."

During this tirade, which was delivered with a fire which Molé might have envied, and Lekain would have thought worthy of imitation, Richelieu bit his lips, muttering to himself: "Has the man understood that the countess is listening? *Peste!* he is a clever dog. He is a master of his craft. In that case I must take care!"

Richelieu was right; the countess was listening, and every word D'Aiguillon spoke sank deep into her heart. She eagerly drank in the charm of this confession, and appreciated his exquisite delicacy in not betraying the secret of their former intimacy to his nearest confidant, for fear of throwing a shadow over a perhaps still dearly cherished portrait.

"Then you refuse?" said Richelieu.

"Oh! as for that, yes, Uncle; for unfortunately I see it is impossible."

"But try, at least, unhappy man!"

"And how?"

"You are here one of us; you will see the countess every day, — please her, *morbleu!*"

"With an interested aim? Never! If I should be so unfortunate as to please her, with this selfish end in view, I should flee to the end of the world, for I should be ashamed of myself."

Richelieu scratched his chin. "The thing is done," said he to himself, "or D'Aiguillon is a fool."

Suddenly a noise was heard in the courtyard, and several voices cried out, "The king!"

"The devil!" cried Richelieu; "the king must not see me here, — I will make my escape."

"And I?" said D'Aiguillon.

"It is different with you, — he must see you. Remain; and for God's sake, do not throw the handle after the axe."

With these words Richelieu stole out by the back-stairs, saying as he left the room, "Adieu till to-morrow!"

CHAPTER XLIII.

THE KING DIVIDES THE SPOILS.

WHEN the Duc d'Aiguillon was left alone, he felt at first somewhat embarrassed. He had perfectly understood all his uncle had said to him, perfectly understood that Madame Dubarry was listening, perfectly understood, in short, that it was necessary to a man of intelligence to be, in this emergency, a man of heart, and to play alone that part in which the old marshal sought to obtain a share.

The king's arrival very opportunely prevented the explanation which must have resulted from the puritanical declaration of Monsieur d'Aiguillon; for the marshal was not a man to remain long a dupe, — especially was he not likely to consent to make another's virtue shine with exaggerated brilliancy at the expense of his own. But being left alone, D'Aiguillon had time to reflect.

The king had in truth arrived. Already his pages had opened the door of the antechamber, and Zamore had darted toward the monarch, begging for bonbons, — a touching familiarity which Louis, when he was in a bad temper, punished by sundry fillips on the nose or boxes on the ears, both exceedingly disagreeable to the young African.

The king installed himself in the Chinese cabinet; and what convinced D'Aiguillon that Madame Dubarry had not lost a word of his conversation with his uncle, was the fact that he, D'Aiguillon, overheard the entire interview between Madame Dubarry and the king.

His Majesty seemed fatigued, like a man who has raised an immense weight. Atlas was less enfeebled when his day's work was done, and when he had held the world suspended on his shoulders for twelve hours. Louis XV. allowed his favorite to thank, applaud, and caress him, and tell him all the particulars of Monsieur de Choiseul's departure, which amused him exceedingly.

Then Madame Dubarry ventured. It was fair weather for politics; and besides, she felt herself strong enough at that moment to move one of the four quarters of the world. "Sire," said she, "you have destroyed, that is well; you have demolished, that is superb: but now you must think about rebuilding."

" Oh! it is done," said the king, carelessly.

"You have a ministry?"

"Yes."

"What! all at once, without breathing?"

"See what it is to want common-sense. Oh!— woman that you are— before sending away your cook, must you not, as you said the other day, have a new one in readiness?"

"Repeat to me that you have formed the cabinet."

The king raised himself upon the immense sofa on which he was lying rather than sitting, using the shoulders of the beautiful countess for his principal cushion. "One would think, Jeannette," said he, "to hear you making yourself so uneasy, that you know my ministry, and wish to find fault with them, or propose another."

"Well," said the countess, "that would not be so absurd as you seem to imagine."

"Indeed? Then you have a ministry."

"You have one, have you not?" she replied.

"Oh! it is my place to have one, Countess. Tell me your candidates."

"By no means; tell me yours."

"Most willingly, to set you the example."

"In the first place, then, the navy, where that dear Monsieur de Praslin was?"

"Ah! something new, Countess, — a charming man, who has never seen the sea."

"Who is it?"

"'Pon honor, it is a splendid idea. I shall make myself very popular, and I shall be crowned in the most distant seas, — in effigy, of course."

"But who, Sire, who is it?"

"I would wager you do not guess in a thousand attempts. It is a member of parliament, my dear, — the first president of the parliament of Besançon."

"Monsieur de Boynes?"

"Himself. *Peste*, how learned you are! You know all these people?"

"I cannot help it; you talk parliament to me the whole day. Why, the man would not know an oar if he saw it."

"So much the better. Monsieur de Praslin knew his duties too well, and cost me too much with his naval constructions."

"Well, the finance department, Sire?"

"Oh! that is a different affair; I have chosen a specialist."

"A financier?"

"No; a soldier. The financiers have crushed me too long already."

"Good heavens! And the war department?"

"Do not be uneasy; for that I have chosen a financier, Terray. He is a terrible scrutinizer of accounts. He will find errors in all Monsieur de Choiseul's additions. I may tell you that I had some idea of putting a wonderful man in the war department, — every inch a man, as they say; it was to please the philosophers."

"Good. But who, — Voltaire?"

"Almost. The Chevalier de Muy, — a Cato."

"Oh, Heaven! You alarm me."

"It was all arranged. I had sent for the man, his commission was signed, he had thanked me, when my good or my evil genius — judge which — prompted me to ask him to come to Luciennes this evening to sup and chat with us."

"Fie! Horrible!"

"Well, Countess, that was exactly what De Muy replied."

"He said that to you?"

"Expressed in other words, Countess. He said that his most ardent wish was to serve the king; but as for serving Madame Dubarry, it was impossible."

"Well, that was polite of your philosopher."

"You must know, Countess, I held out my hand to him, — for his appointment, which I tore in pieces with a most patient smile, and the chevalier disappeared. Louis XIV. would have let the rascal rot in one of those ugly dens in the Bastille; but I am Louis XV., and I have a parliament which gives me the whip, in place of my giving it to the parliament. That is the difference."

"No matter, Sire," said the countess, covering her royal lover with kisses, "you are not the less a clever man."

"That is not what the world in general says. Terray is execrated."

"Who is not? And for foreign affairs?"

"That honest fellow Bertin, whom you know."

"No."

"Then whom you do not know."

"But among them all I cannot find one good minister."

"So be it; now tell me yours."

"I will tell you only one."

"You do not tell me; you are afraid."

"The marshal."

"The marshal! What marshal?" said the king, making a wry face.

"The Duc de Richelieu."

"That old man? That milksop?"

"Good! The conqueror of Mahon a milksop!"

"An old debauchee —"

"Sire, your companion."

"An immoral man, who makes all the women run away."

"That is only since he no longer runs after them."

"Do not speak to me of Richelieu; he is my *bête noire*. The conqueror of Mahon took me into all the bad places in Paris. We were lampooned. No, no! Richelieu, — the very name puts me beside myself!"

"You hate them so much?"

"Whom?"

"The Richelieus."

"I abhor them."

"All?"

"All. What a worthy duke and peer Monsieur Fronsac makes! He has deserved the rack twenty times."

"I give him up; but there are more Richelieus in the world than he."

"Ah! yes, — D'Aiguillon."

"Well?"

The reader may judge whether, at these words, the nephew in the boudoir did not listen intently.

"I ought to hate him more than the others, for he hounds all the bawlers in France upon me; and yet — it is a weakness which I cannot conquer — he is bold, and does not displease me."

"He is a man of spirit," cried the countess.

"A brave man, and zealous in the defence of the royal prerogative. He is a model of a peer."

"Yes, yes, — a hundred times, yes! Make something of him."

The king looked at the countess and folded his arms. "What, Countess! Is it possible that you propose such a thing to me, when all France demands that I should exile and degrade this man?"

Madame Dubarry folded her arms in her turn. "Just now," said she, "you called Richelieu a milksop; the name belongs more properly to yourself."

"Oh, Countess!"

"You are very proud because you have dismissed Monsieur de Choiseul."

"Well, it was not an easy task."

"You have done it, and you have done well; but you are afraid of the consequences."

"I?"

"Of course. What do you accomplish by sending away Monsieur de Choiseul?"

"I give the parliament a kick in the seat of honor."

"And you will not give two! What the devil! Raise both your feet, — one after the other, be it understood. The parliament wished to keep Choiseul; you send him away. They want to send away D'Aiguillon; keep him."

"I do not send him away."

"Keep him, — improved and considerably enlarged."

"You want an office for this firebrand?"

"I want a recompense for him who defended you at the risk of his position and fortune."

"Say of his life; for he will be stoned some fine morning, in company with your friend Maupeou."

"You would encourage your defenders very much, if they could only hear you."

"They pay me back with interest, Countess!"

"Do not say so; facts contradict you in this case."

"Ah, well! But why this eagerness for D'Aiguillon?"

"Eagerness! I do not know him; I have seen and spoken to him to-day for the first time."

"Ah! that is a different affair. Then it is from conviction of his merit? I respect conviction in others, because I never have it myself."

"Then give Richelieu something in D'Aiguillon's name, since you will not give D'Aiguillon anything in his own."

"Richelieu, nothing! Never, never, never!"

"Then something to Monsieur d'Aiguillon, since you refuse Richelieu?"

"What, give him a portfolio? That is impossible at present."

"I understand that; but after some time, perhaps. Remember that he is a man of resources and action, and that with Terray, D'Aiguillon, and Maupeou, you will have the three heads of Cerberus. Remember, too, that your ministry is only a jest, which cannot last."

"You are mistaken, Countess; it will last three months."

"In three months, then, I have your promise?"

"Oh, oh, Countess!"

"That is enough; in the mean time, something for the present."

"But I have nothing."

"You have the Light Horse; Monsieur d'Aiguillon is an officer, — what is called a sword. Give him your Light Horse."

"Very well; he shall have them."

"Thanks!" exclaimed the countess, transported with joy, "a thousand thanks!" and Monsieur d'Aiguillon could hear a very plebeian kiss resound on the cheeks of his Majesty Louis XV.

"In the mean time," said the king, "order supper to be served, Countess."

"No," said she, "there is nothing here; you have overpowered me with politics. My people have made speeches and fireworks, but no supper."

"Then come to Marly; I will take you with me."

"Impossible! my poor head is splitting in pieces."

"With headache?"

"A terrible headache."

"You must go to bed, Countess."

"I am just going to do so, Sire."

"Adieu, then!"

"Au revoir, rather!"

"I am somewhat like Monsieur de Choiseul; I am dismissed."

"Yes, but accompanied, feasted, cajoled," said the giddy creature, pushing the king gently toward the door, and thence to the foot of the stairs, laughing loudly, and turning round at each step. On the peristyle the countess stopped, candle in hand.

"Countess," said the king, turning round and ascending a step.

"Sire?"

"I trust the poor marshal will not die of it."

"Of what?"

"Of the portfolio which he has missed."

"How ill-natured you are!" said the countess, saluting him with another loud laugh; and his Majesty drove off, very much delighted with his last witticism upon the duke, whom he really hated.

When Madame Dubarry returned to her boudoir, she found D'Aiguillon on his knees before the door, his hands

clasped, his eyes ardently fixed upon her. She blushed.
"I have failed," said she. "The poor marshal!"

"Oh, I know all!" said he; "I could hear. Thanks, Madame, thanks!"

"I thought I owed you that," she replied, with a sweet smile; "but rise, Duke, else I shall think your memory is as retentive as your mind is highly cultivated."

"That may well be, Madame; my uncle has told you I am nothing but your admiring and zealous servant."

"And the king's; to-morrow you must go and pay your respects to his Majesty. Rise, I beg;" and she gave him her hand, which he kissed respectfully.

The countess seemed to be deeply moved, for she did not add a single word. Monsieur d'Aiguillon was also silent, as deeply moved as she. At last Madame Dubarry, raising her head, said: "Poor marshal! he must be informed of this defeat."

Monsieur d'Aiguillon looked upon these words as a dismissal, and bowed. "Madame," said he, "I am going to him."

"Oh, Duke! unpleasant news is always soon enough told. Do something better, — stay and have supper with me!"

The duke was stirred by a fragrance of youth and love which inflamed and rejuvenated the blood of his heart. "You are not a woman," said he, "you are —"

"An angel, am I not?" the warm lips of the countess said in his ear, touching him at the same time; and she conducted him to the table.

That evening Monsieur d'Aiguillon might well call himself fortunate, for he gained his uncle's portfolio and ate from the dish of the king.

CHAPTER XLIV.

THE ANTECHAMBERS OF THE DUC DE RICHELIEU.

MONSIEUR DE RICHELIEU, like all the courtiers, had a house at Versailles, one at Paris, one at Marly, and another at Luciennes, — a residence, in short, near each of the palaces or residences of the king.

Louis XIV., when he multiplied his places of residence so much, had imposed on all men of rank, — on all those privileged to attend at the grand and little receptions and levees, — the obligation of being very rich, that they might keep pace at once with the splendor of his household and the flight of his caprices.

At the period of the disgrace of Messieurs de Choiseul and de Praslin, Monsieur de Richelieu was living in his house at Versailles; and thither he returned after having presented his nephew to Madame Dubarry at Luciennes.

Richelieu had been seen in the forest of Marly with the countess; he had been seen at Versailles after the minister's disgrace; his long and secret audience at Luciennes was known, — and this, with the indiscretions of Jean Dubarry, was sufficient reason for the whole court to think themselves obliged to go and pay their respects to Monsieur de Richelieu.

The old marshal was now in his turn about to inhale that delightful incense of praises, flatteries, and caresses which every interested person offered, without discrimination, to the idol of the day.

Monsieur de Richelieu, however, was far from expecting all that was to happen to him; but he rose that morning with the firm resolution of closing his nostrils against the incense, as Ulysses closed his ears with wax against the songs of the sirens. The result which he expected could not be known until the next day, when the nomination of the new minister would be announced by the king himself.

Great was the marshal's surprise, therefore, when he awoke, or rather was awakened by the loud noise of carriages, to hear from his valet that the courtyards of the hôtel, as well as the ante-rooms and salons, were filled with visitors. "Oh!" said he, "it seems I make some noise already."

"It is still early, Monsieur le Maréchal," said his valet, seeing the duke's haste in taking off his nightcap.

"Henceforward," replied the duke, "there will be no such word as 'early' for me; remember that."

"Yes, Monsieur."

"What did you reply to the visitors?"

"That you were not up yet."

"Nothing more?"

"Nothing more."

"That was exceedingly stupid. You should have added that I was up late last night, or better still, you should have— Let me see, where is Rafté?"

"Monsieur Rafté is asleep," said the valet.

"What, asleep? Let him be called, the wretch!"

"Well," said a fresh and smiling old man who appeared at the door, "here is Rafté; what is he wanted for?"

All the duke's bombast ceased at these words. "Ah! I was certain that you were not asleep."

"And if I had been asleep, where would have been the wonder? It is scarcely daylight."

"But, my dear Rafté, you see that I do not sleep."

"That is another thing; you are a minister,— how should you sleep?"

"Oh! now you are going to scold me," said the marshal, grimacing before the glass; "are you not satisfied?"

"I! What benefit is it to me? You will fatigue yourself to death, and then you will be ill. The consequence will be that I shall have to govern the State, and that is not so amusing, Monseigneur."

"How old you are growing, Rafté!"

"I am just four years younger than yourself, Monseigneur. Yes, I am growing old."

The marshal stamped with impatience. "Did you come through the antechamber?" he asked.

"Yes."

"Who is there?"

"Everybody."

"What do they speak of?"

"Every one is telling what favors he is going to ask from you."

"That is very natural. But what did you hear about my appointment?"

"Oh! I would much rather not tell you that."

"What! criticisms already?"

"Yes, and from those who have need of your assistance! What will those say, Monseigneur, whose assistance you need?"

"Ah! Rafté," said the old man, affecting to laugh, "those who would say you flatter me—"

"Well, Monseigneur," said Rafté, "why the devil did you harness yourself to this wagon called a ministry? Are you tired of living and of being happy?"

"My dear fellow, I have tasted everything but that."

"*Corbleu!* you have never tasted arsenic! Why do you not take some in your chocolate, from curiosity?"

"Rafté, you are an idle dog; you think that, as my secretary, you will have more work, and you shrink from it, — you confessed as much, indeed."

The marshal dressed himself with care. "Give me a military air," said he to his valet, "and hand me my military orders."

"It seems we are in the war department?" said Rafté.

"Why, yes; it seems we are there."

"Oh! but I have not seen the king's appointment," continued Rafté; "this is irregular."

"The appointment will come in good time, no doubt."

"Then 'no doubt' is the countersign to-day?"

"You become more disagreeable, Rafté, as you get older. You are a formalist and purist. If I had known that, I would not have allowed you to deliver my inauguration speech at the Académie; it is that which made you pedantic."

"But listen, Monseigneur; since we are in the government, let us be regular. This is a very odd affair."

"What is odd?"

"Monsieur le Comte de la Vaudraye, whom I met just now in the street, told me that nothing had yet been settled about the ministry."

Richelieu smiled.

"Monsieur de la Vaudraye is right," said he. "But have you already been out, then?"

"*Pardieu!* I was obliged to go out. This cursed noise of carriages awoke me. I dressed, put on my military orders also, and took a turn in the town."

"Ah! Monsieur Rafté makes merry at my expense."

"Oh, Monseigneur, God forbid! But —"

"But what?"

"On my walk, I met some one."

"Whom?"

"The secretary of the Abbé Terray."

"Well?"

"Well! he told me that he himself was appointed to the war department."

"Oh! ho!" said Richelieu, with his eternal smile.

"What does Monseigneur conclude from this?"

"That if Monsieur Terray is appointed to the war department, I am not; that if he is not, perhaps I am."

Rafté had satisfied his conscience; he was a bold, indefatigable, ambitious man, as clever as his master, and much better armed than he, for he knew that his master was of humble origin, and that he had been in dependent circumstances, — two defects in his coat of mail which for forty years had exercised all his cunning, strength, and activity of mind. When Rafté saw his master so confident, he believed that he himself had nothing more to fear.

"Come, Monseigneur," said he, "make haste; do not oblige them to wait too long; that would be a bad beginning."

"I am ready; but tell me once more who is there?"

"Here is the list." He presented a long list to his master, who read with increasing satisfaction names prominent among the nobility, in the law, and in finance.

"Suppose I should be popular, hey, Rafté?"

"We are in the age of miracles," replied the latter.

"Ha, Taverney!" said the marshal, continuing to peruse the list. "What does he come here for?"

"I have not the least idea, Monseigneur; but come, make your entrée;" and the secretary, with an authoritative air, almost pushed his master into the grand salon.

Richelieu ought to have been satisfied; his reception

might have contented the ambition of a prince of the blood. But the refined cunning and craft which characterized the period, and particularly the class of society we are speaking of, only too well assisted Richelieu's unlucky star, which had such a severe disappointment in store for him.

Through regard for propriety and respect for etiquette, all the assembly abstained from pronouncing the word "minister" before Richelieu; some were bold enough to venture as far as the word "congratulation," but they knew that they must pass quickly over the word, and that Richelieu would scarcely reply to it. For one and all, this morning visit was a simple demonstration of respect, a mere expression of good-will; at this period such almost imperceptible shades of distinction were frequently understood and acted upon by the general mass of the community.

There were certain of the courtiers who ventured, in the course of conversation, to express some desire or hope. This one would have wished, he said, to have his government rather nearer Versailles, and it gratified him to have an opportunity of speaking on the subject to a man of so great influence as Monsieur de Richelieu. Another said he had been three times forgotten by Monsieur de Choiseul in the promotions of the knights of the order, and he reckoned upon Monsieur de Richelieu's obliging memory to refresh the king's, now that there existed no obstacle in the way of his Majesty's good-will. In short, a hundred requests, more or less grasping, but all veiled by the highest art, were preferred to the delighted ears of the marshal.

Gradually the crowd retired; they wished, as they said, to leave the marshal to his "important occupations." One man alone remained in the salon. He had not approached as the others had; he had asked for nothing; he had not even presented himself. When the courtiers had gone, this man advanced toward the duke with a smile upon his lips.

"Ah, Monsieur de Taverney!" said the marshal, "I am enchanted to see you, truly enchanted."

"I was waiting, Duke, to pay you my compliments and to offer you my sincere congratulations."

"Ah! indeed, and for what?" replied Richelieu; for the cautious reserve of his visitors had imposed upon him the necessity of being discreet, and even mysterious.

"On your new dignity, Duke."

"Hush, hush!" said the marshal; "let us not speak of that. Nothing is settled; it is a mere rumor."

"Nevertheless, my dear Marshal, there are many people of my opinion, for your salons were full."

"In truth, I do not know why."

"Oh! I know very well."

"Why then? Why?"

"It was owing to a single word from me."

"What word?"

"Yesterday I had the honor of paying my respects to the king at Trianon. His Majesty spoke to me of my children, and ended by saying: 'You know Monsieur de Richelieu, I think; pay your compliments to him.'"

"Ah! his Majesty said that?" replied Richelieu, with a glow of pride, as if these words had been the official appointment, the issue of which Rafté doubted, or at least deplored the delay.

"So that," continued Taverney, "I suspected the truth, — in fact, it was not difficult to do so, when I saw the eagerness of all Versailles; and I hastened to obey the king by paying my compliments to you, and to gratify my own feelings by reminding you of our old friendship."

The duke had now reached the excitement of intoxication. It is a defect in our nature from which the highest minds cannot always preserve themselves. He saw in Taverney only one of those expectants of the lowest order, — poor devils who have fallen behind on the road of favor, who are useless even as protégés, useless as acquaintances, and who are reproached with coming forth from their obscurity, after a lapse of twenty years, to warm themselves at the sun of another's prosperity.

"I see what you are aiming at," said the marshal, harshly; "you have some favor to ask of me."

"You have said it, Duke."

"Ah!" grumbled Richelieu, seating himself on, or rather plumping into, the sofa.

"I told you I had two children," continued Taverney, pliant and cunning; for he perceived the coolness of his great friend, and therefore only advanced the more eagerly. "I have a daughter whom I love very dearly, and who is a model of virtue and beauty. She is placed with her Highness the Dauphiness, who has been condescending enough to grant her her particular esteem. Of my beautiful Andrée, therefore, I need not speak to you. Her path is smoothed; her fortune is made. Have you seen my daughter? Did I not once present her to you somewhere? Have you not heard of her?"

"Pshaw! I don't know," said Richelieu, carelessly; "perhaps so."

"No matter," pursued Taverney, "there is my daughter settled. For my own part, I want nothing; the king grants me a pension upon which I can live. I confess I should like to have some emolument to enable me to rebuild Maison Rouge, where I wish to end my days, and with your interest and my daughter's —"

"Eh!" said Richelieu to himself, who until now had

not listened, so lost was he in contemplation of his grandeur, but whom the words, "my daughter's interest," had roused from his revery. "Eh! eh! your daughter! Why, she is a young beauty who annoys our good countess; she is a little scorpion who is sheltering herself under the wings of the dauphiness, in order to bite some one at Luciennes. Come, I will not be a bad friend; and as for gratitude, this dear countess who has made me a minister shall see if I am wanting in time of need." Then aloud, "Proceed," said he to the Baron de Taverney, in a haughty tone.

"Faith, I am near the end," replied the latter, promising himself to laugh in his sleeve at the vain marshal if he could only get what he wanted from him. "I am anxious therefore only about my son Philippe, who bears a lofty name, but who will never be able to support it worthily, unless some one assists him. Philippe is a bold and thoughtful youth, — rather too thoughtful, perhaps; but that is the result of his embarrassed position. You know the horse which is reined in too tightly droops its head."

"What is all this to me?" thought Richelieu, giving most unequivocal signs of weariness and impatience.

"I want some one," continued Taverney, remorselessly, "some one in authority like yourself, to procure a company for Philippe. Her Highness the Dauphiness, on entering Strasburg, raised him to the rank of captain; but he still wants a hundred thousand francs to enable him to purchase a company in some privileged regiment of cavalry. Procure that for me, my powerful friend."

"Your son," said Richelieu, "is the young man who rendered the dauphiness a service, is he not?"

"A great service," replied Taverney. "It was he who forced the last relay for her Royal Highness from that Dubarry who wanted to seize it by force."

"Oh, oh!" thought Richelieu, "that is just it, — the most violent enemies of the countess. He comes at the right time, this Taverney! He advances claims which are sufficient to damn him forever."

"You do not answer, Duke!" said Taverney, rather soured by the marshal's obstinate silence.

"All that is impossible, my dear Monsieur de Taverney," replied the marshal, rising, to show that the audience was over.

"Impossible? Such a trifle impossible? An old friend tells me that?"

"Why not? Is it any reason, because you are a friend, as you say, that you should seek to make me commit treason both against friendship and justice? You never came to see me for twenty years, for during that time I was nothing; now that I am a minister, you come."

"Monsieur de Richelieu, it is you who are unjust at this moment."

"No, my dear friend, no; I do not wish to see you dangling in my antechambers. I am a true friend, and therefore —"

"You have some reason for refusing me, then?"

"I!" exclaimed Richelieu, much alarmed at the suspicion Taverney might perhaps form; "I, a reason!"

"Yes; I have enemies."

The duke might have replied what he thought; but that would have been to discover to the baron that he tried to please Madame Dubarry through gratitude; it would have been to confess that he was the minister of the favorite, — and that the marshal would not have confessed for an empire. He therefore hastily replied: "You have no enemy, my dear friend, but I have many. To grant requests at once, without examining claims, would expose me to the accusations of continuing the Choiseul system. My dear fellow, I wish to leave behind some trace of my administration of affairs. For twenty years I have projected reforms, improvements; and now they shall blossom. Favoritism is the ruin of France; I will protect merit. The writings of our philosophers are bright torches, whose light has not shone for me in vain; they have dissipated all the mists of ignorance and superstition which brooded over the past; and it was full time it should be so for the well-being of the State. I shall therefore examine your son's claims, neither more nor less than I should do those of any other citizen. I must make this sacrifice to my conscience, — a grievous sacrifice, no doubt, but which after all is only that of one man for the benefit of three hundred thousand. If your son, Monsieur Philippe de Taverney, proves that he merits my favor, he shall have it, not because his father is my friend, not because he bears the name he does, but because he is a man of merit. That is my plan of conduct."

"You mean your system of philosophy," replied the old baron, biting his nails with rage, and adding to his anger by reflecting how much humiliation and how many petty cowardices this interview had cost him.

"Philosophy if you will, Monsieur; it is a noble word."

"Which dispenses good things, Marshal, does it not?"

"You are a bad courtier," said Richelieu, with a cold smile.

"Men of my rank are courtiers only of the king."

"Oh! Monsieur Rafté, my secretary, has a thousand of your rank in my antechambers every day," replied Richelieu; "they generally come from some obscure den or other in the provinces, where they have learned to be rude to their pretended friends while they preach concord."

"Oh! I am well aware that a Maison Rouge, of a rank which dates from the crusades, does not understand concord so well as a Vignerot fiddler."

The marshal had more tact than Taverney. He could have had him thrown out of the windows, but he only shrugged his shoulders, and replied: "You are rather behind the time, Monsieur, of the crusades; you remember only the calumnious memoir presented by parliament in 1720, and have not read that of the peers and dukes in reply. Be kind enough to walk into my library, my dear Monsieur; Rafté will give it to you to read."

As Richelieu was bowing his antagonist out with this apt repartee, the door opened, and a man entered noisily, crying, "Where is my dear duke?"

This man, with ruddy visage, eyes dilated with satisfaction, and joyous air, was neither more nor less than Jean Dubarry.

On seeing this new-comer, Taverney started back with surprise and vexation. Jean saw the movement, recognized the face, and turned his back.

"I understand," said the baron, quietly, "and I shall retire. I leave Monsieur the minister in fitting company." And he left the room with dignity.

CHAPTER XLV.

DISENCHANTMENT.

FURIOUS at this very irritating exit, Jean made two steps after the baron; then, returning to the marshal, he said, shrugging his shoulders, "You receive such people here?"

"Oh, my dear fellow, you mistake! On the contrary, I send such people away."

"Do you know who this gentleman is?"

"Alas! yes."

"No, but do you know, really?"

"He is a Taverney."

"He is a man who wishes to make his daughter the king's favorite —"

"Oh, come!"

"A man who wishes to supplant us, and who takes all possible means to do so. But Jean is there, and Jean has his eyes about him."

"You think he wishes —"

"It is a very difficult matter to see what he wishes, is it not? One of the dauphin's party, my dear man; and they have their little assassin too."

"Bah!"

"A young man quite ready to fly at people's throats, — a bully, who pinks Jean's shoulder, — poor Jean!"

"Yours? Is it a personal enemy of yours, my dear Viscount?" asked Richelieu, feigning surprise.

"Yes; he was my adversary in that affair of the relay, you know."

"Indeed! What a strange sympathy! I did not know that, and yet I refused all his demands; only, if I had known, I should not only have refused him, but kicked him out. But do not be uneasy, Viscount; I have now this worthy bully under my thumb, and he shall find it out."

"Yes, you can cure him of his taste for attacking people on the highway. For in fact — Oh, by the by, I have not yet congratulated you!"

"Why, yes, Viscount; it seems the affair is definitively settled."

"Oh! it is all completed. Will you permit me to embrace you?"

"With all my heart."

"Faith! there was some trouble; but the trouble is nothing when you succeed. You are satisfied, are you not?"

"Shall I speak frankly? Yes! for I think I can be useful."

"No doubt of that. But it is a bold stroke; there will be some growling."

"Am I not liked by the public?"

"You? Why, there is no question of you, either one way or other; it is he who is execrated."

"He?" said Richelieu, with surprise; "who is he?"

"Of course," interrupted Jean. "Oh! the parliament will revolt; it will be a second edition of the flagellation of Louis XIV. They are whipped, Duke, they are whipped."

"Explain."

"Why, it explains itself. The parliament, of course, hate the author of their persecutions."

"Ah! you think that?"

"I am certain of it, as all France is. No matter, Duke,

it was a capital stroke of you to send for him that way, just at the very heat of the affair."

"Whom? Whom, Duke? I am on thorns; I do not understand one word of what you say."

"Why, I speak of Monsieur d'Aiguillon, your nephew."

"Well, what then?"

"Well, I say it was well-advised of you to send for him."

"Ah! very good, very good. You mean to say he will assist me?"

"He will assist us all. Do you know he is on the best terms with little Jeanne?"

"Oh! really?"

"On the best terms. They have already had a chat together, and understand each other perfectly, as it seems to me."

"You know that?"

"It is very clear. Jeannette is the laziest dormouse in existence."

"Ah!"

"She doesn't leave her bed before nine, ten, or eleven o'clock."

"Yes; well?"

"Well, this morning, at Luciennes, it was six o'clock at the latest when I saw D'Aiguillon's carriage starting off."

"At six o'clock?" cried Richelieu, smiling.

"Yes."

"In the morning, — this morning?"

"In the morning, — this morning. You can judge that, to get up so early to give an audience to your nephew, Jeanne must be pretty fond of him."

"Yes, yes," said Richelieu; "six o'clock! Bravo, D'Aiguillon!"

"The audience must have begun at five o'clock, — in the night! It is wonderful."

"It is wonderful," repeated the marshal; "wonderful indeed, my dear Jean."

"And so there you are all three, like Orestes and Pylades, with the addition of another Pylades."

At this moment, and as the marshal was rubbing his hands in great glee, D'Aiguillon entered the salon. The nephew saluted his uncle with an air of condolence which was sufficient to enable Richelieu, without understanding the whole truth, at least to guess the greatest part of it. He turned pale, as though he had received a mortal wound. It flashed across his mind that at court there exist neither friends nor relatives, and that every one seeks only his own aggrandizement. "I was a great fool!" he said to himself. "Well, D'Aiguillon?" continued he, aloud, repressing a deep sigh.

"Well, Marshal?"

"It is a heavy blow to the parliament," said Richelieu, repeating Jean's words.

D'Aiguillon blushed. "You know it?" said he.

"The count has told me all," replied Richelieu, "even of your visit at Luciennes before daylight this morning. Your appointment is indeed a triumph for my family."

"Be assured, Marshal, of my extreme regret."

"What the devil does he mean by that?" said Jean, folding his arms.

"Oh! we understand each other," interrupted Richelieu; "we understand each other."

"That is a different affair; but for my part, I do not understand you. Regret! Ah! yes, because he will not be recognized as minister immediately, — yes, yes; I see."

"Oh! there will be an interim?" said the marshal, feeling a ray of hope — that constant guest in the heart of the ambitious man and the lover — once more dawn in in his breast.

"Yes, Marshal, an interim."

"But in the mean time," cried Jean, "he is tolerably well paid, — the finest command in Versailles."

"Ah! a command?" said Richelieu, pierced by a new wound.

"Monsieur Dubarry perhaps exaggerates a little," said the Duc d'Aiguillon.

"But, in one word, what is this command?"

"The king's Light Horse."

Richelieu's furrowed cheeks again turned pale. "Oh! yes," said he, with a smile which it would be impossible to describe, "yes, it is indeed a trifling appointment for such a charming man. But what can you expect, Duke? The loveliest woman in the world, were she even the king's favorite, can give only what she has."

It was now D'Aiguillon's turn to grow pale. Jean was scrutinizing the beautiful Murillos which adorned Richelieu's walls. Richelieu slapped his nephew on the shoulder. "Luckily," said he, "you have the promise of approaching advancement. Accept my congratulations, Duke, — my sincere compliments. Your address, your cleverness in negotiations, is only equalled by your good fortune. Adieu; I have some business to transact. Do not forget me in the distribution of your favors, my dear minister."

D'Aiguillon replied only, "Your interests and mine, Monsieur le Maréchal, are henceforth one and the same;" and saluting his uncle, he left the room with the dignity which was natural to him, — thus escaping from one of the most embarrassing positions he had ever experienced in a life strewn with so many difficulties.

"An admirable trait in D'Aiguillon's character," said

Richelieu, the moment the former had disappeared, to Jean, who was rather at a loss to know what to think of this exchange of politeness between the nephew and uncle, "and one that I admire particularly, is his artlessness. He is at once frank and high-spirited; he knows the court, and is withal as simple-minded as a girl."

"And then he loves you so well," said Jean.

"Like a lamb."

"Oh!" said Jean, "he is more like your son than Monsieur de Fronsac."

"By my faith, yes, Viscount; by my faith, yes!" While replying thus, Richelieu kept walking round his chair in great agitation; he sought, but could not find.

"Ah, Countess!" he muttered, "you shall pay me for this!"

"Marshal," said Jean, with a cunning look, "we four will realize that famous fagot of antiquity, — you know, the one that could not be broken."

"We four, my dear Monsieur Jean! How do you understand that?"

"My sister as power, D'Aiguillon as authority, you as advice, and I as vigilance."

"Very good, very good!"

"And now let them attack my sister; I defy them all."

"*Pardieu!*" said Richelieu, whose brain was boiling.

"Let them set up rivals now!" exclaimed Jean, in ecstasies with his plans and his visions of triumph.

"Oh!" said Richelieu, striking his forehead.

"Well, my dear Marshal, what is the matter?"

"Nothing! I think your idea of a league admirable."

"Is it not?"

"And I enter body and soul into your plans."

"Bravo!"

"Does Taverney live at Trianon with his daughter?"

"No; he lives in Paris."

"The girl is very handsome, my dear Viscount."

"If she were as beautiful as Cleopatra or — my sister, I do not fear her, now that we are leagued together."

"You say Taverney lives in Paris? In the Rue St. Honoré, I think."

"I did not say Rue St. Honoré; it is the Rue Coq-Héron in which he lives. Have you any plan of chastising these Taverneys, that you ask?"

"Yes, Count, I think I have found a capital plan."

"You are an incomparable man. I must leave you; I wish to see what they say in town."

"Adieu, then, Count. By the way, you have not told me who the new ministers are."

"Oh, mere birds of passage, — Terray, Bertin, and I know not who else. Mere counters in the hands of D'Aiguillon, the real minister, though his appointment is deferred for a short time."

"Perhaps indefinitely deferred," thought the marshal, directing his most gracious smile to Jean as an affectionate adieu.

Jean retired. Rafté entered. He had heard all, and knew how to conduct himself; all his suspicions were now realized. He did not utter a word to his master; he knew him too well. He did not even call the valet; he assisted him with his own hands to undress, and conducted him to his bed, in which the old marshal, shivering with fever, immediately buried himself, after taking a pill which his secretary made him swallow.

Rafté drew the curtains and retired. The antechamber was thronged with eagerly listening valets. Rafté took the head valet aside.

"Attend to the marshal carefully," said he, "he is ill.

He has had a serious vexation this morning; he was obliged to disobey the king."

"Disobey the king!" exclaimed the alarmed valet.

"Yes, his Majesty sent a portfolio to Monseigneur, but as he was aware that he owed it to the solicitations of the Dubarry, he refused. Oh! it was a noble resolve, and the Parisians ought to build him a triumphal arch; but the shock was great, and our master is ill. Look to him carefully!"

After these words, whose circulating power he knew beforehand, Rafté returned to his closet. A quarter of an hour afterward all Versailles was informed of the noble conduct and lofty patriotism of the marshal, who in the mean time slept soundly upon the popularity his secretary had gained for him.

CHAPTER XLVI.

THE DAUPHIN'S FAMILY REPAST.

THE same day, about three o'clock, Mademoiselle Taverney left her apartment to attend upon the dauphiness, who had the custom of listening to reading before dinner. The abbé who had held the post of first reader to her Royal Highness no longer exercised his functions, as for some time previous, after certain diplomatic intrigues in which he had displayed a very great talent for business, he had employed himself entirely in important political affairs.

Mademoiselle Taverney set out, then, dressed as well as circumstances would permit, to fulfil her office. Like all the guests at Trianon, she still suffered considerable inconvenience from the rather sudden installation in her new abode, and had not yet been able to arrange her furniture, or make the necessary provisions for establishing her modest household. She had, therefore, on the present occasion, been assisted in her toilet by one of the maids of Madame de Noailles, that starched lady of honor whom the dauphiness nicknamed Madame Etiquette.

Andrée was dressed in a blue silk robe, with long waist, which fitted admirably to her slender figure. This robe opened in front, and displayed a muslin skirt relieved with three falls of embroidery. Short sleeves, also of muslin, embroidered in the same manner as the dress, festooned, and tapering to the shoulder, were admirably. in keeping with a neckerchief embroidered in the peasant style, which modestly concealed her neck and shoulders.

Andree encounters Gilbert at Trianon

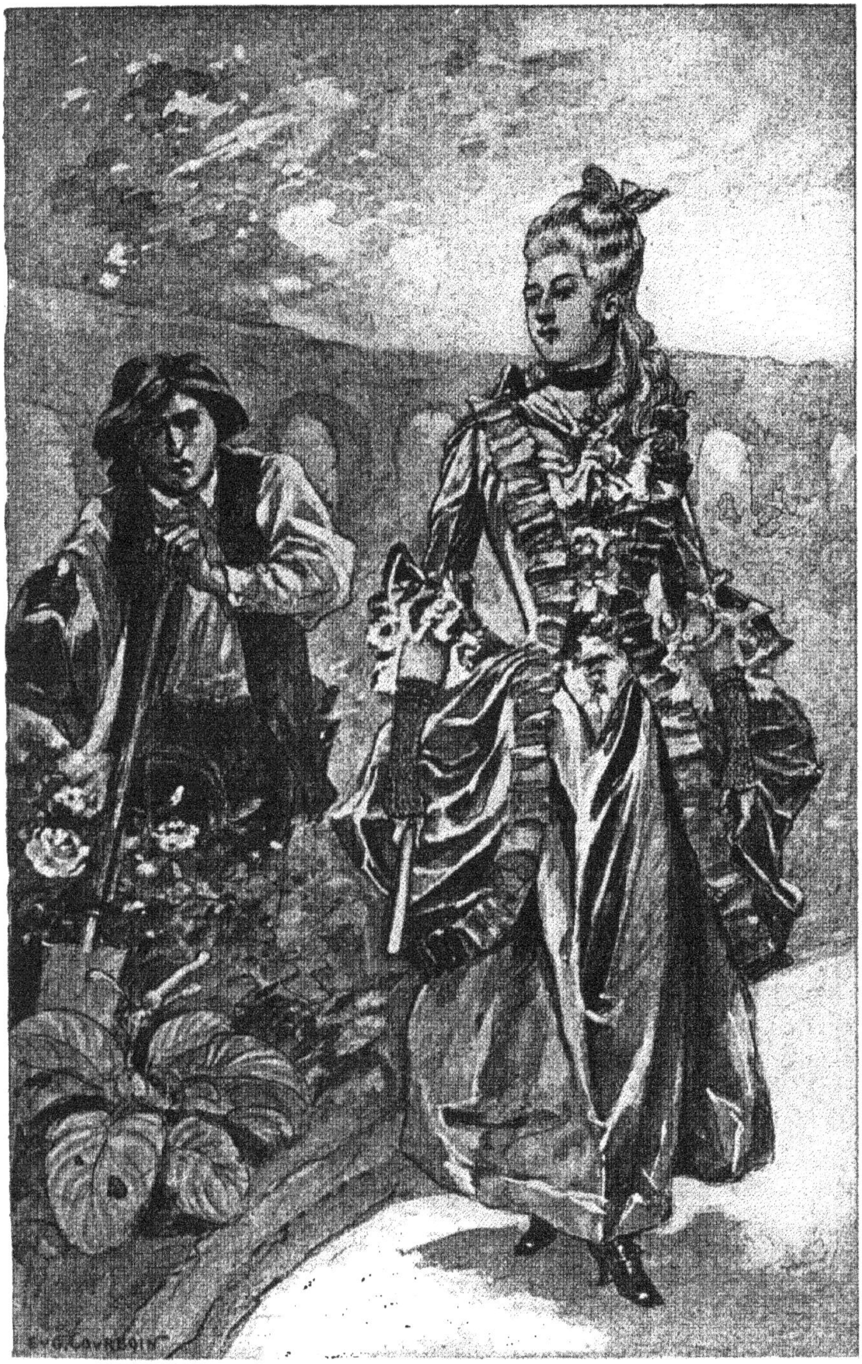

Her beautiful hair, which fell in long and luxuriant ringlets upon her shoulders, was simply tied with a ribbon of the same color as her dress, — a mode of arrangement which harmonized infinitely better with the noble, yet modest and retiring air of the lovely young girl, and with her pure and transparent complexion, never yet sullied by the touch of rouge, than the feathers, ornaments, and laces which were then in vogue.

As she walked, Andrée drew on a pair of white silk mittens upon the slenderest and roundest fingers in the world, while the tiny points of her high-heeled shoes of pale-blue satin left their traces on the gravel of the garden walk. When she reached the pavilion of Trianon, she was informed that the dauphiness was taking a turn in the grounds with her architect and her head-gardener. In the apartment of the first story overhead she could hear the noise of a turning-lathe, with which the dauphin was making a safety-lock for a coffer which he valued very highly.

In order to rejoin the dauphiness, Andrée had to cross the parterre, where, notwithstanding the advanced period of the season, flowers, carefully covered through the night, raised their pale heads to bask in the setting rays of a sun even paler than themselves. And as the evening was already closing in, for in that season it was dark at six o'clock, the gardener's apprentices were employed in placing the bell-glasses over the most delicate plants in each bed.

While traversing a winding alley of evergreens clipped into the form of a hedge, bordered on each side by beds of Bengal roses, and opening on a beautiful lawn, Andrée suddenly perceived one of these gardeners, who, when he saw her, stood up, leaning on his spade, and bowed with a more refined and studied politeness than was to be expected in one of his station. She looked again, and in this workman recognized Gilbert, whose hands, notwithstanding his labor, were yet white enough to excite the envy of Monsieur de Taverney.

Andrée blushed in spite of herself; it seemed to her that Gilbert's presence in this place was too remarkable a coincidence to be the result of chance. Gilbert repeated his bow, and Andrée returned it, but without slackening her pace. She was too upright and too courageous, however, to resist the promptings of her heart, and leave the question of her restless soul unanswered. She turned back; and Gilbert, whose cheek had already become as pale as death, and whose dark eye followed her retreating steps with a sombre look, felt as if suddenly restored to life, and bounded forward to meet her.

"You here, Monsieur Gilbert?" said Andrée, coldly.

"Yes, Mademoiselle."

"By what chance?"

"Mademoiselle, one must live, and live honestly."

"But do you know that you are very fortunate?"

"Oh, yes, Mademoiselle, very fortunate!" said Gilbert.

"I beg your pardon! What did you say?"

"I said, Mademoiselle, that I am, as you think, very fortunate."

"Who introduced you here?"

"Monsieur de Jussieu, a protector of mine."

"Ah!" said Andrée, surprised, "then you know Monsieur de Jussieu?"

"He is the friend of my first protector, — of my master, Monsieur Rousseau."

"Courage, then, Monsieur Gilbert?" said Andrée, making a movement to proceed.

"Do you find yourself better, Mademoiselle?" asked Gilbert, in a trembling voice.

"Better? What do you mean?" said Andrée, coldly.

"Why, the accident."

"Oh, yes, thank you, Monsieur Gilbert; I am better, — it was nothing."

"Oh, you were nearly perishing!" said Gilbert, almost speechless with emotion; "the danger was terrible."

Andrée now began to think that it was high time to cut short this interview with a workman in the most public part of the royal park.

"Good-day, Monsieur Gilbert," said she.

"Will Mademoiselle not accept a rose?" said Gilbert, trembling, and with drops of perspiration standing on his forehead.

"But, Monsieur," replied Andrée, "you offer me what is not yours to give."

Gilbert, surprised and overwhelmed by this reply, could not utter a word. His head drooped; but as he saw Andrée looking at him with something like a feeling of satisfaction at having manifested her superiority, he drew himself up, tore a branch covered with flowers from the finest of the rose-trees, and began to pull the roses to pieces with a coolness and dignity which surprised and startled the young girl.

She was too just and too kind-hearted not to see that she had gratuitously wounded the feelings of an inferior who had unthinkingly committed a breach of propriety. But like all proud natures who feel themselves in the wrong, she preserved silence, when perhaps an apology or a reparation was hovering upon her lips; and she immediately resumed her walk.

Gilbert added not a word either; he threw away the branch and resumed his spade. But his character was a mixture of pride and cunning; and while stooping to his work, he kept his eye stealthily fixed on Andrée's retreating figure. At the end of the walk she could not help looking round; she was a woman.

This weakness was sufficient for Gilbert; he said to himself that in this last struggle he had been victorious. "She is weaker than I am," thought he, "and I shall govern her. Proud of her beauty, of her name, of her advancing fortunes, indignant at my love, which she perhaps suspects, she is only the more an object of adoration to the poor working-man who trembles while he looks at her. Oh, this trembling, this emotion, unworthy of a man! Oh, these acts of cowardice which she makes me commit,— she shall one day repay me for them all! But to-day I have done enough," he added; "I have conquered the enemy. I, who ought to have been the weaker, since I love, have been a hundred times stronger than she."

He repeated these words with a wild burst of joy as he convulsively dashed back the dark hair from his thoughtful brow. Then he stuck his spade deep into the flower-bed, bounded through the hedge of cypress and yew-tree with the speed of a roe-buck, and light as the wind threaded a parterre of plants under bell-glasses, not one of which he touched, notwithstanding the furious rapidity of his career, and posted himself at the end of the diagonal he had made, in advance of Andrée, who followed the winding of the path. From his new position he saw her advancing, thoughtful and almost humble, her lovely eyes cast down, her motionless hand gently lying against her rustling dress. Concealed behind the thick hedge, Gilbert heard her sigh twice as if she were speaking to herself. At last she passed so close to the trees which sheltered him that had he stretched out his arm he might have touched hers, as a mad and feverish impulse prompted him to do. But he knit his brow with an energetic movement almost akin to hatred. and placing his trembling hand upon his heart. "Coward again!" said he to himself. Then he added, softly, "But she is so beautiful!"

Gilbert might have remained for a considerable time sunk in contemplation, for the walk was long, and Andrée's step was slow and measured; but this walk was crossed by others, from which some troublesome visitor might at any moment make his appearance, — and Fate treated Gilbert so scurvily that a man did in fact advance from the first alley upon the left; that is to say, almost opposite the clump of evergreens behind which he was concealed.

This intruder walked with a methodic and measured step; he carried his head erect, held his hat under his right arm, and his left hand rested upon his sword. He wore a velvet coat underneath a pelisse lined with sable fur, and pointed his foot as he walked, which he did with the easy grace of a man of high rank and breeding.

This gentleman as he advanced perceived Andrée, and the young girl's figure evidently pleased him; for he quickened his pace and crossed over in an oblique direction, so as to reach as soon as possible the path on which Andrée was walking, and intercept her course.

When Gilbert perceived this personage he involuntarily gave a slight cry, and took to flight like a startled lapwing. The intruder's manœuvre was successful; he was evidently accustomed to it, and in less than three minutes he was in advance of Andrée, whom three minutes before he had been following at some distance.

When Andrée heard his footstep behind her, she moved aside a little to let the man pass; and when he had passed, she looked at him in her turn. The gentleman looked also, and most eagerly, he even stopped to see better; and returning after he had seen her features, "Ah! Mademoiselle," said he, in a very kind voice, "whither are you hastening so quickly, may I ask?"

At the sound of this voice Andrée raised her head and saw, about twenty paces behind her, two officers of the guards following slowly; she spied a blue ribbon peeping from beneath the sable pelisse of the person who addressed her, and pale and startled at this unexpected rencontre, and at being accosted thus graciously, she said, bending very low, "The king!"

"Mademoiselle —," replied Louis XV., approaching her; "pardon me, I have such bad eyes that I am obliged to ask your name."

"Mademoiselle de Taverney," stammered the young girl, so confused and trembling that her voice was scarcely audible.

"Oh, yes, I remember! I esteem myself fortunate in meeting you in Trianon, Mademoiselle," said the king.

"I was proceeding to join her Royal Highness the Dauphiness, who expects me," said Andrée, trembling more and more.

"I will conduct you to her, Mademoiselle," replied Louis XV.; "for I am just going, as a country neighbor, to pay a visit to my daughter. Be kind enough to take my arm, as we are going in the same direction."

Andrée felt a cloud pass before her eyes, and the blood flow in tumultuous waves to her heart. In fact, such an honor for the poor girl as the proffered arm of the king, the sovereign lord of all France, — such an unhoped-for, incredible piece of good fortune, a favor which the whole court might envy, — seemed to her like a dream. She made a reverence so profound and so expressive of an almost religious veneration that the king felt himself obliged to bow a second time. When Louis XV. was inclined to remember Louis XIV., it was always in matters of ceremonial and politeness. Such traditions, however, dated farther back; they were handed down from Henry IV.

The king offered his hand therefore to Andrée, who placed the burning points of her fingers upon the king's glove, and they continued to advance toward the pavilion, where, as the king had been informed, the dauphiness with her architect and her head-gardener would be found.

We can assure the reader that Louis XV., although not particularly fond of walking, chose to conduct Andrée to the little Trianon by the longest road. Although the king was apparently unaware of his error, the two officers who walked behind perceived it but too plainly, and bemoaned themselves bitterly, as they were lightly clad and the weather was cold.

They arrived too late to find the dauphiness where they had expected, as Marie Antoinette had just set out for Trianon, that she might not keep the dauphin waiting, for he liked to have his supper between six and seven o'clock. Her Royal Highness arrived therefore at the exact hour; and as the punctual dauphin was already upon the threshold of the salon, that he might lose no time in reaching the dining-room the moment the butler appeared, the dauphiness threw her mantle to a maid, took the dauphin's arm with a winning smile, and drew him into the dining-room.

The table was laid for the two illustrious hosts. They occupied the middle of the table, so as to leave vacant the upper end of the table, which, since several unexpected visits of the king, was never occupied in his Majesty's absence, even when there were many guests. At that end of the table the king's cover occupied a considerable space; but the butler, not expecting it to be occupied this evening, was conducting the service from that end.

Behind the dauphiness's chair, leaving the necessary space between for the valets to pass, was stationed Madame de Noailles, stiff and upright, and yet wearing as amiable an expression on her features as she could conjure up for the festive occasion.

Near Madame de Noailles were some other ladies, whose position at the court gave them the right or entitled them to the favor of being present at the supper of their Royal Highnesses.

Three times a week Madame de Noailles sat at the same table with the dauphin and dauphiness; but on the other days she would not for anything in the world have missed being present. Besides, it was a delicate mode of protesting against the exclusion on four days out of seven.

Opposite the Duchesse de Noailles, surnamed by the dauphiness Madame Etiquette, was the Duc de Richelieu, on a raised seat very similar to her own. He also was a strict observer of forms; but his etiquette was undistinguishable to a casual observer, being always veiled beneath the most polished elegance, and sometimes the wittiest raillery. A consequence of this antithesis between the first gentleman of the bedchamber and the first lady of honor of the dauphiness was that the conversation, always dropped by the Duchesse de Noailles, was incessantly renewed by Monsieur de Richelieu.

The marshal had travelled through all the courts of Europe, and had adopted the tone of elegance in each which was best adapted to his character; so that, strong in tact and sense of fitness, he knew both what anecdotes to relate at the table of the youthful couple, and what would be seasonable at the private suppers of Madame Dubarry.

Perceiving this evening that the dauphiness had a good appetite, and that the dauphin was voracious, Richelieu concluded that they would give no heed to the conversation going on around them, and that he had consequently only to make Madame de Noailles suffer an hour of purgatory in anticipation. He began therefore to speak of philosophy and theatrical affairs, — two subjects of conversation doubly offensive to the venerable duchess. He related the subject of one of the last philanthropic sallies of the philosopher of Ferney, — the name already given to the author of the "Henriade;" and when he saw that the duchess was uneasy, he changed the text, and detailed all the squabbles and disputes which, in his office of gentleman of the chamber, he had to undergo in order to make the actresses in ordinary to the king play more or less badly.

The dauphiness loved the arts, and above all the theatre; she had sent a complete costume for Clytemnestra to Mademoiselle Raucourt, and she therefore listened to Monsieur de Richelieu not only with indulgence, but with pleasure.

Then the poor lady of honor, in violation of all etiquette, was forced to fidget on her bench, blow her nose noisily, and shake her venerable head, without thinking of the cloud of powder which at each movement fell upon her forehead, like the cloud of snow which envelops the summit of Mont Blanc at every gust of the north wind.

But it was not enough to amuse the dauphiness, the dauphin must also be pleased. Richelieu abandoned the subject of the theatre, for which the heir to the crown had never displayed any great liking, to discourse of humanity and philosophy. When he spoke of the English, he did so with all the warmth and energy which Rousseau displays in drawing the character of Edward Bromston.

Now, Madame de Noailles hated the English as much as she did philosophers. To admit a new idea was a fatiguing operation for her, and fatigue deranged the economy of her whole person. Madame de Noailles, who felt herself intended by nature for a conservative, growled at all new ideas like a dog at a frightful mask.

Richelieu in playing this game had a double end in view, — he tormented Madame Etiquette, which evidently pleased the dauphiness, and he threw in, here and there, some virtuous apophthegm, some axiom in mathematics, which was rapturously received by the dauphin, the royal amateur of exact sciences. He was paying his court, therefore, with great skill and address, and from time to time directing an eager glance toward the door, as if he expected some one who had not yet arrived, when a cry from the foot of the staircase echoed along the arched corridors, was repeated by two valets stationed at regular intervals from the entrance-door, and at last reached the dining-salon, "The king!"

At this magic word Madame de Noailles started bolt upright from her seat, as if moved by a spring; Richelieu rose more slowly, and with easy grace; the dauphin hastily wiped his mouth with his napkin, and stood up before his seat, his face turned toward the door. As for the dauphiness, she hastened toward the staircase to meet the king and do the honors of her mansion to him.

CHAPTER XLVII.

THE QUEEN'S HAIR.

THE king still held Mademoiselle de Taverney by the hand when they reached the landing-place, and it was only on arriving there that he bowed to her, so courteously and so low that Richelieu had time to see the bow, to admire its grace, and to ask himself to what lucky mortal it was addressed. His ignorance did not long continue.

Louis XV. took the arm of the dauphiness, who had seen all, and had already clearly recognized Andrée. "My daughter," said he, "I come without ceremony to ask you for my supper. I crossed the entire park on my way hither, and happening to meet Mademoiselle de Taverney, requested her to accompany me."

"Mademoiselle de Taverney!" murmured Richelieu, almost dizzy at this unexpected stroke. "Faith, I am almost too fortunate!"

"I shall not only refrain from scolding Mademoiselle for being late," replied the dauphiness, graciously, "but I have to thank her for bringing your Majesty to us."

Andrée, whose cheeks were dyed with as deep a red as the ripe and tempting cherries which graced the epergne in the centre of the table, bowed without replying.

"The devil! the devil! she is indeed beautiful," thought Richelieu; "and that old scoundrel Taverney gave her no more praise than she deserves."

The king had already taken his seat at the table after having saluted the dauphin. Gifted, like his grandson, with an obliging appetite, the monarch did justice to the improvised supper which the butler placed before him as if by magic. But while eating, the king, whose back was turned toward the door, seemed to seek something, or rather some one.

In fact, Mademoiselle de Taverney, who enjoyed no privilege, as her position in the dauphiness's household was not yet fixed, had not entered the dining-room; and after her profound reverence in reply to the king's salutation, had returned to the dauphiness's apartment, that she might be ready, in case it should be required of her, as already it had been two or three times, to read to her Highness after she had retired to bed.

The dauphiness saw that the king was looking for the beautiful companion of his walk. "Monsieur de Coigny," said she to a young officer of the guards who was standing behind the king, "pray request Mademoiselle de Taverney to come up; with Madame de Noailles' permission, we will discard etiquette for this evening."

Monsieur de Coigny left the room, and almost immediately afterward returned, introducing Andrée, who, totally at a loss to comprehend the reason for such a succession of unusual favors, entered trembling.

"Seat yourself there, Mademoiselle," said the dauphiness, "beside Madame de Noailles."

Andrée mounted timidly on the raised seat; but she was so confused that she had the audacity to seat herself only about a foot distant from the lady of honor. She received, in consequence, such a terrific look that the poor child started back at least four feet, as if she had come in contact with a Leyden jar highly charged. The king looked at her and smiled.

"Ah!" said the duke to himself, "it is scarcely worth my while to meddle with the affair; the thing goes on by its own motion."

The king turned, and perceived the marshal, who was quite prepared to meet his look.

"Good day, Duke," said Louis; "do you agree well with the Duchesse de Noailles?"

"Sire," replied the marshal, "the duchess always does me the honor to treat me as a madcap."

"Oh! Were you also on the road to Chanteloup, Duke?"

"I, Sire? Faith, no! I am too grateful for the favors your Majesty has showered on my family."

The king did not expect this blow; he was prepared to banter, but he found himself anticipated.

"What favors have I showered, Duke?"

"Sire, your Majesty has given the command of your Light Horse to the Duc d'Aiguillon."

"Yes, it is true, Duke."

"And for that was needed all your Majesty's energy and skill. It is almost a *coup d'état*."

The repast was now over; the king waited for a moment, and then rose from table. The conversation was taking an embarrassing turn, but Richelieu was determined not to let go his prey. Therefore when the king began to chat with Madame de Noailles, the dauphiness, and Mademoiselle de Taverney, Richelieu manœuvred so skilfully that he soon found himself in the full flow of a conversation which he directed according to his pleasure.

"Sire," said he, "your Majesty knows that success emboldens."

"Do you say so for the purpose of informing us that you are bold, Duke?"

"Sire, it is for the purpose of requesting a new favor

from your Majesty, after the one the king has already deigned to grant. One of my best friends, an old servant of your Majesty, has a son in the gendarmes; the young man is highly deserving, but poor. He has received from an august princess the brevet title of captain, but he has not yet obtained his company."

"The princess,— my daughter?" asked the king, turning toward the dauphiness.

"Yes, Sire," said Richelieu; "and the father of this young man is called the Baron de Taverney."

"My father!" involuntarily exclaimed Andrée, "Philippe! Is it for Philippe, Monsieur le Duc, that you are asking for a company?" Then, ashamed of this breach of etiquette, she made a step backward, blushing, and clasping her hands with emotion.

The king turned to admire the blush which mantled the cheek of the lovely girl, and then glanced at Richelieu with a pleased look, which informed the courtier how agreeable his request had been.

"In truth," said the dauphiness, "he is a charming young man, and I had promised to make his fortune. How unfortunate princes are! When God gives them the best intentions, he deprives them of the memory and reasoning powers necessary to carry their intentions into effect. Ought I not to have known that this young man was poor, and that it was not enough to give him the epaulette without at the same time giving him the company?"

"Eh, Madame! how could your Highness have known that?"

"Oh, I knew it!" replied the dauphiness, quickly, with a gesture which recalled to Andrée's memory the modest but yet happy home of her childhood; "yes, I knew it, but I thought I had done everything necessary in giving a step to Monsieur Philippe de Taverney. He is called Philippe, is he not, Mademoiselle?"

"Yes, Madame."

The king looked round on these noble and ingenuous faces, and then rested his gaze on Richelieu, whose face was also brightened by a ray of generosity, borrowed doubtless from his august neighbor.

"Duke," said he, in a low voice, "I shall embroil myself with Luciennes." Then, addressing Andrée, he added, quickly, "Say that it will give you pleasure, Mademoiselle."

"Ah, Sire!" said Andrée, clasping her hands, "I request it as a boon from your Majesty."

"In that case, it is granted," said Louis. "You will choose a good company for this young man, Duke; I will furnish the necessary funds, if the charges are not already paid and the post vacant."

This good action gladdened all who were present. It procured the king a heavenly smile from Andrée, and Richelieu a warm expression of thanks from those beautiful lips, from which, in his youth, he would have asked for even more.

Several visitors arrived in succession, among whom was the Cardinal de Rohan, who since the installation of the dauphiness at Trianon had paid his court to her assiduously. But during the whole evening the king had kind looks and pleasant words only for Richelieu. He even commanded the marshal's attendance when, after bidding farewell to the dauphiness, he set out to return to his own Trianon. The old marshal followed the king, his heart bounding with joy.

While the king, accompanied by the duke and his two officers, set forth toward the dark alleys which lead from the palace, the dauphiness dismissed Andrée. "You will be anxious to write this good news to Paris, Mademoiselle," said the princess; "you may retire."

Preceded by a footman, carrying a lantern, the young girl traversed the walk, of about a hundred paces in length, which separates Trianon from the offices. In advance of her, concealed by the thick foliage of the shrubbery, bounded a shadowy figure, which followed all her movements with sparkling eyes. It was Gilbert.

When Andrée had arrived at the entrance, and begun to ascend the stone steps, the valet left her and returned to the antechambers of Trianon.

Then Gilbert, gliding into the vestibule, reached the courtyard, and climbed by a small staircase as steep as a ladder into his attic, which was opposite Andrée's windows and was situated in a corner of the building. From this position he could see Andrée call an attendant of Madame de Noailles to assist her, as that lady had her apartments in the same corridor. But when the girl had entered the room, the window curtains fell like an impenetrable veil between the ardent eyes of the young man and the object of his wishes.

At the palace there now remained only Monsieur de Rohan, redoubling his gallant attentions to the dauphiness, who received them but coldly. The prelate, fearing at last to be indiscreet, inasmuch as the dauphin had already retired, took leave of her Royal Highness with the expression of the deepest and most tender respect.

As the cardinal was entering his carriage, a waiting-woman of the dauphiness approached, and almost leaned inside the door. "Here," said she; and she put into his hand a small paper parcel, carefully folded, the touch of which made the cardinal start.

"Here," he replied, hastily thrusting into the girl's hand a heavy purse, the contents of which would have been a handsome salary. Then, without losing time, the cardinal ordered the coachman to drive to Paris, and to ask for new orders at the barrier. During the journey, in the darkness of the carriage he felt the paper, and kissed the contents like some intoxicated lover. At the barrier he cried, "Rue St. Claude." A short time afterward he crossed the mysterious courtyard, and once more found himself in the little salon occupied by Fritz, the silent usher.

Balsamo kept the cardinal waiting about a quarter of an hour. At last he appeared, and gave as a reason for his delay the lateness of the hour, which had prevented his expecting the arrival of visitors. In fact, it was now nearly eleven o'clock at night.

"That is true, Baron," said the cardinal; "and I must request you to excuse my unseasonable visit. But, you may remember, you told me one day that to be assured of certain secrets —"

"I must have a portion of the person's hair of whom we were speaking on that day," interrupted Balsamo, who had already spied the little paper which the unsuspecting prelate held carelessly in his hand.

"Precisely, Baron."

"And you have brought me this hair, Monseigneur? Very good."

"Here it is. Do you think it would be possible to return it to me again after the examination?"

"Unless fire should be necessary; in which case —"

"Of course, of course," said the cardinal. "However I can procure some more. Can I have a reply?"

"To-day?"

"You know I am impatient."

"I must first ascertain, Monseigneur;" and Balsamo took the packet of hair and hastily mounted to Lorenza's apartment.

"I shall now know," said he, on the way, "the secret of this monarchy; I shall know the hidden design of God!"

And from the other side of the wall, even before opening the secret door, he plunged Lorenza into the magnetic sleep. The young woman received him, therefore, with an affectionate embrace. Balsamo could scarcely extricate himself from her arms. It would be difficult to say which was the more grievous for the poor baron, — the reproaches of the beautiful Italian when she was awake, or her caresses when she slept. When he had succeeded in loosening the chain which her snowy arms formed around his neck, "My beloved Lorenza," said he, putting the paper in her hand, "can you tell me to whom this hair belongs?"

Lorenza took it and pressed it against her breast, and then to her forehead. Though her eyes were open, it was by her head and her breast that she saw in her sleep. "Oh!" said she, "it is an illustrious head from which this hair has been taken."

"Is it not? — and a happy head too? Speak."

"She may be happy."

"Look well, Lorenza."

"Yes, she may be happy; there is no shadow as yet upon her life."

"Yet she is married."

"Oh!" said Lorenza, with a sweet smile.

"Well! — what? What means my Lorenza?"

"She is married, dear Balsamo," added the young woman, "and yet —"

"And yet?"

"And yet —" Lorenza still smiled. "I too am married," she said.

"Certainly."

"And yet —"

Balsamo looked at Lorenza with profound astonishment. Although she was asleep, a blush of modesty covered her face.

"And yet?" repeated Balsamo. "Finish."

She again threw her arms around the neck of her lover, and hid her face on his breast. "And yet I am not married," she said.

"And that woman, that princess, that queen," cried Balsamo, "married though she is — ?"

"That woman, that princess, that queen," repeated Lorenza, "is as pure and as chaste as I am, — purer and more chaste, even; for, unlike me, she does not love."

"Oh, fatality!" said Balsamo. "Thanks, Lorenza; I know all I wished to know."

He embraced her, put the hair carefully into his pocket, and then, cutting a lock off the Italian's black tresses, he burned it at the wax-light, and enclosed the ashes in the paper which had been wrapped round the hair of the dauphiness. Then he left the room; and while descending the stairs he awoke the young woman.

The prelate, agitated and impatient, was waiting and doubting.

"Well, Count?" said he.

"Well, Monseigneur, the oracle has said you may hope."

"It said so!" exclaimed the prince, transported with joy.

"Draw what conclusion you please, Monseigneur; the oracle has said that this woman does not love her husband."

"Oh!" said Monsieur de Rohan, with a thrill of joy.

"I was obliged to burn the hair to obtain the revelation by its essence. Here are the ashes, which I restore to you most scrupulously, after having gathered them up as if each atom were worth a million."

"Thanks, Monsieur, a thousand thanks; I can never repay you."

"Do not speak of that, Monseigneur. I must recommend you, however, not to swallow these ashes in wine, as lovers sometimes do; it causes such a dangerous sympathy that' your love would become incurable, while the lady's heart would cool toward you."

"Oh! I shall take care," said the prelate, almost terrified. "Adieu, Count, adieu!"

Twenty minutes afterward his Eminence's carriage crossed Monsieur de Richelieu's at the corner of the Rue des Petits Champs so suddenly that it was nearly upset in a deep trench which had been dug for the foundation of a new building.

The two noblemen recognized each other.

"Ha! Prince," said Richelieu, with a smile.

"Ha! Duke," replied Louis de Rohan, with his finger upon his lips.

And they disappeared in opposite directions.

CHAPTER XLVIII.

MONSIEUR DE RICHELIEU APPRECIATES NICOLE.

MONSIEUR DE RICHELIEU drove straight to Monsieur de Taverney's modest hôtel in the Rue Coq-Héron.

Thanks to the privilege we possess, in common with the devil on two sticks, of entering every house, be it ever so carefully locked, we are aware, before Monsieur de Richelieu discovers it, that the baron is seated before the fireplace, his feet resting upon the immense andirons which support a smouldering log, and is lecturing Nicole, sometimes pausing to chuck her under the chin, in spite of the rebellious and scornful poutings of the young waiting-maid. But whether Nicole would have been satisfied with the caress without the sermon, or whether she would have preferred the sermon without the caress, we can give no satisfactory information.

The conversation between the master and the servant turned upon the very important point that at a certain hour of the evening Nicole never came when the bell was rung, — that she had always something to do in the garden or in the greenhouse ; and that everywhere but in these two places she neglected her service.

Nicole, turning backward and forward with a charming and voluptuous grace, replied : " So much the worse ! I am dying with weariness here ; you promised I should go to Trianon with Mademoiselle."

It was thereupon that the baron thought it proper in charity to pat her cheeks and chuck her chin, no doubt to distract her thoughts from dwelling on so unpleasant a subject; but Nicole continued in the same vein, and refusing all consolation, deplored her unhappy lot. "Yes," she sighed, "I am shut up within four horrible walls, I have no company, I have no air; while I had the prospect of a pleasant and fortunate future before me."

"What prospect?" said the baron.

"Trianon," replied Nicole, — "Trianon, where I should have seen the world; where I should have looked about me; where I should have been looked at."

"Oh! oh! my little Nicole," said the baron.

"Well, Monsieur, I am a woman, and as well worth looking at as another, I suppose?"

"*Cordieu!* how she talks," said the baron to himself. "What fire, what ambition! Oh, if I were young, and if I were rich!" and he could not help casting a look of admiration at so much youth and beauty. Nicole was thoughtful, and at times impatient.

"Come, Monsieur," said she, "will you retire to bed, that I may go to mine?"

"One word more, Nicole."

A sudden ringing of the street-bell made Taverney start and Nicole jump.

"Who can be coming," said the baron, "at half-past eleven o'clock at night? Go, child, and see."

Nicole hastened to open the door, asked the name of the visitor, and left the street-door half open. Through this lucky opening a shadow, which had apparently emerged from the court-yard, glided out, not without making noise enough to attract the attention of the marshal, — for it was he, — who turned and saw the flight. Nicole preceded him, candle in hand, with a beaming look.

"Oh, oh!" said the marshal, smiling, and following

her into the room, "this old rogue of a Taverney spoke to me only of his daughter."

The duke was one of those men who do not require a second glance to see, and see completely. The shadowy figure which he had observed escaping made him think of Nicole, and Nicole of the shadow. When he saw her pretty face he guessed what errand the shadow had come upon; and judging from her saucy and laughing eye, her white teeth and small waist, he had nothing more to learn concerning her character and tastes.

At the door of the salon Nicole, not without a palpitation of the heart, announced, "Monsieur le Duc de Richelieu."

This name was destined to cause a sensation that evening. It produced such an effect upon the baron that he rose from his armchair and walked straight to the door, not being able to believe the evidence of his ears. But before he reached the door he perceived Monsieur de Richelieu in the shadow of the corridor.

"The duke!" he stammered.

"Yes, my dear friend, the duke himself," replied Richelieu, in his most friendly manner. "Oh! that surprises you, after your visit the other day? Well, nevertheless, nothing can be more real. In the mean time your hand, if you please."

"Monsieur le Duc, you overwhelm me."

"You have lost your wits, my dear friend," said the old marshal, giving his hat and cane to Nicole, and seating himself comfortably in an armchair. "You are getting rusty; you dote. You seem no longer to know the world!"

"But yet, Duke," replied Taverney, much agitated, "it seems to me that the reception you gave me the other day was so significant that I could not mistake its character."

"Hark ye, my old friend," answered Richelieu, "the other day you behaved like a school-boy, and I like a pedant. Between us there was but little difference. You are going to speak, — I will save you the trouble; you might say foolish things to me, and I might reply in the same vein. Let us leave the other day aside, therefore, and come direct to the present time. Do you know what I have come for this evening?"

"No, certainly."

"I have come to bring you the company which you asked of me for your son the other day, and which the king has granted. What the devil, can't you understand the difference? The day before yesterday I was a quasi-minister, and to ask a favor was an injustice; but to-day, when I am simply Richelieu, and have refused the portfolio, it would be absurd not to ask. I have therefore asked and obtained, and I now bring it to you."

"Duke, can this be true? And is this kindness on your part —"

"It is the natural consequence of my duty as your friend. The minister refused; Richelieu asks and gives."

"Ah, Duke, you enchant me! You are then really my friend?"

"I should say so!"

"But the king, — the king, who confers such a favor on me —"

"The king scarcely knows what he has done; or perhaps I am mistaken, and he knows very well."

"What do you mean?"

"I mean that his Majesty has, no doubt, some motive for provoking Madame Dubarry just now; and you owe this favor, which he bestows upon you, more to that motive than to my influence."

"You think so?"

"I am certain of it, for I am aiding and abetting. You know it is on account of that creature that I refused the portfolio?"

"I was told so, but —"

"But you did not believe it. Come, say it frankly!"

"Well, I confess that —"

"You always thought me not likely to be troubled by many scruples of conscience, — is that it?"

"At least, I thought you without prejudices."

"My friend, I am getting old, and I no longer care for pretty faces, except when they can be useful to me. And besides, I have some other plans. But to return to your son; he is a splendid fellow!"

"But on bad terms with that Dubarry who was at your house when I had the folly to present myself."

"I am aware of it, and that is why I am not a minister."

"Oh! you refused the portfolio in order not to displease my son?"

"If I told you so, you would not believe me. No, that is not the reason. I refused it because the requirements of the Dubarrys, which began with the exclusion of your son, would have ended in enormities of all kinds."

"Then you have quarrelled with those creatures?"

"Yes, and no. They fear me, — I despise them; it is tit for tat."

"It is heroic, but imprudent."

"Why?"

"The countess has still some power."

"Pooh!" said Richelieu.

"How you say that!"

"I say it like a man who perceives the weak point of a situation, and who, if necessary, would place the miner in a good position to blow up the whole concern."

"I see the true state of the case: you do my son a favor partly to vex the Dubarrys."

"Principally for that reason; and your perspicacity is not at fault. Your son serves me as a grenade; I shall cause an explosion by his means. But, by the way, Baron, have you not also a daughter?"

"Yes."

"Young?"

"Sixteen years."

"Beautiful?"

"As Venus."

"Who lives at Trianon?"

"Ah! then you know her?"

"I have spent the evening in her company, and have conversed about her for a full hour with the king."

"With the king?" cried Taverney, his cheeks in a flame. "The king has spoken of my daughter, — of Mademoiselle Andrée de Taverney?"

"Whom he devours with his eyes, — yes, my dear fellow."

"Ah! really?"

"Do I annoy you in telling you this?"

"Me? No, certainly not. The king honors me by looking at my daughter; but — the king —"

"Is immoral; is that what you were going to say?"

"God forbid that I should speak evil of his majesty! He has a right to adopt whatever morals he chooses."

"Well, what does this astonishment mean, then? Do you pretend to say that Mademoiselle Andrée is not an accomplished beauty, and that therefore the king may not have looked upon her with admiration?"

Taverney did not reply; he only shrugged his shoulders and fell into a revery, during which the unrelenting, inquisitorial eye of the Duc de Richelieu was still fixed upon him.

"Well, I know what you would say, if, instead of thinking to yourself, you would speak aloud," continued the old marshal, moving his chair nearer the baron's. "You would say that the king is accustomed to bad society, that he mixes with low company, and that therefore he is not likely to admire this noble girl, so modest in her demeanor and so pure and lofty in her ideas, and is not capable of appreciating the treasures of her grace and beauty."

"Certainly, you are a great man, Duke; you have read my thoughts exactly," said Taverney.

"But confess, Baron," continued Richelieu, "that our master should no longer force us gentlemen, peers and companions of the king of France, to kiss the vile, open hand of a creature like Dubarry. It is time that he should restore us to our proper position. After having sunk from La Chateauroux, who was a marquise and of stuff to make duchesses, to La Pompadour, who was the daughter and the wife of a farmer of the public revenues, and from La Pompadour to the Dubarry, who calls herself simply Jeanneton, may he not fall still farther, and plunge us into the lowest pitch of degradation? It is humiliating for us, Baron, who wear a coronet on our caps, to bow the head before such worthless creatures."

"Oh! you speak only the truth," said Taverney. "How evident is it that the court is deserted on account of these new fashions!"

"No queen, no ladies; no ladies, no courtiers. The king takes up a grisette, and the people are upon the throne, represented by Mademoiselle Jeanne Vaubernier, a sempstress of Paris."

"It is so, and yet—"

"You see then, Baron," interrupted the marshal, "what

a noble career is open for a woman of mind who should reign at this time over France."

"Without doubt," said Taverney, whose heart was beating fast; "but unluckily the place is occupied."

"For a woman," continued the marshal, "who would have the boldness of these creatures without their vice, and who would direct her views and calculations to a loftier aim; for a woman who would advance her fortune so high that she should be talked of when the monarchy itself should no longer exist. Do you know if your daughter has intellect, Baron?"

"Lofty intellect, and above all, good sense."

"She is very lovely."

"Is she not?"

"Her beauty is of that soft and charming character which pleases men so much, while her whole being is stamped with that air of candor and virgin purity which imposes respect even upon women. You must take great care of that treasure, my old friend."

"You speak of her with such fire —"

"I! I am madly in love with her, and would marry her to-morrow, were I twenty, instead of seventy-four years of age! But is she comfortably placed? Has she the luxury which befits such a lovely flower? Only think, Baron! this evening she returned alone to her apartments, without waiting-women or lackey. An attendant of the dauphin carried a lantern before her! That looks as if she were a servant rather than a lady of rank."

"What can I do, Duke? You know I am not rich."

"Rich or not, your daughter must at least have a waiting-maid."

Taverney sighed. "I know very well," said he, "that she wants one, or at least that she ought to have one."

"Well, have you none?"

The baron did not reply.

"Who is that pretty girl you had here just now?" continued Richelieu. "A fine, spirited-looking girl, i' faith."

"Yes, but — I — I cannot send her to Trianon."

"Why not, Baron? On the contrary, she seems to me perfectly suited for the post; she would make a capital attendant."

"You did not look at her face then, Duke?"

"I, — I did nothing else!"

"You looked at her, and did not remark her strange resemblance?"

"To whom?"

"To — guess. Come hither, Nicole."

Nicole advanced; like a true waiting-woman, she had been listening at the door. The duke took her by both hands and looked her steadily in the face; but the impertinent gaze of this great nobleman and debauchee did not alarm or embarrass her for a moment.

"Yes," said he, "it is true; there is a resemblance."

"You know to whom, and you see therefore that it is impossible to expose the fortunes of our house to such an awkward trick of fate. Is it a pleasant thing that this little minx of a Nicole resembles the most illustrious lady in France?"

"Oh, ho!" replied Nicole, sharply, and disengaging herself from the marshal's grasp, the better to reply to Monsieur de Taverney, "is it so certain that this little minx resembles this illustrious lady so exactly? Has the illustrious lady the low shoulder, the quick eye, the round ankle, and the plump arm of the little minx?"

Nicole was crimson with rage, and therefore ravishingly beautiful.

The duke once more took her pretty hands in his, and with a look full of caresses and promises: "Baron," said he, "Nicole has certainly not her equal at court, — at least in my opinion. As for the illustrious lady to whom she has, I confess, a slight resemblance, we shall know how to spare her self-love. You have fair hair of a lovely shade, Mademoiselle Nicole; you have eyebrows and nose of a most imperial form: well, in one quarter of an hour employed before the mirror, these imperfections, since the baron thinks them such, will disappear. Nicole, my child, would you like to be at Trianon?"

"Oh!" said Nicole, and her whole soul, full of longing, was expressed in this monosyllable.

"You shall go to Trianon, then, my dear, and without prejudicing in any way the fortunes of others. Baron, one word more."

"Speak, my dear Duke."

"Go, my pretty child," said Richelieu, "and leave us alone a moment."

Nicole retired. The duke approached the baron. "I press you the more to send your daughter a waiting-maid," said he, "because it will please the king. His Majesty does not like poverty, and pretty faces do not frighten him. Let me alone; I understand what I am about."

"Nicole shall go to Trianon, if you think it will please the king," replied the baron, with a meaning smile.

"Then, if you will allow me, I will take her with me."

"But still, her resemblance to the dauphiness! We must think of that, Duke."

"I have thought of it. This resemblance will disappear in a quarter of an hour under Rafté's hands, I will answer for it. Write a note to your daughter to tell her of what importance it is that she should have a maid, and that this maid should be Nicole."

"You think it important that it should be Nicole?"

"I do."

"And that no other than Nicole would do?"

"Upon my honor I think so."

"Then I will write immediately;" and the baron sat down and wrote a letter, which he handed to Richelieu.

"And the instructions, Duke?"

"I will give them to Nicole. Is she intelligent?"

The baron smiled.

"Then you confide her to me, do you not?" said Richelieu.

"That is your affair, Duke. You asked me for her; I give her to you: make of her what you like."

"Mademoiselle, come with me," said the duke, rising, and calling into the corridor, "and that quickly."

Nicole did not wait to be told twice. Without asking the baron for his consent, she made up a packet of clothes in five minutes, and light as a bird, she flew downstairs and took her place beside the coachman.

Richelieu took leave of his friend, who repeated his thanks for the service he had rendered Philippe. Of Andrée not a word was said.

CHAPTER XLIX.

THE TRANSFORMATION.

NICOLE was overjoyed. To leave Taverney for Paris was not so great a triumph as to leave Paris for Trianon. She was so gracious with Monsieur de Richelieu's coachman that the next morning the reputation of the new waiting-maid was established throughout all the coach-houses and antechambers, in any degree aristocratic, of Paris and Versailles.

When they arrived at the Hôtel de Hanover, Monsieur de Richelieu took the young girl by the hand and led her to the first story, where Monsieur Rafté was awaiting his arrival, and writing a multitude of letters on his master's account.

Among the various acquirements of the marshal, war occupied the foremost rank, and Rafté had become, at least in theory, such a skilful strategist that Polybius and the Chevalier de Folard, if they had lived at that period, would have esteemed themselves fortunate could they have perused the pamphlets on fortifications and manœuvring, of which Rafté wrote one every week. Monsieur Rafté was busy revising the plan of a war against the English in the Mediterranean when the marshal entered and said, "Rafté, look at this child, will you?"

Rafté looked.

"Very pretty, Monseigneur," said he, with a most significant movement of the lips.

"Yes, but the likeness, Rafté? It is of the likeness I speak."

"Eh! it is true. Ah! the devil!"

"You see it, do you not?"

"It is extraordinary; it will either make or mar her fortune."

"It will ruin her at once. But we will provide against it. You observe she has fair hair, Rafté; but that will not signify much, will it?"

"It will only be necessary to make it black, Monseigneur," replied Rafté, who had acquired the habit of completing his master's thoughts, and sometimes even of thinking entirely for him.

"Come to my dressing-table, child," said the marshal. "This gentleman, who is a very clever man, will make you the handsomest and the least easily recognized waiting-maid in France."

In fact, ten minutes afterward, with the assistance of a composition which the marshal used every week to dye the white hairs black beneath his wig, — a piece of coquetry which he often affected to confess by the bedside of some of his acquaintances, — Rafté had dyed the beautiful auburn hair of Nicole a splendid jet black. Then he passed the end of a pin, blackened in the flame of a candle, over her thick, fair eyebrows, and by this means gave such a fantastic look to her joyous countenance, such an ardent and even sombre fire to her bright, clear eyes, that one would have said she was some fairy bursting by the power of an incantation from the magic prison in which her enchanter had held her confined.

"Now, my sweet child," said Richelieu, after having handed a mirror to the astonished Nicole, "see how charming you are, and how little like the Nicole you were just now. You have no longer ruin to fear, but a fortune to make."

"Oh, Monseigneur!" exclaimed the young girl.

"Yes, and for that purpose it is only necessary that we understand each other."

Nicole blushed, and looked down; the cunning one expected, no doubt, words such as Richelieu knew so well how to say.

The duke perceived this, and to cut short all misunderstanding said: "Sit down in this armchair beside Monsieur Rafté, my dear child. Open your ears wide, and listen to me. Oh! do not let Monsieur Rafté's presence embarrass you; do not be afraid; he will, on the contrary, give us his advice. You are listening, are you not?"

"Yes, Monseigneur," stammered Nicole, ashamed at having thus been led away by her vanity.

The conversation between Monsieur de Richelieu, Monsieur Rafté, and Nicole lasted more than an hour, after which the marshal sent the young girl to sleep with the other waiting-women in the hôtel.

Rafté returned to his military pamphlet, and Richelieu retired to bed, after having looked over the different letters which conveyed to him intelligence of all the acts of the provincial parliaments against Monsieur d'Aiguillon and the Dubarry clique.

Early the next day one of his carriages, without his coat-of-arms, conducted Nicole to Trianon, set her down at the gate with her little packet, and immediately disappeared. Nicole, with head erect, mind at ease, and hope dancing in her eyes, after having made the necessary inquiries, knocked at the door of the offices.

It was ten o'clock in the morning. Andrée, already up and dressed, was writing to her father to inform him of the happy event of the preceding day, of which Monsieur de Richelieu, as we have already seen, had conveyed the intelligence. Our readers will not have forgotten that a flight of stone steps led from the garden to the little chapel of Trianon; that on the landing-place of this chapel a staircase branched off toward the right to the first story, which contained the apartments of the ladies-in-waiting, which apartments opened off a long corridor, like an alley, looking upon the garden.

Andrée's chamber was the first upon the left hand in this corridor. It was tolerably large, well-lighted by windows looking upon the stable court, and was entered through an antechamber, on each side of which was a small room. This apartment, however insufficient, if one considers the ordinary establishments pertaining to the officers of a brilliant court, was yet a charming retreat, very habitable, and very cheerful as an asylum from the noise and bustle of the palace. Thither an ambitious soul could fly to devour the affronts or the mistakes of the day, and there a humble and melancholy spirit could repose in silence and in solitude, apart from the grandeur of the gay world around.

In fact, the stone steps once ascended and the chapel passed, there no longer existed either superiority, duty, or display. There reigned the calm of a convent, and the personal liberty of prison life. The slave of the palace was a monarch when she had crossed the threshold of her modest dwelling. A gentle yet lofty soul such as Andrée's found consolation in this reflection; not that she flew hither to repose after the fatigues of a disappointed ambition or of unsatisfied longings, but she felt that she could think more at her ease in the narrow bounds of her chamber than in the rich salons of Trianon, or in those marble halls which her feet trod with a timidity amounting almost to terror.

From this sequestered nook, where the young girl felt herself so well and so appropriately placed, she could look without emotion on all the splendor which, during the day, had dazzled her eyes. Surrounded by her flowers, her harpsichord, and her German books, — such sweet companions to those who read with the heart, — Andrée defied fate to inflict on her a single grief, or to deprive her of a single joy.

"Here," said she, when in the evening, after her duties were over, she returned to throw around her shoulders her dressing-gown with its wide folds, and to breathe with all her soul, as with all her lungs, — "here I possess nearly everything I can hope to possess till my death. I may one day perhaps be richer, but I can never be poorer than I now am. There will always be flowers, music, and a consoling page to cheer the poor recluse."

Andrée had obtained permission to breakfast in her own apartment when she felt inclined. This was a precious boon to her, for she could thus remain in her own domicile until twelve o'clock, unless the dauphiness should command her attendance for some morning reading or some early walk. Thus free, in fine weather she set out every morning with a book in her hand, and traversed alone the extensive woods which lie between Versailles and Trianon; then, after a walk of two hours, during which she gave full play to meditation and revery, she returned to breakfast, often without having seen either nobleman or servant, man or livery.

When the heat began to pierce through the thick foliage Andrée had her little chamber, fresh and cool with the double current of air from the door and the window. A small sofa covered with Indian silk, four chairs to match, a simple yet elegant bed with a circular top, from which the curtains of the same material as the covering of the furniture fell in deep folds, two china vases placed upon the mantelpiece, and a square table with brass feet, furnished and adorned her little world, whose narrow confines bounded all her hopes and limited all her wishes.

Andrée was seated in her apartment, as we have said, and busily engaged in writing to her father, when a modest knock at the door of the corridor attracted her attention. She raised her head on seeing the door open, and uttered a slight cry of astonishment when the radiant face of Nicole appeared, entering from the little antechamber.

CHAPTER L.

HOW PLEASURE TO SOME IS DESPAIR TO OTHERS.

"Good-day, Mademoiselle; it is I," said Nicole, with a joyous reverence, which nevertheless, from the young girl's knowledge of her mistress's character, was not unmixed with anxiety.

"You! And how do you happen to be here?" replied Andrée, putting down her pen, the better to follow the conversation which was thus opened.

"Mademoiselle had forgotten me, so I came—"

"But if I forgot you, Mademoiselle, it was because I had my reasons for so doing. Who gave you permission to come?"

"Monsieur the baron, of course, Mademoiselle," said Nicole, smoothing with a very dissatisfied air the handsome black eyebrows which she owed to the generosity of Monsieur Rafté.

"My father requires your services in Paris, and I do not require you here at all. You may return, child."

"Oh! then Mademoiselle does not care,—I thought Mademoiselle had been more pleased with me. It is well worth while loving," added Nicole, philosophically, "to meet with such a return at last;" and she did her utmost to bring a tear to her beautiful eyes.

There was enough of heart and feeling in this reproach to excite Andrée's compassion. "My child," said she, "I have attendance here already, and I cannot permit myself unnecessarily to increase the household of the dauphiness by another mouth."

"Oh, as if this mouth was so large!" said Nicole, with a charming smile.

"No matter, Nicole, your presence here is impossible."

"On account of that resemblance?" said the young girl. "Then you have not looked at my face, Mademoiselle."

"In fact you seem changed."

"I think so! A fine gentleman, he who got the promotion for Monsieur Philippe, came to us yesterday, and as he saw the baron quite melancholy at your being here without a waiting-maid, he told him that nothing was easier than to change me from fair to dark. He brought me with him, dressed me as you see, and here I am."

Andrée smiled. "You must love me very much," said she, "since you are determined at all risks to shut yourself up in Trianon, where I am almost a prisoner."

Nicole cast a rapid but intelligent glance round the room. "The chamber is not very gay," said she, "but you are not always in it?"

"I? Of course not," replied Andrée; "but you?"

"Well, I?"

"You, who will never enter the salons of Madame the Dauphiness, — you, who will have neither the resource of the theatre, nor the walk, nor the evening circle, but will always remain here; you will die of weariness."

"Oh!" said Nicole, "there is always some little window or other; one can surely see some little glimpse of the gay world without, were it only through the chinks of the door. If one can see, one can also be seen. That is all I require; so do not be uneasy on my account."

"I repeat, Nicole, that I cannot receive you without express orders from my father."

"Is that your settled determination?"

"It is."

Nicole drew the Baron de Taverney's letter from her bosom. "There," said she, "since my entreaties and my devotion to you have had no effect, let us see if the order contained in this will have more power."

Andrée read the letter, which was in the following terms:—

I am aware, and indeed it is already remarked, my dear Andrée, that you do not occupy the position at Trianon which your rank imperatively requires. You ought to have two maids and a valet, as I ought to have twenty thousand francs per annum; but as I am content with one thousand francs, imitate my example, and content yourself with Nicole, who, though alone, is sufficient for all the domestic service necessary to you.

Nicole is quick, intelligent, and devoted to you, and will readily adopt the tone and manners of the place. Your chief care indeed will be not to stimulate her, but to repress her willingness to serve. Keep her, then; and do not imagine that I am making any sacrifice in depriving myself of her services. In case you should think so, remember that his Majesty, who had the goodness to think of us, remarked on seeing you (this was confided to me by a good friend) that you required a little more attention to your toilet and general appearance. Think of this; it is of great importance.

YOUR AFFECTIONATE FATHER.

This letter threw Andrée into a state of grief and perplexity. She was then to be haunted, even in her prosperity, by the remembrance of that poverty which she alone did not feel to be a fault, while all around seemed to consider it as a crime.

Her first impulse was to break her pen indignantly, to tear the letter she had begun, and to reply to her father's epistle by some lofty tirade expressive of philosophical self-denial, which Philippe would have approved of with all his heart. But she imagined she saw the baron's satirical smile on reading this masterpiece, and her resolution vanished. She merely replied to the baron's order, therefore, by a paragraph annexed to the news of Trianon which she had already written to him according to his request.

"My father," she added, "Nicole has this moment arrived, and I receive her, since you wish it; but what you have written on this subject has vexed me. Shall I be less ridiculous with this village girl as waiting-maid than when I was alone among those opulent courtiers? Nicole will be unhappy at seeing me humiliated. She will be discontented; for servants feel proud or humiliated in proportion to the wealth or poverty of their masters. As to his Majesty's remark, my father, permit me to tell you that the king has too much good sense to be displeased at my incapacity to play the grand lady; and besides, his Majesty has too much heart to have noticed or criticised my poverty without transforming it into a wealth to which your name and services would have seemed a legitimate claim in the eyes of all."

This was Andrée's reply, and it must be confessed that her ingenuous innocence, her noble pride, had an easy triumph over the cunning and corruption of her tempters.

Andrée said no more respecting Nicole. She agreed to her remaining, so that the latter, joyous and animated, she well knew why, at once prepared a little bed in the cabinet on the right of the antechamber, and made herself as small, as aerial, and as exquisite as possible, in order not to inconvenience her mistress by her presence in this modest retreat. One would have thought she wished to imitate the rose-leaf which the Persian sages let fall upon a vase filled with water, to show that something could be added without causing the water to overflow.

Andrée set out for Trianon about one o'clock. She had never been more quickly or more gracefully attired. Nicole had surpassed herself; she had been all politeness, attention, and zeal,— nothing had been wanting in her services.

When Mademoiselle de Taverney had gone, Nicole considered herself mistress of the domicile, and instituted a thorough examination of it. Everything was scrutinized, from the letters to the smallest knick-knack on the toilet-table, from the mantelpiece to the most secret corners of the closets. Then she looked out of the windows to take a survey of the neighborhood.

Below her was a large courtyard, in which several ostlers were dressing and currying the splendid horses of the dauphiness. Ostlers! pshaw! Nicole turned away her head.

On the right was a row of windows on the same story as those of Andrée's apartment. Several heads appeared at these windows, apparently those of chambermaids and floor-scrubbers. Nicole disdainfully proceeded in her examination.

On the opposite side, in a large apartment, some music-teachers were drilling a class of choristers and instrumentalists for the mass of Saint Louis. Without ceasing her dusting operations, Nicole began to sing after her own fashion, thus distracting the attention of the masters, and causing the choristers to sing out of tune.

But this pastime could not long satisfy Mademoiselle Nicole's ambition. When the masters and the singers had quarrelled, and been mystified sufficiently, the little waiting-maid proceeded to the inspection of the higher story. All the windows were closed, and moreover they were only attics, so Nicole continued her dusting. But a moment afterward, one of these attic windows was opened without her being able to discover by what mechanism, for no one appeared. Some one, however, must have opened that window; this some one had seen Nicole, and had not remained to look at her; it was some one very impertinent, — at least, such was Nicole's opinion. But she, who examined everything so conscientiously, wished to examine the features of this impertinent; and she therefore returned every moment from her different avocations to the window, to give a glance at this attic, — that is, at this open eye from which the eyeball was so obstinately absent. Once she imagined that the person fled as she approached; but this was incredible, and she did not believe it. Another time she was almost sure of it, having seen the back of the fugitive, — surprised, no doubt, by a prompter return than he had anticipated. Then Nicole had recourse to stratagem; she concealed herself behind the curtain, leaving the window wide open, to drown all suspicion.

She waited a long time, but at last a head of black hair made its appearance; then came two timid hands, which supported, buttress-like, a body bending over cautiously; and finally, a face showed itself distinctly at the window. Nicole almost fell, and grasped the curtain so tightly, in her surprise, that it shook from top to bottom.

It was Monsieur Gilbert's face which was looking at her from this lofty attic. But the moment Gilbert saw the curtain move, he comprehended the trick, and did not again appear; furthermore, the attic window was closed.

No doubt Gilbert had seen Nicole; he had been astonished, and had wished to convince himself of the presence of his enemy, and when he found himself discovered instead, he had fled in agitation and in anger. At least, Nicole interpreted the scene thus, and she was right, for this was the exact state of the case.

In fact, Gilbert would rather have seen the devil than Nicole. The arrival of this spy caused him a thousand terrors. He had an old leaven of jealousy against her, for she knew his secret of the garden in the Rue Coq-Héron.

Gilbert had fled in agitation, and not in agitation alone, but also in anger, and biting his nails with rage. "Of what use now is my foolish discovery, of which I was so proud?" said he to himself. "Even if Nicole had a lover in Paris, the evil is done, and she will not be sent away from here on that account; but if she tells what I did in the Rue Coq-Héron I shall be dismissed from Trianon. It is not I who govern Nicole, — it is she who governs me. Oh, fury!"

And Gilbert's inordinate self-love, serving as a stimulant to his hatred, made his blood boil with frightful violence. It seemed to him that Nicole, in entering that apartment, had chased from it, with a diabolical smile, all the happy dreams which he from his garret had sent thither every day with his vows, his ardent love, and his flowers. Had Gilbert been too much occupied to think of Nicole before, or had he banished the subject from his thoughts on account of the terror with which it inspired him? We cannot determine; but this we know, at least, — that Nicole's appearance was a most disagreeable surprise for him.

Gilbert saw plainly that sooner or later war would be declared between them; but as he was prudent and politic, he did not wish the war to begin until he felt himself strong enough to make it energetic and effective. With this intention he determined to counterfeit death until chance should present him a favorable opportunity of reviving, — or until Nicole, from weakness or necessity, should venture on some step which would deprive her of her present vantage-ground. Therefore, exercising the greatest vigilance where Andrée was concerned, but at the same time circumspect and careful, he continued to make himself acquainted with the state of affairs in the first apartment of the corridor, without Nicole ever having once met him in the gardens.

Unluckily for Nicole she was not irreproachable, and even had she been so at that time, there was always one stumbling-block in the past over which she could be made to fall.

At the end of a week's ceaseless watching, — morning, noon, and night, — Gilbert at last saw through the bars of his window a plume, which he fancied he recognized. This plume was a source of constant agitation to Nicole, for it belonged to Monsieur Beausire, who, following the rest of the court, had emigrated from Paris to Trianon.

For a long time Nicole was cruel; for a long time she left Monsieur Beausire to shiver in the cold and melt in the sun; and her prudence drove Gilbert to despair. But one fine morning, when Monsieur Beausire had doubtless overleaped the barrier of mimic eloquence, and found an opportunity of bringing persuasive words to his aid, Nicole profited by Andrée's absence to descend to the court-yard and join Monsieur Beausire, who was assisting his friend, the superintendent of the stables, to train a small Irish horse.

From the court they passed into the garden, and from thence into the shady avenue which leads to Versailles. Gilbert followed the amorous couple with the ferocious joy of a tiger who scents his prey. He counted their steps, their sighs, and learned by heart all he heard of their conversation. It may be presumed that the result pleased him, for the next day, freed from all embarrassment, he displayed himself openly at his attic window, humming a song and looking quite at ease, and so far from fearing to be seen by Nicole, that, on the contrary, he seemed to brave her look.

Nicole was mending an embroidered silken mitten belonging to her mistress; she heard the song, raised her head, and saw Gilbert. The first evidence she gave of his presence was a contemptuous pouting, which gave place to a bitter expression, indicating the intensest hostility. But Gilbert sustained this look with such a singular smile, and there was such provoking intelligence in his air and in his manner of singing, that Nicole looked down and blushed.

"She understands me," thought Gilbert; "that is all I wished." Then he began again the same course of conduct, and Nicole trembled. At length she began to wish for an interview with him, in order to free her heart from the load with which the satirical manner of the young gardener had burdened it.

Gilbert noticed that she sought him. He could not misunderstand the short dry coughs which sounded near the window whenever Nicole knew him to be in his attic, nor the goings and comings of the young girl in the corridor when she supposed he might be ascending or descending the stairs. For a short time he was very proud of this triumph, which he attributed entirely to his strength of character and wise precautions. Nicole watched him so well that once she spied him as he mounted to his attic. She called him, but he did not reply.

Prompted either by curiosity or fear, Nicole went still farther. One evening she took off her pretty, high-heeled slippers, — a present from Andrée, — and with a trembling and hurried step she ventured into the attic, at the end of which she saw Gilbert's door. There was still sufficient daylight to enable Gilbert, aware of Nicole's approach, to see her distinctly through the joining, or rather through the crevices, of the panels. She knocked at the door, knowing well that he was in his room; but Gilbert did not reply.

It was, nevertheless, a dangerous temptation for him. He could at his ease humble her who thus came to entreat his pardon; and prompted by this thought, he had already raised his hand to draw the bolt which, with his habitual precaution and vigilance, he had fastened, to avoid surprise.

"But no," thought he, "no. She is all calculation; it is from fear or interest alone that she comes to seek me. She therefore hopes to gain something by her visit; but if so, what may I not lose?" And with this reasoning he let his hand fall again by his side.

Nicole, after having knocked at the door two or three times, retired frowning. Gilbert therefore kept all his advantage, and Nicole had to redouble her cunning in order not to lose hers entirely. At last all these projects and counter-projects reduced themselves to this dialogue, which took place between the belligerent parties one evening at the chapel door, where chance had brought them together.

"Ha! good evening, Monsieur Gilbert; you are here then, are you?"

"Oh! good evening, Mademoiselle Nicole; you are at Trianon?"

"As you see, — waiting-maid to Mademoiselle."

"And I am assistant-gardener."

Then Nicole made a graceful reverence to Gilbert, who returned her a most courtly bow, and they separated. Gilbert ascended to his attic as if he had been on his way thither, and Nicole left the offices and proceeded on her errand; but Gilbert glided down again stealthily, and followed Nicole, supposing that she was going to meet Monsieur Beausire.

A man was indeed waiting for her beneath the shadows of the alley. Nicole approached him. It was too dark for Gilbert to recognize any one; and the absence of the plume puzzled him so much that he let Nicole return to her domicile, and followed the man as far as the gate of Trianon. It was not Monsieur Beausire, but a man of a certain age, or rather certainly aged, with a distinguished air and a brisk gait, notwithstanding his advanced years. When he approached, Gilbert, who carried his assurance so far as almost to brush past him, recognized Monsieur le Duc de Richelieu.

"*Peste!*" said Gilbert; "first an officer, now a marshal of France! Mademoiselle Nicole is promoted."

CHAPTER LI.

THE PARLIAMENTS.

WHILE all these minor intrigues, hatched and brought to light beneath the linden-trees and among the alleys of Trianon, constituted a sufficiently animated existence for the insects of this little world, the great intrigues of the town, like threatening tempests, spread their vast wings over the palace of Themis, as Monsieur Jean Dubarry wrote in mythological parlance to his sister.

The parliaments — those degenerate remains of the ancient French opposition — had taken breath beneath the capricious government of Louis XV.; but since their protector, Monsieur de Choiseul, had fallen, they felt the approach of danger, and they prepared to meet it by measures as energetic as circumstances would permit.

Every great general commotion is kindled at first by some personal quarrel, as the pitched battles of armies are begun by skirmishes of outposts. Since Monsieur de la Chalotais in attacking Monsieur d'Aiguillon had personified the struggle of the third estate with the feudal lords, the public mind had seized on the question, and would not permit it to be deferred or displaced.

Now the king — whom the parliament of Brittany and those of all France had deluged with a flood of petitions, more or less submissive and filial — the king, thanks to Madame Dubarry, had just given his countenance to the feudal party, against the party of the people, by nominating Monsieur d'Aiguillon to the command of his Light

Horse. Monsieur Jean Dubarry had described it very correctly: it was a smart blow in the face of the dear and trusty counsellors sitting in high court of parliament.

"How would the blow be taken?" Town and court asked itself this question every morning at sunrise; but members of parliament are clever people, and where others are much embarrassed, they see clearly. They began with agreeing among themselves as to the application and the result of this blow, and then, when it had been clearly ascertained that the blow had been given and received, they adopted the following resolution:—

"The court of parliament will deliberate upon the conduct of the ex-governor of Brittany, and give its opinion thereon."

But the king parried the blow by sending a message to the peers and princes, forbidding them to repair to the palace, or be present at any deliberation which might take place concerning Monsieur d'Aiguillon. They obeyed to the letter.

Then the parliament, determined to do its business itself, passed a decree, in which, after declaring that the Duc d'Aiguillon was seriously inculpated and tainted with suspicion, even on matters which touched his honor, it proclaimed that that peer was suspended from the functions of the peerage until, by a judgment given in the court of peers, with the forms and solemnities prescribed by the laws and customs of the kingdom, — "the place of which nothing can supply," — he had fully cleared himself from the accusations and suspicions now resting on his honor.

But such a decree, passed merely in the court of parliament before those interested, and inscribed in their reports, was nothing; public notoriety was wanting, and, above all, that uproar which song alone ventures to raise in France, and which makes song the sovereign controller of events and rulers. This decree of parliament must be heightened and strengthened by the power of song.

Paris desired nothing better than to take part in this commotion. Little disposed to view either court or parliament with favor, Paris in its ceaseless movement was waiting for some good subject for a laugh, as a transition from all the causes for tears which had been furnished it for a hundred years.

The decree was therefore properly and duly passed, and the parliament appointed commissioners, who were to have it printed under their own eyes. Ten thousand copies of the decree were to be struck off, and the distribution was provided for without delay.

Then, as it was one of their rules that the person interested should be informed of what the court had done respecting him, the same commissioners proceeded to the hôtel of the Duc d'Aiguillon, who had just arrived in Paris for an important interview, — no less, indeed, than to have a clear and open explanation, which had become necessary between the duke and his uncle, the marshal.

Thanks to Rafté, all Versailles had been informed within an hour of the noble resistance of the old duke to the king's orders, in reference to the portfolio of Monsieur de Choiseul. Thanks to Versailles, all Paris and all France had learned the same news; so that Richelieu had found himself for some time past on the summit of popularity, from which he made political grimaces at Madame Dubarry and his dear nephew.

The position was unfavorable for Monsieur d'Aiguillon, who was already so unpopular. The marshal, hated, but at the same time feared, by the people, because he was the living type of that nobility which was so respected and so respectable under Louis XV., — the marshal, so versatile in his character that, after having chosen a part, he was able to withdraw from it without difficulty when circumstances required it, or when a bon-mot might be the result, — Richelieu, we say, was a dangerous enemy; the more so as the worst part of his enmity was always that which he concealed, in order, as he said, to create a surprise.

The Duc d'Aiguillon, since his interview with Madame Dubarry, had two flaws in his coat of mail. Suspecting how much anger and thirst for revenge Richelieu concealed under the apparent equability of his temper, he acted as mariners do in certain cases of difficulty, — he burst the waterspout with his cannon, assured that the danger would be less if it were faced boldly. He set about looking everywhere for his uncle, therefore, in order to have a serious conversation with him; but nothing was more difficult than this, since the marshal had discovered his wish.

Marches and countermarches were made. When the marshal saw his nephew at a distance, he sent him a smile, and immediately surrounded himself by people who rendered all communication impossible; thus putting the enemy at defiance as from an impregnable fort.

The Duc d'Aiguillon burst the waterspout. He simply presented himself at his uncle's hôtel at Versailles; but Rafté, from his post at the little window of the hôtel looking upon the court, recognized the liveries of the duke, and warned his master. The duke entered the marshal's bedroom, where he found Rafté alone, who, with a most confidential smile, was so indiscreet as to inform the nephew that his uncle had not slept at home that night.

Monsieur d'Aiguillon bit his lips and retired. When he returned to his hôtel, he wrote to the marshal to request an audience. The marshal could not refuse to reply. If he replied, he could not refuse an audience; and if he granted the audience, how could he refuse a full explanation? Monsieur d'Aiguillon resembled too much those polite and engaging duellists who hide their evil designs under a fascinating and graceful exterior, lead their man upon the ground with bows and reverences, and there put him to death without pity.

The marshal's self-love was not so powerful as to mislead him; he knew his nephew's power. Once in his presence, his opponent would force from him either a pardon or a concession. Now, Richelieu never pardoned any one, and concessions to an enemy are always a dangerous fault in politics. Therefore, on receipt of Monsieur d'Aiguillon's letter, he pretended to have left Paris for several days.

Rafté, whom he consulted upon this point, gave him the following advice: "We are in a fair way to ruin Monsieur d'Aiguillon. Our friends of the parliament will do the work. If Monsieur d'Aiguillon, who suspects this, can lay his hand upon you before the explosion, he will force from you a promise to assist him in case of misfortune; for your resentment is of that kind that you cannot openly gratify it at the expense of your family interest. If, on the contrary, you refuse, Monsieur d'Aiguillon will leave you, knowing you to be his enemy and attributing all his misfortunes to you; and he will go away comforted, as people always are when they have found out the cause of their complaint, even although the complaint itself be not removed."

"That is quite true," replied Richelieu; "but I cannot conceal myself forever. How many days will it be before the explosion takes place?"

"Six days, Monseigneur."

"Are you sure?"

Rafté drew from his pocket a letter from a counsellor of the parliament. This letter contained only the two following lines:—

It has been decided that the decree shall be passed. It will take place on Thursday, the final day fixed on by the company.

"Then the affair is very simple," replied the marshal; "send the duke back his letter, with a note from your own hand:—

Monsieur le Duc,— You have doubtless heard of the departure of Monsieur le Maréchal for . . . This change of air has been judged indispensable by the marshal's physician, who thinks him rather overworked. If, as I believe is the case, after what you did me the honor to tell me the other day, you wish to have an interview with Monseigneur, I can assure you that on Thursday evening next the duke, on his return from . . . , will sleep in his hôtel in Paris, where you will certainly find him.

And now," added the marshal, "hide me somewhere until Thursday."

Rafté punctually fulfilled these instructions; the letter was written and sent, the hiding-place was found. Only, one evening, Richelieu, who began to feel very much wearied, slipped out and proceeded to Trianon to speak to Nicole. He risked nothing, or thought he risked nothing, by this step, knowing the Duc d'Aiguillon to be at the pavilion of Luciennes.

The result of this manœuvre was that, even if Monsieur d'Aiguillon suspected something, he could not foresee the blow which menaced him until he had actually met his enemy's sword. The delay until Thursday satisfied him; on that day he left Versailles with the hope of at last meeting and combating this impalpable antagonist.

This Thursday was, as we have said, the day on which parliament was to proclaim its decree.

An agitation, low and muttering as yet, but quite intelligible to the Parisian, who knows so well the level of these popular waves, reigned in the wide streets through which Monsieur d'Aiguillon's carriage passed. No notice was taken of him, for he had observed the precaution of coming in a carriage without a coat-of-arms or other heraldic distinctions.

Here and there he saw busy-looking persons, who were showing each other some paper which they read with many gesticulations, and collecting in noisy groups, like ants round a piece of sugar fallen to the ground. But this was the period of inoffensive agitation; the people were then in the habit of congregating together in this manner for a corn-tax, for an article in the "Gazette de Holland," for a verse of Voltaire's, or for a song against Dubarry or Maupeou.

Monsieur d'Aiguillon drove straight to Monsieur de Richelieu's hôtel. He found there only Rafté. "The marshal," the secretary said, "was expected every moment; some delay of the post must have detained him at the barrier."

Monsieur d'Aiguillon proposed waiting, — not without expressing some impatience to Rafté, for he took this excuse as a new defeat. His ill-humor increased, however, when Rafté told him that the marshal would be in despair on his return to find that Monsieur d'Aiguillon had been kept waiting; that besides, he was not to sleep in Paris, as he had at first intended; and that, most probably, he would not return from the country alone, and would just call in passing at his hôtel to see if there were any news; that therefore Monsieur d'Aiguillon would do better to return to his house, where the marshal could call as he passed.

"Listen, Rafté," said D'Aiguillon, who had become more gloomy during this mysterious reply; "you are my uncle's conscience, and I trust you will answer me as an honest man. I am played upon, am I not, and the marshal does not wish to see me? Do not interrupt me, Rafté; you have been a valuable counsellor to me, and I might have been, and can yet be, a good friend to you; must I return to Versailles?"

"Monsieur le Duc, I assure you, upon my honor, you will receive a visit at your own house from the marshal in less than an hour."

"Then I can as well wait here, since he will come this way."

"I have had the honor of informing you that he will probably not be alone."

"I understand, — and I have your word, Rafté." At these words the duke retired in deep thought, but with an air as noble and graceful as the marshal's was the reverse when, after his nephew's departure, he emerged from a cabinet with a glass door.

The marshal smiled like one of those hideous demons which Callot has introduced in his "Temptations." "He suspects nothing, Rafté?" said he.

"Nothing, Monseigneur."

"What time is it?"

"The time has nothing to do with the matter, Monseigneur. You must wait until our little attorney of the Châtelet makes his appearance. The commissioners are still at the printer's."

Monsieur Rafté had scarcely finished, when a footman opened a secret door, and introduced a personage, very ugly, very greasy, very black, — one of those living pens for which Monsieur Dubarry professed such a profound antipathy.

Rafté pushed the marshal into the cabinet, and hastened, smiling, to meet this man.

"Ah! it is you, Maître Flageot?" said he; "I am delighted to see you."

"Your servant, Monsieur Rafté. Well, the business is done."

"Is it printed?"

"Five thousand are struck off. The first copies are already scattered over the town; the others are drying."

"What a misfortune, my dear Monsieur Flageot! What a blow to the marshal's family!"

Monsieur Flageot, to avoid the necessity of answering, — that is, of telling a lie, — drew a large silver box from his pocket and slowly inhaled a pinch of Spanish snuff.

"Well, what is to be done now?" asked Rafté.

"The forms, my dear Monsieur, the forms. The commissioners, now that they are sure of the printing and the distribution, will immediately enter their carriages, which are waiting at the door of the printing-office, and proceed to make known the decree to Monsieur le Duc d'Aiguillon, who happens luckily — I mean unfortunately, Monsieur Rafté — to be in his hôtel in Paris, where they can have an interview with him in person."

Rafté hastily seized an enormous bag of legal documents from a shelf, which he gave to Monsieur Flageot, saying: "These are the suits which I mentioned to you, Monsieur. The marshal has the greatest confidence in your abilities, and leaves this affair, which ought to prove most remunerative, entirely in your hands. I have to thank you for your good offices in this deplorable conflict of Monsieur d'Aiguillon with the all-powerful parliament of Paris, and also for your very valuable advice."

Rafté gently, but with some haste, pushed Monsieur

Flageot, delighted with the weight of his burden, toward the door of the antechamber. Then, releasing the marshal from his prison, "Quick, Monseigneur," said he; "to your carriage! You have no time to lose, if you wish to be present at the scene. Take care that your horses go more quickly than those of the commissioners."

CHAPTER LII.

IN WHICH IT IS SHOWN THAT THE PATH OF A MINISTER IS NOT ALWAYS STREWN WITH ROSES.

THE Maréchal de Richelieu's horses did go more quickly than those of the commissioners, for the marshal entered first into the courtyard of the Hôtel d'Aiguillon.

The duke did not expect his uncle, and was preparing to return to Luciennes to inform Madame Dubarry that the enemy had been unmasked, when the announcement of the marshal's arrival roused his discouraged mind from its torpor.

The duke hastened to meet his uncle, and took both his hands in his with a warmth of affection proportionate to the fear he had experienced. The marshal was as affectionate as the duke; the tableau was touching. The Duc d'Aiguillon, however, was manifestly endeavoring to hasten the period of explanation, while the marshal, on the contrary, delayed it as much as possible, by looking at the pictures, the bronzes, or the tapestry, and complaining of great fatigue.

The duke cut off the marshal's retreat, imprisoned him in an armchair, as Monsieur de Villars imprisoned the Prince Eugene in Marchiennes, and began the attack.

"Uncle," said he, "is it true that you, the most discriminating man in France, have judged so ill of me as to think that my ambition did not include us both?"

There was no longer room for retreat; Richelieu decided on his plan of action. "What do you mean by that?"

he replied; "and in what do you perceive that I judged unfavorably of you, or the reverse, my dear nephew?"

"Uncle, you are offended with me."

"But for what, and how?"

"Oh! no more of these evasions, Monsieur le Maréchal; in one word, you avoid me when I need your assistance."

"Upon my honor, I do not understand you."

"I will explain, then. The king refused to nominate you for his minister; and because I, on my part, accepted the command of the Light Horse, you imagine that I have deserted and betrayed you. That dear countess, too, who loves you so well—"

Here Richelieu listened eagerly, but not to his nephew's words alone. "You say she loves me well, this dear countess?" he interrupted.

"And I can prove it."

"But, my dear fellow, I never doubted it. I send for you to assist me to push the wheel; you are younger, and therefore stronger than I am; you succeed, I fail. That is in the natural course of things, and on my faith I cannot imagine why you have all these scruples. If you have acted for my interest, you will be a hundredfold repaid; if against me— Well! I shall only return the blow. Does that require explanation?"

"In truth, Uncle—"

"You are a child, Duke. Your position is magnificent,— a peer of France, a duke, a commander of the Light Horse, minister in six weeks; you ought to be beyond the influence of all futile intrigues. Success absolves, my dear child. Suppose — I like apologues — suppose that we are the two mules in the fable. But what noise is that?"

"Nothing, my dear uncle; proceed."

"There is something; I hear a carriage in the courtyard."

"Do not let it interrupt you, Uncle, pray; your conversation interests me extremely. I like apologues too."

"Well, my friend, I was going to say that when you are prosperous, you will never meet with reproaches, nor need you fear the spite of the envious; but if you limp, if you fall — ah, the devil! you must take care; then it is that the wolf will attack you. But you see I was right; there is a noise in the antechamber, — it is the portfolio which they are bringing you, no doubt. The little countess must have exerted herself for you."

The usher entered. "Messieurs the commissioners of the parliament," said he, uneasily.

"Ha!" exclaimed Richelieu.

"The commissioners of the parliament here! What do they want with me?" replied the duke, not at all reassured by his uncle's smile.

"In the king's name!" cried a sonorous voice at the end of the antechamber.

"Oh, ho!" cried Richelieu.

Monsieur d'Aiguillon turned very pale; he rose, however, and advanced to the threshold of the apartment to introduce the two commissioners, behind whom were stationed two motionless ushers, and in the distance a host of alarmed footmen.

"What is your errand here?" asked the duke, in a trembling voice.

"Have we the honor of speaking to the Duc d'Aiguillon?" said one of the commissioners.

"I am the Duc d'Aiguillon, gentlemen."

The commissioner, bowing profoundly, drew from his belt an act in proper form, and read it in a loud and distinct voice.

It was the decree, detailed, complete, and circumstantial, which declared D'Aiguillon seriously affected and inculpated by suspicions, even by deeds, involving his honor, and suspended him from his functions as peer of the realm.

The duke listened to the reading like a man thunderstruck. He stood motionless as a statue on its pedestal, and did not even hold out his hand to take the copy of the decree which the commissioners of the parliament offered him.

It was the marshal who, also standing, but alert and active, took the paper, read it, and returned the bow of the commissioners. They had already withdrawn when the Duc d'Aiguillon recovered from his stupor.

"This is a severe blow," said Richelieu; "you are no longer a peer of France, — it is humiliating."

The duke turned to his uncle as if he had only at that moment recovered the power of life and thought.

"You did not expect it?" asked Richelieu in the same tone.

"And you, Uncle?" rejoined D'Aiguillon.

"How do you imagine any one could suspect that the parliament would strike so bold a blow at the favored courtier of the king and his favorite? These people will ruin themselves."

The duke sat down, and leaned his burning cheek on his hand.

"But if," continued the old marshal, forcing the dagger deeper into the wound, "if the parliament degrades you from the peerage because you are nominated to the command of the Light Horse, they will decree you a prisoner and condemn you to the stake when you are appointed minister. These people hate you, D'Aiguillon; do not trust them."

The duke bore this cruel irony with the fortitude of a hero; his misfortune raised and strengthened his mind. Richelieu thought this fortitude was only insensibility, or want of comprehension, perhaps, and that the wound was not deep enough.

"Being no longer a peer," said he, "you will be less exposed to the hatred of these fellows. Have recourse to a few years of obscurity. Besides, look you, this obscurity, which will be your safeguard, will come without your seeking it. Deprived of your functions of peer, you will have more difficulty in reaching the ministry, and may perhaps escape the business altogether. But if you will struggle, my dear fellow, why, you have Madame Dubarry on your side; she loves you, and she is a powerful support."

Monsieur d'Aiguillon rose. He did not even cast an angry look upon the marshal in return for all the suffering the old man had inflicted upon him.

"You are right, Uncle," he replied, calmly, "and your wisdom is shown in this last advice. The Comtesse Dubarry, to whom you had the goodness to present me, and to whom you spoke so favorably of me and with so much zeal that every one at Luciennes can bear witness to it, — Madame Dubarry will defend me. Thank God, she loves me; she is brave, and exerts an all-powerful influence over the mind of the king! Thanks, Uncle, for your advice; I fly thither as to a haven of safety. My horses! Bourgignon, to Luciennes!"

The marshal remained with an unfinished smile upon his lips. Monsieur d'Aiguillon bowed respectfully to his uncle and quitted the apartment, leaving the marshal very much perplexed, and above all very much confused, at the eagerness with which he had attacked this noble and sensitive victim.

There was some consolation for the old marshal in the mad joy of the Parisians when they read in the evening the ten thousand copies of the decree, which were scrambled for in the streets. But he could not help sighing when Rafté asked for an account of the evening. Nevertheless he gave it, without concealing anything.

"Then the blow is parried?" said the secretary.

"Yes, and no, Rafté; but the wound is not mortal, and we have at Trianon something better, which I reproach myself for not having made my sole care. We have started two hares, Rafté; it was very foolish."

"Why, if you seize the best?" replied Rafté.

"Oh! my friend, remember that the best is always the one we have not taken; and we would invariably give the one we hold for the one which has escaped."

Rafté shrugged his shoulders; and yet Monsieur de Richelieu was in the right.

"You think," said Rafté, "that Monsieur d'Aiguillon will get out of this?"

"Do you think the king will, simpleton?"

"Oh! the king finds an opening everywhere; but this matter does not concern the king, I think."

"Where the king can pass, Madame Dubarry will pass, as she holds fast by his skirts; where Madame Dubarry has passed, D'Aiguillon will pass also. But you understand nothing of politics, Rafté."

"Monseigneur, Maître Flageot is not of your opinion."

"Well, what does this Maître Flageot say? But first of all, tell me what he is."

"He is an attorney, Monseigneur."

"Well?"

"Well! Monsieur Flageot thinks that the king himself cannot get out of this matter."

"Oh, ho! — and who will stop the lion?"

"Faith, Monseigneur, — the rat!"

"And you believe him?"

"I always believe an attorney who promises to do evil."

"We shall see what means Maître Flageot intends to employ, Rafté."

"That is what I say, Monseigneur."

"Come to supper, then, that I may get to bed. It has quite upset me to see that my poor nephew is no longer peer of France, and will not be minister. I am an uncle, Rafté, after all!" Monsieur de Richelieu sighed, and then began to laugh.

"You may have every quality, however, requisite for a minister," replied Rafté.

CHAPTER LIII.

MONSIEUR D'AIGUILLON TAKES HIS REVENGE.

THE morning succeeding the day on which the terrible decree had thrown Paris and Versailles into an uproar, when every one was anxiously awaiting the result of this decree, the Duc de Richelieu, who had returned to Versailles and had resumed his usual mode of life, saw Rafté enter his apartment with a letter in his hand. The secretary scrutinized and weighed this letter with such an appearance of anxiety that his emotion quickly communicated itself to his master.

"What is the matter now?" asked the marshal.

"Something not very agreeable, I imagine, Monseigneur, which is enclosed in this letter."

"Why do you imagine so?"

"Because the letter is from the Duc d'Aiguillon."

"Ha!" said the duke; "from my nephew?"

"Yes, Monsieur le Maréchal; after the king's council broke up, an usher of the chamber called on me and handed me this paper for you. I have been turning it over and over for the last ten minutes, and I cannot help suspecting that it contains some evil tidings."

The duke held out his hand. "Give it to me," said he; "I am brave."

"I warn you," interrupted Rafté, "that when the usher gave me the paper, he chuckled outrageously."

"The devil! that bodes ill," replied the marshal; "but give it to me, nevertheless."

"And he added : 'Monsieur le Duc d'Aiguillon wishes Monsieur le Maréchal to have this immediately.'"

"Pain! thou shalt not make me say that thou art an evil," said the marshal, breaking the seal with a firm hand; and he read the letter.

"Ha! you change countenance," said Rafté, standing, with his hands crossed behind him, in an attitude of observation.

"Is it possible?" exclaimed Richelieu, continuing to read.

"It seems, then, that it is serious?"

"You look quite delighted."

"Of course, — I see that I was not mistaken."

The marshal read on. "The king is good," said he, after a moment's pause.

"He appoints Monsieur d'Aiguillon minister?"

"Better than that."

"Oh! what, then?"

"Read and ponder."

Rafté in his turn read the note. It was in the handwriting of D'Aiguillon, and was couched in the following terms: —

MY DEAR UNCLE, — Your good advice has borne its fruit. I confided my wrongs to that excellent friend of our house, the Comtesse Dubarry, who has deigned to lay them at his Majesty's feet. The king is indignant at the violence with which the gentlemen of the parliament pursue me, and in consideration of the services I have so faithfully rendered him, his Majesty, in this morning's council, has annulled the decree of parliament, and has commanded me to continue my functions as peer of France.

Knowing the pleasure this news will cause you, my dear Uncle, I send you the tenor of the decision which his Majesty in council came to to-day. I have had it copied by a secretary, and you have the announcement before any one else.

Deign to believe in my affectionate respect, my dear Uncle, and continue to bestow on me your good-will and your good advice.

Duc d'Aiguillon.

"He mocks at me into the bargain!" cried Richelieu.

"Faith, I think so, Monseigneur!"

"The king throws himself into the hornets' nest!"

"You would not believe me yesterday, when I told you so."

"I did not say he would not throw himself into it, Rafté; I said he would contrive to get out of it. Now, you see, he does get out of it."

"The fact is, the parliament is beaten."

"And I also."

"For the present, yes."

"Forever! Yesterday I foresaw it; and you consoled me so well that some misfortune could not fail to ensue."

"Monseigneur, you despair a little too soon, I think."

"Maître Rafté, you are a fool! I am beaten, and I must pay the stake. You do not fully comprehend, perhaps, how disagreeable it is to me to be the laughing-stock of Luciennes. At this moment the duke is mocking me in the arms of Madame Dubarry; Mademoiselle Chon and Monsieur Jean are roaring themselves hoarse at my expense, while the little negro ceases to stuff himself with dainties to make game of me. *Parbleu!* I have a tolerably good temper, but all this makes me furious."

"Furious, Monseigneur?"

"I have said it,—furious!"

"Then you have done what you should not have done," said Rafté, philosophically.

"You urged me on, Master Secretary."

"I?"

"Yes, you."

"Why, what is it to me whether Monsieur d'Aiguillon is a peer of France or not, I ask you, Monseigneur? Your nephew does me no injury, I think."

"Master Rafté, you are impertinent!"

"You have been telling me so for the last forty-nine years, Monseigneur."

"Well, I shall repeat it again."

"Not for forty-nine years more, that is one comfort."

"Rafté, if this is the way you care for my interests —"

"The interests of your little passions? No, Monsieur le Duc, never! Man of genius as you are, you sometimes commit follies which I could not forgive even in an understrapper like myself."

"Explain yourself, Rafté; and if I am wrong, I will confess it."

"Yesterday you thirsted for vengeance, did you not? You wished to behold the humiliation of your nephew; you wished, as it were, to be the bearer of the decree of parliament, and gloat over the tremblings and palpitations of your victim, as Monsieur Crébillon the younger says. Well, Monsieur le Maréchal, such sights as these must be well paid for; such pleasures cost dear. You are rich; pay, pay, Monsieur le Maréchal!"

"What would you have done in my place, then, O most skilful of tacticians? Come, let me see!"

"Nothing! I would have waited without giving any sign of life. But you itched to oppose the parliament to the Dubarry from the moment she found that Monsieur d'Aiguillon was a younger man than yourself."

A groan was the marshal's only reply.

"Well," continued Rafté, "the parliament was tolerably well prompted by you before it did what it has done. The decree once passed, you should have offered your services to your nephew, who would have suspected nothing."

"That is all well and good, and I admit that I did wrong; but you should have warned me."

"I hinder any evil? You take me for some one else, Monsieur le Maréchal; you repeat to every one that comes that I am your creature, that you have trained me, and yet you would have me not delighted when I see a folly committed or a misfortune approaching. Fie! fie!"

"Then a misfortune is to come, Master Sorcerer?"

"Certainly."

"What misfortune?"

"You will be stubborn, and between the parliament and Madame Dubarry, Monsieur d'Aiguillon will take the joint; then he will be minister, and you exiled, or in the Bastille."

The marshal in his anger upset the contents of his snuff-box upon the carpet. "In the Bastille!" said he, shrugging his shoulders; "is Louis XV., think you, Louis XIV.?"

"No; but Madame Dubarry, supported by Monsieur d'Aiguillon, is quite equal to Madame de Maintenon. Take care! I do not know any princess in the present day who would bring you bonbons and eggs."

"That is enough for prognostics," replied the marshal, after a long silence. "You read the future; but what of the present, if you please?"

"Monsieur le Maréchal is too wise for me to give him advice."

"Come, Master Witty-pate, are you too not mocking me?"

"I beg you to remark, Monsieur le Maréchal, that you confound dates. A man is never called a witty-pate after forty; now, I am sixty-seven."

"No matter, assist me out of this scrape; and quickly too, — quickly!"

"By an advice?"

"By anything you please."

"The time has not come yet."

"Now you are certainly jesting."

"Would to God I were! When I jest, the subject will be a jesting matter, — and unfortunately this is not."

"What do you mean by saying that it is not yet time?"

"No, Monseigneur, it is not time. If the announcement of the king's decree were known in Paris, I would not say — Shall we send a courier to the President d'Aligre?"

"That they may laugh at us all the sooner?"

"What a ridiculous self-love, Monsieur le Maréchal! You would make a saint lose patience. Stay! let me finish my plan of a descent on England, and you can finish drowning yourself in your portfolio intrigue, since the business is already half-done."

The marshal was accustomed to these sullen humors of his secretary. He knew that when his melancholy had once declared itself, he was dangerous to touch with ungloved fingers.

"Come," said he, "do not sulk at me; and if I do not understand, explain yourself."

"Then Monseigneur wishes me to trace out a line of conduct for him?"

"Certainly, since you think I cannot conduct myself."

"Well, then, listen."

"I am all attention."

"You must send by a trusty messenger to Monsieur d'Aligre," said Rafté, abruptly, "the Duc d'Aiguillon's letter; and also the decree of the king in council. You must then wait till the parliament has met and deliberated upon it, which will take place immediately; whereupon, you must order your carriage and pay a visit to your attorney, Maître Flageot."

"Eh!" said Richelieu, whom this name startled as it had on the previous day, "Monsieur Flageot again! What the devil has Maître Flageot to do with all this, and what am I to do at his house?"

"I have had the honor to tell you, Monseigneur, that Maître Flageot is your attorney."

"Well, what then?"

"Well, if he is your attorney, he has certain bags of yours, — certain lawsuits on hand; you must go and ask him about them."

"To-morrow?"

"Yes, Monsieur le Maréchal, to-morrow."

"But all this is your affair, Monsieur Rafté."

"By no means; by no means! When Maître Flageot was a simple scribbling drudge, then I could treat with him as an equal; but as, dating from to-morrow, Maître Flageot is an Attila, a scourge of kings, — neither more nor less, — it is not asking too much of a duke, a peer, a marshal of France, to converse with this all-powerful man."

"Is this serious, or are we acting a farce?"

"You will see to-morrow if it is serious, Monseigneur."

"But tell me what will be the result of my visit to your Maître Flageot."

"I should be very sorry to do so; you would endeavor to prove to me to-morrow that you had guessed it beforehand. Good-night, Monsieur le Maréchal. Remember, a courier to Monsieur d'Aligre immediately; a visit to Maître Flageot to-morrow. Oh! the address? — The coachman knows it; he has driven me there frequently during the last week."

CHAPTER LIV.

IN WHICH THE READER WILL ONCE MORE MEET AN OLD ACQUAINTANCE WHOM HE THOUGHT LOST, AND WHOM PERHAPS HE DID NOT REGRET.

THE reader will no doubt ask why Maître Flageot, who is about to play so important a part in our story, was called attorney instead of advocate; and as the reader is justified in asking that question, we will satisfy his curiosity.

The vacations had for some time been frequent in parliament, and the advocates pleaded so seldom that their speeches were not worth speaking of. Maître Flageot, foreseeing the time when there would be no pleading at all, made certain arrangements with Maître Guildou, the attorney, in virtue of which the latter yielded him up office and clients on consideration of the sum of twenty-five thousand francs paid down. That is how Maître Flageot became an attorney. But if we are asked how he managed to pay the twenty-five thousand francs, we reply, by marrying Mademoiselle Marguerite, to whom this sum was left as an inheritance about the end of the year 1770, — three months before Monsieur de Choiseul's exile.

Maître Flageot had been long distinguished for his perseveringadherence to the opposition party. Once an attorney, he redoubled his violence, and by this violence succeeded in gaining some celebrity. It was this celebrity, together with the publication of an incendiary pamphlet on the subject of the conflict between Monsieur d'Aiguillon and Monsieur de la Chalotais, which attracted the attention of Monsieur Rafté, who had occasion to keep himself well informed concerning the affairs of parliament.

But notwithstanding his new dignity and his increasing importance, Maître Flageot did not leave the Rue du Petit-Lion-Saint-Sauveur. It would have been too cruel a blow for Mademoiselle Marguerite not to have heard the neighbors call her Madame Flageot, and not to have inspired respect in the breasts of Monsieur Guildou's clerks, who had entered the service of the new attorney.

The reader may readily imagine what Monsieur de Richelieu suffered in traversing Paris — the filthy Paris of that region — to reach the disgusting hole which the Parisian magistrature dignified by the name of "street." In front of Maître Flageot's door, Monsieur de Richelieu's carriage was stopped by another carriage, which pulled up at the same moment. The marshal perceived a woman's headdress protruding from the window of this carriage; and as his sixty-five years of age had not quenched the ardor of his gallantry, he hastily jumped out on the muddy pavement, and proceeded to offer his hand to the lady, who was unaccompanied.

But this day the marshal's evil star was in the ascendant. A long, withered leg which was stretched out to reach the step betrayed the old woman. A wrinkled face, adorned with a dark streak of rouge, proved further that the woman was not only old, but decrepit.

Nevertheless there was no room for retreat; the marshal had made the movement, and the movement had been seen. Besides, Monsieur de Richelieu himself was no longer young. In the mean time the litigant — for what woman with a carriage would have entered that street had she not been a litigant? — the litigant, we say, did not imitate the duke's hesitation; with a ghastly smile she placed her hand in Richelieu's.

"I have seen that face somewhere before," thought Richelieu; then he added: "Does Madame also intend to visit Maître Flageot?"

"Yes, Monsieur le Duc," replied the old lady.

"Oh, I have the honor to be known to you, Madame!" exclaimed the duke, disagreeably surprised, and stopping on the threshold of the dark passage.

"Who does not know the Duc de Richelieu?" was the reply. "I should not be a woman if I did not."

"This she-ape thinks she is a woman!" murmured the conqueror of Mahon; and he made a most graceful bow.

"If I may venture to ask the question," added he, "to whom have I the honor of speaking?"

"I am the Comtesse de Béarn, at your service," replied the old lady, curtseying with courtly reverence upon the dirty floor of the passage, and about three inches from an open trap-door, through which the marshal, with malicious anticipation, expected her to disappear as she bowed the third time.

"I am delighted, Madame — enchanted," said he; "and I return a thousand thanks to fate. You also have lawsuits on hand, Countess?"

"Oh! Duke, I have only one; but what a lawsuit! Is it possible that you have never heard of it?"

"Oh! frequently, frequently, — that great lawsuit. True; I entreat your pardon. How the devil could I have forgotten that?"

"Against the Saluces."

"Against the Saluces, yes, Countess, — the lawsuit about which the song was written."

"A song?" said the old lady, piqued, — "what song?"

"Take care, Madame, there is a trap-door here," said

the duke, who saw that the old woman was decided not to throw herself into the cellar; "take hold of the balustrade, — I mean the cord."

The old lady mounted the first steps. The duke followed her. "Yes, a very humorous song," said he.

"A humorous song on my lawsuit?"

"To be sure! I will leave you to judge, — but perhaps you know it?"

"Not at all."

"It is to the tune of 'The Bourbonnaise;' it runs so: —

"'Embarrassed, Countess, as I stand,
Give me, I pray, a helping hand,
And I am quite at your command.'

It is Madame Dubarry who speaks, you must know."

"That is very impertinent toward her."

"Oh! what can you expect? — the ballad-mongers respect no one. Heavens! how greasy this cord is! Then you reply as follows: —

"'I'm very old, and stubborn too;
I'm forced at law my rights to sue.
Ah, who can help me? Tell me, who?'"

"Oh, Monsieur, it is frightful!" cried the countess; "a woman of quality is not to be insulted in this manner."

"Madame, excuse me if I have sung out of tune; these stairs heat me so. Ah! here we are at last. Allow me to pull the bell."

The old lady, grumbling all the time, made way for the duke to pass. The marshal rang, and Madame Flageot, who in becoming an attorney's wife had not ceased to fill the functions of portress and cook, opened the door. The two litigants were ushered into Maître Flageot's office,

AN OLD ACQUAINTANCE. 535

where they found that worthy in a state of furious excitement, and with a pen in his mouth, hard at work dictating a terrible plea to his head-clerk.

"Good heavens, Maître Flageot! what is the matter?" cried the countess, at whose voice the attorney turned round.

"Ah! Madame, your most humble servant, — a chair here for the Comtesse de Béarn. This gentleman is a friend of yours, Madame? Eh! I cannot be mistaken, — the Duc de Richelieu in my house! Another chair, Bernardet, — another chair."

"Maître Flageot," said the countess, "how does my lawsuit get on, pray?"

"Ah, Madame! I was just now working for you."

"Very good, Maître Flageot, very good."

"And after a fashion, my lady, which will make some noise, I hope."

"Ahem! Take care!"

"Oh! Madame, there is no longer any occasion for caution."

"Then if you are busy about my affair, you can give an audience to the duke."

"Excuse me, Monsieur le Duc," said Maître Flageot; "but you are too gallant not to understand —"

"I understand, Maître Flageot; I understand."

"But now I can attend to you exclusively."

"Don't be uneasy; I shall not abuse your good-nature. You know what brings me here?"

"The bags which Monsieur Rafté gave me the other day."

"Some papers relative to my lawsuit of — my suit about — What the devil! you must know what suit I mean, Maître Flageot?"

"Your lawsuit about the lands of Chapenat?"

"Very probably; and will you gain it for me? That would be very kind on your part."

"Monsieur le Duc, it is postponed indefinitely."

"Postponed! And why?"

"It will not be brought forward in less than a year, at the earliest."

"For what reason, may I ask?"

"Circumstances, Monsieur le Duc, circumstances; you have heard of his Majesty's decree?"

"I think so; but which one? His Majesty issues so many."

"The one which annuls ours."

"Very well; and what then?"

"Well! Monsieur le Duc, we shall reply by burning our ships."

"Burning your ships, my dear friend? — you will burn the ships of the parliament? I do not quite comprehend you; I was not aware that the parliament had ships."

"The first chamber refuses to register, perhaps?" inquired the Comtesse de Béarn, whom Richelieu's lawsuit in no way prevented from thinking of her own.

"Better than that."

"The second one also?"

"That would be a mere nothing. Both chambers have resolved not to render any more judgments until the king shall have dismissed Monsieur d'Aiguillon."

"Bah!" exclaimed the marshal, rubbing his hands.

"Render no more judgments on what?" asked the countess, alarmed.

"On the lawsuits, Madame."

"They will not give judgment on my lawsuit?" exclaimed the Comtesse de Béarn, with a dismay which she did not even attempt to conceal.

"Neither on yours, Madame, nor the duke's."

"It is iniquitous! It is rebellion against his Majesty's orders, that!"

"Madame," replied the attorney, majestically, "the king has forgotten himself; we also shall forget ourselves."

"Monsieur Flageot, you will be sent to the Bastille. Remember, I warn you."

"I shall go singing, Madame; and if I am sent thither, all my fellow-members of parliament will follow me, carrying palms in their hands."

"He is mad!" said the countess to Richelieu.

"We are all the same," replied the attorney.

"Oh, oh!" said the marshal, "that is becoming rather curious."

"But, Monsieur, you said just now that you were working for me," replied Madame de Béarn.

"I said so, and it is quite true. You, Madame, are the first example I cite in my narration; here is the paragraph which relates to you."

He snatched the draft from his clerk's hand, fixed his spectacles upon his nose, and read with emphasis: —

"Their position ruined, their fortune compromised, their rights trampled under foot! His Majesty will understand how much they must have suffered. Thus the petitioner had intrusted to his care a very important suit, upon which the fortune of one of the first families in the kingdom depends; by his zeal, his industry, and, he ventures to say, his talents, this suit was progressing favorably, and the rights of the most noble and most powerful lady, Angélique Charlotte Véronique, Comtesse de Béarn, were on the point of being recognized, proclaimed, when the breath of discord — engulfing — "

"I had just got so far, Madame," said the attorney, drawing himself up; "but I think the simile is not amiss."

"Monsieur Flageot," said the countess, "it is forty years ago since I first employed your father, who proved most worthy of my patronage; I continued that patronage to you; you have gained ten or twelve thousand francs by my suit, and you would probably have gained as many more."

"Write down all that," said Flageot, eagerly, to his clerk; "it is a testimony, a proof. It shall be inserted in the confirmation."

"But now," interrupted the countess, "I take back all my papers from your charge; from this moment you have lost my confidence."

Maître Flageot, thunderstruck by this disgrace, remained for a moment almost stupefied; but rising under the blow like a martyr who dies for his religion, "Be it so," said he. "Bernardet, give the papers back to madame; and you will insert this fact," he added, "that the petitioner preferred his conscience to his fortune."

"I beg your pardon, Countess," whispered the marshal in the countess's ear, "but it seems to me that you have acted without reflection."

"In what respect, Monsieur le Duc?"

"You take your papers from this honest attorney, but for what purpose?"

"To take them to another attorney, to another advocate!" exclaimed the countess.

Maître Flageot raised his eyes to heaven with a mournful smile of self-denial and stoic resignation.

"But," continued the marshal, still whispering in the countess's ear, "if it has been decided that the chambers will not adjudicate, my dear Madame, another attorney can do no more for you than Maître Flageot."

"It is a league, then?"

"*Pardieu!* do you think Maître Flageot fool enough

to protest, to lose his practice, if his fellow-lawyers were not agreed to do the same, and consequently support him?"

"But you, Monsieur, what will you do?"

"For my part, I think Maître Flageot a very honest attorney, and that my papers are as safe in his possession as in my own. Consequently, I shall leave them with him, of course paying him as if my suit were going on."

"It is well said, Monsieur le Maréchal, that you are a generous, liberal-minded man!" exclaimed Maître Flageot; "I will extend your fame, Monseigneur."

"You overwhelm me, my dear attorney," replied Richelieu, bowing.

"Bernardet," cried the enthusiastic attorney to his clerk, "you will insert in the peroration a eulogy on the Maréchal de Richelieu!"

"No, no, by no means, Maître Flageot! I beg you will do nothing of the kind!" replied the marshal, hastily. "Oh, the devil! that would be a pretty action! I prefer secrecy in what it is customary to call good actions. Do not disoblige me, Maître Flageot; I shall deny it, look you, — I shall positively contradict it; my modesty is sensitive. Well, Countess, what say you?"

"I say my suit shall be judged. I must have a judgment, and I will."

"And I say, Madame, that if your suit is judged, the king must first send the Swiss guards, the Light Horse, and twenty pieces of cannon into the great hall," replied Maître Flageot, with a belligerent air which completed the consternation of the litigant.

"Then you do not think his Majesty can get out of this affair?" said Richelieu, in a low voice to Flageot.

"Impossible, Monsieur le Maréchal! It is an unheard-of case. No more justice in France: it is as if you were to say no more bread!"

"Do you think so?"

"You will see."

"But the king will be angry."

"We are resolved to brave everything."

"Even exile?"

"Even death, Monsieur le Maréchal! We have courage, although we wear the gown;" and Monsieur Flageot struck his breast vigorously.

"In fact, Madame," said Richelieu to his companion, "I believe that this is an unfortunate step for the ministry."

"Oh, yes!" replied the old countess, after a pause; "it is very unfortunate for me, who never meddle in anything that is taking place, to be dragged into this conflict."

"I think, Madame," said the marshal, "there is some one who could help you in this affair, — a very powerful person. But would that person do it?"

"Is it displaying too much curiosity, Duke, to ask the name of this powerful person?"

"Your goddaughter," said the duke.

"Oh! Madame Dubarry?"

"Yes."

"In fact, that is true; I am obliged to you for the hint."

The duke bit his lips. "Then you will go to Luciennes?" he asked.

"Without hesitation."

"But the Comtesse Dubarry cannot overcome the opposition of parliament."

"I will tell her I must have my suit judged; and as she can refuse me nothing, after the service I have rendered her, she will tell the king she wishes it. His Majesty will speak to the chancellor, and the chancellor has a long arm, Monsieur le Duc. Maître Flageot, be kind enough to continue to study my case well; it may come on sooner than you think. Mark my words."

AN OLD ACQUAINTANCE. 541

Maître Flageot turned away his head with an air of incredulity which did not shake the countess in the least. In the mean time the duke had been reflecting.

"Well, Madame, since you are going to Luciennes, will you have the goodness to present my most humble respects?"

"Most willingly, Monsieur le Duc."

"We are companions in misfortune; your suit is in abeyance, and mine also. In supplicating for yourself, you will do so for me too. Moreover, you may express yonder the displeasure these stubborn-headed parliament men cause me; and you will add that it was I who advised you to have recourse to the divinity of Luciennes."

"I will not fail to do so, Monsieur le Duc. Adieu, gentlemen."

"Allow me the honor of conducting you to your carriage. Once more, adieu, Maître Flageot; I leave you to your occupations."

The marshal handed the countess to her carriage. "Rafté was right," said he; "the Flageots will cause a revolution. Thank Heaven, I am supported on both sides! I am of the court, and of the parliament. Madame Dubarry will meddle with politics, and fall alone; if she resists, I have my little petard at Trianon. Decidedly, that devil of a Rafté is of my school; and when I am minister he shall be my chief secretary."

CHAPTER LV.

THE CONFUSION INCREASES.

MADAME DE BÉARN followed Richelieu's advice literally. Two hours and a half after the duke had left her she was waiting in the antechamber at Luciennes, in the company of Monsieur Zamore. It was some time since she had been seen at Madame Dubarry's, and her presence therefore excited a feeling of curiosity in the countess's boudoir when her name was announced.

Monsieur d'Aiguillon had not lost any time either, and he was plotting with the favorite when Chon entered to request an audience for Madame de Béarn. The duke made a movement to retire, but the countess detained him. "I would rather you would remain," said she. "In case my old alms-gatherer comes to ask a loan, you would be most useful to me, for she will ask less."

The duke remained. Madame de Béarn, with a face composed for the occasion, took the chair opposite the countess, which the latter offered to her; and after the first civilities were exchanged, "May I ask to what fortunate chance I am indebted for your presence, Madame?" said Madame Dubarry.

"Ah! Madame," said the old litigant, "a great misfortune."

"What! Madame,—a misfortune?"

"A piece of news which will deeply afflict his Majesty."

"I am all impatience, Madame—"

"The parliament —"

"Ah! ah!" growled the Duc d'Aiguillon.

"Monsieur le Duc d'Aiguillon," said the countess, hastily presenting her guest to her lady visitor, for fear of some unpleasant misunderstanding. But the old countess was as cunning as all the other courtiers put together, and never caused a misunderstanding, except wittingly, and when it seemed likely to benefit her. "I know," said she, "all the baseness of those rascals, and their want of respect for merit and for rank."

This compliment, aimed directly at the duke, drew a graceful bow from him to the litigant, who rose and bowed in her turn. "But," she continued, "it is not the duke alone who is now concerned, but the entire population; the parliament refuses to act."

"Indeed!" exclaimed Madame Dubarry, throwing herself back upon the sofa; "there will be no more justice in France! Well, what change will that produce?"

The duke smiled. As for Madame de Béarn, instead of taking the affair pleasantly, her morose features darkened still more. "It is a great calamity, Madame," said she.

"Ah! indeed?" replied the favorite.

"It is evident, Madame, that you are happy enough to have no lawsuits."

"Ahem!" said D'Aiguillon, to recall the attention of Madame Dubarry, who at last comprehended the insinuation of the litigant. "Alas! Madame," said she, "it is true; you remind me that if I have no lawsuit, you have a very important one."

"Ah, yes! Madame; and delay will be ruinous to me."

"Poor lady!"

"Unless, Countess, the king takes some decided step."

"Oh! Madame, the king is well inclined to do so. He

will exile messieurs the councillors, and all will be right."

"But, Madame, that would surely be an indefinite adjournment."

"Do you see any remedy, then? Will you be kind enough to point it out to us?"

The litigant concealed her face beneath her hood, like Cæsar expiring under his toga.

"There is one remedy, certainly," said D'Aiguillon; "but perhaps his Majesty might shrink from employing it."

"What is it?" asked the Comtesse de Béarn, with anxiety.

"The ordinary resource of royalty in France when it is rather embarrassed. It is to hold a bed of justice, and to say, 'I will!' when all the opponents say, 'I will not.'"

"An excellent idea!" exclaimed Madame de Béarn, with enthusiasm.

"But which must not be divulged," replied D'Aiguillon, diplomatically, and with a gesture which Madame de Béarn fully comprehended.

"Oh! Madame," said she, instantly, "you who have so much influence with the king, persuade him to say, 'I will have the suit of Madame de Béarn determined.' Besides, you know, it was promised long ago."

Monsieur d'Aiguillon bit his lips, bowed to Madame Dubarry, and left the boudoir. He had heard the sound of the king's carriage in the courtyard.

"Here is the king!" said Madame Dubarry, rising to dismiss her visitor.

"Oh! Madame, why will you not permit me to throw myself at his Majesty's feet?"

"To ask him for a bed of justice?" replied the countess, quickly. "Most willingly! Remain here, Madame, since such is your desire."

Scarcely had Madame de Béarn adjusted her headdress when the king entered.

"Ah!" said he, "you have visitors, Countess!"

"Madame de Béarn, Sire."

"Sire, justice!" exclaimed the old lady, making a most profound reverence.

"Oh!" said Louis XV., in a bantering tone imperceptible to those who did not know him, "has any one offended you, Madame?"

"Sire, I ask for justice."

"Against whom?"

"Against the parliament."

"Ah! good," said the king, rubbing his hands; "you complain of my parliament. Well! do me the pleasure to bring them to reason. I too have to complain of them, and I beg you to grant me justice also," added he, imitating the reverence of the old countess.

"But, Sire, you are the king; you are the master."

"The king — yes; the master — not always."

"Sire, proclaim your will."

"I do that every evening, Madame; and they proclaim theirs every morning. Now, as these two wills are diametrically opposed to each other, it is with us as with the earth and the moon, which are ever running the one after the other, without coming together."

"Sire, your voice is powerful enough to drown all the bawlings of these fellows."

"There you are mistaken; I am not an advocate, as they are. If I say yes, they say no; it is impossible for us to come to any arrangement. If, when I have said yes, you can find any means to prevent their saying no, I will make an alliance with you."

"Sire, I have the means."

"Let me hear it quickly."

"I will, Sire. Hold a bed of justice."

"That is another embarrassment," said his Majesty; "a bed of justice, remember, Madame, is almost a revolution."

"It is simply telling these rebellious subjects that you are the master. You know, Sire, that when the king proclaims his will in this manner, he alone has a right to speak; no one answers. You say to them, 'I will,' and they bow their assent."

"The fact is," said the Comtesse Dubarry, "the idea is a magnificent one."

"Magnificent it may be, but not good," replied Louis.

"But what a noble spectacle!" resumed Madame Dubarry, with warmth: "the procession, the nobles, the peers, the entire military staff of the king! Then the immense crowd of people; then the bed of justice, composed of five cushions embroidered with golden fleurs-de-lys. It would be a splendid ceremony!"

"You think so?" said the king, rather shaken in his resolution.

"Then the king's magnificent dress, — the cloak lined with ermine, the diamonds in the crown, the golden sceptre, — all the splendor which so well suits an august and noble countenance! Oh, how handsome you would look, Sire!"

"It is a long time since we had a bed of justice," said Louis, with affected carelessness.

"Not since your childhood, Sire," said Madame de Béarn. "The remembrance of your brilliant beauty on that occasion has remained engraven on the hearts of all."

"And then," added Madame Dubarry, "there would be an excellent opportunity for the chancellor to display his keen and concise eloquence, — to crush these people with his truth, dignity, and power."

"I must wait for the parliament's next wrong-doing," said Louis; "then I shall see."

"What can you wait for, Sire, more outrageous than what they have just committed?"

"Why, what have they done?"

"Do you not know?"

"They have teased Monsieur d'Aiguillon a little, but that is not a hanging offence; although," said the king, looking at Madame Dubarry, "although this dear duke is a friend of mine. Besides, if the parliament has teased the duke a little, I have punished them for their ill-nature by my decree of yesterday or the day before, — I do not remember which. We are now even."

"Well, Sire," said Madame Dubarry, with warmth, "Madame de Béarn has just informed us that this morning these black-gowned gentlemen have taken the start of you."

"How so?" said the king, frowning.

"Speak, Madame; the king permits it," said the favorite.

"Sire, the councillors have determined not to hold a court of parliament until your Majesty yields to their wishes."

"What say you?" said the king. "You mistake, Madame; that would be an act of rebellion, and my parliament dares not revolt, I hope."

"Sire, I assure you —"

"Oh! Madame, it is a mere rumor."

"Will your Majesty deign to hear me?"

"Speak, Countess."

"Well, my attorney has this morning returned me all the papers relating to my lawsuit. He can no longer plead, since they will no longer judge."

"Mere reports, I tell you, — rumors, bugbears;" but

while he spoke, the king paced up and down the boudoir in agitation.

"Sire, will your Majesty believe Monsieur de Richelieu, if you will not believe me? In my presence his papers were returned to him also, and the duke left the house in a rage."

"Some one is tapping at the door," said the king, to change the conversation.

"It is Zamore, Sire."

Zamore entered. "A letter, Mistress," said he.

"With your permission, Sire," said the countess. "Ah! good heavens!" exclaimed she, suddenly.

"What is the matter?"

"From the chancellor, Sire. Monsieur de Maupeou, knowing that your Majesty has deigned to pay me a visit, solicits my intervention to obtain an audience for him."

"What is in the wind now?"

"Show the chancellor in," said Madame Dubarry. The Comtesse de Béarn rose to take her leave.

"You need not go, Madame," said the king. "Good-day, Monsieur de Maupeou. What news?"

"Sire," said the chancellor, bowing, "the parliament embarrassed you; you have no longer a parliament."

"How so? Are they all dead? Have they taken arsenic?"

"Would to Heaven they had! No, Sire, they live; but they will not sit any longer, and have sent in their resignations. I have just received them in a mass."

"The councillors?"

"No, Sire, the resignations."

"I told you, Sire, that it was a serious matter," said the countess, in a low voice.

"Most serious," replied Louis, impatiently. "Well, chancellor, what have you done?"

"Sire, I have come to receive your Majesty's orders."

"We will exile these people, Maupeou."

"Sire, they will not judge any better in exile."

"We will command them to judge. Bah! injunctions are out of date, — letters of commandment likewise — "

"Ah! Sire, this time you must be determined."

"Yes, you are right."

"Courage!" said Madame de Béarn, aside to the countess.

"And act the master, after having too often acted only the father," said the countess.

"Chancellor," said the king, slowly, "I know only one remedy; it is serious, but efficacious. I will hold a bed of justice; these people must be made to tremble once for all."

"Ah! Sire," exclaimed the chancellor, "that is well spoken; they must bend, or break!"

"Madame," added the king, addressing Madame de Béarn, "if your suit be not judged, you see it will not be my fault."

"Sire, you are the greatest monarch in the world!"

"Oh! yes," echoed the countess, Chon, and the chancellor.

"The world does not say so, however," murmured the king.

END OF VOL. II.